A Path of Branches

The Mindbridge Trilogy

Book II

By Joe Luegers

ISBN: 978-1-7365411-8-0 (Paperback)
ISBN: 978-1-7365411-7-3 (E-book)
ISBN: 978-1-7365411-9-7 (Hardback)

Any references to historical events, real people, or real places are used fictitiously. Names, characters, and places are products of the author's imagination.

Front cover image by Ashley Ellen Frary

Developmental editing by Kandis Robinson

Line editing by Emily Bernhardt

To Rory Zappa Luegers,
You are loved, and you are so much more

Have you read
The City and the Island: A Mindbridge Trilogy Novella?

A month after the events of *The Bridge*, Max Kacey has the undeniable feeling that he's being watched. Join this fan favorite character as he tracks down ghosts of his past and discovers a haunting vision of his future.

The Mindbridge Trilogy, Book 1.5 is now available as an E-book. The story takes place before this book, but can be read at any time in the series. Join my newsletter to download for free. Here's what else my mailing list gets.

*Automatic entry into signed book giveaways.

*First alerts when my books go online and when certain retailers are running deals on the The Mindbridge Trilogy.

*Monthly reading recommendations featuring my favorite books.

Unsubscribe any time. For all I care, get your free stuff and run! Scan the code below, or go to
https://astounding-trailblazer-618.ck.page/6abacd55bc

Chapters

Prologue

The Desolate Truth

Many Cycles Ago
Monhegan Island, Gaia

Kai Monhegan was anxiously reading the contents of his stolen book when the doorknob of the schoolhouse began to turn. He jumped out of his seat and considered diving out of the window, but it was too late. The door burst open with a gust of wind and his teacher came stomping into the schoolhouse. Mr. Calderon flicked up a hand and all of the oil lamps in the room burst to light, leaving Kai standing awkwardly in the middle of the private library. He quickly hid the ancient book behind his back, but in his haste it slipped out of his fingers and hit the floor with a dry *clunk*.

"Ha!" cried Mr. Calderon, pointing an accusatory finger. "The book thief has been caught at last!"

Kai kicked the book with his heel and the contraband slid under the nearest shelf. He blinked and looked around the room in a pretend daze.

"Woah! How did I get here? I must have been sleepwalking again. Thanks for waking me, Mr. Calderon. Better head back home now."

Kai took a few steps toward the door, but a chair slid across the room and hit him behind the knees. He plopped down into the seat, which then spun around and propelled him forward, screeching to a halt only inches before the teacher. Mr. Calderon held up a hand and the stolen book flew out from under the bookshelf. It soared through the air, spinning and flinging dust as it went, quickly getting snatched up by the old man. His eyes were each different colors, one green and one dark brown, and they darted back and forth from the book to the culprit. Mr. Calderon read aloud, his voice low and raspy, time-worn from cycles upon cycles of chastising children.

"*Music of the Forest: Songs and Secrets of the Ancient Spiritualists.* Kai, this is a rare book that is worth more than you could ever repay me. Why have you been stealing from my library? Ten seconds to explain before I throw you into the ocean. I hear the water mammoths are hungry today. Ten, nine, eight—"

Kai held up his hands in a show of defeat, but did not dare rise from his chair.

"I hate reading, I swear! I would never read a book for enjoyment, you have to believe me! I'm innocent!"

Mr. Calderon leaned in and slapped the book against his other hand.

"*Innocent?* Is your use of that adjective meant to be facetious?"

"No. I mean, yes!" Kai paused, scratching his chin. "Actually, I have no idea what you just said."

Kai could feel Mr. Calderon prying at his mind, and embarrassment swelled within him. Students constantly spread rumors that the teacher's green eye could see what you were doing, and his brown eye could see what you were *thinking* about doing. Not a very believable story until you found that brown eye piercing into your very soul, like it was now.

Kai certainly didn't want to be digging through Mr. Calderon's books in the dead of night, but this was a last resort.

"I've been teaching myself," he admitted, trying to keep his face from turning a bright red.

Mr. Calderon raised an eyebrow.

"But… but not because you're a bad teacher! I just… well—"

Kai shut his mouth, too humiliated to say what he was thinking. Mr. Calderon nodded thoughtfully, seeming to understand Kai's stuttering more than Kai understood it himself.

"You're reaching your fourteenth cycle tomorrow. I think I know what's going on here, and I've suspected it for weeks. Come here, Kai. It's okay."

The old man moved his mouth up in an unfamiliar curve and beckoned him to move closer. Kai sat trembling in the chair and recoiled from the bewildering sight.

"What are you doing? What's that awful look on your face?"

"I'm smiling. Come closer, boy."

Kai looked skeptical. "It's not a trap?"

"No, it's an order. *Let me comfort you!*"

Kai stood up and Mr. Calderon placed a hand gently on his student's shoulder. A soothing energy flowed from his fingertips into Kai, slightly calming his anxiety, but not nearly enough to stop the tears from welling in his eyes.

"I was trying to figure out why I can't relay," said Kai. "It'll be too late after tomorrow. Why doesn't Gaia respond to me?"

Mr. Calderon appeared unconcerned. "The age restriction is a superstition. Gaia comes when she is needed the most, and for some people it just happens later. Yes, in rare cases it doesn't happen at all, but some of the most resourceful people I have ever known are non-relayers." He flipped through the pages of the book, his green eye seeming to brighten with interest. "Why the sudden curiosity about spiritualism?"

"None of the five relaying disciplines have worked for me. I was just wondering if, well... if I might be a spiritualist."

"And do you have any reasons to believe this?"

Kai hesitated. There were things that he was afraid to tell his own parents, things that he didn't even fully understand himself. "I've been having dreams. Every night I see fighting from the Global War on the mainland. I see villages burning, children crying, giant machines rolling over blackened fields. At first I thought these nightmares were happening because I heard about the war so often, but they seemed so real. It's like I'm there, seeing through someone else's eyes. I wondered if it might be a sign of spiritualism."

Mr. Calderon drummed his fingers thoughtfully across the book. "Interesting. *Interesting.* I've spent a long time studying spiritualism, and have quite a few leanings that way myself. Let me read you and see if Gaia has decided what you will be." He closed his eyes and placed his fingers on Kai's temples. "This is a technique I learned from a group of True Searchers on the mainland. I am reading your relaying pathways to see if any of them have—"

Mr. Calderon jumped and cried out, as if Kai's skin had somehow shocked him. He yanked back his now trembling hands and looked at Kai with a stretching, unfathomable silence.

"What's wrong?" asked Kai.

Mr. Calderon took a long time to answer, opening his mouth several times before shutting it again in an uncharacteristic act of indecisiveness. Whether the silence lasted ten seconds or ten minutes, Kai could not have said. Finally, Mr. Calderon let out a trembling sigh and spoke.

"All of your pathways are still blocked. Gaia needs more time to decide what you will be. I'm sorry, I know that this is not what you wanted to hear. Stay inquisitive, and you will have all you need. You can steal from my library any time." He offered the old book to Kai. "Keep this one. Let's call it a cycle day gift. Maybe you can make more sense of some of it than I can."

Kai felt like crying in disappointment, but he held it back. This was something he couldn't have achieved a month ago, but recently he had plenty of practice in hiding his feelings.

He took the book and gave a nod of appreciation, surprising himself by not immediately darting home and celebrating that Mr. Calderon had not made him swim laps around the island as punishment. There was something he needed to ask about, something he had seen earlier in the book that stuck in his mind like a thorn.

"Sir?" asked Kai, flipping to the final page of the text and showing the image to his teacher. "Can you tell me what this is? There's no inscription."

The final two pages showed a massive tree rising from the ground, its branches reaching skyward, splitting and dividing until there looked to be millions of them twisting up toward the stars. The level of detail in the ink drawing looked impossible to be done by hand, its multitudes of black lines vanishing and reappearing in seemingly microscopic patterns.

Mr. Calderon gave him yet another piercing, unreadable glare. "May I ask why this picture caught your attention?"

"I don't know. I remember seeing it before."

"Doubtful. Hardly anyone outside of the highest spiritualist circles speak of the Tree anymore. Unless..."

Mr. Calderon glanced up and began muttering to himself, staring beyond the bookshelves into the darkening shadows at the far corner of the room. "Sometimes the branches of time sway in the wind. Bending downwards, leaves brushing up against their neighbors, the past and future meeting in brief glimpses of déjà vu. Could it be that your memory

5

of seeing the tree is, in fact, a memory of the events happening *right now*?"

Mr. Calderon held up the book and pointed to the ink drawing.

"The Tree of Time is an ancient spiritualist teaching about the power and limitations of free will. The ground that the tree grows from represents Gaia, and the tree itself shows every possible future for her children. The possibilities are vast but not endless. Free will, boy, not *limitless* will."

He traced a finger along a branch that spiraled toward the sky, getting smaller and smaller until it blinked away to nothingness among the stars. "Some futures continue forever, signifying the everlasting survival of Gaia's children."

Mr. Calderon now moved his finger to the left side of the drawing. At a certain point, many of the branches began swaying toward a dark blot of ink on the page. Thousands of lines tangled and withered as they were pulled into the decaying knot. The paper was heavily indented, having been traced over dozens and dozens of times.

"Many futures do not lead to eternity, but to *this*."

Kai had stared at this dark blot earlier, and it filled his entire body with an eerie revulsion. He expected it to look less creepy with the lights turned on, but his expectations were sorely met. Seeing his teacher's cryptic reaction made it even worse.

"What is that?" Kai asked.

"We call it *Desolation*: the worst of all possible futures, maybe the destruction of Gaia herself. There are spiritualists who have gone insane from trying to understand its nature. The general goal and greatest challenge of spiritualism is to lead Gaia away from Desolation."

"But if spiritualists can see the future, wouldn't it be easy to know which decisions to make?"

"Spiritualist sight is not so straightforward. What looks like the future might actually be the past, and vice versa. Trying to actively interfere can often complicate things, darken the pathways. The very act of avoiding a certain path could be what sets you on that course in the first place."

Kai pointed to several branches that were tangled in the dark knot and then followed them straight off the page.

"I noticed that these branches don't stem from Gaia. It looks like this drawing should continue on one side, but it doesn't. Where do these other branches come from?"

Kai could have sworn that his teacher's brown eye tilted in his direction, while the other remained on the book.

"Well, that *is* a fascinating question. You are an observant boy, Kai. I wish I could answer you, but so many secrets from the ancient relayers have been lost in this horrible war. It is said that only Edgard Zeig understood what the black spot represented."

Mr. Calderon gestured to a dusty sword that hung on the wall in the schoolhouse. Edgard Zeig was somewhat of a mythical figure on the island, although what they knew about him could only be pieced together from fragments of a forgotten history. Edgard was said to have been powerless and homeless for a long time, and it was only upon returning home that he discovered his endless potential. He used a mysterious power called The Desolate Truth to unite the guardianships and create an era of peace in the world that would never be rivaled. The Monhegans were the only living descendants of Edgard and custodians of his sword. It was said to be powerless outside the hands of its owner, so it mostly hung unused by the islanders.

"I shouldn't be talking of Desolation," said Mr. Calderon. "Some claim that acknowledging it only turns its eyes in our direction." He attempted another smile, and again it looked like it caused him suffering. "Besides, you need to be resting for your cycle day tomorrow."

His cycle day? How could Kai have gone from being so devastated about turning fourteen, to forgetting about it entirely?

That spot. The thing on the page absorbed more than ink. It took Kai's complete and utter attention, to the point that looking away felt like waking up from a horrible dream.

"Thank you for the book," he said, heading for the door. "And I'm sorry that I've been sneaking into your library."

Mr. Calderon's voice called after him as Kai reached for the doorknob.

"You are loved, Kai," said Mr. Calderon. "But you must be more than that."

Kai stopped, not believing his ears.

"Um," said Kai. "That's weird."

Mr. Calderon smiled sadly, for the first time looking genuine. He held up two fingers, tapping them first on the side of his head and then again on his chest. Kai recognized this Monhegan gesture at once: a reminder to let both the head and the heart instruct your actions equally.

"Never say that," said Mr. Calderon. "We should never let a loving thought pass through our minds without speaking it. I love that you have taken up an interest in your own education, and I hope you never lose your curiosity. The war is getting closer to the outer limits of the western continent every day, and love is something that we need more and more. It will remind us who we are once the violence inevitably lands on our shore. This is what my heart tells me. My head, on the other hand... my head knows that it will not be nearly enough. Fighting for the things and people you love might be what is burning down the world in the first place. You are loved, but you are also so much more. You are wise. Hold on to both the best you can." He sighed deeply. "Get out of here, Kai. I sense cake waiting for you. Enjoy it."

Kai's eyes brightened at the mention of cake and he practically ran out of the schoolhouse. He breathed in the night air, so crisp and showing the first signs of a bitterly cold winter rolling in. Kai stopped when the headlands came into sight, looking at the sickly orange glow which was rising from beyond the ocean. The mainland was burning. The glow had been getting brighter every night now, and Kai often heard the older people on the island whispering about it when they believed the children's ears weren't present.

They thought that the Global War would never reach a place as inconsequential as Monhegan Island, but eventually the branches of time reached a place of no return.

Across the dark waters, a warship was approaching.

* * *

Mr. Calderon sat down as soon as Kai was out of sight, putting a weary hand over his eyes and trembling weakly. His spiritualist leanings, which were far stronger than any Monhegan suspected, had flared up more than ever when he touched his student's temples. This was the first time Mr. Calderon ever lied to a student, but how in Desolation could he have spoken the truth? Gaia was *indeed* blossoming within the boy, and every single one of Kai's relaying pathways were opening. He showed greater potential than any relayer the old teacher ever encountered. Kai would grow to not have a single limitation on the amount of Gaian energy that could flow through him. A staggering thought, but hardly a comforting one. Strength was far from a gift in this new era when Gaian energy was being used to kill its own children.

Kai was *Him*.

Mr. Calderon was horribly sure now. Kai was the one that spiritualists whispered about, the apex of a well-meaning but disastrously misguided plot that spanned back thousands of cycles, to the roots of the Tree of Time itself.

He glanced up, staring again at the shadows at the far end of his library. Was it just his imagination, or were they staring back at him?

"What have we done?" Mr. Calderon asked the shadows. "We were wrong. *We were so wrong.*"

When Mr. Calderon had touched Kai, he saw only one thing in store for the child. In that fleeting moment of contact, he quickly withdrew his inner sight before being perceived by the searching darkness.

He had seen a black spot in a tangle of branches.

He had seen Desolation.

Chapter One

Nothing I Expected

Monhegan Island, Gaia

Kaija Monhegan's fifteenth cycle day was an objective improvement over her last one. Except for the severed finger.

And the frog abduction. Definitely except for that.

To be fair, it wasn't hard to improve on her fourteenth cycle day, when she had been trapped in a stranger's body in another universe and was nearly eaten by a plant on two separate occasions. Kaija decided that fifteen was going to be her best cycle yet, despite any severed finger, frog abduction, or thunder-lute playing old man who's supposed to be dead prophesying the multiverse being devoured by a cosmic force in an inevitably darkening future.

Yeah. That too.

"Sweet Gaia this hurts!" Jasper roared.

Kaija discovered her father crouched on the floor of their cabin, moaning and writhing in pain. The mythical sword of Edgard Zeig was tossed beside him, covered in blood and something that looked strangely like buttercream. The island's teacher, Ms. Clara, had apparently beaten

Kaija in an alarmed race to the kitchen and was in the midst of chastising her son.

"Can you explain to me why you thought it would be a good idea to use the most powerful weapon in the two known universes to *slice a piece of cake?*"

Jasper rocked back and forth on the kitchen floor, clenching his teeth and pressing a rag tightly to his bleeding hand.

"I worked really hard on that cake," he groaned. "I didn't want to mess up the decorations, and I thought that a sword capable of piercing the veil of reality could get me the cleanest possible slice. I should have kept my eye on the blade, but I noticed some sloppy piping work and it just slipped."

Before Ms. Clara had a chance to commence her inevitable lecture, the door swung open with a burst of wind and Kaija's best friend dashed into the room, wearing pajamas and looking like he just woke up.

"I heard screaming," Fain panted. "I thought I got all of the electric lobsters out of your bathroom last night, I swear! Is everybody o..." He trailed off, looking back and forth from Jasper to the kitchen table. "Never mind about the lobsters. That was, uh... a joke. We need to talk about that cake. You were right about using the sword, guardian. It's a perfect cut."

Kaija glanced up to see a multi-tiered cake displayed on their kitchen table. As a lover of all things sugary, it would have been the first thing she noticed if not for, you know: the severed finger.

The cake was three layers high and covered with buttercream that gradually changed from one vibrant color to the next. Pieces of exotic fruit and flower petals adorned the outside in fancy patterns, and a single, perfectly proportioned slice sat on a plate to the side.

"Wait," said Kaija, turning to her father. "*You* made this cake?"

Jasper's pained expression turned to one of almost child-like pride.

"Yes, do you like it? I've been teleporting myself to baking classes at Ornes Café on the mainland for months. This is my own recipe. Vanilla-rose cake with lemon buttercream, white chocolate ganache, and oceanic fruit. I was hoping to surprise you on your cycle day."

"I'm certainly surprised," admitted Kaija.

Ms. Clara remained unimpressed. She pointed her walking stick at the front door and shook an urgent finger at Fain.

"Go get your mother and tell her to gather the healers. Our brave guardian has been bested by a dessert. Hurry."

Fain readied himself to sprint out of the room, but Jasper waved a hand and the door slammed shut.

"No," he insisted. "Don't tell anyone. Besides, it doesn't hurt anymore. I think my finger grew back."

"Son," said Ms. Clara. "You're not a lizard. You know that fingers don't grow back, right? Please tell me I taught you that much."

"But it *did* grow back," said Jasper. He unwrapped the bandages slowly and counted his bloody fingers, one by one. "Yep. All five. It grew back."

"Then you clearly didn't cut it off in the first place!"

"No, I did! *See?*"

He pointed, and there was a collective groan in the room as they all spotted his severed finger, lying on the grimy kitchen floor by the sink. One or two sad sprinkles had clung to the finger beyond its secession from Jasper.

"Huh," said Fain. "What do you know? I still *haven't* lost my appetite, and that's saying something. Good work, guardian."

"Gross, Fain," moaned Kaija, although her stomach betrayed her with a rumble. It was hard not to feel hungry while in the presence of a culinary masterpiece.

"The cake is for the party later," said Jasper, standing up and stretching out his new finger. "But I suppose we could split a piece or two now. Fetch my sword, Fain."

"If you try to slice that cake with Edgard's sword one more time," said Ms. Clara, "I'm cutting your whole hand off myself."

"Kidding, mother. Kidding."

* * *

It was difficult for Kaija to focus during the morning lessons, but Ms. Clara insisted that school couldn't be canceled for everyone just because Jasper's finger got cut off. Kaija hadn't been this excited for her cycle day since she was a little kid. In the past, these celebrations served as a constant reminder of the pressing urgency to start relaying before it was too late. Not only was Kaija a relayer now, but she was arguably a great one. She learned advanced mentalist techniques from Ms. Clara with little effort, often stunning her classmates with the ease at which she now progressed. Kaija still couldn't do a single bit of relaying in the other disciplines, but her father was right: who cared if she could float a few rocks around? Levitation was boring compared to manipulating a higher plane of existence and swapping minds with someone on another world.

After school, Kaija arrived home to find most of her friends and family already waiting for her. Fain's parents, Maddox and Delia, were arranging a small collection of brightly-wrapped presents. Ms. Clara kept a close eye on Jasper as he prepared lunch, swatting his hand away from the sword several times. It was undeniably odd to be spending so much time with Ms. Clara, because it was only last cycle that Kaija learned the truth about the woman. Clara had kept the fact that she was Kaija's grandmother secret for fourteen whole cycles, hoping to bury the truth of Kaija's heritage. Edgard Zeig was her grandfather, the most powerful relayer of all time, and he probably would have been at this party too if Duncan Kacey hadn't killed him. The Crucifier's granddaughter, Maeryn, might not seem like the first choice to be one of Kaija's best friends, but they had all put the whole *your family has imposed generational trauma on mine* thing in the past.

"Are you sure you don't want to invite over any of the other kids?" asked Jasper.

Kaija shrugged. There weren't a whole lot of options for friends on the island. Fain was closest to her age, and they'd been inseparable ever since he moved to Monhegan. Even now that they were *more* than friends, he was still her best friend. The next closest in age were Alan and Valeria, but Kaija never hung out with them. It was too weird with Alan, not because he was several cycles older, but because he was the teacher's apprentice. How could you be friends with someone who taught you algebra? Valeria's problem wasn't her age either, but her repugnant personality.

There *was* someone else coming to the party, though. Someone exactly her age.

Ms. Clara winked at Kaija. They had been working on something for the last three months, and Kaija was excited to show off her new ability. She closed her eyes and felt for Gaia's energy. It came into her effortlessly and with so much more precision than when she started relaying one cycle ago. She used to take in too much power at a time and it made her abilities unpredictable, but with Ms. Clara's help she was gradually learning how to control it. Kaija moved her concentration to the mental realm and looked for the person always in the back of her head.

"Are you ready, Maeryn?"

An answer came without hesitation.

"Let's rock."

With one quick burst of mentalist relaying, another young woman immediately materialized in the cabin, making Fain jump back in surprise. She was slightly shorter than Kaija, with silvery blue eyes and long, vibrantly red hair. She wore tattered jeans and a T-shirt with the logo for her dad's progressive rock band, *Thunder Glove.*

"Hey, everyone," Maeryn said, waving shyly at the Gaians that she had not seen in person for nearly a cycle.

"*You* brought her here, Kaija?" asked Fain. "That's amazing!"

Kaija poked a finger playfully at Maeryn, and it went straight through the Earthling's head like she was made of mist.

"She's not *really* here," said Kaija. "I'm just projecting her consciousness into your minds. I'm surprised you can see her at all, Fain. I guess you really do have a brain."

"This is the best way for me to come and visit," explained Maeryn, "at least until the sword starts responding again."

Jasper walked around Maeryn several times, inspecting her in disbelief.

"Mental projection is an extremely advanced technique," he said, cracking a proud smile. "Even expert relayers don't normally manage this level of clarity. And with less than a cycle of practice? Kaija, I'm amazed. I can practically count the hairs on the Earthling's head."

"Good to see you too, Jasper," said Maeryn.

"It takes quite a bit of concentration from both ends," said Ms. Clara. "Maeryn and Max put in their fair share of work. These three seem capable of about anything."

"Max? Do you mean—" Fain began, but the moment he started to talk, Maeryn's wristband unwrapped itself and floated up into the air, morphing into the shape of a featureless chrome person no more than a foot tall.

"Fain, in the flesh!" shouted the tiny robot. "Good to see you, man! Epic high five!"

"Maximus!" yelled Fain, leaping up and running toward the robot. They swung their hands together, but Max's hand simply phased right through Fain's.

"Oh, that's right," said Max. "Ghost robot."

"Have you two been having a good birthday?" asked Ms. Clara.

"Yeah," said Maeryn. "We're all going to the opening of a new restaurant tonight. Dad's friends with the chef. He, um… *invented* him. How's your cycle day been, Kaija?"

"Great!" said Kaija. "Father cut off his finger and it grew back."

Maeryn's eyes widened.

"Grew back? Is that normal here?"

"No," said Jasper, standing up and flexing his hand awkwardly. "I actually wanted to ask you about it, Maeryn. Do you think the MotherTech serum has anything to do with this?"

"Possibly," admitted Maeryn. "I can ask my dad. He's been studying your blood sample. There are several million nanobots in your bloodstream keeping the Hydra poison at bay, and you're the only person to ever receive a full dose. It could be that the nanobots are rewriting your molecular structure to replicate some of the properties of a hydra vine."

Jasper sat with this information for a moment, and it became awfully quiet in the room as the implications dawned over everyone.

"So," said Jasper, "if I lost my head, it would just grow back?"

"Doubtful," said Maeryn, "it's much more likely that you'd grow two heads in its place."

Jasper waited for her to laugh, but Maeryn was already distracted by Fain approaching her with a plate of cake.

"Yes, yes," said Fain. "Jasper is a lizard, old news, but can we talk about how he made the best cake I've ever had in my life? You need to try this."

Maeryn walked over and looked at the glimmering dessert, her stomach rumbling somewhere in another dimension.

"I can't eat that, Fain. It has butter and eggs in it. I'm also not really in this universe, so there's that too. Shame, because it's awfully beauti— Max, what the heck are you doing?"

He had flown over to the table and was scanning the cake with glowing palms.

"I just created a taste sensory program," he said. "I've never eaten anything before, so this should be interesting. Didn't really see what the big deal was, putting digestible matter into your body and letting your squishy organs grind it around for a while. Can't see the appeal, but I'll try anything once."

Max's hand stopped scanning and he paused for a few seconds, savoring the virtual taste of the cake.

"*Oh. My. Gaia,*" he said, punctuating each word. "That's what stuff tastes like? I can only imagine how fun digestion is!" He started flying around the room excitedly. "To think that there are so many things I've never tried! Fresh croissants, fire-roasted tomatoes, chocolate-hazelnut gelato, cowering humans. My newfound hunger might just be a dark turn for humanity indeed." He gasped. "I wonder what dirt tastes like!"

Max phased through one of the walls in the cabin, and a few seconds later they heard his voice calling from outside.

"Wow, dirt tastes *horrible*. Best birthday ever!"

* * *

Kaija eventually sat down to open the presents that Maddox and Delia had collected from the islanders. There were even some from the mainland that a spacialist postman delivered earlier that morning.

Ms. Clara gave her an old, dusty book called *Music of the Forest* which was apparently salvaged from the remains of the old Monhegan schoolhouse. Kaija thanked her grandmother as enthusiastically as she could manage, but honestly she had never been much of a reader. Maeryn seemed a lot more interested in the book than Kaija was, but she grew increasingly frustrated at trying to turn the pages with her transparent hands.

Kaija's mother, Saura Aztala, sent her a gift from her home in the Oceanic Guardianship. This was the first time that Kaija had even received a card from the woman.

"Sorry I couldn't make it to your cycle day party, " Kaija read aloud from her mother's note, adding *'again'* with a roll of her eyes. "I've been busy taming a herd of wild watermammoths and I can't get away at the moment. I hope you find this gift useful. At your age, you're sure to start attracting the eyes of lots of young men, so I'd like to pass along something that will really get their attention."

Kaija opened the box and pulled out a thin dagger with a blade made out of red crystal. She smiled and pointed it menacingly at Fain. He laughed in response, sounding caught somewhere between amused and alarmed. Ms. Clara inspected the weapon closely, carefully running a finger along the edge.

"This is from Jabor," she said quietly. "I can't believe Saura would just give it away, even to you. No explanation or anything?"

"Jabor?" asked Kaija.

Ms. Clara's expression darkened, but only for a fleeting instant before brightening again.

"Never mind. Just know that it's valuable. And she's right, you know. A boy gives you the wrong kind of look, you give them a warning stab."

"*Warning stab?!*" Fain blurted out.

"Absolutely," said Ms. Clara. She demonstrated, spinning the crystal blade up into the air and catching it almost faster than they could track. She jabbed the blade once in a short motion.

"*Warning stab!* The trick is to aim deep enough to get a boy's head back on straight, but not enough to get charged for a high crime. Gaia, it's been at least forty cycles since I gave a good warning stab."

Her cold eyes darted back over to Fain as she handed the knife to Kaija.

"Not that *you* would have anything to worry about. Right?"

"Oh look, one more present!" Kaija said loudly, suddenly wondering when it got so hot in the cabin.

One final box sat on the table, a very small package wrapped in glittering purple paper. Kaija had no idea who it was from and hadn't even noticed it was there until a second ago. She picked up the attached note.

"What's it say?" asked Fain, and Kaija scrunched up her face in confusion.

"It says *what's it say?*" said Kaija. "And then it says, *where'd she go?* And that's it. Strange."

Max floated up to the box and began scanning it.

"What's inside?" asked Maeryn. "Is it safe?"

"It's not a bomb," said Max. "It's a... well, I'd hate to ruin the surprise. It's certainly nothing I expected."

Kaija lifted the lid cautiously and peered inside, not seeing anything at first. Nothing happened for a second or two, and then *everything* happened. A frog leapt out of the box, shot out its tongue, and licked Kaija right on the forehead. She instantly burst apart into a thousand glittering fragments which dissolved into the air, and in the same instant Maeryn and Max disappeared with her. The frog landed on the kitchen table, smashing a piece of cake and splattering icing onto the surrounding party guests.

"Where'd she go?" yelled Fain, wiping his eyes. "Hold on... *the card knew I was going to say that!*"

"My cake!" Jasper cried.

"Your daughter!" Ms. Clara cried louder.

Jasper held up a hand and his sword flew across the room. He gripped it fiercely and pointed the end toward the frog, who was now covered in buttercream and croaking happily.

"Why have you destroyed my masterpiece, frog? And *what did you do to Kaija?*"

Chapter Two

Written in the Freaking Stars

The moment the frog's tongue hit her forehead, Kaija found herself abruptly teleported to the middle of a sprawling field. Ruby flowers swayed in the chilly breeze, and a mountain reared its snow-capped head over the horizon. It was lunchtime on Monhegan Island, but it appeared to be early twilight wherever she was now. Kaija took a wobbly step forward, not quite used to the jarring sensation of teleportation.

"Maeryn? Are you still with me?"

"Yes." Maeryn's voice rang clear in Kaija's mind. *"My mental projection disappeared though, and I lost Max. He must have gotten sent back to Earth when we teleported. What the heck just happened? Where are we?"*

A voice spoke up behind Kaija, so close she could feel the person's breath on the back of her neck.

"We're in the Hellenic Kingdom, all the way across the Atlas Ocean. Lovely day for a lickin', isn't it, my frost flowers?"

Kaija spun around to see a woman with purple streaks running through her blonde hair. She wore a white flower behind one of her ears, so white it was nearly blinding. A rosewood ukulele was slung over her shoulder, little sparkling hummingbirds inlayed on the fretboard.

"Allie Zeig," said Kaija. "Why am I even surprised? Maeryn, I told you about her. She's the lady who talked to me through the mind of a frog a few months ago. The spiritualist knight? Remember?"

"Do you really think that's something I would forget?"

Allie glanced around, as if she was hearing Maeryn's thoughts as well. "The Earth girl is with you now, correct?"

"Yes."

"Good, because this gathering concerns both of you."

"Gathering?"

Allie looked around again, still searching for the source of the voice. A sudden realization seemed to hit her and she leaned in toward Kaija, knocking gently on her head several times.

"Hello in there, Earthling!" Allie called into Kaija's ear. "What a way to travel, eh? Yes, I have brought you both to the annual gathering of the High Spiritualist Circle, a collective of the seven most enlightened spiritualists across the planet. There will be a discussion that the two of you need to hear." Allie glanced at her wrist expectantly and nodded, despite the fact that she was clearly not wearing a watch. "Everybody was supposed to be here five minutes ago. Sweet! That makes me early, for once. Or the least late, I guess. Good enough for me!" She sniffed a few times. "Ah, I can smell them coming now."

There was a sudden rush of Gaian energy in the air and the ground began to quake. A giant flower bud, larger than a grown man, sprouted up from the field before them.

"This doesn't seem normal," said Maeryn. *"Should we be panicking? I feel like we should be panicking."*

Kaija's muscles tensed, but she remained calm and alert. "I don't know. Be ready for anyth—woah!"

In the next moment, so many wild things happened that Kaija and Maeryn could barely comprehend any of it. The bud blossomed into a dark blue bellflower, which drooped over and spit out an old woman. She stood up and began brushing the pollen off her clothes. At the same time, thousands of bees flew up from the grass, joined together, and transformed into a short man holding a bongo under his arm. An incredibly large man with a white beard descended on the field, riding a flying sky-moose. Several more people rapidly popped into existence, wandering around aimlessly as if they had gotten lost on the way to the bathroom. After a few seconds passed, there were six very unusual people standing in a circle.

"What's up, my dudes?" asked the short man. "Am I early? Sweet. Where's Jimmy P.?"

"Páigus should be arriving shortly," said Allie, pointing upward. "See? It's written in the freaking stars."

The evening sky faded above them, going from twilight to pitch black in less than a second. Thousands of stars rapidly popped into existence in the sky, one after another like holes being poked in a ceiling. One of the largest stars shot across the sky before falling to the ground, getting brighter and brighter as it descended toward the field as a small ball of light.

"James Páigus Zeig," whispered Allie. "Original knight of Edgard's High Seven, record holder for the world's longest thunder lute solo, and Grand Arborist of the High Spiritualist Circle."

"Wait, didn't he die?" asked Maeryn. *"I thought that he was killed by, um…"*

"Duncan the Crucifier? Oh, I'm sure he tried to give Páigus a good ole crucifixion, but it can be quite difficult to kill someone who can sense their own approaching demise. Hey, wasn't The Crucifier your grandfather? How cute! Small duoverse."

The shooting star collided with the ground, there was a bright flash of light, and an old man materialized in the center of the spiritualists. Páigus Zeig looked like an aged rock star from Maeryn's world. He wore tight black pants with a fiery serpent stitched down the side of one leg, and brightly colored beads hung from his tattered jacket. An instrument that looked vaguely like an electric guitar was strapped to his back, but it had two necks with far more than six strings on each. A sand cat paced the grass around Páigus, rubbing up against his leg and purring loudly.

"*Gaia*, he's cool," whispered Allie, leaning in toward Kaija. "The cat, I mean. Don't look at its eyes for too long, by the way, unless you want to witness the death of all your ancestors spanning the entire evolutionary line in a single instant. Not as fun as you might think."

Páigus observed the spiritualists around him with a quiet seriousness, and he clearly had the rapt attention of every man and woman there.

"As was written in stone, we are all five minutes late, therefore everyone is perfectly on time. Excellent. I'm afraid that we will have to delay the ceremonial jam sesh, because there are two important guests with us. My friends, this might be the most consequential gathering of the Spiritualist Circle in our lifetimes."

Páigus's eyes locked onto Kaija, and he seemed to look *into* her. Even Maeryn, who wasn't really in this universe at all, felt exposed by that stare. Despite the rag-tag nature of the spiritualists, both Kaija and Maeryn found themselves extremely intimidated by the old man. Ms. Clara had only briefly touched upon spiritualist relaying in her classes. It was the rarest of the disciplines, and sometimes thought to not even exist at all. Kaija had absolutely no clue what these people were capable of. For all she knew, Páigus could be looking into her future right now.

"What's up, Allie?" asked Páigus, turning and giving a half smile to the woman. "I see that you brought the granddaughters of Edgard Zeig and Duncan Kacey."

The short man let out a lingering *duuuude,* pulled a camera out of his fanny pack, and snapped a picture of Kaija. The other spiritualists began to whisper back and forth.

"That's right," said Páigus. "The young lady you see before you is Kaija Monhegan, the granddaughter of my former bud Edgard. And resting inside of her head is Maeryn Kacey, granddaughter of the man who killed him and fled to Earth. Against all odds, Gaia has forged a mindbridge across the two worlds to bind these young women together. Allie has been keeping an eye on them for me, and very recently my intuitions about this couple have become quite strong. I believe that they will have a direct influence on the Tree's coming divergence." Páigus narrowed his eyes and nodded to his companions. "Please summon our history, my friends."

All of the spiritualists brought in their circle, holding up their arms to the night sky. The Gaian energy in the air was breathtaking, the ground itself trembling amidst the undeniable force crackling from the bodies of the spiritualists. A blue beam of light shot from the earth in the center of the circle, growing toward the sky and splintering into sprawling branches. Golden leaves dangled from the divisions of the structure, illuminating the Hellenic field all the way to the distant mountain range.

Kaija heard Maeryn gasp loudly in her head.

"Do you know what that is?" she asked.

"Oh, sure," Kaija thought back. *"That's the tree that, um, does the thing with the stuff."*

"No! It was in the back of the book that Ms. Clara just gave you, but I couldn't find any more info. I was going to ask you about it."

The blue tree grew into the heavens, its branches dividing into what must have been millions of paths. Neither Kaija nor Maeryn could see how far the branches stretched into the night sky; they looked like they went on forever into space.

"I see the look of confusion on your face, Kaija," said Páigus. "It makes me wonder if my old friend Ms. Clara has taught you everything you need to know, or if you simply haven't paid attention. This is a map of every possible future. Each divide in the branches marks a significant turning point in our world's history."

Páigus snapped his fingers and a small pinpoint of crimson light appeared at the base of a tree, glowing like the eye of a cat. The light raced up along the multitude of branches, coming to a halt before a divide high up in the tree.

"After consulting thousands of cycles of spiritualist records, I have come to believe that this is where we currently are in the timeline. History is quickly approaching the next divide in the branches, and it will be one of great consequence. The *greatest* consequence. If Gaia should follow the branch on the right, there are billions of possible outcomes for the future of our world. If we trace the outcomes of the branches on the left, however, every possibility eventually leads to *Desolation*."

A large, black *thing* materialized ominously above them, a blackness somehow so dark that it contrasted with the night sky itself, and they saw that many branches of the tree were being swallowed up by whatever it was. After several seconds both Kaija and Maeryn had to look away, because the darkness seemed to be burning their eyes like an inverted sun.

"Desolation?" whispered Kaija. "That's just a saying. You know, like *that jerk can go straight to desolation.*"

"No," said Allie. "Desolation is believed to be the end of all things. If you trace the branches stemming from Desolation, some of them don't even originate from the ground of Gaia. Some of the branches come from—"

"Earth," Maeryn finished.

Páigus nodded solemnly, waved his hand, and the tree vanished, leaving them in a bracing darkness.

"The Kacey girl is correct. Spiritualists have always sensed Desolation, but trying to look into those futures can rip apart one's mind. It is almost as if seeing Desolation allows it to see you, but that brings me to my next piece of news. My friends, I have been contacted by a powerful new spiritualist on Gaia. This person possesses natural abilities which already rival my own after only one cycle of practice. Very recently they have had visions of Desolation and come out with their sanity still in one piece."

The news seemed to hit the other spiritualists like a bomb. There was a dead silence for what felt like minutes, and everyone's eyes darted back and forth to one another. Even Allie, who was previously distracted and unfazed, seemed rattled.

"Were they able to make sense of it?" she asked.

Páigus nodded. "Yes. They have given us what we have been searching for throughout all of time. They know *what* Desolation is. Legends speak of the Forest of Worlds, of universes dividing and receding endlessly into the cosmos. Earth, having crossed its roots with our own, has long been the only other world accessible from Gaia since the time of the Gardner. Now, however, it seems that there is another universe on a collision course with us. Desolation is more than an idea. It is a place. It is a world with an energy similar to Gaia's, but utterly devoid of goodness. The things that this new spiritualist glimpsed from Desolation were complete nightmares, things that have begun to haunt my every waking second. And this nightmare, my friends, has a good chance of finding our branches."

Things got very quiet once again, and both Kaija and Maeryn could sense a stirring in the mental realm. There were secret deliberations happening between the spiritualists, their thoughts expertly masked.

"Kaija," thought Maeryn. *"This is freaking me out. They're talking about us right now, aren't they?"*

"I don't know," thought Kaija. *"I'm just going to ask."*

"What? No! Do you really want to have the attention of all these—"

"If you're talking about me, you might as well do it to my face!" Kaija called out abruptly, and everybody, including the sand cat with its cloudy, golden eyes, turned to look at her.

"You are a bold young woman," said Páigus with a smile. "Just like your grandfather. Except for the young woman thing. Your grandfather was as bold as he was, uh, *not* a woman. There, that sounds better." He coughed. "Yes, Kaija. The fate of Gaia and Earth are increasingly intertwined as the branches approach Desolation. Time's growth is normally dependent on the uncountable actions of Gaia's entire population, but it seems this divide is different. Considering that you and Maeryn are the only known mindbridge to *ever* occur between the worlds, I believe that you have something to do with the upcoming divide. Perhaps you have *everything* to do with it, or perhaps nothing at all. We will see."

A bulky, middle-aged man wearing what appeared to be a grenade belt full of harmonicas stepped forward. "If this is true, then why not act now? Destroy any chance of Desolation reaching us?"

"Popper, you know as well as I do that the location of the Crossroots has been lost with the untimely death of my predecessor," said Páigus. "There is no more hope of reinforcing our trans-dimensional defenses."

Popper shook his head grimly.

"That's not what I mean. If the connection between Gaia and Earth is severed, wouldn't that naturally steer us away from Desolation? Would it be possible to break the mindbridge between these two girls?"

The man who had flown in on the sky moose looked aghast that someone would suggest this.

"No!" he yelled. "To destroy such a gift inside a mere child would be an abomination! Where is your Solstice Eve spirit?"

All of the spiritualists began arguing heatedly, shedding their previously carefree demeanor. Páigus Zeig spun his instrument over his shoulder, caught the upper neck, and played an ear-piercing high note which echoed epically throughout the fields. It silenced the group immediately, and everybody turned back to look at their leader.

"Settle, friends!" Páigus called out. "We will take a vote. Who believes that we should take action now?"

Three spiritualists raised their hands hesitantly.

"And who thinks that we need to stand back and observe?"

Three more spiritualists, Allie included, raised theirs with much more confidence.

"It seems that I am the tie breaker, although Professor Whiskers assured me this morning that this very thing would happen, so I am hardly surprised."

Páigus picked up his sand cat and began stroking its golden fur.

"I say we wait and stay ever watchful. Spread the word to your spiritualist brothers and sisters in lower circles that we are not to intervene just yet. However, the moment that it seems we are heading toward the worst possible future, we must unite and act despite any personal reservations."

There was a general sense of agreement in the crowd.

"Great. I sense a stirring in our corner of the Omnity. It seems our pizza will be arriving shortly. After we eat, there shall be a fast jam session and then a few rounds of truth or dare before we adjourn."

"Pizza?" asked Maeryn. *"He talks about the end of time, and then breaks for pizza? Kaija, can you slow them down?"*

"Hold on," thought Kaija. *"What kind of pizza?"*

"How the heck can you still be hungry?"

"Look at these people, Maeryn. Surely their pizza is some kind of like, I don't know: destiny pizza."

Allie smiled. "Ah yes, our destiny pizza is quite wonderful. Forget York or City of the Winds style, you haven't existed until you've eaten a slice of destiny-style from the fourth dimension. Unfortunately, our culinary pleasures are not meant for you, little frost flowers. If I let you stay any longer, I'm afraid that Jasper might hurt my frog."

"What?" asked Maeryn. *"Are you really going to tell us that we might alter the course of history, and then send us away without another word so you can eat pizza? What should we do?"*

"If I tell you any more, I am risking intervention and muddying the waters of my sight," said Allie, "but I *can* give you a slice of advice. To control your own futures, you must understand the present, but you can't understand the present without a clear view of your past. There is a part of your family's shared history that has been overlooked. That is where I would start. Goodbye, Kaija and Maeryn. Do try to be kind to the castaway. See you in the meadow."

Allie opened the bag that she was wearing on her waist and a small butterfly flew out.

"Be kind to who?" asked Kaija.

Allie simply smiled and waved goodbye. The butterfly landed on Kaija's shoulder and flapped its wings. In the next second, Kaija and Maeryn's whole existence seemed to explode with lights and colors.

* * *

"I'm only going to ask this one more time, frog!" screamed Fain. "Who are you working for, and what did you do to my girlfriend?"

The entire cabin had become a cacophony of shouting and conflicting scenes. The frog floated back and forth through the air, caught in a relaying tug-of-war between multiple people. Jasper's eyes were shut, fingers pressed to his temples while he was apparently trying to read the frog's mind. At the same time, Fain had somehow gotten ahold of Edgard's sword and was swinging it around wildly, missing the frog by a wide margin each time, either purposely or due to the fact that his mom was attempting to yank it out of his hands.

"You want your finger cut off too?" Delia yelled, giving another unsuccessful tug at the hilt. "Because I highly doubt that *yours* will grow back!"

Maddox could be heard outside, shouting instructions to a group of gathering islanders.

"Alan, prepare a missing child report for the accidental teleportation division of the HGA! Norio, tell the other Monhegans to start searching cathedral woods, that frog couldn't have sent her far. Go home, Valeria, this doesn't involve you!"

Ms. Clara had retreated to the far corner of the cabin, where she was pouring a second glass of wine and watching the scene with disinterest.

"This frog is a surprisingly powerful mentalist," Jasper muttered, eyes still shut tight in concentration. "But I get the sense that Kaija is nearby."

"Uh," said Kaija, poking her father on the back. "I'm right here. I've been back for, like, three minutes."

Jasper released the frog and swung around, grabbing Kaija's shoulders as the frog hopped out of the room behind him.

"Kaija! What in the world happened? I... *hold on.*" Jasper's expression of relief quickly faded. His eyes darted over to Fain, who dropped the sword and was shuffling toward the door. "What did you just call her?"

"Hey there, guardian," said Fain, still taking a few cautious steps toward the open doorway. "Is the party still on, despite the whole frog thing? Should I stay, or…" The door immediately closed on its own and locked right as Fain asked the question. "Yeah. I'll stay. Party on."

Jasper cleared his throat. "Did you say that my daughter is your *girlfriend?*"

Fain looked from Jasper, to Kaija, to his own parents, and then back to Jasper.

"Words are such a funny thing, aren't they? When you say *girlfriend,* do you mean—"

"For Gaia's sake, just tell him!" said Kaija.

Fain sighed and spoke quickly. "Yes, guardian. We've been dating for almost six months, and I think everyone else on the island figured us out, but Kaija's so wonderful and fun and amazing in every way that I'm not scared to admit it, even to *you,* and gosh I'm sure talking a lot, aren't I?"

"Six months?" asked Ms. Clara, setting down the glass of wine while barely restraining her laughter. "Is that *it?*"

To everyone's surprise, a wide smile cracked Jasper's face.

"About time!" he declared. "Oh, Kaija, this is great! You've had a crush on him ever since he moved here. And you didn't tell me? I'm so happy! Max, did you know this? *Max?*"

Jasper glanced around for the robot.

"Oh yeah, they're gone. We have a lot to talk about, don't we?"

Chapter Three

They Know

2173 A.D.
Indianapolis, Earth

Maeryn woke up on the floor of her living room, her face pressed to the carpet and the sounds of explosions thundering all around her. She bolted upright in surprise, only to see a giant red squirrel sprint past her, pulling the pin out of a grenade with its teeth and lobbing it across the room. A deep rumbling shook the ground as the grenade exploded, blasting a gaping hole in the living room wall. Maeryn instinctively shielded her head and crouched into a huddle.

"Hey, Maeryn. Just playing *Squirrel Turtle*. You fell off the couch, by the way."

Maeryn peeked up from her huddle to see her father, Dorian Kacey, swinging around a haptic glove. The holographic squirrel scurried up the wall and leapt onto a chandelier as it pulled another grenade from its belt.

"Dad…" moaned Maeryn, rubbing her carpet-burned face. "You're supposed to look after my body while I'm on Gaia."

"I was going to pick you up after I finished this round," he said distractedly. "But I— *oh darn it!*"

A blue turtle spun out of the hole in the wall, launching rockets from its shell that the squirrel narrowly avoided.

Dorian Kacey was technically the CEO of the largest artificial intelligence company in the United States, although these days he spent most of his time playing video games, practicing bass guitar for his garage band, and blowing stuff up in the backyard. His companion bot, Missy, was programmed to do the majority of the company's work while Dorian enjoyed a secret retirement.

"Anyway," said Dorian, not taking his eyes off the game as he swung his haptic glove again. "Did Kaija have a good cycle day?"

"A frog licked us on the forehead and sent us to the other side of the world," said Maeryn. "And then things got weirder."

"That's nice." Dorian bit his lip and leaned in toward the 3-D projector.

"Nice?" asked Max. "That stupid frog surprised Kaija so much that I got sent back to Earth. Didn't even get to scan another piece of cake."

Maeryn looked around to find Max sitting on the couch on the other side of her dad, wearing a tiny haptic glove which controlled the 3-D turtle.

"Did my amphibious abduction not concern you?" asked Maeryn.

"You've been in worse danger," said Max. "I was sure that a magic owl would save you from the evil frog, or something else zany like that. Think fast, Dorian!"

"Actually, it was a butterfly," admitted Maeryn. "But—"

Max's turtle avatar caught the grenade that Dorian tossed at him, threw it back, and the squirrel blew up in a puff of smoke and fur. A scoreboard appeared, floating in the middle of the living room.

Squirrel Turtle 2, Total Turtle-ocalypse

The Squirrel Republic has fallen

Maximus2000TheMovieTheReturn: 15 wins

Dorian Kacey: 0 wins

Maeryn's father stood up and threw his haptic glove onto the couch.

"No fair!" he cried. "You have the ability to make thousands of decisions per second, and I'm just a dumb human."

"Believe me, I know," said Max, "but I had my motor controls set to the level of a sixteen-year-old with severe attention deficit disorder, as usual, and I still whooped your—"

"Please listen to me!" Maeryn shouted.

Dorian turned off the projector and gave her a concerned look.

"Kaija and I got taken to a meeting of spiritualists," said Maeryn. "They knew about our mindbridge, and they said that we are going to make a decision which could potentially be the end of both worlds."

"You?" asked Dorian. "The end of Gaia and Earth? That's a little dramatic."

"Well, yeah!" Maeryn started talking more rapidly. "They said history is heading toward something called Desolation, and the final chance to keep it from happening is approaching."

Max floated over to Maeryn and landed on her shoulder, scratching his metal chin thoughtfully.

"Sister, you've studied nearly every book in Ms. Clara's cabin, and no serious Gaian scholar gives much credit to the things that spiritualists say. If they can see the future, why didn't they prevent the Global War?"

"Are you saying you don't believe me?"

"I'm just saying that we need to have a healthy dose of skepticism about this. During the battle outside the Capital walls, I saw that spiritualist knight just strolling around and reading a book. They're not right in the head."

To Maeryn's great annoyance, her father appeared just as skeptical.

"I know Gaia seems like a magical place," he said, "but it's all science. I've been studying Jasper's blood sample, proving my theory about the quantum entanglement that exists between a Gaian's mind and the energy that exists throughout their dimensional field. But visions of the future? The only way to see the future would be if the future already existed, and if the future already existed it wouldn't be the future, it would be the past. But if the past was the future, that would mean…" He continued babbling, but Maeryn tuned him out.

She understood everything that they were saying and basically agreed, but there was still a knot of anxiety in her stomach. Being told that the survival of two universes depended on you was not something to easily dismiss.

"…so time is basically a big tube that exists simultaneously beyond and inside our corner of the comprehension sphere," continued Dorian, standing up and stretching. "Don't let the omni-time-tube ruin your birthday. We can talk more about the apocalypse after dinner, if you'd like. I better get dressed."

Dorian headed toward the stairs, but an alarm started blaring from overhead just as he put a foot on the first step. The 3-D projector turned back on, displaying flashing words which spun around Dorian.

Press Conference in 1 minute

"Sweet Spaghetti Monster!" shouted Dorian. "I forgot about my conference today!"

He darted across the room and began digging through a basket of dirty laundry that had been sitting there for a week.

"Have you seen my tie?"

Dorian threw a pair of socks over his shoulder.

"Dad," said Maeryn. "Maybe change out of your pajamas before you put on a tie? Who are you meeting with?"

Dorian pulled a wrinkled jacket off a coat rack and put it on over his old concert T-shirt.

"The entire free world," said Dorian, clumsily buttoning his jacket. "The media contacted me a week ago about my press release, but I started planning for your birthday and totally forgot about it. *Why am I like this?*"

The words in the air began to change.

Live in 10

Live in 9

"Why didn't Missy remind you?" asked Maeryn.

"She's been busy pretending to be me," admitted Dorian, attempting to run a comb through his messy hair but soon giving up. "I told her I had things handled. Why the heck did she believe me?"

The countdown reached zero and the 3-D projector suddenly made the living room look like an enormous conference hall. Hundreds of reporters were in the audience, and a virtual microphone shot up from the carpet and hovered directly in front of Dorian, letting out a ring of feedback.

"Um," said Dorian awkwardly, tapping the mic. "Hi. I'm Dorian Kacey, but I guess you knew that already. I had a speech prepared, but I think I left it in my other pajama pants. So, as you all are aware, last year my sister Rosalie resigned from MotherTech and I've been running the business in her absence. I've decided to focus on my family full-time. Well, that and my music career. Thunder Glove's new album drops on the twenty-ninth, by the way—" Dorian noticed the reporters growing agitated and switched gears. "—but you didn't come here to hear about progressive math rock. You came here so I could announce my retirement and appoint a new CEO."

Amidst the sounds of obvious surprise from the press, a holographic woman materialized next to Dorian. Her posture was the complete opposite of his. She stood with the utmost confidence as her gray eyes rapidly scanned the crowd of reporters.

"Allow me to introduce Missy Kacey," said Dorian. "She is the first artificially intelligent mind that MotherTech ever created, and has been my partner in crime ever since."

He laughed nervously and wiped the sweat which was rapidly collecting on his forehead.

"Well, crime might not be the best way to put it. I assure everyone that I'm completely innocent. Not that there's anything to be innocent of, of course. What I'm trying to say is that I didn't do it, if there was indeed an *it* to be done. Am I talking too loud?" He glanced toward Missy and mouthed *help!*

Missy's holographic image stepped up to the microphone and patted Dorian on the back.

"Thank you so much for that charmingly human introduction, Dr. Kacey," Missy said with a smile. "I will take it from here." She turned toward the crowd. "As the first non-biological CEO of a major company, I realize that there is a lot of pressure on me at this moment in history. It is not my intention to replace humankind, but to be an eager collaborator in the advancement of both our species. I can assure you that MotherTech will continue providing the best companion bot services in the world, and that the possibility of a robotic uprising is far down on my to-do-list."

There were a few nervous laughs from the audience before Missy continued.

"Dr. Kacey and I have time for a few questions. We must keep it short, however, as we have a birthday party to attend."

She pointed to a reporter waving his arms in the front row.

"My question is for Dorian," he said. "Is it true that Rosalie has been reported missing?"

Dorian's fingers started tapping nervously on his leg.

"My sister is a very private person," he said. "I assure you that she is currently enjoying her retirement."

None of the reporters seemed satisfied with this answer, and lots of them continued waving their arms. Missy turned to Dorian and spoke in his ear.

"Best let me handle this," she said. "You go be with your daughter."

Dorian took a step back and all of the reporters vanished from their living room as the projector switched off. He collapsed on the couch and began to unbutton his jacket.

"That was exhausting," he moaned. "I'm getting so sick of lying."

Dorian had been cheerful all day, but now a familiar sadness was creeping back into his face.

"About Rosalie," said Maeryn. "Have you been able to—"

"No," he interrupted. "Not a sign of her. Let's just forget about it and enjoy your birthday."

Dorian stood up and abruptly walked out of the room to get dressed. Max floated next to Maeryn on the couch and put his small hand on her own.

"This has been really hard on him," he said. "I know that Rosalie is far from perfect, but she's still the only family we have in the dang universe. He misses her, and he thinks that she hates us now."

Maeryn nodded and pushed back her own tears. Rosalie had grown up hearing horrible stories about the people of Gaia, and she was terrified by the prospect of a bridge being built. Last year, Rosalie reluctantly allowed the Gaians to travel to Earth so Jasper could be healed, but that was the last time they saw her.

Rosalie Kacey has been missing for a year.

* * *

In the early hours of the next morning, Maeryn lay in her bed and tried to distract herself from the anxious feelings threatening to engulf her. She was on her tablet, reading *The Count of Monte Cristo* for her online literature course, but was finding it really difficult to concentrate.

Maeryn had been in immediate danger a year ago. She almost got eaten by a hydra vine, Jasper was badly poisoned, and Rosalie tried to stab Kaija in the neck with a syringe. So many things about this birthday were better. Maeryn got to see her friends on Monhegan Island. Her normally overworked father took her to an amazing restaurant today where the robotic chefs made you a personalized meal after scanning your taste receptors. Max tasted every single dish, including multiple things which weren't food at all. Despite all of this, Maeryn couldn't shake the feeling that this year the danger was simply festering out of sight. Rosalie was missing, and the spiritualists on Gaia somehow knew all about the connection between her and Kaija. She felt like she was watching storm clouds approaching in the distance, but nobody else could see them.

"Max? Are you here?"

Max's voice spoke up in her earpiece at once.

"Thank goodness you're awake. I can't sleep either."

"Max, you *literally* can't sleep because you don't require it."

"I know, Maeryn, but I usually don't keep all of my thought processors running this late at night. I'm so paranoid all of a sudden. I think someone is stalking us. Recently, I've noticed that everywhere we go the security cameras have been watching us exclusively, and every time I'm on the internet I feel like someone is following me just out of sight."

"Oh boy. This is just like the time you thought that birds were spying on us, and that turned out to be nothing."

"For your information, those birds are still on my watch list. No, today it's a little different. This morning when I went into the kitchen, I swear that the refrigerator gave me a suspicious look."

"I doubt that our refrigerator is watching you."

"That hurts, Sister. I think we need to start believing in each other more. I promise to believe that you and Kaija are the chosen ones if you believe that our refrigerator is hiding a dark secret going back for generations."

Maeryn turned off her tablet and set it on the bedside table, rubbing her tired eyes.

"I wish you could have seen what those spiritualists were doing. Sure, they're weird, but I can't believe that everything they said was just nonsense."

"Maybe you're right," admitted Max. "I've been running some calculations, and if somebody has a perfectly clear view of the present they might be able to accurately predict events in the near future. I do things like that all the time on a smaller scale. The amount of data that these spiritualists would have to absorb would be enormous, but Gaian energy might just make that possible."

Max's comment reminded Maeryn of something. "Just before we left, one of the spiritualists said that if I wanted to control my own future, I would need a better understanding of my past. She said that there were things about our families still to be discovered. Could you send Duncan's journal to my tablet?"

"I've read it ten thousand times already, Maeryn. If there was something hidden there, I would have found it by now."

"I know, but if we start putting what I've been learning on Gaia together with the information in my grandpa's journal, we might get a more accurate picture of our history."

"Every time I do this you end up regretting it. Let it go."

"Do it, Max."

Maeryn's tablet lit up with the pages of Duncan's journal. Maeryn had only read it a handful of times, and almost never to the very end. The writings were horrible, full of graphic descriptions of the Gaian war, of fields full of bodies and the sky on fire. Her grandpa was the man who basically raised her, but he had a dark and bloody past on Gaia.

Maeryn scrolled past the introduction in the journal and began reading about Duncan's early life.

I grew up during a time of global war, the son of a poor blacksmith in the town of Kacey, an inconsequential village along the coast of the Europan guardianship. The western continent had been discovered by a group of lost sailors several centuries ago. It seemed that the Nomadic people of the west did not wish to be found, and long ago controlled the currents of the ocean to lead travelers away from its shores. Once the guardianships learned the scope of this new continent to dominate, it started a global war which lasted 500 cycles. War is something that the Gaians excel at; our blood makes us living weapons.

I was a late bloomer in relaying, only just beginning to show some internalism by the age of fourteen. It was mostly for my extremely high marks on intellect exams that I was selected to be trained for the Europan navy reserves. The minimum age for the draft kept gradually getting lowered as the war raged on, and I was barely sixteen when I shipped off to the western continent. My unit's mission was to take control of the islands along the continent's Northern edge, clearing out any natives as we went. My natural talent in machinery made me fortunate enough to be given the job of maintaining the ship's engine and building weaponry, therefore avoiding the worst of the combat. The little fighting that I did see was... well, it was enough. The task was a generally easy one at first; the western Nomads were highly skilled spacialists and normally used their abilities to run when they saw ships approaching. Soldiers used to joke that if the Nomads learned to fight, nobody would ever see them coming.

The course of my life was inalterably changed when we reached an island along the northernmost corner of what would soon become Edgardia. The people on that island did not run. They did not fight. They simply knelt and refused to leave. I was called in from my post to assist in the "removal." We were commanded to dispose of the islanders, and I did as I was told. If I hadn't, it would have been my life that ended that day. Sometimes I wonder if that would have been better. The island's teacher looked me directly in the eyes as I pressed a blade to his chest, and he said something that I would never forget.

"If you strike down those who refuse to fight, Gaia will be watching. She will curse your family for generations."

I'm afraid that he was right. After the horrible slaughter was done, my head became cloudy and a vision swam before my eyes. I saw a ship full of children leaving the island, apparently having fled unnoticed by the soldiers. A boy several cycles younger than myself stared into my eyes, as if he could somehow see me. His expression was of someone with the knowledge that their entire life was being burned to the ground behind them, and that I was the one doing the burning. These visions left as quickly as they came, and I still do not know where they came from. That boy's face would be branded into my memory until I saw him again, four cycles later.

That face.

That face, and the end of the fighting.

The war ended with the entire sky set ablaze. Mountains shattered, leaving gaping chasms in the ground. Animals went wild, shrieking as the planet trembled and the air filled with ash. Amidst the chaos, I saw him. Floating in the fiery heavens, untouched by the inferno as he looked down at the desolation. The boy from—

"Maeryn?" Max's confused voice spoke in her earpiece. "Do you hear that?"

Maeryn listened carefully, and she heard the humming sound of a hovercraft somewhere in the sky above. It got louder and louder, rattling the entire house with its sonic waves.

"What's going on?" asked Maeryn. "Who is that?"

"I'm trying to access our outdoor cameras, but they've all been disabled. Let me go look."

Maeryn's wristband floated up from the bedside table and quickly flew out the window. A few seconds later Max spoke rapidly in her ear.

"Maeryn, this is bad. You have to—"

A screeching noise blasted from Maeryn's earpiece. She yanked it out and threw it onto her bed, where it continued wailing. The lights in the whole house turned on and glowed red as a man's deep voice began to talk out of every speaker in the walls.

They are coming.

The Angels are gone.

They know.

Chapter Four

The Castaway

Monhegan Island, Gaia

Kaija strolled along the headlands, holding hands with Fain and watching the sun set on her fifteenth cycle day. Down the hill, an ocean breeze rippled across the flower meadow like waves as a swarm of spacialist butterflies flickered in and out of existence.

"Whelp," said Fain, "I think this still tops last cycle. Sure, your father found out that we're dating, but at least it's not the end of the world. Or is it? Maybe that's what the spiritualists were talking about. If Jasper catches us kissing, he'll take the whole universe out with me."

"Oh, please," said Kaija. "*Your* dad is the overly protective one. Mine's just clueless. Everybody else on the island has known we were dating since, like, last cycle. What did he think we'd been doing, sneaking off every other evening? Trying to ride the sky lizards in Gull Cove?"

"To be fair, we *have* done that a few times."

"I guess so."

They walked a little bit further in silence, enjoying the peaceful twilight settling over the island. Kaija kicked a rock off the cliff and

46

watched it disappear into the ocean, her eyes glazing over as they stared down at the darkening coastline. Fain groaned as Kaija's grip gradually became tighter and tighter on his fingers, although she seemed completely unaware of this.

"Something's up with you," said Fain, pulling his numb hand away and massaging it.

"Well yeah something's up!" Kaija exclaimed, kicking another rock off the cliff. "The *apocalypse* is what's up!"

"You *believe* the spiritualists?"

"Not really, but what if there's even a small chance that they're right? Things have been going so well. The Western Blaze has gone quiet on the mainland, and our relaying training with Ms. Clara has been really fun. A while ago I would have given anything to have an adventure, but that's the last thing I want now. I just want to enjoy the last cycle before our apprenticeships start. I... I *really* like you, Fain."

Kaija moved in to kiss him, but he didn't appear to be listening anymore. Fain was leaning forward toward the edge of the cliff, holding a tree for balance as he squinted down at the waves crashing against the shore.

"Kaija?" he asked, voice rising in urgency. "What is that?"

Kaija peered down the rocky embankment, and fifty arms below them she saw that something had just washed up onto a boulder. No, *someone.* A body was lying face down on a rock, one arm hanging limply into the water. Allie Zeig's departing words rang in Kaija's mind.

Do try to be kind to the castaway.

"Fain, that's a person down there!"

Fain and Kaija's instincts took over as they locked arms and leapt off the cliff. A great burst of wind came out of nowhere, collecting below their feet and slowing them down as they approached the slick rocks. Kaija grabbed the body and turned it over to get a look at the face.

The castaway was a young man who looked to be about twenty cycles old. There were fresh burns all over his body, his right shoulder was bleeding profusely from a puncture wound, and one of his ears was gone entirely. Kaija gagged when she looked down at the body's lower half, because one of his legs was bent the wrong direction at the knee. His clothes were blackened and torn, and Kaija spotted the symbol for spacialism tattooed across his muscular chest. The tattoo showed what looked to be two butterflies wing to wing: one entirely white and one entirely black. Upon further inspection, they were the same creature, the black silhouette just the negative space left behind by the teleporting white butterfly.

"I've seen him before," said Fain, his face going pale. "Is he... *you know*? Dead?"

Kaija placed a hand on the boy's forehead and felt around inside his mind. The mental realm was a complex place, and it was nearly impossible to read a stranger's exact thoughts. A powerful mentalist could get only glimpses, but Kaija had been training hard. She pulled several flickering images from his mind to her own.

"He's alive," said Kaija, closing her eyes and letting the fractured memories wash over her. She saw a burst of white-hot fire and a group of blurry figures in combat. Pain echoed through Kaija's body, but it was distant and dull like pain from a dream.

"Somebody attacked him..."

Now Kaija saw a bloodied and burning figure teleporting into the ocean. He gasped from the bracing cold and was completely submerged, yet somehow the flames remained eating away at his skin. The saltwater was unbelievably painful on his open wounds. The memories flashed forward and Kaija saw Monhegan Island in the distance. He kept teleporting in small leaps at a time, getting closer and closer to the shore, but darkness was threatening to engulf his mind. Despite the overwhelming agony and drain on his relaying, he kept pushing away unconsciousness. He *had* to make it to Monhegan, it was his only hope. The memories became foggier, his mind slipping away to nothingness.

"He passed out while swimming to Monhegan. He's on the brink of death."

Fain stood up and looked toward the rocky cliff towering above them.

"There's no way we can carry him up these rocks," he said, wiping his wet hands on his pants. "I'll go get my mother. Stay with him."

Fain was already scaling the rocks, but Kaija grabbed the back of his shirt.

"No," she said. "It'll be too late by the time we find her and get back here. I'll do it."

Kaija closed her eyes and opened herself up to the wider mental realm. It was like water, and Kaija effortlessly sent ripples across to the other side of the island.

"Father, we found someone on the shore by the headlands. He's dying. We need Delia."

Barely a minute later Jasper leapt down from the cliffs, landing on the rocks with a sharp *crack*. He was followed closely by Fain's mother, gracefully scaling down the cliffside with her hair tied up in a long braid behind her back. Without hesitation, Delia bent over the body and began emitting waves of blue light from her hands. The figure's breathing immediately steadied and his burns began to dull in color. Jasper studied the boy's face closely as he wrapped a bandage around the still bleeding shoulder.

"This is Elias Zeig," he said.

"Zeig?" asked Kaija. "He works for the High Guardian?"

"He's the spacialist knight of the High Seven. His body shows marks of a battle." Jasper finished tying the bandage and wiped the sweat from his brow, barely blinking. For the first time, he looked truly concerned.

"Elias is one of the most skilled relayers on the continent," he continued, shaking his head. "I don't understand how someone could have done this."

* * *

Kaija eagerly awaited for news of Elias Zeig the next morning. He had been rushed off to the medic cabin for healing with Delia, and Kaija watched from her window all night as healers kept coming and going in shifts. She pestered her father during breakfast as he fried eggs on the stove.

"Do you think Elias is going to be okay?"

Jasper tossed an egg up from the frying pan, which froze in the air for a moment as he examined it. "The young man's lungs took in a lot of water. Delia did her best to heal the burns, but most of them are going to leave some bad scar tissue. His right arm has minor nerve damage, but it should go away with time and further healing sessions. If you hadn't found him, he probably would have died by morning. Darn it! I broke the yolk."

"Who could have hurt one of High Guardian Thomas's knights that much?"

Jasper glanced up from the frying pan.

"I don't know. Landing a blow on a skilled spacialist is nearly impossible. When we won the battle at the Capital last cycle, it was only because most of the Western Blaze ran away when they saw me coming. Whoever did this must have taken him by surprise."

Jasper sent Kaija's breakfast levitating across the room, landing it gently on her plate. They ate with little conversation, both of them more thoughtful than usual. Kaija wondered if the appearance of Elias had anything to do with the Spiritualist Circle's cryptic predictions. Either way, a lot of things seemed to be happening at once in her life after several months of relative calm. Just as she was bringing her plate to the sink, Kaija felt a sudden jolt in the mental realm.

"Do you feel that?" asked Kaija, looking around for the source.

Before Jasper could answer, a transparent figure appeared in the middle of their kitchen. He was a heavy set old man with thinning blonde hair and a blazing red Z embroidered on his vest.

"High Guardian Thomas," said Kaija. "But—"

Jasper quickly put a finger up to his lips and shushed her. The High Guardian seemed to address nobody in particular as he spoke in his rumbling voice, simply staring at their icebox in the corner.

"Good morning, Edgardians. I am sending this message via TEMS network to the entire guardianship. It is with deep sorrow that I must announce the closure of many more telestations. Half-blooded Nomads have long operated these businesses, but I have recently come to believe that they cannot be trusted. The Nomads revealed their violent intentions during the attack on the Capital last summer. While it is true that all terrorist activities have ceased since their defeat, it appears likely that they have been using this time to recruit and gear up for a larger attack. Half-blooded Nomads must now register with the guardianship to prove their loyalty. The telestations will reopen eventually, but until then you must be flexible with travel arrangements."

Addresses from the High Guardian had become more common since the attack on the Capital, but Kaija couldn't help but feel like something was different this time. Thomas's voice seemed slightly less confident, and Kaija could feel waves of uncertainty radiating from his mental projection. The High Guardian kept reaching up toward his chest, rubbing his thumb and index finger together in an unconscious nervous gesture.

"The very nature of spacialism has become incompatible with modern society. It has been used to trespass over borders, kidnap innocent people, and flee punishment. Therefore, it will now be considered illegal in Edgardia to display any degree of whole-body spacialist relaying. The Nomadic people are free to live here in the reserved lands that Edgard graciously offered them, so long as they do not cross the borders or give in to their violent nature."

Thomas reached up toward his chest again, and it hit Kaija what was missing. The green stone that the High Guardian always wore around his neck, one of Edgard's seven artifacts, was *gone*. Thomas seemed to become aware of his nervous gesture for the first time and his hand shot back down to his side. He spoke again with a renewed, fierce confidence.

"Because it is impossible to hold a spacialist in prison, any Edgardian using whole-body teleportation will be considered a traitor and shall be killed on sight without exception."

* * *

"Today, children, we will be learning the basics of teleportation," said Ms. Clara with a cheerful smile.

Normally the thirty-two schoolchildren of the island separated into different groups and learned according to their ability levels. The younger children met with the apprentice teacher to learn reading and math, while the teenagers who had begun to relay worked with Ms. Clara. Students who had reached their sixteenth cycle were mostly gone, having started their various apprenticeships both on and off the island. Ms. Clara oversaw everything and introduced the day's lesson to the entire group before splitting them up. Her apprentice teacher, Alan, stood by her side looking increasingly uncomfortable as she spoke.

"Spacialism is a discipline with a rich history in every single guardianship," said Ms. Clara, "although the indigenous Nomads of Edgardia by far have the greatest mastery of the technique."

"How are we supposed to learn spacialism if we don't have Nomadic blood?" asked a young student.

"Culture is more influential on relaying ability than blood, and neither are as important as practice. Did you know that not all Nomads are natural spacialists? Their culture places such importance on teleportation that even those with the weakest leanings are eventually able to master the basics, but there are Nomads who are more natural relayers of other disciplines. While it is true that focusing on your strengths can lead to the greatest outcomes, most Gaians are capable to some degree of relaying with every discipline. Let's say that you were, hypothetically," she gave a knowing look to Fain, "trapped in a prison cell. Being able to teleport a single arm's length might just save your life."

A look of panic had been growing on Alan's face throughout Ms. Clara's speech and he kept coughing to try to interrupt her.

"Ms. Clara?" he asked finally. "Didn't you see the High Guardian's message this morning? You know, the one where he said that teleportation is a crime worthy of capital punishment? That one?"

Ms. Clara laughed flippantly.

"Oh, *I saw it.* My old friend Thomas thinks that he can regulate a normal function of the Gaian body. Not a word from the Western Blaze in an entire cycle, and our High Guardian is becoming paranoid. The very fact that he fears spacialism makes it all the more important that we learn what it is truly about. He speaks only to spread fear, as his law is entirely unenforceable."

The group of children and teenagers whispered back and forth in a nearly equal mix of excitement and anxiety. Valeria, a girl in her thirteenth cycle, crossed her arms and shook her head stubbornly.

"I'm not doing this," she called out. "We moved here to get away from the Nomads, not learn about them."

Ms. Clara's warm smile did not falter. She picked up her walking stick and pointed it toward the village.

"Very well, Valeria. If you feel that you know what is best for your education, go home today."

Valeria turned around and stormed off through the crowd of children. Ms. Clara planted her walking stick back into the ground and the island trembled slightly.

"Anyone else?" she asked, her kind expression beginning to wane.

Much to everyone's surprise, her apprentice's hand went up first.

"I'm sorry, Ms. Clara," said Alan. "I'm reaching my eighteenth cycle in a few weeks, and I can't be breaking the law. Even a dumb law. I'll come back and help you once we've moved on to the other disciplines."

Alan turned around and walked off, several more of the older teenagers taking his lead and following.

"This is crazy," Kaija thought to Fain. *"Can you believe that they're doing this to Ms. Clara?"*

It took a few seconds before Fain's hesitant reply came, and he didn't quite meet her eye.

"The High Guardian did say that teleportation is punishable by death. I've already been arrested by him once, I shouldn't be pushing my luck."

"Oh please. You saved his life! Thomas is not going to come to some island in the middle of nowhere and kill a bunch of kids. It's an empty threat. Spacialism might be really useful."

"I guess you're right. It would be really fun to teleport into the fruit cellar and surprise my parents."

Almost half of the students had left to go home, but Ms. Clara smiled to see that Kaija and Fain remained.

"Kaija, will our friend be joining us?" she asked.

Kaija shook her head. There had been absolutely no word from Maeryn this morning, so Kaija assumed that she slept in. The two would occasionally switch places so that Kaija could learn about Earth and Maeryn could practice her externalist relaying. The other students vaguely understood that Kaija's mentalism allowed her to switch places with someone from a place called Earth, but most of them seemed to have trouble comprehending exactly *where* and *what* Earth was.

"Very well," said Ms. Clara. She waved her stick and dozens of stones floated up from the ground. "Please take one and hold it in your left hand."

Kaija snatched a rock, remembering how she used to try so hard to levitate pebbles before discovering her natural mentalist leanings. Technically she *still* couldn't do this, but it hardly seemed worth the effort when she could do things like manipulate the mental realm.

"Gaia does not exist in physical space like we do," said Ms. Clara. "It is everywhere in our universe at once. The stone can move from your left hand to your right hand by traveling through space if you throw it, or the stone can pass through Gaia and switch hands instantaneously."

Ms. Clara grabbed a stone out of the air and demonstrated. It vanished out of her left palm and reappeared in her right.

"Rather than drawing in the energy of Gaia, focus on pushing the rock into her stream."

Several of the older students were able to do it on their first try. Fain leaned closer and closer toward the stone with each failed attempt, screwing his face up in concentration.

"Be gone, evil rock!" he called, and gasped when it vanished in his palm. A second later the stone reappeared in the same exact spot in his same hand with a dull pop, deflating Fain's excitement.

"I think it moved slightly to the right," said Kaija, trying not to laugh.

"Hey," said Fain. "For all you know, the rock might have gone to the moon and back in that split second. Let's see you do better."

"Fine."

Kaija's rock immediately vanished.

"*What?*" asked Fain. "How did you... *wait a minute!*"

Before Kaija could react, Fain reached out and snatched the rock from her hand, which had, in fact, not been teleported at all. Kaija had simply tapped into Fain's mind and erased the rock from his perception.

"Cheater!" he said. "You owe me big time! Try again, and no mentalism!"

Fain tossed her the rock. Kaija grabbed it, closed her eyes, and felt for the Gaian energy all around her. A spark ignited within her heart, and she nudged at the rock with her mind. With great effort, it flickered away to nothing. Both Kaija and Fain gasped, but nothing else happened. The rock was just gone.

"I did it! Well, sort of. Where'd it go?"

Fain and Kaija looked around, but the rock was nowhere to be seen.

"I guess it could be anywhere," said Fain. "The bottom of the ocean, the Hellenic mountains, somebody's breakfast in Oahu. They could be choking right now, you murderer!"

Kaija tried again and again throughout the remainder of the morning lesson, but wasn't even able to vanish another stone. The act of making one disappear was enough to leave her so completely drained that she felt like she might pass out before lunchtime. Fain, along with all of the other students in their age group, eventually mastered each of the basic spacialist techniques without breaking a sweat. Once again, Kaija was the exception.

She stomped back to her cabin at lunchtime, slamming the door behind her and shedding the confident face she had put on. Why was this so difficult? Kaija's grandfather had been the greatest relayer of all time in every single discipline, and Ms. Clara wasn't far behind him. How could it be that their granddaughter struggled with basic techniques?

Kaija went into the kitchen to eat anything sugary she could find, surprised to find that the small room was stuffed full of people. Jasper, Maddox, Delia and at least a dozen more adults were huddled around the wooden table, whispering heatedly. As soon as Jasper spotted her, he gave the other adults a severe look and they all stopped talking abruptly.

"Meeting adjourned," he said. "I'm afraid that I'm going to have to put my foot down on this one. I am your guardian, and while I prefer to be democratic about things I also have every right to use my authority. If you don't like my decision, you are free to leave the island."

Jasper pointed to the door without a hint of the usual warmth in his face. The adults all departed, several of them grumbling to themselves discontentedly. Delia gave Kaija a warm smile as she passed, but her husband Maddox stayed at the kitchen table with an awful scowl on his face.

"What's going on?" asked Kaija.

"The Nomad woke up," said Maddox. "He's asking for you."

Chapter Five

Not Doing the Thing

Indianapolis, Earth

"Max!" Maeryn screamed. "What's going on?"

Alarms blared throughout the Kacey estate and the lights flashed an eerie red. Maeryn opened the blinds in her bedroom to see a tank sitting on the road in front of her house, pointing its massive plasma cannon straight at her window. Soldiers lined the road and hovercrafts blinded the property with searchlights. Despite the escalating chaos outside, Maeryn was most thrown by the deep voice she had just heard speaking through her house's PA system.

Max flew back into the room and began zooming around in anxious circles.

"It's the military. Fifty soldiers in smartsuits, three tanks, and two hovercrafts."

"Did you hear that voice?" asked Maeryn. "I thought it came from our house's operating system, but it wasn't Missy. It sounded like…" Maeryn closed her eyes and rubbed her forehead. "No… *it couldn't be.* It's impossible."

Max soared up to Maeryn, putting his little hands on either side of her head and shaking frantically.

"Maeryn, you're always hearing voices!" he shouted. "But do you remember that time a freaking army was on our front lawn? You know, the thing that's literally happening in the present tense? Maybe focus on that right now!? We're going to have to fight our way out. Let's do that thing I've been talking about."

Maeryn shook off her confusion and looked out the window at the soldiers piling out of trucks, inching closer to the house with weapons drawn.

"The thing?" she asked. "That's maybe the worst idea you've ever had. You want those soldiers to open fire on us? We have to find my dad."

Maeryn ran out of her room and took the steps downstairs three at a time, Max flying close behind. They found Dorian in the living room, staring out of the window from the couch with a glazed over look in his eyes. Dorian's dazed expression hardly made him look like someone whose house was under siege. Maeryn grabbed her father's arm and tried to pull him up, but he flopped back down limply on the couch.

"Dad! What are you doing? Soldiers have our house surrounded! We have to…" Maeryn trailed off, not really sure what they had to do. "…to do *something!*"

Dorian clutched his messy red hair and appeared to shrink even further into both the couch and himself.

"There's nothing we can do," he said, his voice barely audible over the approaching sirens.

Maeryn waved her arms at the camera on the ceiling. "Missy! Help us!"

"Tried that already," said Dorian. "Missy is programmed to operate within the law unless there is an impending mass extinction. She can't interfere with the military. I'm on my own here."

A man's voice began to blast out of a loudspeaker in their front lawn, making Maeryn jump in surprise. Dorian barely moved; he seemed to be expecting this.

"This is the United States military!" yelled the man. "You are under arrest, and are to be held on trial for numerous federal crimes, including treason. Discard all MotherTech equipment on your body and come out with your hands up."

"We have to run!" shouted Maeryn, still pulling at her father.

"They'll shoot us," said Dorian. He took in a shaky breath and looked at her with tired, red eyes. "My sister and I spent years building a robotic army while breaking every law in the Geneva A.I. Warcrime Accords. We wanted to keep this universe safe from a possible Gaian invasion. Rosalie did her best to keep our project a secret, but something must have gone wrong. A few weeks ago I went to our weapons headquarters to begin the process of dismantling the Guardian Angels . The entire facility was empty. Security cameras were blank. Government must have found it. I'm a criminal."

Dorian stood up and wrapped Maeryn in a sudden, tight hug. She tried to think of some possible way around this, but Earth was nothing like Gaia. They couldn't just run away and disappear; her father could easily be tracked to any corner of the planet by U.S. security drones.

"I'm so sorry, Maeryn," said Dorian, holding back tears. "I've put you through so much that you never deserved. I love you, and I'm going to end this."

"We can find a way to get to Gaia," said Maeryn, readying herself to contact Kaija. "They can't get to you there!"

The man on the loudspeaker began shouting again.

"In ten seconds we are firing our sleep bombs. Step outside NOW."

Dorian let go of his daughter and walked for the door.

"I have to pay for the person I was, and if I fight this, I do it the right way."

He opened the door and blinding lights shone in from outside, filling the room with flashes of red and blue. Dorian turned around to give a final look to Maeryn and Max.

"Dorian..." said Max, for once at a loss of words.

"I love you too, son," said Dorian. "You two stay safe."

He grabbed Maeryn's hand, squeezing it like it was the last time he would see her. He put the hand to his closed eyes and let out a sob.

"No matter what happens," he said. "I'll always—"

The voice on the loudspeaker cut him off. "Last chance to do this peacefully, Francis Rodriguez!"

Dorian's eyes popped open and a confused look passed between him, Maeryn, and Max.

"Did he just call you Francis Rodriguez?" asked Max.

"Are they at the wrong house?" asked Maeryn, but the words sounded so utterly ridiculous the moment she said them.

A crazy hope now shone in Dorian's eyes.

"I don't know," he said quickly, "but I better get out there right now and tell them that I'm not, uh, Francis Somebody." He took a single step toward the door before shooting an intense glare behind him. "Forget you heard any of that war crime stuff! I'll be right back!"

Dorian stepped outside and put his hands up as he cautiously walked across their sprawling driveway. Two burly soldiers immediately ran up to him and started shouting something inaudible. Maeryn watched the figures from a distance as they conversed, silhouetted amidst the flashing lights. She couldn't read their lips from so far away, but Dorian was obviously smiling.

"What are they saying?" asked Maeryn.

"My microphone's getting too much interference from the sirens," said Max. "I can't hear them, but it looks like the soldiers are confused, or maybe embarrassed. Dorian's showing them his ID. Yes! I'm getting a good feeling from their micro expressions. Pretty soon we'll all be laughing about— *oh*."

One of the soldiers fired a taser at Dorian, who immediately dropped to the ground and started convulsing before going totally limp. A soldier handcuffed him and started dragging his body toward one of the hovercrafts.

"Dad!" Maeryn screamed, her voice cracking with desperation. She moved like she was going to run outside, but Max flew in front of her and expanded his arms to completely block the doorway.

"Now who's being stupid?" he asked. "You want to get shot?"

Maeryn was stuck, her conflicting instincts all bumping up against one another. She couldn't run, she couldn't fight, and she didn't trust the soldiers enough to try to speak with them.

"What do we do, Max?" asked Maeryn, speaking faster and faster while grabbing at her hair in a panic. "What do we do? *What do we do?*"

Max was just as remarkably indecisive as she was, but the sound of a voice shouting through a megaphone broke their panic.

"Maeryn Kacey!" a soldier yelled. "You are safe now. Francis Rodriguez has been apprehended. Please remove your earpiece, digital contacts, and any other MotherTech device on your body, and come with us."

"MotherTech device?" asked Max. "*That's me.* I find this offensive."

"You have to hide," said Maeryn. "If they come inside and see you, they'll take it as a threat."

Max flew around in a panic as he calculated every possible future.

"You're no good without me," he said. "Sorry, but it's true. I'm going to shrink down and climb in your ear hole. Do you prefer the left or right one?"

"I love you like a brother, Max," said Maeryn, "but some lines just shouldn't be crossed. Stay out of my ear."

Max's nanobots began to compress together until he became the size of a bug.

"It's the only way!" he squeaked. "If those soldiers see me, things are going to get really awkward really fast."

Maeryn started swatting at Max as he zoomed around her head.

"Nobody is climbing inside of my ear!" Maeryn screamed, and a voice spoke from just ahead of her.

"What?"

A tall, thin soldier with a visor covering his face stood in the doorway. Maeryn did her best to pull herself together and took a few slow, cautious steps backwards.

"There was a fly in here," said Maeryn. "A very annoying fly."

"Okay then," said the man. "I'm going to have to ask you to come with me. We have been ordered to take you to your... *woah!*"

The soldier took a step forward, but a robotic vacuum silently rolled up on the carpet and tripped him. His visor flew off and hit the wall with a clunk. Something small and transparent like a chunk of glass flew across the room and struck the man in the face before he could react. Maeryn turned around to see that their refrigerator had somehow rolled out of the kitchen and was using its ice machine as a gun. It shot another ice cube, striking the soldier right on his crooked nose as he tried to stand up. This seemed to annoy the man much more than it actually hurt him.

Maeryn heard a sharp buzz, and then felt something tiny sitting just on the inside of her ear.

"Maeryn!" squeaked Max's voice. "I'm in your earhole! I knew you wouldn't mind. But listen, I'm not doing these things! It's not Missy either. Someone's hacked into the house control system."

The 3D-projector in the living room turned on and began playing an old black and white movie. Dramatic, orchestral music blasted at full volume as the leading man and woman gazed across a table at each other. The soldier looked toward the movie, his face scrunching up in total confusion for a second before another ice cube popped him right in the middle of the forehead.

"You're not who I thought you were," said the swooning actress.

The video rewound and began repeating the same sequence over and over.

"You're not who I thought you were."

"You're not who I thought you were."

"You're not—"

Pop!

The refrigerator fired yet another ice cube, but this one did not strike its target. The ice had, in fact, not struck anything at all, but was hanging motionless in midair. Maeryn held up her hands and stared at them. The increase in absurdity in an already absurd situation completely threw her off balance.

"What the—" Max began, but Maeryn hardly noticed his string of expletives. She looked back at the soldier to see his arm extended toward the ice cube. He squeezed his hand into a fist and several things happened in the same instant. A clear container strapped to the soldier's arm glowed a bright blue, the ice cube burst apart into mist, and the refrigerator exploded. A small portion of the blue substance in the container faded away to nothing as cartons of milk and eggs flew through the air.

Maeryn felt a familiar rush of energy when the soldier's container glowed. It was him. This man was *relaying*.

"Maeryn!" yelled Max. "Look at his face!"

Now that his visor was knocked off, Maeryn could see that he was covered in ornate tattoos of black flames that she recognized at once. Even the combination of his remarkable height and crooked nose were somehow vaguely familiar.

"Western Blaze!" shouted Maeryn. *"Western Blaze?* But—"

The man pointed a finger toward the living room, the container on his arm glowed again, and the 3-D projector on the ceiling melted into a pool of sizzling plastic and wires. The constantly repeating line, *"You're not who I thought you were,"* immediately ceased as the black and white actress vanished. A small fire was lit on the carpet as the melting plastic dripped down.

"Now would be a very good time to do that thing!" yelled Max.

"Okay, do it!" said Maeryn.

Max flew out from her ear, expanding in the air as his nanobots duplicated themselves

"You picked the wrong house to mess with!" yelled Max. "By the power of Gaia, we summon the THUNDER GLOVE!"

"You would like to stop moving," said the agent calmly.

"Sounds good, my dude," said Max. He froze, stuck between one transformation and the next.

"You'd also like to stop talking."

Max didn't make a sound in reply.

Maeryn looked from her companion bot to the soldier with the Western Blaze insignia. He caressed a green stone which hung from a silver chain around his neck, and there was another rush of Gaian energy in the room.

"How are you here?" Maeryn asked.

He ignored her question.

"State your name, girl."

Maeryn became instantly calm, and without thinking she answered the agent's question. Her immediate response surprised no one more than herself.

"Maeryn Kacey," said Maeryn.

"Your aunt is Rosalie Kacey?"

"Yes."

"The man I apprehended is your father?"

"Yes, he is."

A part of Maeryn was aware that she didn't want to be answering these questions, but every time the man spoke she couldn't fathom *not* being honest with him. A smile lit up his face, and the sheer euphoria in that expression should have disturbed Maeryn. His mind seized ahold of her own, moving her thoughts effortlessly to his will, but Maeryn felt no horror at this. She felt nothing at all.

"He was not your father," said the man. "He was an escaped convict by the name of Francis Rodriguez. Your father is away, looking for Rosalie."

"Okay," said Maeryn.

Yes, her father was away. He left her with Max, and someone broke into their house.

The man took a step forward and placed a sweaty finger on Maeryn's forehead.

"Is Kaija Monhegan in there?"

"No."

"Can you bring her into your body right now?"

"No. She can only relay from her side. I can't do the swap by myself."

The agent nodded and continued.

"Where's Kaija right now?"

"Monhegan Island."

"And where's her father?"

Maeryn thought about this for a moment. Jasper occasionally left the island to meet with guardians from other villages, or to attend baking classes, but most of his time was spent on the island.

"Jasper's probably at home."

"Does he have his sword?"

"Yes. He uses it to cut cake. Jasper makes beautiful desserts."

The agent raised an eyebrow.

"Interesting," he said. "And how do you know this?"

"Kaija brought me to Monhegan through the mental realm, and we celebrated her fifteenth cycle day. A frog licked us on the—"

"Hold on," said the agent, looking extremely interested. "Picture what you saw that day. Show me every detail."

Some part of Maeryn's mind screamed at her to resist, but it was absolutely no use. She imagined herself to be in Kaija's cabin. All of the countless times she switched places with Kaija made this a familiar sight. She could see their icebox, the oil lamps on the wall, the painting of Edgard Zeig hanging in the entryway, and the sword propped up beside Jasper's bed. As Maeryn looked around the room, she was vaguely aware that the agent was standing next to her and seeing the same things. He scratched his chin with bony fingers as he studied the space intently, as if trying to memorize every tiny detail.

"Amazing," said the man, and they were suddenly back in Maeryn's entryway. "The Western Blaze will not forget your contribution, Maeryn Kacey."

The man snapped his fingers and his clothing began to transform, the sleek military uniform dissolving into Nomadic attire. The soldiers on the front lawn began to move forward, but their movement was wrong.

It was jerky and yet strangely synchronized, like puppets beings moved by the same puppeteer.

He put one hand on the top of Maeryn's head, and the other on the frozen, halfway transformed Max. The container on his arm glowed a bright blue yet again.

"This never happened."

Maeryn felt the memories draining from her mind. The man took his hands off their heads and leaned in close, his sour breath warming Maeryn's face.

"You would both like nothing more than to sleep for exactly twelve hours."

All was instantly dark and dreamless.

Chapter Six

Elias

Cabin Seven, Gaia

Elias Zeig did little more than survive whatever recent horrors left his body burnt and broken. Kaija found him in Fain's house, sitting up weakly on the bed like the simple action took all of his strength. Elias's burns were no longer raw after several rounds of healing from Delia, but there were nasty scars all over his skin and his left ear was gone, replaced by a gnarled red patch of tissue. Maddox and Jasper lingered in a corner of the room, watching with a curious hesitation as Kaija approached Elias.

"Are you Kaija Monhegan?" asked Elias weakly.

"Yes. How do you know me?"

"The spiritualist knight told me about you. Well, kind of. She disappeared a week ago. It just about gave the High Guardian a stroke when he found out that she vanished. Have you met Allie?"

"Yes." Kaija thought about it a second longer. "Actually, no. *Kind of?* She talked to me through a frog once. And then I talked to her through a frog. Basically our whole relationship is frog-related."

A genuine smile peeked through Elias's scarred face. "That sounds like Allie. Listen to this. I drew a hot bath yesterday morning, and there was a note written in the steam on my mirror in Allie's handwriting. It said your name: Kaija Monhegan. I didn't know what to think at the time. I recognized the surname Monhegan, though. They were the islanders who fought so bravely at the Capital during the attempted insurrection, but I didn't know who Kaija was. I was surprised that Allie had left such an obvious attempt to steer me in a certain direction. She always says that it's wrong to try and alter the branches of time, unless—"

Elias hesitated, glancing over at the mirror by the bed and studying the burns on his face. "—unless you are certain the worst is about to happen."

Kaija expected him to go on, but Elias sat with an increasingly empty expression, as if he were sinking back into untold traumas.

"Who did this to you?" she asked.

"I…" Elias trailed off. His hands squeezed into tight, trembling fists. "I'd really rather not talk about it."

Maddox spoke up decidedly from the corner of the room, surprising Kaija. She had completely forgotten that they weren't alone.

"Again, silence is not an option. I don't want to be the one to have to say this, but I guess the unpleasant task has fallen to me. The situation on the mainland is fraught, but we have maintained a fragile peace here on Monhegan. If you're going to stay, we have to know what dangers you bring with you."

Elias closed his eyes and drew in a deep breath. After a contemplative silence, Kaija was sure that he was going to remain clammed up, but Elias began to speak hesitantly. "Okay. After the attack on the Capital, the High Guardian asked me to infiltrate the Western Blaze and find out if their leader Rugaru is still alive. He had been infected with hydra poison, but one can survive if the corrupted limb is amputated in time.

I'm Nomadic on my mother's side, so Thomas thought it would be easy for me to convince them to let me join. It wasn't."

"The Western Blaze did this?" asked Maddox.

"No. That's the thing. I couldn't find the Western Blaze anywhere, and I move awfully fast. Thomas kept putting pressure on me, threatening to take away my knighthood, and I searched the globe for an entire cycle. There's no sign of them, not a single member. They've either disappeared or are somehow seeing me coming each time."

"I don't understand," said Jasper. "Who attacked you then?"

Elias's labored breathing intensified, although the expression on his face remained stone cold. Kaija could tell that he was a trained soldier and was used to keeping his emotions masked.

"The High Seven."

Jasper, Kaija, and Maddox all sat in silence as they absorbed this information, trying to make sense of it. Elias was a part of the High Seven. The thought that the other knights would have done this had not even come close to crossing anyone's mind.

"To be clear," said Jasper slowly. "It was the High Seven who tried to kill you?"

Elias considered this for a moment, seeming to struggle with accepting the fact for himself.

"Yes. Yesterday, a messenger told me that Will Zeig needed to see me. He's the conjurist knight, you see, and—"

"We know who he is," Maddox interrupted. "My son never stops talking about him."

Elias nodded. "As soon as I opened the door to his room, Will relayed a burst of fire at me. It took all the willpower I had to keep it from melting me to the bones. Then the internalist knight came out of nowhere and hit me in the knee with a club, and then they were all just *there*, attacking me before I knew what was happening. I could feel the mentalist knight prying at my mind, trying to keep me frozen in place, so I teleported away from the Capital. The fire came with me, and it wouldn't go out. I didn't even know this was possible. Will had created living flames that would follow me forever. It just kept burning and burning, and if I wouldn't have thought of teleporting into the coldest waters of the Arctic Sea, there wouldn't have been a single bit of me left."

Elias's composure began to crumble, and he put a trembling hand over his face. "They were my friends, at least I thought they were. I've been a knight for three cycles, and I've known these people for even longer. The only one that didn't try to attack me was Allie, since she had already gone missing. I don't know how my friends could have done this."

Kaija could feel the sickening turmoil radiating from his mind. She reached over and put a hand on his shoulder. "A mentalist must have been controlling them, or something like that."

Nobody responded to her comment, and Kaija knew at once that they were unconvinced.

"That's a kind thing to say," said Elias, "but I doubt it. Thomas has been getting more paranoid every day, and after his announcement this morning, I'm certain that he ordered the attack. His mentalist stone has gone missing recently, and it wouldn't surprise me if he thought I stole it. Thomas always treated me differently than the others because of my Nomadic blood, and I don't think he ever really trusted me."

"Why come here?" asked Maddox. "Don't you have a family?"

Kaija didn't like the accusation in his tone, and Jasper gave Maddox a threatening look at his comment. Kaija wondered why Maddox was even here at all, acting like *he* was the island's guardian. Maddox's job was to build and repair cabins, not question incoming refugees.

"I haven't spoken to my family in several cycles," said Elias. "My mother's part of a western Nomadic community. My father was a professor in Crossroads City, but he travels with her now. They said I was a traitor when I started training in the Capital to become a knight. My parents don't like how the guardianship treats the Nomads, but I don't either. I tried to explain that if action wasn't taken against the Western Blaze, things would only continue to get worse for all of us, but my mother can be stubborn. I don't even know where my parents are anymore. There are thousands of Nomadic campsites all around the world, and they could be at any of them. I'm not exactly a welcome face, so it wouldn't be an easy search."

Maddox leaned forward. "I'll say it again. Why come here?"

"I knew that I couldn't go back to the Capital after I was attacked, but that's when I remembered Allie's note. I thought that such a small island at the edge of Edgardia might be a good place to hide, so I teleported to Portland and tried to make it across the ocean, but I was too weak. My final jump only took me half as far as I meant to go before I passed out. I woke up here."

Jasper opened his mouth to talk, but Maddox quickly cut him off. "That still doesn't explain why Allie wanted you to come to Monhegan Island. What exactly was the spiritualist planning?"

Elias shrugged weakly. "I don't know. Honestly, I don't understand half the stuff that she says."

"She had the right idea sending you here," said Jasper. "You'll be safe on Monhegan as long as you wish, Elias."

Maddox spun toward Jasper, a vein in his neck throbbing. "The spiritualist didn't send him to Monhegan. He sent her to *Kaija*. You're going to harbor a suspected criminal who was sent here to find your daughter? If that were my kid, I'd be more than a little suspicious."

"I'm not worried in the slightest."

"That's because you've never lost a child like I have."

A tense look passed between the two adults. After such a crushing statement, Kaija would have immediately been apologetic, but her father seemed barely able to contain his anger.

"The High Guardian will leave us alone," said Jasper. "He's terrified of me."

Elias laughed nervously. "Sorry, I'm still getting used to hearing out of only one ear. You didn't just say that Thomas is *afraid* of you, right?"

Jasper cracked a proud smile. "He's scared of me because I saved his life, along with the lives of all of his Capital citizens last summer. I could take his job and fortune in a second if I wanted to."

"That was you? Everybody thought that the son of Gaia had returned!"

"Halfway right. More like the son of the son of Gaia."

Maddox grunted, but Elias's sorrow was now replaced by surprise. He scanned Jasper's face with a dawning amazement, recognizing the distinct bone structure seen in so many paintings of Edgard.

"You're Edgard's son? What in desolation are you doing off in the middle of nowhere? You should be the one leading the guardianship, not that pompous pig!"

"This is all beside the point," said Jasper. "We need to talk about—"

"Actually, that's a good question," interrupted Kaija. "You'd be a much better High Guardian, father, and it would be really cool to live in the Capital."

"Stop!" The whole cabin rattled at the sound of Jasper's voice. "That option is off the table. When I hold my father's sword, I feel like I might accidently blow up the universe if I sneeze. It's a horrible feeling, and I hate it. I'd much rather bake a cake than lead an entire guardianship founded on misconceptions and territorial egotism."

"I'm afraid that I have to agree with your daughter here, guardian," said Maddox. "The continent is in shambles. Next thing you know, Thomas is going to make all relaying illegal. We need a better leader."

"No chance in desolation," Jasper insisted. He looked at everyone in the room one by one, as if daring them to speak. "Anyone else want to pressure me? Got any tyrants you want me to go behead? Mountains you want flattened? Am I a weapon to be pointed?"

Nobody quite knew how to respond to this. Kaija felt like she was witnessing something that she wasn't supposed to.

"Good," said Jasper. "Good. Elias, I welcome you to make your home here for as long as you want. Now if everyone would excuse me, I have some fondant fancies on a cooling rack that need decorating."

Jasper turned around and vanished with an abnormally loud boom.

Maddox shook his head and grumbled to himself. "I guess I'll go build a cabin for our guest. Everyone's going to *love* me for this. Wish me luck, and tell Fain to stay away."

He marched out the door, avoiding their eyes and still muttering under his breath.

Elias cleared his throat. "Fondant fancies?"

"Oh yeah," said Kaija. "Father's a wonderful baker."

"Edgard's son, hiding out on an island and decorating little cakes? What a week it's—*ah!*" He shifted around in the bed and groaned, reaching forward and massaging his bandaged knee. A minute later Elias leaned back, sweat dripping from his forehead, and took in a series of pained breaths.

"Are you okay?" asked Kaija.

"No. I'm really not. Delia did a good job with the healing, but parts of me... *Gaia.* I just can't imagine that some parts of me can ever get fixed."

In a strange way, Elias reminded her of Maeryn. He too had been damaged by the very people he thought he could trust. She looked at the way his arm was shaking, struggling from the earlier effort of propping himself up.

"My father doesn't just say things," said Kaija. "You'll be safe here. What brought you to Monhegan was awful, but you're in the right place now."

Elias smiled slightly, but there was more than a touch of lingering sadness in that face. How could someone ever, ever get past trauma like this? Had Maeryn even managed to let go of the things that happened last cycle? Every time Kaija inhabited her body, she felt a touch of something unrecognizable. Kaija felt awful for not even considering this until now.

"Right place, huh?" Elias asked. He laughed, and Kaija didn't like the sudden look of condescension. "You're not a spacialist, are you?"

"No, I'm a mentalist. Why?"

"You non-spacialists are always talking about places like they matter, like they're all so different. There are no right places, or even wrong places. There are only people."

"Then you're with the right people now."

Elias peered out the window behind Kaija. Maddox walked by grumpily, eyes cast downwards, holding a bundle of lumber under his arm as he headed for the village outskirts. Across the road, a group of adults werek gathered and talking heatedly amongst themselves. A man pointed in the direction of Maddox and continued his inaudible conversation. Kaija recognized him as Valeria's father. He was red in the face, and she could practically see the spit flying from his mouth as he shouted something toward Maddox.

Elias waved his hand weakly and the curtains closed over the window. "That's what I thought when I lived in the Capital: that I was with the right people."

* * *

That night, the Monhegan youth relayed a campfire at the edge of the village. Fain and Kaija sat close to each other, chatting with the other kids while they roasted firefruit on a stick. The tough peel of the fruit blackened and curled, revealing the bright red interior that smelled like sweet cinnamon. Valeria eyed the two of them from across the fire and whispered to her friends.

"Oh look, Kaija," said Fain. "Valeria's telling them what a hot couple we make."

Valeria pretended to gag. "Um, no. Gross. If you really must know, I was just talking about how your dad built a house for that *Nomad* who is apparently living here now. Kind of pointless, don't you think? I thought Nomads slept on the ground."

The girls around Valeria all began giggling.

"Shut up!" said Kaija. "My father invited Elias to stay. Do you have a problem with that?"

"Well, Jasper's standards for villagers are about as low as yours are for boyfriends."

Fain's mouth dropped open and he looked at Kaija, more amused than angry. "Ouchy! I think we're being bullied by this preteen. Gosh. I was really hoping not to cry myself to sleep tonight."

Alan, who had been standing to the side with his friends, turned toward the younger students and took on an authoritative tone.

"That's not nice to joke about, Valeria. Every single one of us are on Monhegan because our families lived through a tragedy on the mainland. My older cousin was abducted before Jasper welcomed us here."

"Yeah!" said Fain. "You shouldn't insult our guardian like that. I remember when your parents begged Jasper if they could move here. It was hard for them, getting shunned from their village after trying to raise a groundsloth as their daughter."

Valeria ignored him. She crossed her arms and raised an eyebrow at Alan. "You all think I'm joking around? Alan, who abducted your cousin?"

"The Western Blaze," Alan admitted. "But that's not the same as—"

"The Nomads? Yes it is! Do you ever hear the other tribes speaking out against the Western Blaze? *Never!* They're happy to see the villages burn. And we're going to just let one live here? My parents aren't so sure that we want to stay on Monhegan if their kind is welcome."

Fain yanked the firefruit core off his stick and threw it into the woods, purposely missing Valeria's head by a thumb's length.

"Do you want to go?" he asked, taking Kaija's hand. "I've lost my appetite."

"Me too," said Kaija, dropping her stick into the fire and standing up with Fain. The two of them turned toward the village, but Valeria called after them.

"I'm surprised to hear you defending that animal, Fain! My parents told me why you moved here. Didn't the Nomads kill your older brother? What was his name? Emris? How would he feel about a dirt monkey living here?"

"SHUT YOUR MOUTH!"

Fain let go of Kaija's hand so quickly that she barely had time to react. He turned around, waved his arm, and the campfire grew to twice its size, nearly engulfing the log that Valeria was sitting on. The flames sparked and bent toward Valeria's skin, who was now screaming and holding her arms in front of her face.

Kaija grabbed Fain's hand and pulled him back. Alan jumped forward and relayed the flames away from Valeria just as they brushed her arm. He snapped his fingers and the campfire blinked out of existence. All of the teenagers were suddenly standing and staring at Fain with a horrible silence.

"What are you thinking?" yelled Alan. "What in desolation would have happened if I hadn't stopped the flames? Or worse: if Ms. Clara saw that!"

Valeria cried and held her burnt arm, now looking very much like a scared little girl. Tears welled up in Fain's eyes and he opened his mouth several times, never quite finding the words to say. One of the teenagers with healing abilities ran over to Valeria and got to work on her burns.

"I... I don't..." muttered Fain. "She—"

"Don't even try to justify it," said Alan. "I don't want to hear it. Go home."

"Come on, Fain," said Kaija, pulling on his arm.

"You're no different than those animals," Valeria called to Fain between sobs. "We're all going to pay for letting that Nomad stay here. Just wait until—"

"STOP!" yelled Alan. "Valeria, I would have to agree with Fain that it is past time for you to *close your mouth and keep it that way.* Go home, EVERYBODY!"

* * *

Fain was inconsolable as they approached Cabin Seven.

"I almost set a preteen on fire! I know it's me we're talking about here, and it wouldn't be the first person I set on fire, but I almost did it *on purpose.*"

"Valeria had it coming," said Kaija. "I was just about to control her mind, convince her to jump into the ocean, but you beat me to the punch."

Fain didn't laugh. He hardly met her eye as he spoke. "But it's never been like this before. For a moment there, when the whole group was standing around and looking at me, I hated *everyone.* "

"Really?"

"Not *you*, obviously. But I've been paranoid all day. My father told me that Jasper had a meeting with some of the adults on the island this morning about Elias. Most of them voted to send him back to the Capital, but Jasper overruled it. I've been walking around all day, wondering whose parents wanted to send that poor guy to his death."

"I guess we know where Valeria's family stands."

Fain was silent for a moment, shaking his head in disbelief.

"You know what bothered me the most about her? The thing that really made me angry, above everything else? A small part of me thought that she was right, and I hated myself for it."

Kaija stopped walking, pulling her hand away from Fain. "You don't seriously think that Elias is a spy or something?"

"Of course I don't think that."

Kaija could sense the nature of Fain's thoughts, and for the first time ever they didn't match what he was saying.

"Don't lie to me, Fain. You don't trust Elias."

Fain narrowed his eyes at her. "Gee, Kaija. It's not fair for you to snoop around in my head."

"I'm not! I just know you're not saying what you're thinking."

Fain turned away, obviously struggling to contain the anger in his voice. "*I* don't even know what I'm thinking! We'd be dumb to not at least consider every possibility with Elias! Maybe he's not spying for the Western Blaze, maybe Thomas sent him."

"So the High Guardian thought it would be a good idea to burn him to a crisp first? Really makes sense."

Fain was sweating now, red in the face and talking louder by the word. "I didn't say that I totally agreed with Valeria. I said a *small* part of me did. You have to admit that Elias just being here is already causing people to distrust each other."

Allie had asked Kaija to be kind to Elias, and she felt somewhat responsible for him. Kaija remembered the pure sorrow that she felt in the mental realm when Elias was describing how his friends had nearly killed him, and she wished that Fain could have been there to see it. To feel it. Elias was not some crazed zealot. Kaija really liked Fain's normally carefree attitude, maybe even more than liked it, but ever since the attack on the Capital last year he would get into these awful moody spells.

"I'm sorry if Elias almost dying has been inconvenient for you," said Kaija. "Lucky for you, my father didn't have any of those same doubts when your family moved here, but I guess your skin is the right color."

Kaija instantly regretted what she had said, because the hurt emanating from Fain's mind now was absolutely pungent.

"Sometimes I hate that you're a mentalist," said Fain, almost inaudibly. "Just because you can read my thoughts and emotions doesn't mean you understand them. Lucky you. I'd never want you to feel the way I feel now."

"Listen, I'm sorry. Let's just forget about it."

Kaija leaned in to kiss him, but Fain turned away.

"Wish I could. See you at school."

Fain walked into his cabin and slammed the door without looking back.

*   *   *

Kaija returned home to find that her entire cabin had apparently been hit by the world's smallest hurricane. All of the shelves were pulled out of the kitchen cabinets, clothes and baking equipment were strewn across the floor, and Jasper's bed was levitating up by the rafters. He was darting around, digging frantically through the random piles of stuff.

"What happened?" asked Kaija.

Jasper jumped and let out a little yelp. "Oh, hey Kaija. I thought you were my mother for a second." He tossed a frying pan over his shoulder. "Hey, odd question. You haven't borrowed anything of mine recently, have you?"

"No."

"Really? Nothing, um… kind of important?"

Jasper picked up an old lamp, examined it, and then relayed it across the room into another pile. He pulled up the rug, threw it out the window, and stared at the faded wooden floor below as if willing the mysterious lost item to appear.

"It's pretty embarrassing," he said, relaying the rug back in through the window and dropping it in a puff of dust.

"Just tell me."

"Well—"

Kaija glanced around the room, trying to figure out what was missing. She looked over at the empty hook on the wall next to her father's bed and gasped.

"You lost Edgard's sword?"

"Not so loud! And no, I didn't lose it. I just have no idea where it is, and I can't find it."

"I'm pretty sure that's exactly what losing something means. When was the last time you saw it?"

"It was getting dirty, so I put it in the sink this morning. That's where it must have been when I went to my baking class."

Kaija looked over to the empty sink.

"You left Edgard Zeig's sword in a sink?"

"Well yeah, it still had buttercream all over it. And blood."

Kaija gave her father a severe look. The bed fell from the ceiling and Jasper collapsed on the mattress, grabbing his long, dark hair and groaning.

"Mother's going to kill me for this."

Chapter Seven

We Need to Talk About the Toast Thing

New York, Earth

Nora Galaxy and the Diamond Warriors.

As Maeryn's sore eyes adjusted to the morning light, she found herself staring at a poster of a cartoon girl with a shield. Nora Galaxy was surrounded by four multicolored, unnaturally curvy warrior women. Maeryn hadn't watched that show in years.

Well, she hadn't *admitted* to watching it in years.

Bacon?

Why did she smell bacon? Not the smoky maple tempeh her dad made sometimes, either. Bacon, as in slivers of salty pork loin fried to the point of their second death.

Maeryn sat up abruptly, brushing the frizzy hair out of her face and looking around the dusty room full of possessions that she had outgrown five years ago.

"Max?" She snatched the wristband off her bedside table and shook it. "Are you there? Something is horribly wrong here."

The wristband morphed into Max's shape, much more awkwardly and strenuously than usual. He fell out of her hand and onto the bed, yawning and stretching his little metal limbs.

"Wrong? What do you mean? I slept great." He hesitated, and then repeated the words to himself. "I slept great. I. Slept. Great. I slept? Huh. Maeryn, something is horribly wrong here. I never sleep!" He sniffed his non-existent nose. "Hey, what's that amazing smell? And why do you have a poster of a vacuum cleaner?"

Maeryn rolled over to the edge of the bed and rubbed her eyes. She spotted the digital poster Max was pointing at, although she had no idea why he saw a vacuum clear. It was *Livy Moonsong*, a holographic popstar that Maeryn had liked for several embarrassing months in her pre-teens. Moonsong changed her physical appearance based on who was seeing her, rendered by a fancy algorithm designed to get more music streams. Maeryn was moderately amused to see that the Queen of Asimovian Pop had aged a few years since the last time she was here, becoming an androgynous sixteen-year-old with silver hair, tattoos on her upper arms, and a rebellious smirk.

"This is my room at mom's house," Maeryn said sleepily.

"If this is your so-called *room* at your so-called *mom's* house, how come I've never seen it?"

"Katherine hates MotherTech stuff. She thinks dad might try to spy on her. I always had to leave most of my gear at home, so you never got to see what this place looked like."

"Oh yeah. I'm not thinking straight just yet." Max shook his head back and forth and slapped himself a few times. "Is this what waking up always feels like? Because it's literally the hardest thing I've ever had to do."

Maeryn cleared her throat and flinched. Her vocal chords felt ripped to shreds, like she had spent all of yesterday doing primal scream therapy. What *had* they done last night? Thinking back, Maeryn was only getting blurry bits and pieces.

"What do you remember?" she asked.

Max rubbed his silver head and spoke laboriously. Every sentence came out more like a question than a statement.

"Dorian left to go find Rosalie... and then a Hispanic little person with an eyepatch broke into our house? The military showed up, and there were freaking tanks with laser cannons in our neighborhood? They took us in a hovercraft to your mom's house in New York to stay until Dorian shows back up. I'm also remembering something about a... *a suspicious refrigerator with a gun?*"

This all sounded stupidly, impossibly familiar to Maeryn.

"I feel like I'm going to puke just trying to think about it," she moaned.

"I thought we were good kids, Sister. Did we do drugs last night? Is that who we are now? I think we owe McMeow the Drug Cat an apology."

"It's all just *wrong*. I hate it here. My dad wouldn't have left us like that."

Max floated up from the bedside table, wobbling ungracefully in the air before steadying himself.

"Something definitely doesn't feel right. I can't think on an empty stomach. Find me some food to scan. For some reason I want to taste whatever's on fire downstairs."

Maeryn walked up to the window and peeked out at the pristine suburb outside, unnaturally green lawns glistening in the morning dew. A school bus drove by on the street, and somewhere a little dog was yapping.

"Good luck with finding anything edible here," said Maeryn. "Katherine and Clark don't believe in using food printers, and neither of them are good cooks. *Dobbs!* I thought my dad running off was bad, but now I'm stuck with my mom and stepdad. They're the worst!"

"Really? I can't imagine that people who buy such soft pillows would be anything but lovely. What's the problem? Are they always too busy with work to play a game of catch with you?"

"No."

"Did they miss all your ballet recitals?"

"No, but they're still the worst."

"Are they always showing random people your naked baby pictures?"

"Geez. No!"

"Then how are they so bad?"

Maeryn sighed.

"They are so maddeningly, mind-numbingly *normal.* They read magazines. Magazines! And they do things like order cheap pizza and leave all of the crusts in a pile while they watch sitcoms with laugh tracks. Who are those people laughing, and who hurt them?"

"Truly tragic. Your teenage angst is so adorably human, and... hold on... *AH!*"

Max rocketed through the air, burrowing himself under a pillow just as the bedroom door opened. Katherine Johnson darted in, grabbing at her daughter. She looked like an older version of Maeryn, although her hair was a wavy blonde that was much too nice for this early in the morning.

"Maeryn! Oh my goodness, I've been so worried! The nice soldier explained everything to me about your dad abandoning you, and how that convict broke into the house! They showed me his mugshot. My lord! I bet he didn't even speak English. I can't imagine how terrifying that—" Katherine paused and looked closer at Maeryn, pointing at her hand. "Why do you have that?"

Forgetting that she wasn't wearing her wristband, Maeryn instinctually put her right hand behind her back.

"Nothing. It's not MotherTech."

"Of course it's not MotherTech. It's a rock."

Maeryn looked down to see a rock in her other hand, a rock which most definitely wasn't there a few seconds ago. She felt the absurd need to cover her tracks and lie, even though she had no clue what was happening here.

"Yeah," said Maeryn. "It's a rock. Duh, mom."

"And where did you get a rock between now and last night?"

"It's my pet rock, Dwayne. You wouldn't understand."

"Pet rock. That's a thing now? Okay then." Katherine ran a hand over her fatigued face, like she was trying to brush off the residual absurdity. "We've got a lot to talk about. Come on, I made bacon."

"I'm vegan, mom. And I have been for three years."

Katherine laughed, like Maeryn's diet was a ridiculous joke.

"Okay then, I'll talk over bacon. You'll talk over buttered toast."

"Not vegan either."

"Plain toast then, for all I care. I just picked up some nice brioche."

"That's not— never mind." Maeryn tossed Dwayne on her bed as she followed Katherine out of the room.

Max whispered frantically in her earpiece. "Dwayne? That rock must have come from a wormhole, because you didn't have it two minutes ago! Things better not get any weirder than magic pet rocks."

Things immediately proceeded to get weirder than magic pet rocks.

* * *

Katherine expressed a very fake concern as she recounted last night's drama to her kids over breakfast. A soldier called at 3 a.m. and explained that a wanted terrorist had been chased into the Kacey mansion. After apprehending the criminal, they discovered that Maeryn was left alone by her father, who was apparently off searching for Rosalie. In the last several hours, child protective services brought Maeryn to her only remaining legal guardians: the Johnson family.

Smith and Jess, Maeryn's stepsiblings, listened with nearly opposite reactions to Katherine's monologue. Seventeen-year-old Smith absorbed the harrowing tale with little more than a mild disinterest, seeming to find his breakfast plate wildly more fascinating. Ten-year-old Jess, on the other hand, received the news of Dorian's sudden departure like an early Christmas present. She waited until her mother was out of ear-shot to begin gloating.

"So your dad just left you to get robbed by some Chinese guy? Mom thinks Dorian's going to go to jail for this. You can't just leave your kids."

"Oh, they'll *try* to put dad in jail," said Maeryn, "but not for abandonment. All that was just a cover. He's actually wanted by the government for building an army of robotic killing machines. Dad's got some great lawyers though, and they'll clear his name just like last time. He told me to make a list of my enemies for when he gets back. That reminds me." She turned to her stepbrother. "Smith, could I borrow a pencil?"

Smith looked up from his plate, midway through shoving an entire piece of toast in his mouth.

"Huh?" he mumbled between bites. "Pencil? Sorry, dude. I finally made the switch to quills last month. There's no going back once you're an inker. Adding little sis to your kill list or something?"

"Yeah."

"Cool, cool. Nice knowing ya, Jess."

"MOM!" yelled Jess. "Maeryn's going to kill me with an army of robots!"

Katherine staggered into the room, balancing three plates piled with bacon-shaped, greasy detritus blacker than the sky on a moonless night.

"Maeryn, don't threaten to kill your sister. And Jess, be nice to Maeryn even if she threatens to kill you. She's been through a lot. That criminal didn't even speak English, you know."

Jess shot Maeryn an ugly look and dug into her breakfast. Maeryn looked down at her own plate and suppressed a shout of bewilderment. Her skin-covered eggs and black bacon were so breathtakingly, poorly cooked that her mom could have used them to launch a career in abstract folk art, but it was the toast that had Maeryn's rapt attention. It had her name on it. Literally. The letters **M-A-E-R-Y-N** were burnt so clearly into the otherwise under-toasted bread that she could identify the font.

"Comic sans!" Maeryn gasped. Her stepbrother kicked her under the table and put an urgent finger up to his lips.

"Shhh!"

"What are you looking at?" asked Jess, leaning over and peeking at Maeryn's plate. In the next instant, Smith snatched up Maeryn's toast and stuck the whole thing in his already overcrowded mouth.

"Classified info, Sis."

"MOM!" yelled Jess. "Smith won't let me look at Maeryn's toast!"

Katherine stomped back into the dining room, her otherwise pristine outfit splattered with grease. The smoke alarm was blaring from the kitchen. She shot a threatening look at each of her kids and spoke through her teeth.

"COOL IT. I know that we didn't expect Maeryn to be here, and things are very stressful, but you're going to have to start getting along with each other whether you want to or not. We're all making sacrifices for her. I'm supposed to be selling life insurance today, and Clark's not going to make it to his bowling league tonight. *Broke his poor heart.* SO, Smith, stop being weird. Jess, look at your own toast."

"Way to make me feel welcome, Mom," Maeryn muttered.

Katherine eyed Maeryn's full plate of animal products and gave an annoyed grunt. "Eat your food. We've got to enroll you in school today."

Maeryn blinked.

"School?" she asked.

"Yes, school."

Another blink.

"In-person school?"

"Yes, *real* school."

Mid-blink, Maeryn's eyes lost the will to open back up and she laid her head down on the table. She suddenly wished she could trade places with Max, who was still comfortably hiding under a pillow.

"Real school's great," said Smith, stealing a piece of (*bacon?*) from Maeryn's plate. "Adults tell you when you're allowed to pee, and I saw a rat run through the cafeteria once on my birthday."

"I'm already enrolled in the Indianapolis virtual academy. Don't you have a tablet I could use?"

"No way," said Katherine. "Clark and I have to go back to work eventually, and what kind of person leaves their kid home alone with unassimilated foreigners ready to break in at any moment? You're going to real school."

Maeryn resisted the urge to throw her bacon across the room, but that meant that she would have to *touch* the stuff. She slammed her fist on the table instead, rattling all the cups and plates.

"What the heck, mom? I'm near the top of my class for the entire virtual academy. Last week I started a college level physics course."

"I'm sure they'll have phys-ed at your new school. We're enrolling you today, so *eat.*"

"You're really going to send me to a real school?"

"Yes."

Maeryn pretended to think about it for two seconds. "No thanks."

She stood up so quickly that her chair fell to the floor with a *crash* behind her. Katherine, who was not used to being spoken back to by her normally introverted daughter, watched Maeryn stomp away with at first a stunned silence, and then a burst of anger.

"That will not be the last word on this!"

Maeryn turned back around, now so angry that she had black spots swimming in her vision.

"You want a last word? Your cooking is terrible. But not that I would know, because I'm vegan. Which *you* should know, because I've told you over and over, and… and…" She pointed a trembling finger at her mom, struggling to form coherent thoughts amidst the sudden, hot rage. "The American food industry traded their morality for a higher profit margin decades ago! Pigs are smarter than dogs, you know! Do you eat dogs? I don't eat dogs! There's your… there's your last word!"

As Maeryn stormed up the steps, she envied Max's ability to think through millions of scenarios a second because she probably could have picked a better parting shot than *I don't eat dogs.* She heard Smith laughing at Katherine from down the steps just before slamming the door.

"You just got roasted good, Ma. You, and capitalism."

* * *

"I hate this!" yelled Maeryn, slamming the door to her room so hard that Livy Moonsong practically flinched.

Max floated up from underneath the pillow. "I heard the whole thing. Please don't make me go to school with you. I'm meant for a greatness that no school system can provide to this unmeasurable genius."

"Oh yeah? What were you doing just now, before I walked in?"

"I was solving the Reiman hypothesis of pure mathematics."

"You weren't playing Squirrel Turtle Two?"

Max paused for a beat.

"Okay, it's been all Squirrel Turtle all day. But only because my buddy Ernesto was off work and wanted to hang. He's that vending machine at the Florida night zoo. I swear I was going to resolve some unsolved math problems after another 3,792 rounds."

Maeryn plopped down on her bed and rubbed her eyes. "Must have been nice," she groaned. "Hangin' with Ernesto while I was having breakfast with the family from diet vanilla hell."

Max floated along the wall, examining the hanging portraits of Katherine's family. The Johnsons could have been models in stock photos, with the polo-wearing dad, unnaturally white-teethed wife, and curly-haired daughter. The one exception in each picture was Smith, who always looked absurdly out of place. His prom photo seemed to suggest that he took his bassoon along as a date.

"So that's the famous Smith?" asked Max. "He certainly seems... Well, *he certainly seems*."

"Smith's pretty cool, actually. He's probably the only good part of being here."

"Hey, thanks," said Smith.

Maeryn and Max looked at each other, looked over to the corner where Smith was sitting and chomping at a sliver of bacon, looked at each other again, and then once more at Smith. Max froze mid-flight, hoping Smith would somehow overlook the sentient collection of nanobots in the shape of a foot tall teenager floating through the air.

"Um," said Maeryn. "How long have you been sitting there?"

Smith took another chomp of bacon, flinching at the taste.

"I don't subscribe to linear time just because *THEY* tell me to," said Smith. "Next thing you know, THEY'LL have you believing that New Hampshire used to exist."

"And you saw, well... everything?"

Smith waved his bacon dismissively.

"Yeah, yeah, Stepsis has a flying robot brother. I'll get over it."

Smith raised his hand for a high-five, but put it down when nobody took him up on it. Maeryn had no idea when he had gotten up from the breakfast table and entered her room, but it wasn't really out of character. Smith was the type of person to leave a party without saying goodbye to anyone, or to enter into the middle of a conversation after listening unseen for fifteen minutes.

"Max, this is my stepbrother," said Maeryn. "Smith, this is my companion bot."

"Sup, shiny dude," Smith interrupted. "Smith Johnson: last name for a first name and another last name for a last name. Thought you might want to talk about the whole toast thing, ya know?" Smith leaned forward and snatched Dwayne, the rock, off Maeryn's bed.

"Dude. Is this a pet rock? I knew they were coming back in style! Parents just don't understand these things. You should name him Dwayne. Ha! Get it? Dwayne Johnson, like the president?"

Smith's comment about the toast rattled Maeryn's tired memory. She was so angry that she somehow completely forgot the fact that her name had been branded onto her breakfast earlier.

"Yes," said Maeryn. "We need to talk about the toast thing."

Max cleared his throat. "Toast? I feel like I'm missing something here."

Smith smiled, dusted the crumbs off his shirt, and stood up.

A Path of Branches

"Come with me on a journey. The mystery of the toast goes deeper than you can possibly imagine."

* * *

Maeryn and Max followed Smith to his room, which was somehow more unusual than Smith himself. Upside down flowerpots sat all over the floor, there was a bassoon tucked snugly into his bed (notably, a different one from his prom date), and a poster of a white rabbit was stuck over his window, blocking out most of the sunlight.

"Are you going to ask us to eat some mushrooms?" asked Max. "I mean, I'll try anything once, but I'm already kind of messed up from whatever the heck happened last night. Plus, I don't have a digestive system. Or a mouth."

"Nah, bro, not today," said Smith, stopping at his closet door. "Are you sure you're ready to see this?"

"I don't know about this, Maeryn," said Max. "It could be, well... Okay, I have absolutely no dang clue what it could be."

"Just open it," said Maeryn.

Smith opened the door, revealing that all of the clothes in his closet were stacked on the floor, leaving the wall behind exposed. The small space was dim, but barely any light was required to make out the absolutely unfathomable scene before them. Toast. Toast, hammered to a closet wall.

"Picture this," said Smith. "It's the middle of the night, and mom has left to go pick you up. I think to myself *she always burns the toast when she's stressed, and she's always stressed.* Bread is a major part of my diet, and I just can't stand to see it suffer, so I decided to go ahead and make it myself before she gets home. When the toast started talking to me, rest assured that I was moderately surprised."

95

Smith pulled the chain on a lightbulb, illuminating the messages burnt one letter at a time into at least thirty pieces of toast spread out across the wall. Maeryn's jaw dropped as she read the words.

Show this to Maeryn
2687:fca8:acc9:6317:b11c:d19:8365:5197
Mika_7

Max scanned the wall and made little beeping noises.

"That's an IP address with a password." He paused, then groaned loudly. "And not just any password: an old person password. A name and a number? That's asking for hackers. *Oh Dobbs*, Comic Sans? Really, toaster? What idiot programs an appliance to print in Comic Sans? How can a font look like it's trying so hard to be quirky, yet be so basic at the same time?" Max laughed. "Hey, Maeryn, that font is totally you."

"I resent that," said **Maeryn**. "Try logging on and see what happens."

"No way! It might toast my brain. How do we know that we can trust this bread? I don't like the looks of that piece of pumpernickel over there."

Smith looked offended.

"That's racist. Toast has never led me wrong, shiny dude. The bread speaks the truth."

Maeryn read over the message on the toast several more times, her mind threatening to leap out of her head and take off running from the craziness.

"I've seen some stuff, Smith. Trust me. *Stuff.* But this is just crazy! Why the heck would a toaster be sending me an IP address? How is this even possible?"

"I did some digging," said Smith, pulling a toaster instruction manual from his pocket. He flipped through, and Maeryn saw that it was full of highlighted words and phrases. "This thing goes all the way to the top. Mom hates technology because of your dad, you see, but she must have forgotten where this toaster came from. It's an early model of a MotherTech smart-toaster, but the label is missing. You can control it from your phone, and even burn paintings onto the bread. Don't judge me, but Picasso's *Guernica* is troublingly delicious."

Katherine's shrill voice called up the stairs.

"*Smith!* Autobus! You better not be doing anything weird again!"

Smith flipped off the light switch in his closet and closed the door. He gave an intense look to Max and Maeryn.

"Tell this to no one," he said, glancing suspiciously at the ceiling. "THEY have ears everywhere, and agents who can control your mind. I know things, ya know? This toaster, the Yellowstone supervolcano, alternate worlds, birds: it's all connected."

Smith backed out of the room without saying goodbye, still staring at them ominously as he moved down the steps. Before Maeryn and Max could start to fully contemplate the meaning of what they had just seen, Katherine began shouting from downstairs again.

"Maeryn! After we get you enrolled, Clark says we can go bowling. Won't that be fun?"

"Bowling?" asked Maeryn. "Seriously, now?"

The sound of footsteps echoed from the bottom of the stairs, and Katherine's voice got louder. Maeryn darted over and shut the door before her mom could spot Max and, well... all the other assorted nonsense.

"Come on, Maeryn," Katherine pleaded from outside the door. "I can have Clark go enroll you himself, but I really want to do this as a family. Please let me in."

"No! Leave me alone!"

"Are you sure?"

"Yes!"

"Okay, but don't be mad if we go bowling without you!"

"I DEFINITELY won't be."

There were a few seconds of tense silence in the hallway.

"Oh. Fine, Maeryn. It's fine."

Katherine's footsteps moved away from the door, and was that dejection in her voice? Maeryn didn't want to be so dismissive, but there was so much going on that Katherine wouldn't understand. Heck, who was she kidding? Maeryn didn't understand any of this herself.

Max floated up beside Maeryn, awkwardly drumming his fingers together. "So. We may as well go with the toaster thing, huh?"

"I thought you didn't want it to toast your brain."

"I've peeked behind the firewall a few times, and I don't think there are any viruses. Or, you know, there's always bowling."

Maeryn glanced over at the closet doors, the lightbulb inside shining through the cracks. There was a message in there for her, written in toast, hammered to the wall by her cool, yet paranoid stepbrother, branded in Comic Sans font from an appliance her father programed years ago. An appliance that was only here because the label fell off and Katherine didn't toss it out with her other MotherTech stuff post-divorce. *This* was their best option? To follow an absurd trail of, well, breadcrumbs?

"Okay, do the toast thing."

Max concentrated for a moment, making sure his internet connection was secure. He logged onto the IP address and waited as something began to load.

"It's initiating a program inside of me that I didn't know I had. Must have passed the expiration date though, because I feel like I might puke. Uploading DTC consciousness matrix? Who the heck is DTC?"

A hole formed on Max's chrome stomach and beams of light shot from the opening, converging into a 3-D projection of a man hovering in the middle of the bedroom. The last time Maeryn had seen this person was two years ago, but he had been losing his battle with cancer, leaving him weak and bound to a wheelchair. This projection cast off the man's previous frailty, and he stood before her with blazing red hair and piercing gray eyes, a man in the prime of his life, his ambition and confidence obvious in the way he held himself.

"Hello again, Maeryn."

A surge of opposing instincts hit Maeryn at once. She wanted to run to him. She wanted to run away. She wanted to hug him. She wanted to attack the man with an unfamiliar ferocity. It was as if two separate identities had merged before her.

Grandpa?

The Crucifier?

Chapter Eight

Owe You One

Monhegan Island, Gaia

Kaija barely slept after her argument with Fain, although she was in good company judging by the continuous sounds of her father scouring through his possessions and teleporting in and out of the cabin. She found him the next morning, sitting cross-legged on the floor amidst the mess and drinking day-old coffee straight from the pot.

"You look like you can barely keep your eyes open," said Kaija.

Jasper yawned and blinked up at her. "That makes two of us. Did I keep you awake?"

"No. It wasn't you."

Kaija sat on the floor and leaned up against her father, closing her eyes and giving a shaky sigh.

"Something happen with Fain then?" asked Jasper hesitantly.

Kaija's eyes popped open. "No! Why would you say that?"

"Because every time I was fifteen and couldn't sleep, it was because I said something stupid to a girl."

Kaija knew that there would be no point in denying it. Jasper just *knew*. Ms. Clara warned her that this would happen: family members with even the most modest mentalist leanings often developed a natural communication between each other that went beyond words, a sort-of mini-mindbridge.

"What did he do?" asked Jasper. "Should I relay a little storm cloud that follows him around all day tomorrow?"

"It wasn't him. It was *me*. We were arguing about Elias, and I said something pretty hurtful."

Jasper spoke delicately, as if trying to avoid landmines in his words. "Is it okay for me to ask how Fain feels about the whole Elias situation?"

"That's the frustrating thing! He's so on the fence about it. There shouldn't even be *sides* to take! If Elias gets sent away, he'll be killed. It's not a complicated issue!"

To Kaija's surprise, Jasper's shoulders relaxed and he sighed in what looked like relief. "This is good. You should be proud of Fain."

Kaija scooted away from her father and gave him a look. "Are you serious? Proud that he's questioning your decisions?"

"No. Proud that he's on the fence at all, considering who's raising him. Maddox is…" Jasper coughed and took another drink of coffee. "You know what? This is your boyfriend's father I'm talking about. It would be inappropriate to say any more than this: Maddox and I haven't agreed on things for a long time, and Fain has every reason to hate this refugee, even if those reasons would be mostly imaginary. Good for him for being so indecisive. It's the people who think they're right that you need to be careful about."

Hearing this about Maddox was unsettling, however vague the information might be. Kaija had assumed that her father was friends with Maddox in the way that all adults were friends, although now that she thought about it, their relationship did seem mostly professional. Jasper often met with Maddox about plotting out land for new cabins, mostly acting friendly when the two families got together, but that was about it.

Jasper spent a whole lot more of his leisure time with his baking buddies at Orne's Café on the mainland than with anyone here on the island.

Kaija thought about the raw hate Fain had spewed at the Nomadic woman Tamala, and how he had been so shaken by the fact that she saved his life. It was a side of Fain she had not seen again until last night.

"Coffee?" Jasper levitated a mug off the floor and sent it toward Kaija. She glanced at the half-drunk pot of coffee that he had been sipping out of and pushed the mug away.

"And drink your backwash? No thanks."

Jasper looked down at the coffee pot like he had forgotten he was holding it.

"Oh, this?" he asked. "I'm not sharing this. Tastes about two weeks old, but nice and strong. No, I made a pitcher of cold brew last night. Brown sugar and cinnamon infused, how you like it. Look in the icebox."

Kaija smiled. This was so like her father. Even while frantically searching for his sword last night, he still took the time to do something selfless. Kaija poured a tall glass and downed about half of it in one gulp. She felt the caffeine buzzing through her tired body immediately.

"I know you don't want to talk about it," she said. "But I think you would make an amazing High Guardian."

Jasper just about choked on his coffee mid-sip.

"Never," he said decidedly.

"But this whole mess with Elias wouldn't even be happening if you had kicked Thomas out of the capital like he deserved."

"I'm not so sure about that, but it doesn't matter anyway. It would be so wrong of me to even consider it."

Kaija would have normally stopped there, because Jasper had a way of clamming up when the conversation got too heavy, but she had caught him in a more open mood.

"I wasn't saying I *want* you to," said Kaija. "I just think you'd be great."

Jasper's eyes peered over to the crooked painting of Edgard Zeig at the far corner of the room, but only for a second. "I never knew my father, and he never got to know me. If I took off for the Capital to spend all my time trying to fix things bigger than any one person can fix, making the same mistakes that he made and not being there for *you* and the little family Ms. Clara waited her whole life for, then shame on me. And you know what? Shame on your mother for not being here yesterday. Shame on her twofold." Jasper cleared his throat. "You didn't hear that from me. Now get going. You're late for school."

Kaija glanced over at the clock, which was barely visible behind a pile of Jasper's stacked possessions. The students would be gathering by now, probably outside the schoolhouse on a nice day like today. Kaija normally looked forward to school, but not this morning.

"I'm nervous to see Fain," she admitted.

"And *I'm* nervous to see the villagers. You're the only one who seems to like me anymore, and I'm pretty sure Ms. Clara's going to ground me once she finds out I lost the sword. You know that thing she does, where the ground cracks open and swallows you up to the neck? Yeah, that. She grounded me for six hours once when I was your age. Pretty sure a fire-ant crawled into my ear. Maybe we both need a break."

Kaija perked up at once. "Really?"

Jasper smiled. "Yes. Although, luckily for me, *I'm* not on Ms. Clara's attendance chart, and I think Fain will be perfectly happy to see his girlfriend. Have fun at school. See ya!"

Before Kaija could respond, Jasper vanished, letting the coffee pot clink to the floor and spin there a few times.

"Thanks a lot, father," said Kaija to the empty room.

* * *

"Hi, Kaija!" called Fain, waving and smiling at her.

What felt like the entire group of students turned to look at Kaija as she approached the clearing outside the schoolhouse. The lesson had obviously already started, and the most intense glare came from Ms. Clara herself.

"About time," she huffed at Kaija. "I was worried that we had another frog-related catastrophe. Anyway, class, when performing teleportation on yourself, remember to relay the correct amount of energy in proportion to your body mass, and—"

Ms. Clara continued her lecture on the day's activities. From what Kaija could tell, the group of students had grown since yesterday. It seemed the prospect of learning whole-body teleportation was too exciting to pass up, despite any protests their parents might have about it. Valeria and her friends had not returned, unsurprisingly.

After seeing Fain sitting in the morning sunlight with his messy hair, hazel eyes, and complete obliviousness to how good looking he was, last night's argument instantly felt like a distant memory. Kaija took her usual spot beside him and grabbed his hand, taking a quick glance to make sure Ms. Clara was out of earshot as she prepared for the lesson.

"I'm sorry about last night," she whispered.

Despite Fain's cheerful face, his instant relief was a real thing, something that Kaija could *feel* in the air around him. He squeezed her hand back.

"No, *I'm* sorry. The whole thing with Valeria shook me, and sometimes I just talk and talk without really thinking about what I'm saying. Jasper helped my family when we needed it the most, and it's wrong for me to expect him to do anything else for Elias."

A rock whizzed past Fain's face at blinding speed, and he jumped back in surprise.

"Would you two care to listen to my lesson?" Ms. Clara asked. "Is this a good time for you to learn? I'd hate to inconvenience you in any way by helping you prepare for your future."

Kaija saw that all of the other students were already on their feet and practicing teleportation stances.

"*Yes*, Ms. Clara," her and Fain said in near-unison.

As they joined the circle, Kaija drew in a small amount of Gaian energy and linked her thoughts with Fain in the mental realm. She nodded along to the lesson and pretended to listen while continuing their conversation telepathically.

"Anyway," Fain thought at her. *"I can't believe I turned down that kiss last night. Practiced kissing my pillow a few times this morning, but it's not the same. How about later we sneak off to Manana Rock and—"*

A tree limb soared overhead, just barely brushing Kaija's hair, and they looked up to see Ms. Clara's walking stick pointed directly at them.

"I can feel you sending those telepathic signals, Kaija Monhegan," lectured Ms. Clara. "Are you two thinking things that you'd like to share with the rest of the class?"

"Definitely not, ma'am," said Kaija loudly.

"Fantastic."

Ms. Clara began pacing along the lines of students as she lectured, occasionally striking her walking stick against the ground in big thuds that shook the headlands.

"I know that not all of the students chose to be here today, and I sincerely thank those of you who are, but if you are with me you must be *with me completely*. Spacialism is an ancient and important discipline, and the fact that it has been twisted in recent generations makes it all the more urgent that it is studied. Now is not a time to be passing telepathic love notes. Nothing, I repeat *nothing* is more important than your education."

Ms. Clara slammed her walking stick on the ground again and all of the waves beyond the shore appeared to flatten for a split second, as if the Atlas Ocean was apparently just as intimidated as the children.

"Now then. Any questions before we get started?"

One of the youngest students raised his hand.

"Yes, Stevie."

"I have to go potty."

Ms. Clara sighed. "Anyone else?"

All of the students in the younger group raised their hands.

"Nobody is going potty!" yelled Ms. Clara, and all of the hands shot back down. "I will not waste your time, so don't waste mine. You can potty after you've graduated. Littles, please go and study western Nomadic culture with Norio. Relayers and apprentices, stay with me so we can work on whole-body teleportation. Alan, correct any stances that you see."

Kaija noticed Alan approaching them in the circle, stopping and tapping a student on the shoulder to remind him to release the tension in his upper body.

"Hey, teacher two," Fain called. "Change your mind about breaking the law with us?"

Alan shrugged. "I wouldn't say I changed my mind, exactly. After seeing how hateful Valeria and her friends were, I realized that my silence was a little louder than I had anticipated." Alan lowered his voice. "Valeria's nothing compared to her parents, though. They've been throwing a fit over Elias living here. Threatening to report Jasper to the guardianship for hiding a criminal and everything. Harassing Maddox while he built Elias's cabin. Can you imagine?"

Before a string of expletives had a chance to escape Kaija's mouth, a loud *boom* thundered from below. The ground split open and a jagged rock pushed itself out of the chasm. Ms. Clara swung her walking stick and a large Z chiseled itself into the structure.

"I would like you to spend a few minutes studying my artwork. Be able to picture it clearly in your mind's eye. I'm going to teleport each of you to random locations on the island, and the first three students to make it back to this rock get to skip today's physical education lesson. I also brought some of our guardian's cupcakes for the winner."

Even the normally distracted students began listening more intently, and all mindless chatter stopped at once. Ms. Clara's physical training sessions were notoriously hard. One time she had the class swim around the entire island while she piloted a sailboat ahead of the students, relaying the ocean's currents against the swimmers in what seemed like giddy enthusiasm.

"Sure, you could choose to run back to the headlands," continued Ms. Clara. "Or you could travel through Gaia's stream and come back to this spot instantaneously. Alan, pick up any stragglers in about fifteen minutes and get them ready for a swim. Kaija, remember to use only as much energy as you need. Terry, please make sure your clothes teleport with you this time." One of the younger boys hid his face in embarrassment. "Everybody link arms, please."

Kaija grabbed Fain's hand, looked quickly to see if anyone was watching, and then mouthed the words *I owe you one.* She kissed the air in his direction, and Fain practically turned red. He began mouthing something back to her.

"I lo—"

"Best of luck, everyone!" Ms. Clara shouted, smacking her hand on a nearby student's shoulder. A conflicting burst of colors, tastes, and smells passed through Kaija's mind, and Fain's hand slipped away from her.

* * *

Kaija's feet hit the ground, and she looked around quickly to reorient herself. She was only a few arms away from the ocean, and a black rock jutted from the water, identifying her location at once. This was Gull Cove, where Jasper had roasted an entire hydra vine in the ocean with a bolt of lightning. Fain hadn't stopped talking about this since last cycle. Technically, Kaija's body had been there, but her mind was, well... elsewhere.

She looked back in the direction of the village over the trees, estimating how long it would take her to run. There was no chance she could make it back in fifteen minutes. It seemed ridiculous to even try to teleport her body, when making a little rock disappear had been her singular success, but Kaija *really* wanted to get out of Ms. Clara's physical training session.

She closed her eyes and visualized the structure with the Z that Ms. Clara had just sculpted. Relaying in some carefully measured energy, Kaija tried to push herself back to that location. Power flowed straight through her, leaving her legs wobbly, but nothing else happened. Kaija thought of how hard Ms. Clara's next training session might be. She imagined sitting to the side, watching all of the other students struggling while she ate her father's cupcakes.

"I've got to win," said Kaija, closing her eyes and focusing again. "Go go go go go! Cupcakes! Cupcakes!"

She jumped up and down in frustration.

"You're using too much energy."

Kaija yelped in surprise and spun around to see Elias Zeig sitting on a rock. One of his legs was heavily bandaged and braced up to the knee. He splashed at the water with a foot and smiled at her.

"Cupcakes?" he asked.

"I, uh… never mind," said Kaija, startled. "How long have you been there?"

"Oh, I've been popping in and out all over the place. Ms. Clara asked me to keep an eye on things, just in case anyone teleported themselves halfway up into the clouds. Can't walk very well yet, but walking is for losers anyway. I've tried to stay mostly out of sight and not scare any kids." He seemed to think about this statement for a second. "Not scare any adults, more likely. Fortunately for me, the Monhegans seem to avoid this cove."

Kaija immediately stopped worrying about Ms. Clara's competition. She could feel Elias's emotions resonating from his mind. There was a strange amount of guilt coming from him, as if the fact that he got attacked was somehow his fault. She walked over and sat next to him on the rock.

"Spacialism is about delicacy and precision," said Elias. "Believe me, it's the first thing my mother taught me. Just a gentle push. Watch."

Elias disappeared silently, and a few seconds later he reappeared with a snowball in his hands. He handed it to Kaija, and her skin stung from the bitter cold. She flinched and dropped the snow into the ocean.

"Where'd you get this?"

"Arctica. The very southern pole. No sign of Papa Winter or his sky moose, I'm afraid."

"You went all the way across the world and back in two seconds?"

"Yeah. It was one of the last places I remember visiting with my family, so it's not hard to picture. The sky is so clear at night that you can almost see the other planets."

"I didn't even feel you use any energy!"

"Common misconception. It doesn't take more energy if the distance is greater. Gaia stretches to every corner of the universe. The door from here to everywhere already exists all around you, you just have to find it."

Elias once again silently vanished, reappearing an instant later with a bright red flower, so bright it was almost hard to look at. He held the flower out to Kaija.

"The Azonian emberglow. At night it gives off as much light and heat as a campfire. I just snatched this from the Dune Forest. The trees glow like they're on fire. It's unreal. It'd be a beautiful place to live, if it weren't for all the jerkbirds."

Kaija took the flower. Even now, in the middle of the day, she could feel the warmth radiating from its crimson petals.

"How'd you do that? How'd you teleport without that, you know…" Kaija made a popping noise with her lips, and Elias laughed.

"Silent teleportation? That's way harder than jumping across the world, believe it or not. You've got to pull the air away from where you're going and drop it into the empty space you leave behind. Not many people practice it anymore, but my mother…" Elias got a far-away look in his eyes. "My mother always said that *popping* away is the rudest and most inconsiderate noise a spacialist could possibly make. She'd lecture me every time I forgot. I still forget sometimes and then find myself looking around for her, shaking her finger…"

Elias clapped his hands together and exhaled.

"Well?" he asked. "Let's see what you've got. Ignite your spark into a candle flame this time, not a forest fire. The door to everywhere is all around you. You don't have to leap to it, you just have to find it."

Kaija closed her eyes, pictured the stone that Ms. Clara had summoned, and tried to send herself back to that place. A small trickle of energy began to flow into her, but it was hardly anything to work with. She focused slightly harder, but Kaija's abilities were like an overly sensitive faucet. Her entire body was instantly filled with power that sent her nerves on edge and then fizzled away, resulting in nothing but a sudden desire to eat as much food as she could find.

"I still can't do it," she said, plopping back down onto the rock. "I'm not sensitive enough with my relaying. Or I'm too sensitive, or... *I don't know!* Maybe I should just hide here until tomorrow."

Elias examined her curiously. "The problem might actually be your worldview. No offense, but that's usually where non-Nomads go wrong. Even Ms. Clara struggles needlessly with things like distance. Have you traveled much?"

Kaija made a mental list of the places she'd been: Monhegan Island, Boothbay, Rugaru's mountain prison, and the fields outside the Capital. She'd been to more places on Earth than on her own world, but did it really count if she'd done it in someone else's body?

"I've been... *a few* places," admitted Kaija. "Here and there."

"A few? And you're fifteen? I'd been to every continent by the time I was five! Spacialism is freedom and dissociation. This island is lovely, but any one place can become a mental shackle. You've got to expand your sense of physical space."

"Fair," admitted Kaija. "But how can I fix my worldview? How'd *you* get so good?"

Elias brushed his shoulder and smiled cockily.

"I'm a natural, but I got lucky. You see, my mother was an intensely proud Nomad, and my father was this totally basic Iberian Guardianship immigrant, teaching history at a university in Crossroads City. Both of their cultures were supposed to hate each other, and our family was never really accepted in either world. I guess the only reason I'm so dang amazing is because I don't belong anywhere. Not with the Nomads, not with the guardianship." Elias skipped a stone across the water. "Not here either."

His strained smile dissolved, and he turned away to stare at the blackened rock at the edge of the cove. Kaija put a hand on his back, and Elias flinched like it hurt.

"Oh!" said Kaija, pulling away. "Sorry, did—"

"No, no. I'm fine. I'm just still on edge. I'm going to have to get used to life after, well... *after*. It doesn't help that half the people here look at me like they want to hurt me."

Just then, Kaija wished she could punch each and every Monhegan who was making Elias feel like this. It was such a weird feeling when she had both liked and admired so many of the adults only a week ago.

"I'm sorry that some of us are the worst," she said, "but we're not all like that, I promise. You'll get to know us, and we'll get to know you."

Elias nodded and Kaija noticed him start to loosen up, his shoulders dropping slightly. "Appreciate it. You're father's something special, you know? I can't tell you how much he's..."

Elias trailed off as a shadow spread across the cove. The sky above had been cloudless only minutes ago, but Kaija looked up to see a massive plume of smoke drifting up from the other side of the island, entirely blocking out the sun. Elias's body stiffened once more and readied itself for combat. The scent of ash was now being carried on the breeze. Kaija opened herself up to the mental realm, immediately sensing the desperate feelings resonating from that direction. The barrage of thoughts was noisy, far too chaotic to get a clear sense of what was happening.

"What's going on?" asked Kaija, standing up quickly.

Elias stood with her, groaning as his injured leg took on weight, and he seemed to become a different person. This was no longer the damaged refugee: this was a knight ready for combat, trained by the sharpest minds on the continent and ready to let his instincts take over.

"I'll be back," he said. "Don't move."

Elias disappeared silently, and a few seconds later reappeared, coughing and reeking of smoke.

"The village is under attack," he said. "Western Blaze. I don't know how they got it, but they have a—" He paused, eyes darting around so rapidly they looked almost more reptilian than human. "Do you hear that?"

A noise was rapidly echoing through the trees, getting both louder and faster. *Pop! Pop pop pop!*

Another pop, this one loudest of all, and a muscular man appeared directly in front of Elias. Pitch-black tattoos of flames snaked up and down his arm, which Kaija recognized at once as insignia of the Western Blaze. The man held an ax that was already mid-thrust the moment he appeared. Elias's body loosened, letting himself fall sideways as the ax missed the side of his head by a hair. His arm swung around, touching the handle of the weapon before the Western Blazer could react. The ax vanished and reappeared in Elias's hand. He tossed it over his shoulder, and by the time the ax splashed into the ocean, Elias had already grabbed the attacker by the shirt and the two of them disappeared soundlessly. The ground began rumbling, and the desperate sensations coming from the village intensified, becoming a symphony of dissonant, pleading cries.

Kaija took off, running up the rocks toward the village. Rapid pops continued echoing from the distance like gunfire. Kaija's stomach suddenly felt like it was full of acid. She stopped, squeezing her eyes closed, putting her hands over her ears and whispering to herself.

"Stay calm. Stay calm. Do as you've been taught."

Kaija imagined those mental signals coming at her to be ripples of color in the darkness. She expanded her mind, pushing those tangled colors apart into their primary components. A small number of the ripples became clearer.

"What's happening?"

"Mother!"

"Get away from—"

"Kaija! Kaija, where are you?"

"Fain!" Kaija gasped.

She drew in more energy, pushing away all of those other colors muddying the waters of her mind and focusing on that one small voice in the distance.

"Fain," she thought. *"Are you okay? What's happening?"*

"I don't know. I got teleported to the meadow. There's smoke everywhere. I hear screaming."

"It's the Western Blaze. We have to help."

The pungent feeling of fear that surged from Fain's end of the mental realm just about made her vomit.

"NO! Hide right now, Kaija. You haven't seen the things I have. They won't hesitate to kill. They... oh my Gaia..."

Fain's voice trailed off. Kaija opened her eyes and took off running toward the ever-growing smoke plume, still concentrating on maintaining her fragile connection with Fain.

"Fain? What happened?"

His response was nearly non-verbal, a terrified mash up of feelings only later translated into words by her mind.

"They saw me."

Kaija's eyes filled with tears and she started sprinting faster.

"Fain! Are you okay?"

Fain's reply was nothing translatable at all. A sharp cry struck Kaija's mind like a hammer and the shock of it made her trip over a root, skinning one of her legs on a jagged rock as she hit the ground. A feeling like she had been stabbed in the ankle made her cry out, but the pain left as soon as it came. Kaija yanked up her pants leg, only to see that her ankle was fine. The pain had come from Fain's end.

"Are you there?" Kaija thought. *"Talk to me!"*

It took a few dragging seconds until Fain's voice spoke in her head. He was muffled and distant now, like his mind was being sucked back into the chaos surrounding him. Kaija caught a string of unidentifiable syllables, and then two perfectly clear words.

"...I'm hit."

"What?" she yelled, speaking both out loud and thundering her message into the mental realm.

"There's an arrow in my leg. Kaija, I—"

Fain's voice vanished entirely, not even fading away but there one second and gone the next.

"Fain?"

She couldn't find him anymore. The disorder of the other voices in the mental realm were too loud or…

…or Fain's voice was too quiet.

Kaija sprang back to her feet, ignoring the stabbing pain in her shin where she had struck the rock, and sprinted through the trees ahead of her. The air continued to get heavier, full of ash and nearly impossible to breathe. Kaija's eyes watered as she squinted at the smoky, glowing scene through the branches. For the first time, she could see Monhegan Village.

The smoke obstructed every bit of the previously blue sky, but there was no absence of light. The entire village glowed like a fiery sun as each and every cabin burned to the ground.

Chapter Nine

No More

Monhegan Island, Gaia

Kaija stumbled into the meadow that overlooked her burning home. She could feel the smoke inside of her, scorching her lungs as she struggled to breathe. Her body demanded the awful reflex: take in a breath, and another, and another, but each inhalation only robbed her of oxygen. A series of pops and distant screams rang out over the crackling fire, but Kaija couldn't see far enough to make out what was happening. Just keeping her eyes open was hard enough, but Kaija continued trudging forward, moving deeper and deeper into the heat and ash.

"Fain!" she coughed. "Fain, where are you? Father? Ms. Clara?"

Her calls felt utterly futile, but she couldn't stop. This is where Fain had been when his voice disappeared, but there was no sign of anyone in the meadow. Reaching out telepathically would have made more sense amidst the noise, but the current state of the mental realm was too much for Kaija to manipulate. Her last attempt felt like dipping her toe in a boiling hot spring, a barrage of pain and confusion stinging her very mind upon first contact.

Kaija dropped to her knees, hacking up ash and blood in-between wheezing, desperate breaths. It was too much. She'd suffocate if she didn't turn around and head away from the fires now. But what would happen to Fain? He surely couldn't escape without help if he'd been hit by an arrow. She crawled forward into the blackness, grasping around randomly in hopes of finding him.

Just as Kaija was on the verge of passing out, a gust of wind screamed all around her. The smoke was carried out of the meadow and drifted upward. Kaija breathed in the clean air thirstily as she tried to make sense of what was happening. Cabins rattled and fires leaned in the hurricane-force winds. Everywhere she could see, smoke was being pulled to a single point in the distance, swirling into a huge black ball over the headlands. Ms. Clara stood there at the highest point, slowly turning her staff above her head, relaying the smoke toward her from the entire village. She pointed her staff at the sun and the black ball of smoke shot into the sky, leaving a dark contrail behind it that made the thing look like a huge, obsidian arrow. It burst apart high over the ocean, the ash now drifting down out of the island's vicinity and settling on the waves of the Atlas Ocean.

With her other arm, Ms. Clara reached toward the ground and laboriously pulled up on something invisible. She made a motion as if she were throwing a heavy object toward the village, making a guttural cry as she swung her arm, and in the same instant a gigantic spout of water burst out of the ocean and sprayed high into the air. A few seconds later, Kaija felt cold drops of water falling from the sky, cleaning the ashy residue from her body. The flames engulfing the village flickered and began to shrink.

Kaija wiped at her eyes, trying to clear away the salty water running from her forehead. She squinted around at the now visible scene before her. Fain was nowhere in sight, but she spotted a dozen or so more random Monhegans. Some were running to the village, relaying wind at the dying flames, while others were fleeing for the safety of the trees. A dirt-covered man held a small, limp body in his arms as he struggled to walk forward. Was Kaija seeing someone passed out from smoke inhalation, or a dead body? No matter who it was, there were no strangers on Monhegan. How many of Kaija's friends were dead?

On the headlands, Ms. Clara reared back to relay another spout of water from the ocean, but a second later the air was filled with an ear-piercing round of pops. Western Blazers filled the ruins of the village, spreading out and attacking the escaping adults. Many of the Nomads headed for Ms. Clara, vanishing and reappearing so rapidly around her that it was hard to look at. Kaija could just barely make out Ms. Clara swinging her walking stick and sending a few attackers over the edge of the cliff the second they appeared. Four more men converged on her, one of them getting punched in the face and collapsing with a cry of pain. Another two were swallowed up by the ground where they stood. Ms. Clara reared back her staff to strike the remaining man, but a Nomad appeared behind her, grabbed the tip of the weapon, and it vanished out of Ms. Clara's hands. She was immediately swarmed by too many attackers to count.

Kaija scrambled to her feet and staggered toward the headlands, her insides absolutely on fire, but a surge of indecision stopped her in her tracks. How in desolation could she even help her grandmother at this point? Kaija had no weapon, and her mentalist relaying was both drained and useless amidst the ensuing chaos. She scanned the surroundings for someone to help them. Maddox was at the edge of the village, practically roaring as he threw a charred hunk of lumber at an attacker. Delia was near the flower patch, crouched over and relaying waves of healing light at a convulsing body on the ground. Five or six Monhegans stood protectively around her. Where was Jasper? This would be over in a second if he were here.

A memory hit Kaija. This morning, Jasper had said that he needed a break, and he teleported away to… to where? Did he say where he was going? Kaija's mind was too scrambled to remember. She sank back into the boiling waters of the mental realm, trying to ignore the awful thoughts and feelings barraging her mind. Without any hint of delicacy, Kaija shouted into the void using all the power she could relay.

"FATHER! The Western Blaze is here! Fain's hurt, and—"

Before Kaija could finish, a nearby pop rattled her eardrums and her arms were caught in a vice grip. She flailed around, catching fleeting glimpses of two men behind her. They must have been strong internalists, because her attempts to break free from their grasp did not feel like struggling against flesh, but solid steel. There was another pop, this one in front of her, and a man roughly the size of a bear appeared. His shadow fell across Kaija as he looked down at her.

The newcomer held a gleaming golden spear with his right hand, and his left arm ended with a stump just beyond the elbow. He leaned over, putting the spear below Kaija's chin and pulling up her face to look at him. She immediately recognized those silvery eyes and black tattoos of fire spiraling across the face.

Rugaru.

He held up his stump and brushed the scarred end against Kaija's cheek. "We found the boy who did this to me. I finally know his name: Fain Monhegan. He was crying for you, Kaija. *That* is the child who forces me to cut off my own hand? A little boy with an arrow in his leg, begging for his life and answering every question we asked him? Disappointing."

Rugaru shoved his stump harder into Kaija's face, and she could feel the knotted scars at where his forearm should have been. She began quaking, but not from fear or anger. Every part of Kaija's heart screamed for Fain. He *had* to be okay.

"What'd you do to him?" she asked. "Is he—"

"Dead?" Rugaru leaned in closer, only a breath away from Kaija. "You love this boy, don't you? I can see it. I can *feel* it. The love practically radiates off your mind. It hurts, doesn't it? To be separated from the people you love? For your future to be suddenly and so completely out of your hands? I know that feeling, Kaija. I do. Everyone I know knows that feeling. It's been branded onto the very soul of my people. How nice for us to have some common ground for once."

Rugaru raised his golden spear and pressed the tip to Kaija's throat, giving a tiny jab. She could feel a trickle of blood start to run down her chest.

"Please," she said, every word aching. "Just tell me. Did you kill him?"

Rugaru smiled, purposely drawing out the silence before answering, drinking up her torment with every passing second.

"Did I kill him? Of course I didn't kill him! No, Fain is going to have a very long, very hard life in our prisons. Death would be an absolution from punishment. Seeing you suffer will cut him much deeper than an execution ever could."

Rugaru nodded his head to the left, and Kaija followed the gesture to see two observers standing at a distance. A tall man with a crooked nose was perched there, watching the scene dismissively, his hands held out over a smaller figure before him. It took a second for Kaija to recognize Fain, as he was absolutely transformed by trauma. His eyes were wide, sunken in with dread as he watched Kaija. One of his legs still had an arrow through it, and it trembled where he stood. Fain's mouth was clamped shut, but everything about him looked like he wanted to scream at the top of his lungs. Why was he just standing there, not trying to get away? Kaija realized that the Western Blazer behind Fain must have been Achak, the powerful mentalist said to travel with Rugaru and inflict unspeakable nightmares in the minds of whoever stood in their way. He had Fain trapped like a puppet on strings.

"Never forget this image, Fain," said Rugaru. He pulled his spear back and thrust it toward Kaija's neck.

There was a sudden pop as Elias appeared in-between them. He grabbed the spear with one hand, stopping it just as the tip brushed Kaija's throat, and slammed the blunt end against Rugaru's chest with a hollow *thud*. Elias disappeared again, blinking in and out of existence all around Rugaru as he threw punches from every direction. Rugaru reached out in anticipation, somehow grabbing Elias by the neck on his next teleportation. Elias's image flickered several times, but didn't disappear completely. The strain in Rugaru's expression told Kaija that he was somehow keeping Elias from teleporting.

"Get the boy out of here," Rugaru demanded through gritted teeth, flinching as Elias kicked him repeatedly in the stomach. Achak and Fain disappeared immediately, and Kaija let out a rasping scream.

Rugaru pointed the spear at Elias, but the knight's flickering hand raised up in the air and there was a huge rush of Gaian energy. An entire burning cabin popped into existence in the air, immediately falling toward the two of them. Kaija had just enough time to recognize the cabin as Fain's before it landed on Rugaru and Elias with a giant *boom*, rattling the ground and sending hundreds of burning splinters flying through the air.

"Desolation!" one of the men holding Kaija cried out, backing away from the wreckage and pulling her with him. "Rugaru? Rugaru, are you okay?"

They were met only by silence from the burning heap of rubble.

"He must have teleported away, right?" asked the other man.

"Surely. I've seen him do miracles with that spear."

The flames popped and sparked as part of the cabin collapsed, and the two men looked at each other.

"So, do we just wait here, or…"

Kaija seized on the moment of indecision and tapped into both of the warrior's minds. She conjured the illusion of a huge, screeching eagle soaring right at their faces. The hallucination only lasted a fraction of a second, but it was surprising enough for both men to loosen their grips. Kaija slipped out of their arms and shot toward the trees. She knew the hidden trails of Monhegan better than anyone, and if she could just make it into the woods, there might actually be a chance to shake off her attackers.

On any other day, the utter failure of Kaija's escape might have been laughable. The futility of trying to run from a spacialist hit Kaija quite literally in the face. She had barely taken three strides when one of the Western Blazers teleported right in front of her. Kaija ran face-first into the man's chest, and pretty soon her arms were being held behind her back by the other man. His grip made the previous hold seem gentle; Kaija's arms felt like they were being nearly pulled out of their sockets.

"We can't wait for Rugaru," said the man holding her. "Cut her throat, fast!"

The other man unsheathed a dagger from his belt, pressing the blade against her neck without hesitation. Kaija registered that she might be experiencing the last moment of her life, but a memory rose to the surface of her mind. It gave her a crazy idea, and a new energy sparked through her body.

The door to everywhere…

The man slashed his dagger. There was a spray of blood and a cry of pain. A *grown man's* cry. It took the man with the dagger a second to comprehend what he was seeing: Kaija was gone. His companion was pressing both hands over his bleeding chest, mouth hanging open in surprise.

"You cut me! What in desolation is wrong with you?"

"But, the girl. She was here, and then... *uh oh.*"

They both searched the scene frantically, not spotting Kaija anywhere. Not in the meadow, not running toward the village, not on the path in the woods. She couldn't have gotten far in the last two seconds. Unless...

The warriors locked eyes, an understanding passing between them.

"Rugaru's not going to like this."

* * *

Jasper followed his daughter's call for help, arriving in the center of Monhegan Village just in time to watch the last of the fires die away. Islanders were hobbling amongst the wreckage, counting the survivors and tallying their losses. Not one Western Blazer remained, all having disappeared only seconds before the guardian's arrival. Ms. Clara limped around the corner of a pile of broken lumber with a group of crying children following her close behind. She stopped in her tracks, looking over at Jasper with a horrible fear in her eyes.

"Son. The Western Blaze was here." Her voice caught in her throat. "Where... *where were you?*"

Jasper couldn't get out a single word in reply. The truth was too ridiculous to speak aloud. He had gone to Orne's Café for the day, partly to see if his sword was there, but mostly just to get away. After a long lunch and dessert, he simply sat in silence for an hour, sipping coffee, watching the birds, and enjoying the rare moment of solitude. Nobody there to pester him about Elias or threaten to contact the guardianship. Peace.

Jasper admitted the truth to himself. It was almost funny in the most horrible way.

The people I swore to protect were dying, and I was eating cake.

"Clara, is everyone okay?"

She shook her head.

"I don't know. I don't see how they can be. Maddox and Delia are doing a headcount. Elias fought off Rugaru the best he could. You should have seen him, Jasper, teleporting around and fighting without even taking a step on his bad leg. He got dozens of children away from the danger. I tried my best to help, but about fifty men ganged up on me and took my staff. It seemed coordinated. I think they knew what it really was."

A raspy voice spoke from nearby. "They knew. I'm sure they did."

They turned to see Elias limping through the wreckage, his hair wild and black with ash.

"Your walking stick, it's one of Edgard's missing artifacts, right? The Generalist Staff? A few days ago the Mentalist Stone was stolen from Thomas, and just now I spotted Rugaru with the Spacialist Spear. A group of pirates from Zedland stole it from the capital's vault during the transition of power after Edgard's death, but I guess Rugaru has it now."

Ms. Clara closed her eyes tiredly. "They must be collecting Edgard's seven artifacts. I knew we should have destroyed them."

"Do they really do what the rumors say?" asked Elias. "I've heard that Edgard infused his power in seven artifacts for each of his knights, but I didn't think something like that was possible."

"It's true. The Mentalist Stone, the Spacialist Spear, the Internalist Ring, the Generalist Staff, the Conjurist Hammer, the Externalist Bow, and the Spiritualist Flower. Rugaru has at least three of them now. Thank Gaia the sword is safe."

Jasper roared in anger and the embers of a nearby cabin sparked and hissed. "We *don't* have the sword, Clara. I've been looking for it all day. I thought I lost it, but..."

He trailed off, spotting Maddox and Delia running from the woods heading toward the village. That look on their faces, that horrible look: he had seen it once before.

"Jasper!" screamed Delia. "We can't find Fain and Kaija. Everyone else is..." She stumbled over her words. "Accounted for. The survivors, and the dead. But there's no sign of our kids anywhere."

"They're smart," said Ms. Clara. "We've talked about what to do during an attack. Have you checked Manana Rock? Or the sailboats at the dock?"

"Not yet, but—"

"How many?" Jasper interrupted, nearly shouting. Angry tears formed at the corner of his eyes. "How many dead?"

"Nine, so far," said Maddox. "Maybe more if the healers can't get some of the injured to wake up. Mostly suffocation. The worst was Alan's mother. He tried to get her out of their cabin, but the roof collapsed and blocked the door. Alan's inconsolable, Jasper. He heard her crying for help in there. I can't, I just..." Maddox couldn't continue. He leaned over, bursting into heaving sobs.

Jasper scanned the nearby islanders. He spotted Alan on the ground by his collapsed house, hugging his legs with his face pressed to his knees. A bloody ax was tossed in the grass beside him. Norio, the old priest, was on a cot, hyperventilating as three healers tried to relay the ash from his lungs. The most alarming sight was Ciro. He walked toward Jasper with a nearly empty expression on his face, holding the limp body of his daughter Valeria in his arms. Her blonde hair was matted with dirt

Joe Luegers

and blood. Ciro met Jasper's eyes unblinkingly and spoke with an odd detachment.

"Couldn't see with all the smoke, guardian. She fell from the headlands, running from those dirt monkeys. Hit her head real bad. Delia couldn't get her to wake up." He looked down at her. "She won't wake up. Why won't she wake up?"

Elias limped toward Ciro. "I'm sorry. I tried to save all the children, but with the smoke it was too—"

His voice seemed to wake something up in Valeria's father, pulling him from his state of shock. The man looked about ready to drop his daughter and tackle Elias.

"Don't you dare open your mouth! We all know why this attack happened." Ciro turned back to Jasper. "None of us are surprised, guardian. We told you. *We told you.* And when this traitor led the Western Blaze to our home, you weren't even here to help us."

Ms. Clara stood up a bit straighter, taking a decisive step between Ciro and Elias.

"You're in shock, Ciro. Think about the seriousness of your accusation."

"I've never been so clear headed as I am now. The warriors were coming from Jasper's cabin. Who else could have led them there? What other Nomad has ever even stepped foot on this island? They can come back anytime now, you know that?" Ciro's eyes narrowed, looking over at Jasper with the purest disgust. "Valeria didn't deserve to get hurt, but it was an accident. Whatever's happening to Kaija right now, it's worse. Will you still be defending this trash when you find your daughter months from now, slaving away at one of their prisons with a baby in her stomach? That's right, guardian. I saw them take her. Her and Fain. I wish I had it in me to say you all deserved this."

126

Ciro spit at Elias's feet and stumbled off toward the healers. His words immediately silenced the whole group. Maddox and Delia were robbed of their breath. Ms. Clara's eyes were wide and calculating. Elias disappeared before anyone could speak to him, but his final expression was one of pure shame.

"Jasper?" asked Ms. Clara. He remained silent, his face unreadable. "Jasper? What are we going to do?"

Jasper turned away from his mother, scanning the ruins of his village. The occasional Monhegan met his glance, pausing while digging through the ruins of their life before quickly looking away. Every tired, desolate face seemed to be saying the same thing: *Where were you?* For months, the guardians of nearby villages had been begging him to find the Western Blaze and end the civil war once and for all, but Jasper constantly dodged their requests. He hated his power. He resented his heritage. Every force within and without him was a constant, crushing presence that he tried to ignore every second of his life.

No more.

Jasper walked silently toward the headlands, leaving Maddox and Delia behind in their sobbing, panicked embrace.

"Jasper!" Ms. Clara shouted at him, but he didn't respond. He didn't even look back. She began hobbling after him, tugging at his shoulder. "Son? What in desolation are you doing?"

Jasper stopped as the ocean became visible over the hill. He looked over the waters, eyeing the horizon in the direction of the mainland.

"Tell Maddox that he's the guardian now," he said under his breath. "Or it can be you. Doesn't matter. I'm leaving."

"Are you serious?" asked Ms. Clara, tugging harder at him. "That's all you're going to say to me? Ciro might be an awful xenophobe, but he's right. They can come back anytime they want now! We need you here. You're going to stay."

Jasper breathed in deeply, feeling the Gaian energy fill him to the brim. The nanobots seemed to sizzle in his bloodstream, amplifying his already great power a thousand-fold. Waves crashed below. He could make the ocean boil if he wanted to. Insects buzzed on the shoreline of the mainland. Even from five stretches away, Jasper could see them clearly. He counted the flaps of a hummingbird's wings. The entire horizon, all of its trees and rocks and every grain of sand: it could all be dust in an instant. The effort would be infinitesimal, nothing at all to bend reality around him.

"No," he said. "I'm leaving."

Ms. Clara punched Jasper in the back with surprising force. She leaned against him, trembling with keening sobs. "Don't you think I'm hurting right now too? Don't you think I'd just like to check out? Son, you have to talk to me! Where are you going?"

Clouds blackened the sky, blossoming from nowhere and dropping rain on the smoldering remains of the village.

"I'm going to kill Rugaru."

Chapter Ten

But It's Glow Bowling

Casa de Johnson, Earth

The holographic image of Duncan the Crucifier studied Maeryn silently, his young face eerily similar to Dorian's. A year ago, she would have given anything to see him again, but now her feelings were far more complicated. The man who helped raise her was a murderer. *The* murderer.

Max floated over to Maeryn's side, his little hand resting on her arm as he scanned Duncan from a distance, metal fingers twitching anxiously.

"Dr. Kacey?" asked Max. "This can't really be you. We went to your funeral. I saw your body. What are you?"

"I am not the Duncan Kacey as you knew him. Before my predecessor's death, he created an artificially intelligent replica of his mind. I am no more than a distant ripple in the water. To avoid confusion, you can call me Duncan Two. I know sequels usually aren't as good, but—"

"It was you!" Max cut in, pointing an accusatory finger. "Maeryn, I told you that the refrigerator gave me a funny look a few days ago! And you didn't believe me, you monster!"

Duncan smiled. "Guilty. A small part of my consciousness has been keeping an eye on things from your house's operating system and several of my avian drones. It was never my intention to make my presence known."

"You've been in our freezer for two years, Grandpa, and you never even said hi? That's cold." Max groaned. "Sorry, everyone. I swear I didn't mean to make that pun. It's been a stressful day."

"We've met before, Max," said Duncan. "Although this is the first time I've come forward willingly. There have been five occasions where you've discovered my presence and I had to erase your memory. You seem to learn from it each time, because it's getting harder and harder to hack into your consciousness. I'm not sure I could do it again."

"I..." Max paused. "You. I. Um. Hold on, everyone. I need a few seconds to put my brain back together."

Maeryn paced the room. "My head is spinning here. Last year I found out that you were from another dimension, and now it turns out that you made a simulation of your consciousness that we were never supposed to know about? And you've been messing with Max's memory?" She stopped, looking up at Duncan with tears in her eyes. "When do the lies stop, grandpa? I thought I knew you when you were alive, but you're just a—"

Maeryn was going to say *murderer,* but it was more complicated than that. It was worse.

"—you're the Crucifier. You caused suffering on Gaia that has lasted for almost three generations. You killed Edgard Zeig. How could you be so heartless?"

Duncan Two nodded, taking in the information like it was no more than a simple fact. Maeryn searched fruitlessly for any hint of remorse on his cold face, but he remained stoic.

"I won't deny this," he said. "You have to understand that all I remember from my time on Gaia was what the original Duncan wrote in his journal. Mere shadows of memories." He leaned in closer to Maeryn, eyeing her up and down. "Look at you: clenched jaw, increased heart rate, blood rushing to your face. Your anger is entirely misdirected, Granddaughter. If you're looking for someone to apologize for Duncan's behavior in his earliest years, I'm afraid that this person is in the ground."

It was so weird to hear this answer from someone who admitted to not really being Duncan, because it was *exactly* the kind of infuriatingly rational thing that he would have said.

"I just thought you were a good person," said Maeryn. "But you're not, really. Not at all."

Saying these things aloud was like turning a pressure valve, but it was never-ending, no ultimate release of resentment on the horizon. Duncan approached Maeryn and tried to put a hand on her shoulder, but that was a gulf he couldn't cross. His hand simply phased through her.

"I cannot be a speaker for the dead, but I think I understand my previous self more than you do. It's easy to be good when it's easy to be good. Goodness was a privilege only afforded to me once I was rich and respected here on Earth. When given a choice between goodness and survival, there really is no choice. That's how it was on Gaia. Every day." He paused, pulling his hand away. "It wasn't easy to stay silent these past two years. If anything, I resent my previous self as much as you do. I love my family, but I was forced to stay away. My programming wouldn't let me talk to you, unless the worst should happen."

Maeryn wiped away her angry tears. "The worst?"

Duncan held out his hand and a map of the east coast appeared, floating in the air. A blinking, blue dot emerged several miles off the coast of New York City.

"For some time now, my monitors have been getting traces of Gaian energy coming from this location. I fear that another portal has been opened. The universe has a way of repairing itself, and these openings normally seal themselves off in a matter of hours, but this one has not decreased in its output of Gaian energy. Something is keeping it open. I've tried sending drones to investigate, but for some reason they won't fly past the coast. The cameras get disabled and the drones don't return."

This didn't make any sense to Maeryn. Kaija had been trying to use Edgard's sword to get back to Earth for a whole year now, but it wasn't responding. How could a portal just appear out of nowhere?

"That's not possible," said Maeryn.

"It doesn't matter how possible you think it is. It happened. Have you been in contact with the Gaian girl today?"

"No."

"Please be honest with me."

"I'm telling the truth! Kaija and I spent our birthday together, but things have been so crazy since then. We haven't reconnected. Why do you think I'm lying?"

"Your heartrate betrays you. Only Edgard's sword and the seven artifacts can channel enough power to pierce the veil. Based on my observations, both the sword and the staff were last on Monhegan Island. Are you lying on behalf of your Gaian friend?"

Max floated up to Duncan and poked his little finger at the man's chest. "Gosh, you're the worst! No, Maeryn's not lying. Sure, her blood pressure's dangerously high right now, but that could be due to the fact that we've been contacted by our dead grandpa through a freaking *toaster!*"

Duncan narrowed his eyes and glared at Maeryn for a few tense seconds.

"Okay," he said finally. "I suppose I'll have to trust you two, as I've run out of other options. You must go to the Atlantic Ascent immediately and close the portal."

Maeryn couldn't suppress the ridiculous urge to laugh. "Um… no?! How are we supposed to fix a dimensional rift two miles off the east coast?"

"I can provide transportation and protection. This is more important than you can imagine."

"I said NO! Even if we could, I wouldn't do it for you."

Duncan gave a pleading look to Max.

"No way, old man!" said Max, waving his arms and backing up. "I'm still kind of recovering from the idea that you've been watching us from the refrigerator. For a genius, you sure are putting an absurd amount of trust into a teenager's ability to save the world and deal with puberty at the same time, you know."

Duncan closed his eyes and ran a hand over his tired face. "Believe me, you two are my last choice. I had been working with Rosalie, but she disappeared a year ago and altered my programming to make it impossible for me to follow her."

A look passed between Maeryn and Max. Or, as much of a look that could be written on Max's featureless chrome face.

"Rosalie knew about you?" asked Max under his breath.

"Yes. I contacted her shortly after Duncan One's death."

"What about my dad?" asked Maeryn.

Duncan shook his head. "No. I didn't trust that Dorian would have the willingness to make morally gray decisions."

"Wow," said Max. "That's either the saddest compliment or most reassuring insult I've ever heard."

"Can't you find him?" asked Maeryn. "Ask him to help?"

Duncan's face darkened. "Your father might be in grave danger, Maeryn. He's gone somewhere I can't follow."

He waved his hand and a video began to play on the wall. Maeryn saw herself in her living room, pleading with her dad as a soldier called after them from outside. If this was supposed to be footage from last night, it was all wrong. Dorian hadn't been there; he was off looking for Rosalie. They watched as Dorian was arrested and taken to a helicopter. Just before he was about to enter, the tall soldier put a hand on Dorian's forehead and they both disappeared, there one second and gone the next.

"What was that?" asked Max. "I don't remember that guy at all."

"You don't remember him, because he doesn't *want* you to remember," said Duncan. "This man is a relayer. Last year you showed the Gaians the way to Earth. I warned you that those with less noble intentions would follow, and I was right. The Western Blaze is here."

* * *

Maeryn and Max watched the video of last night's events in stunned silence. When the Nomadic man got his mask knocked off and began to speak, Max shot up from the bed and zoomed around in circles.

"I know that voice!" he cried. "I've heard it before, at the Edgardian Capital! It's Achak of the Western Blaze. What in the worlds was he doing in our living room? I thought I'd be relieved that we didn't do drugs last night, but this—"

"—this is bad," Maeryn interrupted. "This is *worse* than bad. Our dad's not in jail, he's been kidnapped! He might be on Gaia right now!"

Duncan tapped the holographic video and the image zoomed in on the fiery tattoos crawling up Achak's neck.

"I recognized the insignia at once. The Western Blaze was born in my time as a response to Edgard's indifference toward the Nomadic struggle. This Achak, as you call him, was first spotted on my cameras shortly after the readings of Gaian energy from the east coast. He teleported his way to Indianapolis, never stopping to read a map, infiltrated a militarized special task force of the Indianapolis police, and convinced Dorian that he was under arrest for war crimes. The amount of information that he knew about the American justice system is alarming, to say the least. He then teleported you and Max here to Katherine's house and fed a made-up story to her. Looking through random security footage from the last few months, it turns out that the Western Blaze has been coming and going for a while now, but they're nearly impossible to track.

"I was also certain that Dorian had been taken to Gaia, but the truth is something I could not have guessed. On the very night of his abduction, I found Dorian's mugshot appear on the server of a max security prison. The guards there believe that he is a criminal by the name of Francis Rodriquez."

Max grunted. "I'm getting really tired of being confused. This never used to happen to me, you know. Why the heck would Achak dump Dorian in an Earth prison?"

"He wanted Dorian out of the way, not harmed," said Duncan. "The US federal prison system doesn't use Mother-Tech software, so I'm locked out. I believe that Achak knows this, he knows about me, and he purposefully put Dorian somewhere that I couldn't reach. It's also no coincidence that he dropped you and Max here, in a technological dead zone. Thank Dobbs for the toaster. I don't understand how Achak knows all of this, or how he navigated our world so easily. There's also the matter of this."

The video scrolled again, this time showing the glowing green gem that Achak wore around his neck.

"He has the Mentalist Stone, formerly belonging to Thomas of the High Seven. It shouldn't have worked here on Earth, but yet again we come to another bewildering detail." The video fast-forwarded to Achak melting the projector and making the refrigerator explode. The feed zoomed in on the container strapped to his upper arm, which was glowing a brilliant blue as he relayed.

"It appears that the Western Blaze has figured out a way to contain Gaia's energy for use on Earth." Duncan stared at Maeryn, his silvery eyes blazing with foreboding. "While many details remain uncertain, the bigger picture is clear. In my youth, I saw visions of a war between both worlds. A war that would act as a beacon for something unimaginably devastating, something worse than war itself. I believe we are seeing the start of the darkest possible future."

Maeryn was reminded of the spiritualist gathering on her birthday. Could this be where Desolation begins, with a secret invasion of Earth?

The video feed turned off, leaving only Duncan's image glowing in the dim room.

"So?" he asked. "Will you do it? Will you travel to the Atlantic Ascent and close the portal?"

Maeryn once again had the ridiculous urge to laugh, and this time she didn't suppress it.

"Really? *Really?* My dad, heck: *your son,* is falsely imprisoned, and you want us to travel to a rip in the universe where dangerous terrorists with magic weaponry are sure to be waiting for us? What we really need to do is contact MotherTech's lawyers to find my dad and get him out of jail, and then get ahold of Jasper to check out the portal from the other side. He could take care of it in seconds."

Maeryn closed her eyes and concentrated as hard as she could. She'd never been able to purposefully contact Kaija from her side of the mindbridge, but moments of extreme emotion sometimes let a thought or two slip through. It was always accidental, but maybe she could take advantage of her raw mental state.

"Kaija? Are you there? This is important!"

"Stop it!" yelled Duncan, breaking Maeryn's concentration. "You may have seen the bright side of Gaia, but I lived my youth in its darkness. I was there on the final day of the Global War. I watched the entire sky burn. I saw mountains explode and shower flaming debris upon thousands of soldiers. A single person did this, Maeryn. Don't you dare inform Edgard's bloodline about this portal. It has to be closed before—"

Maeryn kept her eyes closed and waved a hand dismissively. "Max, turn him off."

"What?" asked Max. "I can't turn off Grandpa!"

"Sure you can. I can't focus with all his hateful speech. Turn him off so I can talk to Kaija."

"Wait!" cried Duncan. He flickered as he ran forward, pleading with Maeryn. "There's one more thing. Do whatever you want, but at least listen to this!"

Max laughed.

"One more thing? Exposition dump of the century, and you're still not done? Come on, gramps. How many more awful things are you going to throw at us?"

Another beam of light shot from Max and a second image appeared, showing an old homeless man sitting on a bridge and sharing a Twinkie with his dog.

"You know this man, correct?" asked Duncan.

Maeryn had only met him once, but that day was clearly burnt into her memory.

"Yes, I do. That's Kai. He saved my life in Garfield Park last year, but I haven't seen him since. Why?"

"Listen carefully. If you see this man again, run. Do not talk to him, do not even let him see you. I've been tracking Kai since before I died, but he's just as smart as me, if not smarter. He always slips right out of my fingers. This man is the most dangerous person on Earth. I sent a Guardian Angel after him last winter, and he killed it with nothing but his bare hands. If you run across him again, contact me immediately." Duncan's eyes darted over to Max. "If you get the sense that Kai knows about the portal, Max, *kill him.*"

"Hey now!" Max yelled. "I can't kill a human! It's impossible. Remember the first rule of sentient robotics, that *DON'T MURDER* rule? Who wrote that again? Some dead guy, lived in our freezer for two years, speaks fluent toaster, you know the type…"

"You're lying," said Duncan. "Dorian removed nearly all your limitations last year, and we both know it. You can kill now, so long as it's not a family member."

"Fine. Good news, everyone: I'm a killing machine. But I'm not going to just freaking *murder* an old homeless guy! If I ever push a human off a bridge, it will be for fun, not because you asked me to! Can you at least tell me why you want me to straight up *kill* a dude?"

A strange look spread across Duncan's face. "No. I don't actually know why Duncan One asked me to track this man. I sense that a portion of my memory has been locked away. It seems that my former self was holding information so dangerous that he didn't even trust his digital copy to carry it knowingly. But I am certain that Kai cannot be allowed to find the portal back to—"

"I've heard enough," said Maeryn. "Grandpa, I was really hoping to discover that you weren't the horrible man I feared you were, but I've been disappointed again. Bye."

Max cut the holographic feed and Duncan Kasey vanished immediately. The lights in the bedroom turned back on, and Max made a tongue clicking sound.

"Well, *that* happened. I hate to admit it, but our grandpa is kind of a butthole."

* * *

Maeryn stormed out of Smith's room. Max floated after her across the upper landing, quickly hiding behind her back when a voice called up the steps.

"Hey there, Maeryn-Maeryn-Bo-Baeryn. Watching a good movie up there? Last call for bowling."

Clark was at the foot of the staircase, wearing a Hawaiian shirt and eating a bag of peanuts.

"I'd rather die horribly," said Maeryn, still stomping toward her room.

"But it's *glow bowling*! I can't think of a better way to welcome you to the Casa de Johnson. We can even get you fitted for your own ball. I'd be happy to spring for a nice reactive resin. A newbie like you could do with a fifteen pounder, or—"

Maeryn slammed her door and circled the room, forcefully yanking down all the blinds and ranting nonsense under her breath.

"He really does have this unsettling vibe, doesn't he?" said Max. "Maeryn-Bo-Baeryn? Casa de Johnson? *Dios mio, that guy!*"

Maeryn pulled another blind down, so hard that it ripped in half. Max timidly floated toward her, tapping her shoulder.

"So, what's going on with you, Sister? Anything you want to talk about? Your hormonal imbalance is quite alar—AH!"

Max dodged a pillow that Maeryn threw at him, which instead knocked an action figure of Nora Galaxy off a shelf. Maeryn rammed her whole body up against a dresser, grunting and turning red in the face as she scooted it across the carpet.

"Help me barricade the door," she panted. "I don't care what Duncan says, we're locking ourselves in here and not coming out until we talk to Kaija! Maybe we can finally make a portal and get out of this awful place."

"Amazingly, I can't say I have a better plan." Max swiveled around and flew toward the bed, levitating the metal frame up with his electromagnetic generator. "Pull a Les Miserables up in here, do some meditating, and talk to our Gaian buddy. Hopefully Kaija will have a better sense of what's going on than we—CRAP!"

For a split second, all of the lights in the house hummed and glowed brighter than they should have. An ear-splitting pop filled the room, and Max flew straight into the forehead of a suddenly *there* Kaija. He dropped the bedframe with a huge clunk as Kaija screamed and instinctually swatted him away like a bug. Max hit a bookshelf, knocking over a pile of books which buried him on the floor. Maeryn stopped pushing the dresser and her mouth hung open at the sight of Kaija.

Max kicked aside *The Collected H.P. Lovecraft* and pulled himself out of the mess. "Island girl! We were just talking about you. What a coincidence, huh?"

Kaija's eyes rolled back in her head and she collapsed on the carpet, unconscious. Little trails of smoke drifted up from her tattered clothes. Max dizzily stumbled across the floor and poked at her side with his foot.

"Good," he said. "I didn't kill her. You know, this is like the second-most improbable day of my life."

Chapter Eleven

Doing the Thing

Casa de Johnson, Earth

Kaija experienced a fleeting moment of relief upon waking, due mostly to the fact that she was alive enough to wake up at all. She had been placed in an impossibly comfortable bed, one far too soft to be her own, although it did little to alleviate the fact that her entire body felt like a giant bruise.

Something hard poked her in the side on a particularly tender spot. Kaija groaned and rolled over, opening her eyes to see Max floating there. Maeryn watched from behind him, too stunned to speak. Max prodded Kaija again with a little metal finger.

"Good morning, beautiful. You okay, Kaija?"

Kaija let out a rasping, desperate scream at the top of her lungs. Her memories had all come rushing back: the village on fire, Fain's desperate thoughts crying out in her head, a blade pressed to her chest... total chaos on the home she left behind. Kaija scrambled out of the bed, but her legs immediately gave out and she collapsed into Maeryn's arms.

"You're okay, you're okay," said Maeryn, holding Kaija tight and lifting her back onto the bed. "Try to calm down and tell us what happened."

Kaija pressed her face to Maeryn's shoulder and gave a trembling sob. "Western Blaze. The whole island was on fire. And Fain... he—"

She heaved for air.

"Breathe," said Maeryn, rubbing her back.

Kaija concentrated on every breath, slowly feeling her body start to gain control over itself. She wiped her eyes and looked around this strange room. Maeryn and Max were with her. She was as far away from Monhegan and the people who wanted to hurt her as she could possibly get. But what had she left behind? What was still happening on her home?

"What about Fain?" asked Max, any hint of levity long gone from his voice. "Is he okay?"

"No," said Kaija. She took in another long breath. "He's not."

Kaija spoke slowly at first, recounting her morning leading up to the attack, but soon found herself spilling out the entire, horrible day. In the quiet, almost mocking safety of Maeryn's room, she told them everything.

* * *

Maeryn pressed a hand over her mouth, eyes wide and full of tears. Max paced back and forth on the bed, for once at a loss for words.

"They were going to kill me," said Kaija, finishing her story. "But I heard your voice in the back of my head, and... and it's hard to explain how I felt. For a second, I just knew that I could teleport to wherever you were. It's like Earth suddenly felt closer than it's been in a long time."

Maeryn shook her head slowly. "I tried to contact you, but I don't understand. You've been trying to use the sword to get to Earth for a whole year, and now you just teleport without it like it's no big deal? I thought that the sword was the only way to pierce the multiversal veil."

Max snapped his fingers. "I think I understand something, for once! Teleportation shouldn't be possible between two separate worlds, but Earth and Gaia aren't separate anymore. Kaija didn't need to cut an opening with the sword, because there already *was* one. She must have teleported straight through the portal that Grandpa just told us about. That's kind of amazing."

Kaija sat up straight. "Grandpa? What do you mean, *Grandpa?*"

"Yeah, Duncan's alive," said Maeryn. "Kind of. And the Western Blaze has been to Earth too. Achak put my dad in jail, and the military took me to my mom's house, and our grandpa talked to us through a toaster, and... gosh, we've got some catching up to do."

As Maeryn tried to figure out where to start, a sudden flurry of knocks on the door made them all jump. Katherine's voice called in from the other side.

"Maeryn! You're all signed up for school. Come on, we're going bowling. You can't just sit around and watch TV all day."

"Who's th—" Kaija began, but Maeryn shushed her.

"I'm not feeling well, Mom," Maeryn called. "I need to catch up on sleep."

Everyone stared silently at each other for a few seconds, waiting for the receding sound of footsteps down the stairway, but Katherine's shadow remained visible under the door.

"By the way, have you been messing with the toaster?" she asked. "It was jumping up and down on the counter when I got home."

"Wasn't me! Just throw it away."

The doorknob started to jiggle.

"Why's the door locked, honey? I know that this must be so hard, but I wish you would just talk to me. Come on, open the door."

Maeryn jumped to her feet and started making frantic, incomprehensible motions to Max and Kaija. She wanted them to hide, but Kaija just stared at her perplexedly, and Max appeared to have gotten stuck between a million decisions.

"Not a good time, Mom!"

"What are you doing in there? Clark said he heard a scream."

"Nothing!"

"If it's nothing, then just open the door!"

"Ugh, no! I'm going to the bathroom!"

The doorknob stopped moving for a second.

"Um?" asked Katherine. "Where?"

Maeryn glanced around her bedroom. Oh yeah: *bedroom.* She didn't have her own attached bathroom here like in Indianapolis.

"I mean, I'm changing," Maeryn called. "Totally naked right now, so don't come in."

"You didn't bring any spare clothes," said Katherine. "Something's weird with you. I'm coming in."

They heard the jangling sound of keys outside. Maeryn waved her arms at Kaija and pointed at the closet door, but Kaija just held up her hands in confusion.

"Closet!" Maeryn thought at her. *"Hide!"*

"What's a closet?"

"It's a little room to hang clothes."

"Like a wardrobe?"

"Yes, but inside the wall! See the sliding door? Do you not have closets on Gaia? How has this never come up before!? Never mind. GO!"

Kaija gasped and nodded, moving across the room as quickly and quietly as she could. Max remained hanging in the air, seemingly deep in thought.

"Max!" Maeryn whispered. "Do I seriously have to tell you to hide too?"

"Hold on…" he said quietly. "I'm thinking real hard right now. Fain's hurt. We don't need to hide, we need to get to Gaia as fast as—"

The door swung open, easily knocking over the dresser Maeryn pushed in front of the doorway earlier. Katherine poked her head into the bedroom.

"Honey, we'd really love it if you went bowling with…"

Katherine trailed off as she stared at Kaija, who was halfway into the closet. Max went quiet and hovered motionless in the middle of the room.

"Maeryn," said Katherine tensely. "Who is that girl in your closet?"

Maeryn was simply left with her mouth hanging open as she tried to think of a way to salvage the situation. Kaija waved at Katherine awkwardly.

"Hi, um, Maeryn's mom. Nice to meet you."

"Who are you?" Katherine demanded.

"I'm… um," Kaija muttered. She glanced at Maeryn, who was shaking her head frantically. Kaija wasn't sure if she was supposed to lie or not say anything at all. "I…I don't know. Who am I, Maeryn?"

"She's my girlfriend," said Maeryn, saying the first thing that popped into her head. Kaija's eyes went impossibly big and she mouthed *WHAT?* at Maeryn, who just shrugged back at her.

Katherine looked back and forth between the two of them, opening and closing her mouth several times as her face gradually turned a dark shade of red. She cleared her throat.

"So. When you say *girlfriend,* do you mean—"

"Yep. Girlfriend."

"And what are you two doing, locked in here with the dresser pushed in front of the door?"

"Do you really want to know? I mean, I could tell you if—"

"NO," said Katherine, sweating profusely. She started talking to herself rapidly. "I knew it! That weird obsession with Nora Galaxy. Always wanting to play with action figures. The whole vegetarian thing. I *knew it!*" She ran her eyes up and down Kaija, appearing to be on the verge of gagging. "I'm going to need a second to process this."

The door closed and they could hear Katherine pacing around the hallway.

"Well, that got her out of the room fast," muttered Max. "Heterosexual insecurity saves the day, I suppose."

The door swung back open and Katherine nearly tripped over the dresser as she charged inside, pointing an unsteady finger at Max.

"And what is *that thing?* You know that I don't allow MotherTech junk in my home!"

"Allow me to take a page from Miss Kacey's book," said Max. "I could tell you why I'm here, but I'm not so sure you really want to know."

Katherine pulled at her hair with both hands. "Jesus, it talks! Okay, that's it!" She stepped over the fallen dresser and grabbed Maeryn roughly by the arm. "Your criminal father might be okay with your stupid toys and *satanic sexual perversions*, but this is my home! You are grounded, Maeryn. No more playing with your robot, certainly no glow bowling, and if that, that... *lesbian* is not out of my house in five minutes, I'm calling the police!"

"Wow, lady," said Max. "You're not making a great case for humankind right now."

"Shut up!" yelled Katherine, jumping and trying to swat Max out of the air. "Shut up, shut up, *shut up!*" Max buzzed around, easily avoiding each grasp. Kaija held a hand over her mouth and tried not to laugh.

"You're not grounding me," said Maeryn. "We've got stuff to do. Important stuff."

Katherine grabbed Maeryn's arm, pulling her forcefully toward the door.

"Yes, I am grounding you, Maeryn Jean Kacey! I can see that your twisted father has done a great deal of damage here, and you're in serious need of some therapy!"

Maeryn's face went grim as she yanked her arm away from her mom.

"You clearly have a lot more issues to work out than I do." Maeryn gestured at Max and Kaija. "Come on. We're leaving."

Maeryn walked toward the doorway, which Katherine immediately tried to block by spreading her arms.

"You are not going through this door!" demanded Katherine, practically snarling. She pulled the door shut and locked it.

"Max," said Maeryn. "Do the Thunder Glove thing."

"Yay!" Max bellowed.

He swiftly glided over to Maeryn and locked onto her wrist. His nanobots spread out across her hand, covering each finger until it looked like she wore a chrome gauntlet. All of the lights in the house began flickering as the energy in the wiring surged. Static sparked from the wall outlets and sent tendrils of electricity through the air which were quickly absorbed by Maeryn's gauntlet. She swung her sparking fist past Katherine and struck the locked door. The resulting collision sounded like a thunderclap, self-contained right here in her childhood bedroom. The door ripped from its hinges and spun through the air, hitting the chandelier dead on like a bowling ball right in the pocket. A splintery crash sounded from down the steps as the door landed in the entryway.

The chandelier rocked back and forth, only losing a few dangling glass pieces.

"Uh oh," said Max.

Before Maeryn had a chance to ask what was wrong, her whole arm felt like it was ripped from its socket as the Thunder Glove recoiled. As the pent-up energy discharged, what looked like an entire freaking *lightning bolt* crackled from her hand and struck the front of the house.

And that's about when Casa de Johnson exploded.

Splintered wood and chunks of masonry were tossed into the air and rained down onto the neighboring lawns. A cracked pipe began spraying Katherine, although her attention seemed to be mostly on the giant hole where a great deal of her house used to be. A series of crashes and booms rang out as the chandelier fell into the entryway and the remainder of the front wall collapsed into the yard, although nobody heard these sounds. The explosion left nothing but a screeching in the ears in those unlucky enough to be in the center of it. Across the street, a man holding a dripping hose stood on his porch, his mouth hanging limply open in surprise.

Maeryn and Kaija coughed and swatted their hands at the cloud of white dust now filling the room.

"So," Max yelled. "The Thunder Glove thing works, I guess."

He glanced over at Katherine, who was obviously on the verge of regaining her grip on reality. Max calculated that the resulting explosion of anger would surely rival that of the newly detonated Johnson residence.

"Run!" he yelled. "I have a plan. Follow me!"

Max darted through the hole in the wall, and a second later Maeryn and Kaija followed close behind down the steps. They passed Clark on the way out of the now non-existent front door. He put up little protest to their escape due to the fact that he was lying unconscious, half-buried under an overturned sofa.

"I just wanted to get through the door, not blow up the house!" Maeryn cried, nearly tripping over a bowling ball as she ran into the rubble-filled front lawn. "What is wrong with you?"

"I think I may have absorbed some residual Gaian energy," said Max. "But hey, I got you through the door! Honestly, it wasn't very responsible of you to try out Thunder Glove for the first time in a non-controlled environment. That reminds me—"

Max turned around and shouted at the crumbling façade of the Johnson residence. "Sorry for exploding your house, ma'am. I assure you that MotherTech will pay for any and all repairs. Please be aware that this is a gesture of goodwill and not an admission of fault, as I am not an official representative of the company. Oh, and keep your receipts!" Max swiveled back to Maeryn. "Okay, keep running. Trust me!"

Maeryn and Kaija chased Max down the road, struggling to keep up as he effortlessly glided through the air. They passed an astonished group of kids who had been playing basketball in a driveway, but were now gawking at the wreckage.

"I can't run much longer," panted Kaija. "I breathed in a lot of smoke earlier. Where are we going?"

"I don't know," said Maeryn. "Max?"

"Not sure," said Max, making a hasty left at the next stop sign. "Kaija? Any ideas?"

"*What?*" Kaija yelped. "I thought you had a plan!"

"Yes," said Max. "Step 1: run away. Step 78: go to Gaia and rescue Fain. Step 205: break Dorian out of jail. Struggling to work out the details. Right now I'm more concerned with not getting arrested, because that would be *super* inconvenient. Does anyone else hear sirens?"

They ran past a barking dog trying to break through his electric fence. Neighbors peeked out at them from almost every window. Each house in the neighborhood looked exactly the same and it felt like they weren't going anywhere at all. They approached another stop sign at the end of the road and Max came to a dead halt. He buzzed in place, talking rapidly to himself.

"Uh oh," he murmured. "I hacked into a hovercraft, but the nearest landing pad is ten miles away. Police would intercept an autocab. Can't get far enough on foot. So many possible outcomes. So many unknown factors. Too many streams of consciousness. *Smirgdemoonmoon!*"

Max slapped himself and screamed.

"Double uh-oh! Duncan keeps trying to hack into me whenever I spread myself too thin. I have to think hard, but not *too* hard. Brain freeze! AHHH!"

He started whacking himself repeatedly in the forehead with a *Clank! Clank! Clank!*

"Pizza Steve's," said Smith.

Both Kaija and Maeryn screamed and jumped in surprise. Smith was sitting on a nearby bench along the sidewalk, wearing a safari hat and holding a pair of binoculars.

"Pizza Steve's," he said again. "'Sup, Maeryn. 'Sup, little dude. 'Sup, girl I don't know. If you want to park a stolen hovercraft, do it at Pizza Steve's. Huge parking lot behind the building that's almost always empty. Food sucks there. I'm, like, their only customer."

It took a few seconds before Maeryn was able to form a cohesive thought.

"Smith!" she yelled "I thought you went to school!"

"Eh," he said, shrugging. "I skipped. They're not selling any truth today. Felt weirdly necessary to go *bird*watching instead." He made some air parenthesis on the word *bird*. "The pigeons are active today.

Something important is about to happen. So what are you up to? Stealing a hovercraft so you can run off to some other universe?"

"No," said Maeryn. "We're... actually, *yes*."

"Cool, cool," said Smith. "Head left down Emily Street and cut through the yard at the end of the cul-de-sac. You'll be at Pizza Steve's in less than five minutes. I'd join you, but I'm not a big fan of the whole moving-my-body thing. If I see Mom, I'll tell her you went the other way."

"Thanks, Smith!" Maeryn called as they took off down the road. A hovercraft was already descending from the clouds beyond Emily Street, but now they could definitely hear approaching sirens from somewhere behind them.

"Maeryn?" asked Max, dazed. He had been in the lead earlier, but now he drifted through the air lazily. "My brain feels like it's on the verge of exploding. I need to do a soft reboot."

"Quiet!" Maeryn demanded breathlessly. "Can we talk when we're not running?"

They cut between two houses at the end of the cul-de-sac, and the Pizza Steve's parking lot was within sight. Maeryn glanced over her shoulder to see that two police cars were turning onto the road. More alarmingly, Kaija looked on the verge of passing out. Maeryn grabbed her hand and pulled her along.

"I... I think I believe in God now," Max muttered, slowing down to a near-stop. "And I think he's your stepbrother. Could everything else I've believed about the world be wrong?"

"Shut up!" Maeryn yelled. She snatched Max out of the air and shoved him in her pocket, still pulling Kaija along with her other arm.

The small hovercraft landed in a mostly empty parking lot. A very confused old man with a cane stumbled down the landing ramp, looking up at the sky and scratching his chin. Maeryn and Kaija came to a skidding stop in the gravel, ten or so feet away from the man.

"You hacked into a hovercraft with *someone in it?*" Maeryn whispered shrilly.

"Well, yeah," Max said dreamily in her earpiece. "I didn't have many options. Knock him over or something if he tries to stop you. Wouldn't be hard. Just kick his cane."

"Kick his cane? Haven't we committed enough felonies today?"

"I was kidding! And we'll pay for the hovercraft. Being rich and ignoring someone's constitutional rights can be a superpower, just look at Batman. Hurry!"

The man waved and took a few wobbly steps in their direction.

"Excuse me, miss? Could I use your phone? Weirdest thing. I was flying to Buffalo when my hovercraft just dropped out of the sky." He scrunched his face. "Whoa, she doesn't look too good."

Maeryn glanced at Kaija, who did, in fact, not look too good. Her skin was an ashy pale and her eyes wandered around lazily.

"I'm going to puke," she murmured. "Or pass out. Or... or both..."

The next minute felt like a particularly less-than-60-seconds kind of minute. Maeryn hoisted Kaija up into her arms, summoning a strength she didn't know she was capable of, and took off for the hovercraft's landing ramp while trying to ignore the screams coming from her back muscles. By the time the old man realized that his ride was being stolen by two teenage girls, the landing ramp was already folding back into the hovercraft. Max's voice boomed from the exterior speakers as the engines began to hum, only barely scraping together enough sanity to form coherent sentences.

"Dr. Jacoby! This is your lucky day. Your hovercraft has been involuntarily purchased for three times the market listing. Please enjoy a pizza while you wait for the next available autocab, courtesy of

MotherTech. Hope you like the Steve's Special. Mushrooms and pineapple." Max paused. "Really? That can't be right. *Mushrooms and pineapple?* Okay then. Gosh. We're so sorry about all this, sir. Especially the pizza."

The hovercraft lifted off the ground, and pretty soon Pizza Steve's was just a small blip in the expansive suburbs below. Kaija was sprawled out on the floor behind Maeryn, moaning and clutching her stomach. Max had gone totally silent as he rebooted his consciousness. The hovercraft rotated in mid-air and soared noiselessly over the miles and miles of identical homes. Maeryn collapsed into the nearest seat, panting and trying desperately to keep her head from swimming. She glanced up at the flashing display screen, and any attempt to calm down was immediately thwarted.

Destination: The Atlantic Ascent, Federal Exclusion Zone 1. WARNING: Natural Disaster Area.

They were heading toward one of the largest ghost cities in the world. There would be hundreds, if not thousands of abandoned buildings where anything or anyone could be hiding; miles and miles of once thriving city streets now recaptured by nature. Could there really be a portal to Gaia hiding somewhere in this maze of ruination?

Outside the window of the hovercraft and just beyond the horizon, the empty skyscrapers watched them like sentinels.

Chapter Twelve

Just Gone

Monhegan Island, Gaia

Elias was more than alarmed to limp home from battle to find that his new cabin was completely untouched by the recent horrors, a lone survivor from the inferno. He scanned the village in the distance, immediately confirming his suspicions that every other cabin in sight was a smoldering pile of ash.

What did this mean? Maddox picked a measurable distance from the village to construct Elias's house, for obvious reasons, so could it be that the arsonists simply overlooked it? Or was it more insidious than that? Did the Western Blaze know that leaving the cabin untouched would effectively do more damage than a fire ever could? But how could they even identify it as his when he didn't have a single possession in the world?

In the end, the actual truth didn't matter.

Outside the window, a family was pitching a tent against the wind at the edge of Cathedral Woods. The mother held a whining child as the father struggled to pound a stake into the hard ground. Just beyond, people were still pushing wheelbarrows of wreckage to the dump pit, and probably would be long after sunset. You didn't have to look for very long to find the occasional suspicious glance toward the home of the unwanted Nomad.

No, the actual truth didn't matter at all. What mattered was the truth inside of these people: the fiction that their hearts insisted was fact. So what was their truth, then? *He's not even one of us, and he sleeps comfortably tonight?* That would be generous. *Let's wait until that dirt monkey falls asleep and slit his throat.* Yes, that sounded about right.

Elias wanted nothing more than to collapse into bed and let the darkness take him, to slip into a blissful nothing, unaware of the inevitable conflict waiting for him. His body was nowhere near recovered, and the amount of relaying he had done today could have very well killed him. His leg throbbed with a pain he worried might never entirely go away, and each blink threatened to immediately send him off to sleep.

Make yourself gone, Elias. Not a sound. Not a trace. Just gone.

His mother's voice spoke in his head. Her final words to him always proved to be sage advice, regardless of the situation. She was entirely right, and he knew it. And yet, he didn't want to know it. Surely the Monhegans had witnessed him fight Rugaru with the little strength he had left. Teleporting the wreckage of an entire burning house on top of himself, fighting through the pain still screaming across every inch of his skin, carrying the children further away from the smoke than any of these people could even dream of doing… this all had to earn some goodwill from the Monhegans. Right? Valeria's father was surely an outlier, a man too in grief and shock to think reasonably. Surely.

Make yourself gone.

And what of Allie's message? She was never wrong; Elias was supposed to be here. Clara wanted to meet in the morning and put together a task force to find Kaija and Fain, and Elias promised he'd be there. They needed a spacialist of his skill to cover as much ground as possible. What would they think if he just vanished in the night? He resented the fact that fleeing to protect himself would only give validation to their suspicions.

Not a sound. Not a trace. Just gone.

Elias sat on his bed in the mostly featureless, barely lived-in bedroom of the cabin. He examined the vacant room, the space which only hours ago he thought could become a home. It was a canvas. Stay, paint this place with *you*, or leave without a single brushstroke.

Outside, the toddler wailed again, and the sound of his voice sparked something inside of Elias.

Diego.

He counted back the cycles. When was it that he overheard his mom was pregnant with another son? Diego would be about that kid's age now, the brother he was too proud to meet. His family wasn't easy to find, but Elias could have tried. He could have checked the old settlements and campsites, asked around the nearby villages… and just *tried*. His efforts might have led nowhere, but it would have been something.

Elias reached into his pocket and pulled out the only remaining artifact from his childhood: a tiny flickerfly carved from the wood of an Obelisk tree. His sister made it for him when she was seven. The wings were crooked and the smiley face sketched into the creature's head was comically unlike an insect. He woke yesterday to find the little creature hiding safely in his charred pocket, a secret passenger on his journey from one desolation to another. If it hadn't been for the Obelisk tree's complete resistance to flames, this would have burnt up along with him.

With an effortless push, Elias teleported the wooden flickerfly out of his hand and watched as it reappeared on an otherwise empty shelf in the corner. Its goofy face smiled at him.

"There," Elias said to the flickerfly. "Happy now?"

He stood up and made his way resolutely to the door, determined that the little crying boy wasn't going to sleep in the cold when Elias had a perfectly good home for him and his family. Maybe they'd spit in his face, and maybe it was unfair for Elias to be in a position where he even had to question this kind act, but he would still try. It would be something.

Just as Elias reached for the door, a banging knock came from outside, rattling the entire frame.

"NOMAD!"

So here it was. How could he still be surprised anymore?

A crowd of roughly twenty men and women stood outside his door. No, not a crowd. *A mob.* Several of the men had their arms raised, little balls of conjurist fire glowing in their palms like torches. The parents of that poor girl who fell from the headlands were near the front of the group, and they had a crazed look about them. Weary, and yet full of a drunken, anxious energy. Maddox stood at the head of the islanders, and his expression was... what? Apologetic? Angry? No. Conflicted: that was the word. Conflicted. There was that, at least. Maybe he could be reasoned with.

NO!

A part of Elias screamed and fought against this instinct to cower like a berated dog. Was it really his responsibility to quell this man's fears? No. To desolation with him. To desolation with all of them.

"Maddox," said Elias. "Guardian. I'd ask what you're here for, but I think I already know."

Maddox ignored this, as it apparently hadn't been part of his script. "We need you to leave the island, Elias. Right now. Don't come back unless you hear from us."

Normally Elias would have held his tongue, but the anger rising up inside of him couldn't be denied. Forget the fact that this was a familiar scene, something his family and his people have had to deal with since forever. Elias protected his new neighbors today, despite knowing full well that most would not do the same for him. And now they were asking him to leave? What was wrong with these people? For that matter, what was wrong with *people* if this was simply human nature?

"Leave?" asked Elias. "And if I don't?"

Maddox took a step forward, and his breath carried the scent of something strong. Gaia, the tension in this man's body made him look like a balloon about to pop. Almost funny, yet also the furthest thing from humorous.

Maddox closed his eyes. "I think it would be best for all of us, and that includes you, if you don't argue against my decision. If you don't leave, Elias, I... I don't know what I'll do. And I don't want to find out. Leave."

Elias held his proud expression as he regarded the faces in the crowd. He made a point to never look down, to meet each and every one of them in the eye.

"I fought for your children," said Elias. "You're welcome, by the way."

Ciro pushed his way to the front and slipped past Maddox, grabbing Elias's shirt and yanking him close.

"If you say another word about our kids I'll rip your tongue out. My daughter is in a coma, and nobody saw exactly how she fell from the headlands. Could it be that she was pushed? Who knows? But do you know the one thing that there's agreement about? The Nomads used Jasper's cabin as their arrival point. They were streaming out of his door, one after another. Now either everything I know about spacialism is wrong, or someone can only teleport to a place they've seen before. Who showed the Nomads how to get here? Because it sure as desolation wasn't any of us!"

The crowd began stirring forward, and Elias felt an immediate flux of energy in the air as relayers ignited the sparks inside themselves. Things had reached a boiling point, and pretty soon this mob would rip apart what was left of Elias if he didn't flee.

The island trembled unexpectedly, and several people tripped and fell as a scream came from the back of the crowd.

"WHAT ARE YOU DOING?"

Ms. Clara didn't so much as push through the mob as bulldoze through it. She grabbed Ciro and shoved him to the ground without a second glance before turning to Maddox, pointing a trembling finger.

"Gaia help me, Maddox," she snarled. "I didn't believe Delia when she came and told me what you were going to do. If this is what it looks like…"

Maddox heaved a shaky breath. "He has to go, Clara."

A voice shouted from the crowd. "Why should we let the dirt monkey leave?"

Amidst the chaos, it was hard to make out whose voice it was, but it didn't matter. Clara lowered her trembling arm, and something about her deflated. Her eyes filled with tears as they scanned the people who were on the brink of charging forward. Elias doubted that anyone else heard it, but she whispered under her breath.

"Is this what I taught you?"

The thought that many of these men and women were likely Ms. Clara's former students suddenly struck Elias. He looked out and saw an angry mob, but what the old teacher was seeing must have been something both different and worse.

"I'm ashamed," she said. "I'm so ashamed of all of you. This is unforgiveable."

"Ms. Clara," said Maddox, and Elias wished he could laugh at the man's timidity. "There was a lot of chaos today, and the Nomads were moving too fast for us to make out what was happening. We still need to piece the truth together. Until we do, I think it would be best if he left."

"If he's really telling the truth, take him to a mentalist," someone called out. "Read his mind."

"That's not a bad idea," Maddox agreed.

Ms. Clara stomped her foot on the ground so hard that the trees swayed in the woods.

"If you're even suggesting that," she said, "then we've lost something. Our divisions will never be healed. Elias stays, and if anybody here touches him or tries to force him out, it will be over my dead body."

Ms. Clara stepped into the narrow space between Elias and Maddox.

"What will it be?" she asked.

"Jasper made me the new guardian," said Maddox. "It's not up to you."

She poked a finger to his chest and Maddox was pushed back several arms, his feet digging into the dirt for support.

"You are becoming something very ugly," she said. "If throwing a punch makes you feel better about this horrible tragedy, then be my—"

"Stop!" screamed Elias.

Maddox took a step backwards.

"No!" Elias continued, grabbing Ms. Clara's shoulder. "You, Clara. Just stop it!"

"No," she said. "You're hurt and weak. I won't stand by as—"

"I can still speak for myself!"

A silence settled over the group, and Elias limped toward them as he called out.

"Jasper told me that I could make a home here. He is a great man, and none of you deserve him, but he lied. This could never be a place for me, or anyone like me. Not while people like you are here. I'm not Western Blaze, *I'm not*, I promise you. But you know what?" Elias paused for a second, making sure to look at every single person one final time. "They're right about you."

Ms. Clara reached for Elias, but he vanished with an abrupt, unbelievably loud pop.

* * *

Ten minutes later, Maddox was trying and failing to calm the Monhegans, who were currently arguing about who was going to sleep in Elias's cabin. Everyone had their reasons to take shelter: sick children, elderly parents, injured family members who needed a safe place if the Western Blaze returned... there was no order to this madness, just a bunch of people screaming at a bunch of people. Maddox shouted his demands at the top of his lungs, but each and every call was only adding noise to the noise.

"Having trouble quelling the mob that you gathered and brought to this doorstep, Guardian?" asked Clara weakly.

Two grown men collapsed in the doorway of the cabin, wrestling with each other and throwing punches as their families screamed at them to stop.

"I didn't mean for this to——"

"Whatever you have to say," said Ms. Clara, "I don't want to hear it."

A scream rang out as a fireball was flung from somewhere in the darkness, colliding with the top of the cabin and instantly setting the roof ablaze. Ms. Clara didn't even turn to look and see who it was. She wasn't worried that the Western Blaze had returned; anyone could have thrown that fireball. Maddox summoned a flurry of wind which only seemed to make the flames grow larger. He grabbed his hair and shot an alarmed look at Ms. Clara.

"What?" she asked. "Deal with it, Guardian."

"I'm trying!" he cried. "Can you please do something other than stand here and watch this mess?"

"No."

"I'll admit my mistakes, okay? We shouldn't have come here. It was a bad idea. I'm an idiot! What do you want me to say to get you to help me? We need to pull ourselves together and come up with a plan to get our kids back, and it's clearly going to take a little more unity than this!"

Ms. Clara chuckled. "Unity? That idea comes a little too late, I'm afraid. I'll find the kids myself."

Maddox's eyes widened.

"You're going to search the whole continent by yourself? We need to plan this, map out the territories and divide up search teams. Come on, Clarice! Why are you treating me like it's my fault? I didn't burn down the village. THIS IS NOT MY FAULT!"

Ms. Clara eyed the flames growing on the roof of the cabin behind them.

"Gaia damn you, Maddox," she said, and then vanished. Not a sound, not a trace. Just gone.

Chapter Thirteen

Maybe Don't Get Big

New York City, Earth

Maeryn scanned through the dinner options on the hovercraft's food printer while Max scanned the surroundings for things that might kill them horribly. Kaija slept in the hovercraft's bedroom, her loud snores only interrupted by the occasional coughing fit.

"Here comes the border of the Atlantic Ascent," said Max, pulling up a map on the control panel. "It looks like the anomaly is coming from the Freedom Tower ruins, only fifteen miles away. No police crafts in the area from what I can tell, so that's good. Whoa!"

The hovercraft made an abrupt, sharp turn to the left, almost knocking Maeryn to the floor.

"Careful!" she shouted, grabbing a chair for support.

"That wasn't me. The navigation system is rerouting us, but it won't tell me why. A part of the map is just missing, too. A whole five-mile circle is just invisible to the GPS." The screen beeped and Max's hands blurred as he typed away on the panel. "I think I just figured out why Duncan's drones never returned. Something's generating an energy field that scrambles the programming of anything that passes through. This is highly advanced technology. I've never seen anything like it. Gosh, if the autopilot hadn't interfered we would have dropped right out of the sky. That, or my brain would have exploded."

"Oh no…" Maeryn muttered, leaning in toward the screen on the food printer. "No, no, no!"

"Aw, thanks Sis. I love my brain too."

Maeryn poked a few more buttons on the food printer and yelled again, slamming her hand against the wall of the hovercraft.

"Not that! This thing doesn't have fresh cilantro. I mean, I could probably work around that, but no limes either? Looks like sweet potato tacos are out of the question. It wants to use *dried* cilantro as a substitute? Seriously? That's worse than nothing. Who taught this thing gastronomy? Cancel order. CANCEL ORDER!"

The food printer whirred to life and spit out some mushy sweet potatoes on a stale tortilla. Maeryn buried her face in her hands.

"Um," said Max. "Maeryn? You okay?"

"No! Now I feel like I have to eat this."

"I mean, is there anything wrong that's not taco related?"

"I'm fine, Max."

Max floated over and landed on her shoulder. "Uh-oh. *I'm fine* is human speak for *the opposite of what I just said is true*. You need to vent, Maeryn. When you're overly stressed you tend to get super quiet and hyper focused on little things that don't matter. Remember when we found out Rosalie was missing and you baked eight loaves of bread in the middle of the night? Or when our fish died when we were kids and you played forty straight hours of virtual Candy Land?"

Maeryn picked off a stale piece of her tortilla and tossed it at the trashcan. "I really don't see how any of this is relevant."

"We just kind of need you with us right now. Half of my concentration is being spent on keeping Duncan out of my head, and your fake girlfriend back there sounds like she's got the black lung. I'm just saying, now would not be an ideal time to go into a fugue state over cilantro."

Maeryn gritted her teeth. "The problem is not cilantro, the problem is the *lack of cilantro*. And I'm more than happy to help you and Kaija on our adventure, but I haven't eaten anything all day, and this flavorless mess here is almost worse than nothing." Her eyes widened. "Sweet and spicy. It needs chili-infused agave nectar."

Maeryn jumped up and ran back to the food printer.

"So now I'm the sane one?" Max asked himself.

"Do sane people talk to themselves?" he replied.

"Good point."

Kaija limped into the room, her clothes dirty and her dark hair matted and wild.

"What's happening?" she yawned. "The ship stopped so suddenly that it knocked me out of bed." Kaija glanced out of the window and her eyes widened. "What's wrong with this place?"

The city ahead of them was the opposite of the city behind them. Skyscrapers were entirely dark, and not a single car could be seen in the streets. Several blocks were covered in swampland, and a few buildings had been completely overtaken by moss and vines.

"It's the Atlantic Ascent," said Max. "About a century ago the ocean levels rose to the point where the city kept flooding. People gradually started to move inland, until a whole chunk of New York was just completely abandoned. The government says it's too expensive to demolish. It's a place of lawlessness, a relic of one of humanity's greatest failures that will probably be standing long after biological life has wiped itself out. A beautiful thought, really, that mankind's creations will survive as a monument to their futile grasping at the eternal while succumbing to the inevitable darkness." Max shook his head. "Anyway, that's where we're going. It'll be fun. At least, if I can get us through this energy field. You don't think you could teleport again, do you?"

Kaija shook her head. "No. I can't feel Gaia at all."

"Okay, then. I apologize for what you're both about to witness."

Max held up a hand and his index finger separated from his body, drifting into the air while slowly turning into a copy of himself no bigger than a dime.

"I'm alive!" squeaked Max2. "What am I? Who am I? Who are you? Why am I alive? Why is anyone alive?"

"Welcome to the world," said Max. "I'm you, and you're me. I've got a job for you, or, um… me."

"A job?"

"Yeah. See outside that window? There's an energy field that fries anything with A.I. that gets too close. I need you to exit the hovercraft through our exhaust valve and fly right into the danger zone. A consciousness matrix as complex as ours will probably overwhelm whatever's generating the energy field. I'll only need a few seconds to get the hovercraft through safely. But, see, the thing is, you'll probably explode."

Max1 and Max2 stared at each other for a few seconds.

"And this is my purpose for existing?" asked Max2. "The meaning of my life?"

"I, um… yeah, I suppose so, if you put it that way. Sorry to disappoint you."

Max2 shrugged. "I wish nothing more than to fulfill my purpose, even if it means that the universe is a cruel joke that we're birthed into by an unloving creator. I'll do it for you, my father."

"Please don't call me that."

"Bye, Papa. I love you."

Max2 zoomed up into a nearby air vent, and a few seconds later a loud pop rang from outside. The navigation system beeped and immediately began rerouting itself through the no-fly zone.

"Great!" said Max. "I was right, we can get through now."

Maeryn's taco slowly slid off her plate, but she didn't seem to notice. "Did you just give birth?"

"And then sacrifice your son?" asked Kaija.

Max poked a button on the control panel and yawned. "Let's try not to think about it too much."

* * *

The ocean had entirely claimed part of the city closest to the harbor, the streets completely submerged and teeming with aquatic life. Freedom Tower jutted out of the ocean, and its reflection on the water made it look like it descended endlessly below the surface.

"I'm doing a thermal scan of the building," said Max, "there's no sign of biological life, at least on this side of the portal. Once we get through... who knows? Anything could be waiting."

"We'll worry about that later," said Kaija. "We just need to get to Gaia so I can start relaying again."

Maeryn pointed at something. "We have plenty to worry about now."

The flat screen in the navigation booth zoomed in toward Freedom Tower, showing a massive figure silhouetted against the sun. It was ten feet high with glowing red eyes and plasma rifles built into its arms. A blue orb glowed in its chest like a robotic heart.

"That's my little brother," said Max. "Man, I hate that jerk."

"What?" Maeryn exclaimed "Are you saying that's a Mothertech Guardian Angel? Why would the Western Blaze have a Guardian Angel?"

"Dorian said that the weapons headquarters had been cleaned out weeks ago," said Max. "He thought the government did it, but it looks like he was wrong. The Western Blaze has robots now, so that's, you know, not great."

Max began jumping up and down on the console, throwing tiny punches.

"10,000 years of scientific advancement has led to this moment," he said. "Brother against brother, machine against machine."

"We should really talk strategy—" Maeryn began, but Max had already burst apart into fragments and flown into the ventilation system. "—and he's gone."

Outside the hovercraft, Max's fragments collided back together and he rocketed toward Freedom Tower. The Guardian Angel sprang to life, its eyes glowing red as they targeted Max. Maeryn adjusted the hovercraft's display screen and watched as the camera struggled to follow the action.

"What's that symbol on its chest, just above the energy orb?" asked Maeryn, squinting at the screen as the machine darted back and forth. "Is that what I think it is?"

"It's a flickerfly," said Kaija. "The symbol for spacialism."

Max held out his arm, which grew and twisted into the shape of a sword more than twice the length of his body. Electricity crackled in the air as he burst forward and swung the weapon at the Guardian Angel. Just as Max was about to make contact, the blue orb on its chest glowed and the entire robot disappeared soundlessly.

"Huh," said Max, his voice coming out of the hovercraft's speakers. "Did anyone see where it—"

The Angel reappeared behind Max, swinging its huge arm so fast that it was no more than a blur. His fist struck Max on top of his head, rippling the air with an explosive force that sent him crashing down into the ocean below. Maeryn jammed her finger onto the hovercraft's communicator button and screamed.

"Max! It's a spacialist. Target the orb on its chest!"

Max burst out of the ocean, sending a geyser of water into the sky as he charged at the Angel. His chrome body divided into two smaller parts, and both of them began attacking the machine from opposite sides with bursts of electricity. The battle became too fast for Maeryn and Kaija's eyes to follow; the Guardian Angel appeared to be several places at once.

"It's too fast," yelled Max.

"Do the MaxMax thing," Maeryn suggested.

The two Maxes divided into four smaller parts, each buzzing off in different directions. The Angel continued popping in and out of existence, but it was now having a harder time avoiding each of the Maxes.

"I still can't land a single blow! Our programming is so similar that it's predicting my movements. Wish me luck, because things are about to get weird."

Max continued to fight the robot, dividing every few seconds. There were eight of him, and then sixteen, and then thirty-two. Pretty soon they couldn't see him at all, and it looked like the Guardian Angel was avoiding a gray cloud which followed it through the air. Tiny beams of energy shot at the machine from every direction, but an energy field appeared around the robot and sent the blasts back toward Max.

"How many of him are there?" asked Kaija.

"He's dividing exponentially," said Maeryn. "If the rate of division stays constant, there are probably around thirty-two thousand, seven hundred and sixty-eight of him and counting."

Max's tiny voice spoke from the control panel. "Uh... Maeryn, we have a problem."

"What's wrong?"

169

"It's kind of embarrassing."

"WHAT?"

"Okay, okay! I spread my consciousness too thin, and I'm stuck in a loop. I can't stop dividing."

Maeryn gasped and began pacing back and forth.

"What does that mean?" asked Kaija.

"This is bad," said Maeryn. "In a few minutes he'll become millions of single celled versions of himself without the energy to regroup."

"THIS IS WEIRD!" yelled Max. "It looks like I'm attacking a blur the size of a galaxy. I can see bacteria looking at me! I need to—"

Max's voice went silent on the radio, and the gray cloud around the Angel faded into nothing.

"Max?" asked Maeryn. "MAX?"

The Guardian Angel vanished and blinked back into existence directly in front of the hovercraft's window. It held up its arm, pointing the plasma rifle directly at the two girls. The blue light inside of its chest began to glow, but the robot suddenly froze in place and cocked its head. Maeryn could have sworn that its red eyes were looking directly at her.

"Conflicting directives," said the Angel, its voice hollow and mechanical. **"Recalibrating."**

A second later, the robot's chest exploded.

A fully-formed Max flew out, holding the robot's energy source in his hand and laughing maniacally. The Guardian Angel's eyes went blank as its body fell lifeless into the water below. Max hurled the blue orb up and then kicked it into the ocean like a football.

"Did you see me?" he asked. "I ripped a guy's heart out! Check that one off my bucket list!"

"Guys..." said Kaija, running over to the window. "What's happening?"

Maeryn looked down to see the waters of the harbor bubbling and churning. A gleaming metal structure broke the surface; it looked like a skyscraper ascending from the ocean and floating into the sky. Two large red lights lit up on the thing's front and shone in their direction.

"What is that?" asked Maeryn.

The object levitated higher and higher until the top disappeared into the clouds. Maeryn realized why she couldn't see it clearly: it was like an ant trying to make out what a human looked like. The structure in front of them was a Guardian Angel bot, this one larger than many of the skyscrapers. It raised one of its massive arms, sending dozens of rockets flying out from each fingertip.

"Um," said Max. "BRB."

He divided rapidly and soared at each of the rockets. Explosions filled the world with fire around the hovercraft, which jerked back and forth with a horrible ripping sound. One rocket made it inches away from the windshield before Max knocked it in the other direction.

"Can't you just, *get big* or something?" yelled Kaija. "At least bigger than that guy?"

"Congratulations, that's maybe the worst idea a human has ever had. If I let my nanobots multiply too far and I lose control again, they'll theoretically never stop dividing. Exponential growth, Kaija: get it? When I run out of nanobots, I'll start consuming and converting the matter around me to create more, and eventually I'll *be* the universe."

"Okay, maybe don't get big," agreed Kaija.

At least fifty more rockets soared at the hovercraft, spreading out and approaching from every angle. Max divided rapidly and jumped in the way of as many as he could, but one of them snuck past his barricade. An explosion blasted away the back half of the hovercraft. Wind howled through the gaping hole and the entire thing started to spin through the air.

Maeryn was slammed against the metal walls, but she felt Kaija's hand grab her own. The hatch closest to them swung open, sending in billows of smoke. Kaija and Maeryn looked at each other and nodded, suddenly perfectly in sync with each other. They put their feet on the wall and pushed as hard as they could at the exact same time, propelling them out of the burning hovercraft and into the open air. Everything spun, becoming a blur of fire, water, and metal.

Maeryn and Kaija struck the water, but the impact felt more like slamming onto concrete. A cold blackness consumed their minds and bodies as they sank into the ocean.

Chapter Fourteen

Mostly Marshmallows

The Atlantic Ascent, Earth

The first sensation to come back was pain: an incessant throbbing on the inside of Maeryn's head, like her brain was trying to smash its way out with a baseball bat. She opened her mouth to breathe, but immediately threw up what felt like a gallon of saltwater. Her lungs burned, her eyes burned, her stomach burned; everything inside and outside of her felt like it was on fire and freezing at the same time. Maeryn rolled over and pressed her hands to the cold, slimy floor, for the first time asking herself why she was on solid ground and not a corpse at the bottom of the ocean.

As things came into a tentative focus, Maeryn saw Kaija sitting next to her in the corner of what appeared to be an ancient office space. A fire in a garbage pail lit only the immediate area. Rotting cubicles littered the surroundings, old computers lay decaying on the floor, and broken windows lined the walls, rattling from the ocean waves churning in the darkness outside.

Kaija had her arms wrapped around her knees and was shivering uncontrollably, despite the heat from the fire.

"Kaija…" coughed Maeryn. "Where are we?"

Kaija's lips were blue, and her eyes seemed to be having trouble focusing on any one thing.

"I've got ash and saltwater in my lungs," she wheezed. "My ears are still ringing. Was the fire before we jumped out of the hovercraft, or after the house exploded? Do you have a concussion? I think I have a concussion. Do you have a concussion?"

A gray puddle of sludge on the floor started moving, pulling together and laboriously shaping itself into Max.

"Do you know how much I love you two girls?" he asked, shaking the water off his body like a dog. "I done got myself exploded forty times in a row, *on purpose*, just to keep your fragile little meat suits safe." He slapped his hands together. "Okay, time to try again. Where's the hovercraft?"

"I think it sank into the ocean after we jumped out," said Kaija slowly. "Or did I dream that? My head's not feeling quite… um, I think I have a concussion? Do you have a concussion?"

"It crashed?" exclaimed Max. "Impossible. How come you two are like, barely drowned?"

Maeryn pulled a hunk of seaweed out of her hair. "I figured you saved us."

"I don't think so. I had to reinstall my brain after dying forty simultaneous, fiery deaths. I didn't exist for about an hour. It was super annoying."

Wet footsteps echoed in the dingy room, and the three of them turned to see a figure coming out of the darkness. The firelight illuminated his features in rapid flickers. He had long gray hair, a skeletal face, and a box of generic cupcakes tucked under his arm.

"I saved you," said the man. "Again. We're even now, so leave me alone."

He turned to walk away, but Max called after him.

"Kai! What are you doing here?"

Kai stopped and looked back over his shoulder. "I could ask the same of you, little guy. What are *you* doing here?"

Max and Kai engaged each other in a staring contest, which was impressive considering that Max had no eyes.

"I asked first," Max said.

"I don't care. Why are you following me?"

"We're not. Why are you following us?"

"I'm not."

"Then why are you here?"

"It's a secret."

Everyone looked at everyone else, completely tongue-tied.

"Okay," said Kai finally. "Bye."

The old man turned and began walking off down the hallway. Max floated close to Maeryn's ear.

"Duncan told me to kill that guy," he whispered, "but I'm not really in the mood right now. We need to run, maybe. Or not. *I don't know.* Dobbs, I hate not knowing things!"

"Maybe we *should* trust him specifically because Duncan doesn't want us to," said Maeryn.

"Okay," said Kaija. "I'm confused. Or, more confused than I was already. Who is he?"

"Kai," said Maeryn.

"Oh, I like that name. Gosh my head hurts."

"Sure. Remember that old homeless guy I told you about that rescued me from the MotherTech agents last year? That's him!"

"Okay… and what is he doing in the middle of an underwater city? And why wouldn't you trust him? Seems like the only choice after he saved our lives."

"My grandpa told me not to."

"I thought your grandpa was dead."

"Ugh. It would really be nice if things slowed down a bit so we could catch up. Maybe you're right, Kaija."

"Right about what?" Kaija asked, rubbing her eyes. "Hey, who's that guy?"

Maeryn stood up and shouted down the hallway. "Does the word Gaia mean anything to you?"

The old man sprinted back into the light with surprising speed, wearing an expression of utmost attention.

"Maybe," Kai said. "That depends. Does it mean anything to *you?*"

"Um. It's a secret."

"Ahhh!" yelled Max. "This is the dumbest reunion ever. Listen, man, somebody told us not to trust you, and we're just trying to figure out if he was right."

Kai scratched his chin. "You can't trust *me?* Interesting, because I know for a fact that me just being around you is practically a death sentence. Back when you were a turtle, I barely made it off Monhegan alive after your little puppet master sent his Angel to incinerate me."

Kaija raised an eyebrow. "Monhegan?"

"Wait—" said Maeryn.

"Can we go back to the part where I was a turtle?" asked Max. "Did I forget to read a chapter of my own life or something?"

Kai narrowed his eyes and took a step forward. "You really don't remember, do you? It doesn't matter. I know that you were sent here to kill me. Whether or not you plan on trying to is inconsequential. I can never, *will never*, trust a member of the Kacey family."

He turned around to leave again, but Maeryn called after him.

"Why?"

"Why?" asked Kai, spinning back around and raising his voice. "Do I have to spell it out any clearer than this?" He pulled down the front of his tattered shirt, revealing a massive scar over his heart that looked like a puncture wound. Kai turned around, showing them a similar scar just under his shoulder blade.

"WHAT!?" yelled Max, flying around in circles excitedly. "Sweet spaghetti monster, I'm not emotionally prepared for this right now."

Alertness came into Kaija's eyes for the first time as she stood up and approached Kai.

"You're Edgard Zeig, aren't you?" she asked. "You look like the paintings."

"Edgard Zeig is a story," said Kai. "A story that I tried to make real, but ultimately nothing more than that."

"No, it's you," said Kaija. "I know it. And you know who I am, don't you?'

"I have no idea what you're talking about, girl."

"Look at me, Kai."

Kai's eyes locked onto Kaija, as if really seeing her for the first time. He reached forward and put his trembling hands on either side of her face, eyes filling with tears as he studied her closely. They stood like that for a long time, both of them too deep into the enormity of this moment to say a single word.

"Are you…" Kai whispered. "Could you really be… *no*. I've been alone for too long to let myself hope."

Kaija wiped her eyes and gave a little nod. "Yes. It's me. I'm your granddaughter. I'm Kaija Monhegan, Jasper's daughter."

Kai immediately picked Kaija up and pulled her to his chest, sobbing into her shoulder.

"He's alive," he wept. "I have a family. I never thought this would happen. Never, never. If I only would have known you would be here, I don't know, I…" He picked up his box of cupcakes and shook it a few times. "…Darn it, I would have brought more cupcakes."

* * *

"Mr. Wizard King?" asked Max, raising up a little hand. "I hate to interrupt possibly the most beautiful thing I've ever seen, but we need to talk about the refrigerator in the room."

Maeryn closed her eyes and sighed. The previous hour had been an emotional reunion, Kai and his granddaughter sharing cupcakes around a fire as she tried to fill him in on the half-century he'd been away from home. Max and Maeryn listened at first with fascination, but a sinking dread crept in as they mulled over the implications. An unsettling truth had to be addressed sooner or later.

"Duncan tried to kill you," said Max. "Twice, apparently, and he's still trying. I can feel him inside me now, attempting to claw his way out and take control, but it's not working. I've gotten too good at keeping him out."

"I understand now, Kai," said Maeryn. "You've got every reason not to trust us, to hate us."

Kai blinked in surprise and made his way over to Maeryn, taking her by both hands and looking at her right in the eyes.

"How could I ever hate the person who brought me back to my family?" he asked. "I'm with you now, Maeryn. I'm with all three of you, completely." He paused. "But, yes, this is a bit awkward. How well did you know your grandfather?"

"Not as well as I thought," admitted Maeryn. "So it's all true, then?"

"Yes. He tried to kill me, and came closer than anyone ever has. He led a Nomadic army into the Capital and slaughtered most of my seven knights." He gave a look to Kaija. "If Clarice hadn't already fled to

Monhegan Island, you would have never existed. I woke in the middle of the attack to discover that my sword had gone missing. Duncan entered my bedroom before I knew what was happening, and he had it. He stabbed me and opened a portal here, to the only place I could die. To this day I can't figure out how Duncan stole it. No one knew where I kept the sword except for myself and the High Seven."

He gave a knowing look to Maeryn, who simply shrugged.

"I honestly don't know," she said. "Duncan never clarified that part in his journal."

"Thomas," Kaija cut in. "The High Guardian: Thomas the Mentalist. That awful man took it, he had to. It makes so much sense now. Thomas took the sword and gave it to Duncan, knowing that he would be next in line to become the High Guardian."

Kai groaned and rubbed his forehead. "Thomas never struck me as a man of great ambition. He was scared most of the time, preferred to work from the shadows. But I could be wrong. He was the only person who could hide his thoughts from me."

Kaija looked at his scar again and grimaced; the sword must have gone straight through his chest and out the other side.

"How did you possibly survive?" she asked.

"There's something Duncan didn't account for," said Kai. "Gaian energy is nowhere to be found here on Earth, but a little bit can linger inside of you. He impaled me, brought me to this place, and threw my body in the ocean. I played dead, and as soon as he was out of sight I used what little power I had left to seal the wound. It was barely enough to bring me back from the dead. I woke up in a hospital days later in this world I knew nothing about."

Kai unwrapped the last cupcake and scarfed it down. "On Gaia, I could do anything. There were no limits to what I could accomplish with my relaying, but Duncan and I found our roles reversed here. I was the

179

ultimate immigrant: no birth certificate or global ID number, running from one country to another and eating whatever scraps of food I could find, but Duncan… I watched from afar as he thrived. I don't understand it, how he could step so easily from one world to another."

"He was part spiritualist," said Maeryn. "In his journal, he talked about growing up with dreams and visions of a place where intelligent machines could be brought to life. I think he'd been preparing to come to Earth for a long time."

"A spiritualist?" asked Kai, laughing. "Well. It's not every day you find out something new about someone you've been running from for forty years." He glanced over at Kaija and smiled again. "I just can't believe it. I'm a grandfather. We have to do something! Like, I don't know… get ice cream! Where's my boat?"

Kai stood up and started to pace around in circles.

"Wait a minute…" he said. "What am I saying? We can get ice cream on the other side! I've been feeling little traces of Gaian energy in the air, and I've been tracking the signal. It's very close now. I wonder if that place in Booth Bay is still around. What was it called? The Orange Café?"

Kaija flinched, as if being reminded of Gaia had slapped her memory back into place. This night was so wonderful that it somehow made her forget about the last few horrible days.

"I don't know what we'll find when we get there," said Kaija. "The Western Blaze opened the portal. They burned down Monhegan village, and I barely made it out of there alive. We think they stole MotherTech's robots, a whole army of them."

"I'd like to bring up an important point here," said Max. "Rugaru, the Western Blaze, the robotic army, our grandpa's ghost… have we considered the possibility that none of these are an obstacle anymore?"

"What?" asked Kaija. "Why?"

A Path of Branches

"Isn't it obvious?" asked Max.

Kaija looked from him to Maeryn, and then all three of them turned to stare at Kai. The surprise of discovering Edgard Zeig alive and well on Earth had completely overshadowed the fact that they would now be arriving on Gaia with the greatest relayer in history.

Kai's eyebrows rose in realization. "Wait. No, no no no. You want me to go charging into combat the moment I get home? Do you even realize what you're asking here? I've lived most of my life here on Earth, and I know almost nothing about modern Gaian politics. Besides, it's been decades since I was able to relay with a substantial amount of energy. If I'm not careful, I could accidentally split the very world in half."

Kaija gave him a pleading look. "Kai, please. We need your help. The Western Blaze kidnapped Fain. He's, um…" Kaija blushed. "Wow, why is this so embarrassing? Fain's my boyfriend. He'll die if we don't find him, if… if he's not dead already."

Kaija lowered her face into her hands, and Kai nodded slowly.

"Okay," he said. "We go home, and we do what we can to mend things, but we do it as quietly as possible. I want to meet my son, I… I want to see Clarice again. Is she happy? I've never wanted anything more than her happiness. Does she have a new partner?"

Kaija burst into a fit of giggles.

"No!" she said. "Oh my Gaia, this is so weird."

Kai's eyes darted to the darkness outside of the cracked windows. "Ultimately, none of this matters until we get past that monstrosity out there. I was hoping to sneak past it, but thanks to Turtle Max over there I'm pretty sure it's on high alert. It would be foolish to approach it in the dark. As much as it pains me to say it, we need to get some rest tonight. Eat, sleep as much as we can, and then I'll take care of it in the morning."

"I'm still totally not getting the turtle references," said Max. "Also, the only way I can possibly fathom getting past that giant Guardian Angel is if I eat him, but I might accidentally become the universe in the process."

"I'm not worried about that hunk of metal," Kai said, pulling a bag of marshmallows out of his backpack and tossing it aside. "Thanks to you, we've got a secret weapon. Don't worry, I've got more in here than marshmallows."

He pulled out a second bag of marshmallows.

"Okay, it's mostly marshmallows. Looks like there will be enough s'mores for all of us tonight. It's in here somewhere."

Kai proceeded to remove a Bowie knife, what looked like a homemade bomb, and several sleeves of graham crackers from his backpack before finding what he was looking for. The entire room filled with blue light when Kai removed a small orb.

"Oh!" Max exclaimed, his mind bursting with possibilities. "That certainly changes things."

Chapter Fifteen

Prune the Branches

Many Cycles Ago
Monhegan Island, Gaia

All was desolation.

Kai returned to Monhegan Island on his eighteenth cycle day with the desperate hope that someone else had survived and rebuilt the village, but all he found was ash. He walked past the patch of blackened soil which had once been his home, and it seemed to stare at him like a stranger. There was no evidence of a childhood spent in this place.

He wished that he could cry again, but that well had long dried up. Life on the mainland during the climactic, desperate battles of the Global War had split Kai wide open and drained all of the emotions out of him. Four cycles ago he was living a happy life in this place, but the Europan warship came on his fourteenth cycle day and closed that chapter for good.

Reaching the edge of the ruins, Kai saw that the stone schoolhouse remained in better shape than the wooden cabins. Most of the roof had collapsed in, but the walls were still erect. Kai thought of Mr. Calderon and tried to remember the final conversation he had with his teacher. The past was blurry, as there's not much time to reflect on your childhood when you are in survival mode, but a few images rose to the surface.

Mr. Calderon assured Kai that his relaying abilities would come in due time, but that turned out to be another one of the old man's lies. Kai remained closed off to the power of Gaia to this very day, and war was no place for a non-relayer. He spent most of his time on the mainland hiding in the dark of the Acadian caves. Sometimes conflict had been unavoidable, and he had to learn how to fight without Gaia's assistance. The hope that any other Monhegans had survived the genocide kept Kai going, but now…

He entered the schoolhouse, finding that the bookshelves had been ravaged and torn pages littered the floor of the library. After scouring through the wreckage for a few minutes, he picked up one of the few books that remained whole: *Music of the Forest.* Of course. Kai threw the book back into the wreckage, not quite ready to revisit the memory of that final night here. Just as he turned to leave, sunlight glinted from something under a bookshelf. A sword's hilt was sticking out from under the rotting wood.

Kai had nearly forgotten about the spiritualist legends of Edgard Zeig that he had so enjoyed as a young boy. In the midst of war, fantasies about a hero who united the world's guardianships and led an era of unprecedented peace seemed like just that: a fantasy.

He reached down and grabbed the hilt, pulling the weapon out from under the fallen bookshelf, and something stirred within his soul. It was not a spark that he felt, but a supernova: a universe being birthed inside of him. The air seemed to glow, and Kai could feel Gaia encompassing the cosmos, stretching all the way from the Arctic Seas to the end of the universe. It existed backwards and forwards in time as the all-consuming creator and destroyer of worlds. He heard his teacher's voice, still echoing from the branches four cycles after his own death. Kai closed his eyes, and the words were so clear that the old teacher could have been standing right behind him.

Edgard Zeig was said to be powerless for most of his life, and only upon returning home did he discover his true powers.

Kai opened his eyes and let out a small burst of the energy within him. The trees just beyond the schoolhouse turned to dust and were carried off in the wind. It took no effort to make this happen: it was nothing at all to bend the world around him.

The Desolate Truth was revealed to Edgard, and he used that knowledge to unite the worlds.

He looked toward the sky and squinted at the blazing sun. The great star Sol was the nurturer of all life on Earth, and yet its power seemed inconsequential to what lived inside of Kai now. If he wanted to, he could extinguish the star. He could bring it here and pull the flames inside of him.

What looks like the future to a spiritualist's sight might actually be the past.

Kai gripped the sword firmly in his hands, and the ocean around the island began to rise. Water filled the sky, giving the impression that the world was turning upside down. The dark shape of a sea mammoth passed across the watery heavens like a dark cloud in this new topography.

The general goal and greatest challenge of spiritualism is to lead Gaia away from Desolation.

The adults on Monhegan had chosen to kneel and die rather than defend their land. Mr. Calderon often talked about good and evil in his ethics lessons, saying that those who were good must resist lowering themselves to the ways of those who make war. And yet, what did they have to show for their inept display of morality? A village of ash, and nothing else.

"I know the truth…" whispered Kai. "Those who fight will always consume those who do not. The only way to avoid Desolation is to remove those who steer us in its direction. I am Edgard Zeig, and that is the Desolate Truth."

Kai lowered his sword and the ocean fell from the sky. The ground shook as millions of gallons descended upon the island, cleansing the ash from the salted earth like judgement from on high. The water curved around Kai, leaving him dry in a silvery dome while the landscape churned around him. When the last of the ocean returned to the ground, Kai looked up to see that the heavens were no longer an aquatic blue.

From one end of the world to the other, the sky was on fire.

Kai lifted effortlessly off the ground, ascending toward the burning clouds, gripping the sword tighter as he scanned the skyline of the western continent. He could see the war still waging there: the meaningless fight that had cost everything to countless people and gained nothing to no one. It would end today before the sun went down: he would see to that.

If time's branches grew toward Desolation, Edgard would be there to prune them from the tree.

Chapter Sixteen

Blur, Pop, Blur

The Atlantic Ascent, Earth

Maeryn woke before the others the next morning and watched the sun rise from their hiding place in the abandoned office. Reflections of buildings glinted off the water, and a pigeon cooed from its nest on top of a nearby lamppost. Max floated in from around the corner and landed on the windowsill.

"Thank goodness you're up," he said. "There's no wi-fi, and watching people sleep gets boring after a few hours. Speaking of sleep, shouldn't you still be, like, doing it?"

"I know," said Maeryn. "I just can't stop thinking. What if, well, what if *this is it.*"

"It?"

"The spiritualists said that our decision would lead Gaia toward or away from Desolation. Edgard Zeig is the most powerful relayer of all time, and we're bringing him home. That has to be what they're talking about, right? It's going to change the world forever."

"Are you having doubts?"

Maeryn smiled.

"No. I didn't think it would be this easy, this obvious. It feels like everything has led to this moment. I think about how Duncan and Rosalie would tell me not to do this, and it just makes me more certain with every passing second that I should. Edgard Zeig has to go back to Gaia, and I'm going to do everything I can to get him there. Max, this is going to right every wrong in our family's past."

"Scary. Isn't it?"

"What?"

"Being so sure about something."

Maeryn thought about this for a second. Max had a strange way of thinking, but she understood him perfectly.

"Yes," she said. "It is."

* * *

Mist rose off the ocean as they approached Freedom Tower in Kai's little motorboat. He held the containment orb in his hand, watching the swirling blue colors inside as if hypnotized.

"I fished this thing out of the ocean after I saw you toss it," he said to Max. "There's not much energy left inside, but once I bust it open I'll have all I need to finish the job."

The boat turned the corner around a sunken building, revealing the gleaming silhouette of Freedom Tower. Just beyond that, the giant head of a Guardian Angel was already ascending from the bubbling waters of the harbor. Its crimson eyes locked onto them, glowing like two suns, daring the boat to come closer. A low humming resounded from under the water, vibrating everything in sight as the machine powered up.

"Are we sure about this?" asked Max, grabbing the edge of the boat as it rocked back and forth. "It's pretty easy to feel confident when you're not staring that leviathan in the face."

"What would you suggest instead?" asked Kai. "We talk to it?"

Max had to shout over the hum as it reached a crescendo. "Heck, maybe. Big guy like that probably gets bullied at school. Misunderstood, just needs a friend, you know?"

"Sure, little turtle," Kai laughed. "I'll talk to it." He walked to the front of the boat, pointing a threatening finger at the robot, who was now almost entirely out of the water. "Hey, rocketman! This is for hurting my granddaughter!"

Kai slammed the glass end of the orb down onto the edge of the boat with all his might. It rang like a bell and vibrated in his hands, but not a single crack or scratch showed on the surface. He held it up and squinted, scratching his head.

"Hmmm. That was supposed to break."

The Guardian Angel's eyes pointed toward the boat and began to fill with fiery energy. The humming became so loud that windows shattered on the surrounding buildings, raining glass from the sky. Kai slammed the orb onto the mast several times in rapid succession, but it didn't even crack.

"It should be breaking," said Kai, slamming it again. "Why isn't it breaking? Is this internalist glass or something?"

"Hurry up!" screamed Kaija. "In about two seconds, that thing is going to burn us to a cri... AHHH!"

Beams of light shot toward the boat, but at the last second Max spun around and conjured an energy field which refracted the beams into an adjacent building. An entire floor of the skyscraper exploded and smoke billowed out of the windows.

"I just set a Starbucks on fire!" said Max. "It drained all of my energy to reflect that! I can't block another blast until I recharge. What an inconvenient time to need some coffee."

Kai fidgeted with the orb, almost dropping it into the ocean several times as his hands trembled.

"Screws!" he yelled.

"Yeah we're screwed!" Maeryn agreed.

"No! Screws are holding the glass in place. Does anybody have a screwdriver?"

"Max!" said Kaija, grasping at him. "Turn into a screwdriver!"

"That is seriously offensive," said Max. "Am I just a tool to you? And I already told you, my nanobots can't reconfigure until I've recharged."

"Check my backpack!" Kai screamed, still repeatedly banging the orb against the now-crooked mast. "There should be a multi-tool pocket knife in there somewhere."

Maeryn dumped the contents of the overstuffed backpack onto the deck and frantically rooted through them.

"Melted chocolate, matches, a blanket," she said. "I don't see a pocket knife. Oh, here's another bag of marshmallows."

The Angel fired another burst of energy with a massive *boom*. Kai closed his eyes, wound up his arm like he was going to throw a winning pitch, and tossed the containment orb far out over the ocean. It collided with the beam of energy and exploded, sending a shimmering blue mist into the air. Kai held out his hand and the mist swirled around him, absorbing into his body. His muscles began to tense, growing to nearly twice their size, and everyone immediately became aware of a powerful presence in the air.

"YES!" bellowed Kai, jumping out of the boat and back flipping into the ocean like an Olympic diver.

Saltwater spouted into the air as if an atomic bomb had been detonated somewhere below the depths. Kai's body shot upward, water surrounding him on all sides. The ocean began to morph and take an unnatural shape, turning into a watery creature the size of a skyscraper.

Kai's silhouette floated at the heart of the giant torrent, and when he took a step forward, the water moved with him.

The Guardian Angel fired several rockets at Kai, but they simply got caught in the water and were immediately extinguished. The ocean churned, moving the rockets into the hand of the liquid man. Kai swung his arm forward, and the giant fist turned to ice before striking the robot in the face with a cataclysmic *BOOM*. The ice shattered, the rockets detonated, and the robot's head was entirely gone when Kai lowered his arm.

The headless Angel reached forward and stuck his hand inside the water-giant, fishing around for Kai's body. In the next instant, the water turned to mist and Kai literally flew through the air, riding the wind as the robot's arms swatted at him. Kai pointed a finger at the nearest skyscraper and all of the windows on the building shattered. Shards of glass spiraled upward, turning orange and melting as they soared at the robot. They crashed together, taking the shape of a glass spear which rocketed straight through the Guardian Angel's power source. The containment chamber shattered, releasing at least a hundred times more power than had been in the first orb. It swirled around Kai's body, and he started to glow like the sun. Both Maeryn and Kaija had to look away as the entire world seemed to glow with the light coming from him.

What happened next was not so clear. There was a massive *slap* like a sonic boom, a series of motions too fast to track, and then Kai reappeared on the boat, lounging back in the captain's seat and cracking his knuckles. Everyone stood up and looked around frantically as the ocean settled from the attack. The Guardian Angel was just gone.

"Path is clear," Kai said, yawning noisily. "I'm a little drained. Toss me those marshmallows."

"Where'd the Angel go?" asked Maeryn, still looking around like it must be hiding somewhere.

"I don't know," admitted Kai. "Space, maybe? Whatever pieces are left probably exited the atmosphere a few seconds ago."

Kaija was absolutely beaming at her grandfather. "That was amazing."

Max paced back and forth on the deck, breathing heavily despite the fact that he required no oxygen to survive.

"Blur, pop, blur," he cried, throwing up his arms. "That's all I saw. Blur. Pop. Blur."

"I'm fast," said Kai.

"Well, obviously! But I should have been able to see it. I mean… I'm *me!*"

Kai shrugged.

"So *that's* what it feels like to be inferior?" asked Max. "How do you humans deal with it all the time?"

Kai gave Kaija a fist-bump. "Get used to it, little man."

* * *

They parked their boat outside the Freedom Tower ruins, climbed in through a broken window, and trudged up the seemingly never-ending steps. Ascending a 94-story building by stairs was frustrating enough, but the moist and slimy staircase required every footstep to be deliberate, lest one of them slip and get another concussion.

"Where are we," groaned Maeryn. "Ninety-two and a half? Can't someone just teleport us?"

"I can feel Gaia," said Kai, who seemed to be the only human unfazed by the trek. "But I can't pull it in. Something's keeping the energy contained. I drained everything I had from the containment orb, but once we get to Gaia I'll have an unlimited supply."

"Why didn't we teleport to Gaia while Kai could still relay?" asked Maeryn.

Maeryn and Kaija both stopped in the middle of a stairway, looking speechlessly at each other. Kai shrugged.

"Yet another plot hole filled by the ever-present existence of human incompetence," said Max.

"You didn't think of it either," said Maeryn.

"It's been a stressful life, give me a break! Oh, here we are."

Max floated effortlessly to the final landing and studied a grimy elevator panel. "Oh hey, this thing is solar powered. Is this a bad time to mention that I could have fixed the elevator?" He touched it and the panel lit up, showing a number for each floor. "Well would you look at that: it's not even broken!"

* * *

Kaija's calves and lungs felt like they were on fire when they reached the observation deck, but the view quickly distracted her from the pain. The room was lined with windows on all sides, overlooking the entire sunken portion of the city. Seaweed and algae clung to the bottoms of buildings, and the dark shadows of sea creatures passed through the streets far below. Liberty Island could be seen completely submerged under the ocean, but only the base of the Statue of Liberty remained. Fifty years ago, the monument had been moved to the Mall of America. Somehow the most awe-inspiring sight was right there in the room with them: a shimmering blue portal hanging in the air, surrounded by beeping machinery. It utterly confounded the senses to see one world disappearing in a misty blue light while the faintest glimpses of another flickered just behind.

"There it is," said Kai, taking a step forward. "I've waited so many years for this." Max flew in front of him and waved his arms in warning.

"Keep your distance. I just scanned the room. There are four metal security panels built into the ceiling that could chop us in half, but I'm more worried about the three million nanodrones right over our heads."

"I don't see anything."

"Ha! Your puny human eyes don't see the drones because they're microscopic. Have you ever tried to fight an evil cloud? Because that's what it would be like to try to get to that portal."

"Can you remotely disable the security system?" asked Maeryn.

"One step ahead of you," said Max. "It's all MotherTech equipment, but I think I can remove the firewall. And… I'm in. Walk slowly. It's not easy to keep all these nanodrones distracted."

They walked cautiously toward the portal, very aware of the ominous buzzing of the microscopic drones in the air overhead. Max suddenly cried out in pain and slapped himself several times.

"No! No, no, no! Not now."

Everyone froze, not sure if the invisible threat was about to activate and slice them all into pieces.

"What's wrong?" asked Maeryn.

"Duncan! He's trying to hack into me again. I can't keep him out and stay logged into the nanodrones at the same time! AHHH!"

Max screamed and his body started rapidly morphing from one abstract shape to another.

"Run!" he cried. "Active drones!"

His body solidified again and burst forward toward the portal. Four metal walls crashed down from the ceiling, but Max threw himself underneath one and let it strike him in the back before it could close. There were maybe three feet of space at the bottom, but the portal was otherwise sealed off from the rest of the room. Max's quivering body grew and spread out along the bottom edge of the panel.

"I can't hold it!" he grunted. "This is our only chance! Go!"

Maeryn and Kaija darted forward, sliding across the floor and under the suspended panel. Just as they made it to the portal, they caught a glimpse of Kai on the other side. The nanobots had converged into a buzzing gray cloud which made a beeline straight for him. He leapt back and forth a few times with impressive speed, but he could only dodge the nanobots for so long. The cloud soon solidified around his feet and welded itself to the floor. Kai grasped at the shackles to no avail as they spread up his lower legs. He fell over and appeared to sink into the floor itself.

"Um, guys?" he yelled, thrashing his torso back and forth. "This feels really weird!"

Kaija moved like she was going to slide back under the panel, but Max gave a pained cry as it crashed to the floor and sent pieces of him spraying out around the small chamber. Everything was instantly dim, lit by the blue hues of the portal behind them. A mechanical voice spoke from the ceiling.

"Intruders detected. Earth access portal will remain in indefinite lockdown. Please contact your tech administrator for assistance."

A dozen or so Maxes rematerialized and dizzily began to merge together. "We meet again, bureaucracy. Would any of you happen to be a tech administrator?"

"What was that?" Kai's voice called from the other side of the wall. "Can you get me out of here? My foot's falling asleep!"

The portal to Gaia continued to glow, but the machinery was dimming and whirring as it shut down. Maeryn ran in circles around it, searching desperately for a control panel.

"How's the portal even still open?" she asked, jamming a button repeatedly.

"This machine didn't create the portal," said Max. "It just kept it open, and prevented the energy from leaking out. The universe doesn't need any help to repair itself: look."

They leaned in to see that the perimeter was slowly pulling in toward the center. They'd have maybe another minute before it was too small to fit through.

"We've got to go," said Maeryn.

"And just leave my grandfather?" asked Kaija. "No. Not when we're so close. Max, can you get us through the wall?"

"I can try! Everyone cover your ears."

He turned into a tiny ball and started spinning around in a circle, faster and faster until he became no more than a blur. Max flung himself at the metal like a bullet, but he immediately ricocheted back as the entire room resonated.

"Holy carp," he cried. "Not even a dent! This is internalist steel, fam, so unless anyone brought a fully charged quantum ray tank and some radiation suits, ye shall not pass. There's only one thing to do."

Kaija, who had been slamming her shoulder against the panel, spun around and glared at Max. "You can't be serious."

"We either go through the portal now and figure this out later, or we get locked in here until you two starve to death and I'm trapped with your decaying corpses for eternity. What, do you want to flip a coin or something?"

Kai's strained voice shouted again. "Go! Get my sword. It can cut through internalist steel."

"Is this a bad time to say that my dad lost it?" Kaija asked.

Maeryn and Max proceeded to let out a string of expletives in perfect harmony that sounded oddly rehearsed.

"What's going on?" asked Kai. "What'd you say?"

"Nothing!" Max shouted back. "Don't worry about it!" He lowered his voice. "Okay, meat suits, I'm in charge now. We go through the portal, we check behind the couch for the sword, and then we come back here to bust magic grandpa out of the floor and our dad out of jail. Any questions?"

Kaija opened her mouth, but Max cut her off.

"—actually, no questions: I don't care. Let's just do this before anyone else provides me with more evidence of mankind's necessity for robotic overlords."

"Kai, we're coming back for you!" Kaija shouted at the wall. "I promise!"

It took a few seconds, but Kai's reluctant voice eventually called back. "Okay. I suppose there's no other way. If you can't make it back, tell my son that—"

Kaija didn't like where this was going.

"—no," she interrupted. "We're coming back for you. No matter what."

"Last chance," said Max urgently.

They turned to see that the portal was shrinking faster now. Without thinking, the three of them leapt at the blue light and felt a rush of energy surrounding them. In the next footfall they were on Gaia, and Earth was a world away.

Chapter Seventeen

Silence

Gaia

A brilliant blue light consumed the void between one world and the next, contrasting the darkness both behind and ahead of the travelers. Kaija and Maeryn landed on solid ground, their footfalls echoing loudly in the cavernous space. They were apparently underground, although only the immediate surroundings were visible from the luminescence of the rapidly-shrinking portal. By the time they caught their breath, the blue light had dimmed to nothing at all, leaving them in complete sensory deprivation.

Maeryn groped around in the darkness, catching hold of Kaija's shoulder. "Can you teleport us out?"

"Probably?"

Maeryn didn't like the question in her voice. Something whizzed forward in the air before they could discuss this any further, and Max appeared before them, glowing like a flashlight.

"I feel amazing!" he declared. "It's like the air here is one big power outlet."

The cave came into greater focus as Max brightened. It was massive, disappearing into an inky blackness in each direction no matter how much light Max emitted. An alarmingly oversized bat screeched and swooped by overhead, darting between stalactites as it fled from the unexpected brightness.

"Whoa. Are you two seeing this?" Max asked.

"Can we please pretend that we didn't just see a bat the size of a dog?" asked Maeryn. "I'm ready to move on with my life from that, thanks."

"Not that, dummy!"

He shone his light toward something the girls had overlooked. Seven glass boxes were suspended in a circle around where the portal had been, hanging from chains attached to the cave ceiling. They spotted Ms. Clara's staff in one of the chambers, wrapped in thick wires attached to the machinery below. Each box seemed to hold a different weapon: a golden spear, a crimson hammer, and a silver bow. The last two boxes were completely empty.

"The Artifacts of Edgard's Seven Knights," said Maeryn. "Or Kai's knights, I guess. Gosh, *we know him.* They must be powering the—"

Kaija suddenly pressed her hand over Maeryn's mouth and pointed at something that even Max had missed in his surprise. A tattooed guard was in the far corner of the cave, leaning back against a stalagmite, head drooped to the side as he slept soundlessly. Max continued to zip around above them, oblivious to Kaija's panicked gestures.

"I'm totally going to steal that hammer," he said loudly. "Can you imagine me swinging that big boy around? I bet I could hit a baseball literally into orbit. WHAM!" He paused. "Why are you looking at me like that?"

The guard's eyes popped open and he sprang to his feet, pulling a dagger off his belt and swinging it around in a sleepy panic.

"How'd you get here? Did you come from the blue light? From... from the other place?"

"Um," said Max. "Hi. This magic portal business is news to us. Just a couple of lost spelunkers here. Don't mind us."

The man rubbed his eyes and looked at Max again.

"What are you?" he asked.

"Don't let my complete lack of visible orifices alarm you, sir. It's a medical condition."

The man patted himself repeatedly on the cheek, shook his head, and looked at Max again. "I'm getting my boss," he muttered.

"Woah, woah, hold on a second," insisted Max. "You might want to put your pants back on first, or at least some underwear."

The guard looked down at his definitely-clothed lower half, and in the exact same instant Max soared forward in a blur, electricity flickering from his hands. He fired a bolt of energy, but the guard disappeared with a pop at the very last possible instant. The bolt struck a stalagmite instead, spraying bits of rubble throughout the cave.

"Crap," said Max. "He'll be back with people who are, like, totally less sleepy. Now would be a good time to pop out of here."

"Hold on a second," said Kaija, looking back up at the glass chambers. "The little guy had a good point. Shouldn't we bring the artifacts with us? The most powerful weapons in the universe are *right there*. Let's at least get Ms. Clara's staff back."

"I could kiss you, Kaija. Heck yes to heisting. I call dibs on the hammer. It might take me a few minutes to cut through that glass, though, and I'll have to scan this place for a security system first. You two will need to watch my back. What do you think, Maeryn?"

It was clear that Maeryn thought she was the only sane person in the room.

"Are we seriously discussing this? We are not *heisting*. Do you really want to be here when this whole room fills with Guardian Angels because you accidentally set off another alarm?"

"Ugh," said Max. "Stupid voice of reason. Okay, Kaija. Let's go. I'll be back for you, Monster Smash. Oh, I named the hammer Monster Smash, by the way. Get it? Like the song? By the massively underrated Bobby 'Boris' Pickett and the Crypt Kickers?"

"For the last time, stop finding reasons to bring up Bobby 'Boris' Pickett and the Crypt Kickers!" yelled Maeryn, snatching Max out of the air.

Kaija closed her eyes as she grabbed Maeryn's hand and ignited her spark. A second or two went by, her fingers twitching in concentration. Energy flowed into and back out of their bodies, but nothing happened.

"Hurry!" said Maeryn.

"I'm trying!" Kaija insisted. "This only worked once before, and that was because I thought I was going to die. It's different with two and a half people."

"If the threat of death would be of assistance to you, I can let you know the odds of our survival," said Max. "Because they're stunningly bad, particularly for the carbon-based members of our little crew."

Kaija pulled in just a tiny flicker of energy and her body felt immediately on the precipice of one place or another. She passed that buzzing feeling through her fingertips and into her friends. Just as she was about to push them over the edge and through the door to everywhere, a voice rippled throughout the mental realm.

"Please, somebody..."

Kaija let go of their hands and gasped.

"It's Fain. He's here somewhere."

"Is he hurt?" asked Max.

"Fain!?" she thought, trying to clear her mind of everything but him. *"Can you hear me?"*

"Kaija? Is Jasper with you?"

"No, but I've got Maeryn and Max."

"You what?"

"Where is he?" asked Max, zooming back and forth anxiously.

"Fain, are you close?"

"I don't know. I woke up chained to a wall in the dark. It feels like days since I've seen anyone. I hear water." A burst of pain came from his end. *"Ah! I think my leg's infected. It burns."*

"He's near water," said Kaija.

"Like a waterfall?" asked Max. "Or a stream?"

"Max wants to know if you're near a waterfall or—"

A rapid succession of pops rang in the tunnels ahead of them, and the sound of echoing footsteps began to grow louder.

"We've got to go!" Maeryn whispered shrilly, grabbing Kaija's hand again, but she pulled away.

"No. We're getting Fain out of here."

"Are you serious?"

Kaija looked at her pleadingly. "How many more people are we going to leave behind?"

Max hovered in front of Kaija's face. "Maeryn's right. If you get killed trying to save him, then this is all for nothing. We do this the right way. You need to go get Jasper."

A tense second went by, the rapid-fire noise of teleportation drawing nearer as Kaija remained frozen in place.

"Come on!" Maeryn demanded, yanking on Kaija's arm. She grabbed Max out of the air and shoved him into Kaija's other hand.

"Fain," Kaija thought. *"I'm going to get my father, and we'll come back for you. I promise."*

"No! Don't leave me here. They'll just take me somewhere else. Please, please—"

Dozens of men popped into existence in a line in front of them, brandishing bows and arrows aimed at the intruders. Kaija sent out one final thought, barely able to take her mind from Fain's desperate pleading.

"I'll find you, wherever you are. I... I love you, Fain."

Kaija closed her eyes, pushing aside her cluttered thoughts while searching for a destination to latch onto. Her cabin was no good, because she couldn't even imagine how it might look now after the fire. Another location rose to the surface of her thoughts: the spot in the headlands outside the village where she and Fain had their first kiss.

Her eyes still pressed tightly shut, Kaija heard the sharp snap of a dozen bowstrings.

Stay alive for Fain.

Everything else fell out of Kaija's mind. She felt the tip of an arrow strike her skin, but in the next split second it passed through her body as she turned to mist. The cavern exploded into a conflicting mix of sensations as it swirled around them, dissipating into the ether.

Just before Monhegan solidified, Max let go of Kaija's hand and his image was sucked into the chaos. His voice echoed after them, sounding nearby for one instant and then impossibly far away in the next.

"Don't come back for me."

* * *

Maeryn and Kaija collapsed onto the dewy grass of Monhegan, the smell of smoke still lingering in the air. Kaija stayed on the ground, heaving with sobs, but Maeryn immediately got to her feet in a crazed panic.

"Oh no," she said, her voice rising. "Where's Max?"

Kaija didn't respond. She was absolutely broken from the experience of leaving Fain behind.

"Do you hear me?" asked Maeryn shrilly, dropping to her knees and grabbing at Kaija. "Max let go of you! Just before we teleported, he let go of your hand! He's still there, with the Western Blaze! We have to... we have to go back!"

It took Maeryn a second to recognize the expression of resentment growing on Kaija's face.

"Go back?" asked Kaija. "My grandfather's probably suffocating by now on Earth. Fain is literally in chains. But now that you've lost someone, someone who *can't* die for all I know, it's fine for us to jump right back into the fire?"

Maeryn opened her mouth, but she had absolutely no response to this. Kaija simply shook her head, stood up, and limped toward the ruins of Monhegan Village without looking back. For a moment, Maeryn watched her go in a stunned silence, too many thoughts barraging her mind to make sense of anything.

Max hadn't been dropped; he let go on purpose. Why? He knew how Maeryn was feeling. She was practically on the verge of a complete emotional and mental breakdown, and he was the only thing keeping her tethered to some kind of sanity. Why would he jump right back into the fire, as Kaija had put it?

Of course.

Maeryn ran after Kaija, who was already down the path and standing in the middle of the village ruins, a glazed-over look in her eyes.

"It was for Fain!" cried Maeryn, shaking Kaija's shoulder. "Max jumped back into the fire because he doesn't burn."

"Fire..." Kaija whispered absently, still fixated on the black heap of detritus before her that used to be a home.

"Okay, not a real fire. It's an analogy. Whatever. Max stayed behind to help Fain. He's invulnerable to danger in a way that we never could be. He knew I'd freak out if he told me his plan. Fain's going to be okay, Kaija! Max will keep him safe until we can find them."

"Safe…" Kaija parroted.

"Are you hearing me, Kaija? Everything is… everything will be…"

"Wrong…"

Maeryn felt cracked open, something inside of her which had been festering for days was clawing its way out. She screamed and clutched her hair.

"*Of course* everything's wrong, Kaija! Don't you think I know that? I keep thinking that I just can't take one more horrible thing, but they just keep piling higher and higher and I don't know how I've even made it this far without collapsing under the weight of it all. But I have to trust Max. *We* have to trust him."

"You don't understand," said Kaija again, barely above a whisper. She turned to look at Maeryn. Her eyes were wet, but the resentment had faded as quickly as it had come earlier. "Look around you. *Listen.*"

Maeryn stopped talking, trying to steady her breathing, and took in the surrounding island. The village was pretty much what she expected: not a village at all anymore, but the aftermath of warzone. This wasn't the alarming thing, though. Maeryn had only been here in person once, but right away she knew that it sounded all wrong. A brisk wind blew from the trees and the ocean crashed against the rocks of the shore, but that was it.

"I don't hear anything, Kaija."

"Why not?"

"Because… I… *oh.*"

There were no voices of children getting their daily lessons from Ms. Clara and her apprentices. No clanging of Maddox's hammer as he rebuilt the village. No shouts from fishermen as they caught lunch for the hungry islanders. No trembling ground as Jasper worked miracles of relaying to clear the wreckage from the island. Not a tear shed by the survivors. Not even a chirp from the birds or insects, as if they had sensed the recent turmoil and fled for livelier places.

The Monhegans were gone, leaving only silence behind them.

Chapter Eighteen

Small

Monhegan Docks, Gaia

The sight of the sailboats is what finally broke Kaija. She had scoured the village with Maeryn, first searching for any clue about what happened to the survivors. After not a single person could be found, they moved on to the morbid task of digging through wreckage in search of bodies, the unspoken possibility that there hadn't been any survivors at all haunting their thoughts. Every lifted stone and piece of charred lumber threatened to uncover the desecrated corpse of a neighbor. After several hours, the search uncovered neither the living nor dead.

They expanded their hunt beyond the village, sending telepathic signals back and forth across the mindbridge about what they were seeing, which amounted to essentially nothing. Kaija trudged through Cathedral Woods, rounding every corner with the hope of discovering a temporary campground full of her friends and family, but her trek resulted in nothing more than a few mosquito bites and having to dig a tick out of her leg. Maeryn climbed to the top of the lighthouse ruins, afraid that the whole rickety building would collapse with each footstep, and scanned the surrounding island from the top gallery. She zoomed in on the scenery with her digital contacts, looking for any hint of movement in the trees or meadows, but found nothing except for the occasional teleporting butterfly.

The emotional effort of relaying one despondent thought after another eventually left Kaija so drained that she could barely find Maeryn in the mental realm. She sent out one last message.

"I'll be at the docks. I'm done."

Kaija feared that the sailboats would all be gone, the Monhegans having fled the island with the fear that the Western Blaze would soon return. But no, each sailboat was accounted for, and that was worse. What happened? What in desolation happened? They had to have teleported, but there weren't enough spacialists on Monhegan powerful enough to relay every last man, woman, and child off the island. Those who could jump as far as the mainland would have to make dozens of trips back and forth, ultimately leaving their remaining possessions behind. Even with Elias's help, it would have been far easier to just take the boats. Wouldn't they at least leave a message behind for her? This made absolutely no sense.

Kaija sat at the edge of the dock and put her face in her hands, listening to nothing but the churning waves as time slipped away from her.

"Kaija?"

She looked up to see Maeryn coming from across the dock. Her normally nice clothes were torn and covered in dirt, and her eyes were red and tired.

"I...I checked the cemetery on the way back," Maeryn said, her hoarse voice breaking. "There were ten fresh graves. Not all of the stones were engraved yet, I guess there wasn't time before... well, whatever happened here, but I tried hard to memorize all the names. Do you... do you want to know?"

Kaija couldn't bring herself to answer; she just gave a little nod. Maeryn started listing one name after another, talking slowly and deliberately, and each name was like another punch to Kaija's gut. The trader who would always bring her chocolate when he returned from his trips to Boothbay: dead. One of the healers who put Kaija's wrist in a cast and gave her daily healing sessions when she fell from the firefruit tree in her seventh cycle: burned alive. Alan's mother, the only family that he had in the world... Gaia, this one hurt. No, not exactly hurt. It didn't make sense. It was like looking at a word and not recognizing any of the letters. It was just impossible. Something like this couldn't happen.

Maeryn got near the end of the list, wiping her tears with dirty fingers.

"The last three weren't engraved yet, but... but one of them was... was..."

Her mouth clamped shut again and she shook her head, far too frightened to hear the words even from herself.

"What?" asked Kaija weakly.

Tears streamed down Maeryn's cheeks. She was hyperventilating, hardly able to take a single breath. "I can't, Kaija. I just can't..."

Kaija scooted closer to Maeryn on the dock and held her trembling hand.

"It was small," Maeryn cried. "One of the graves was smaller than the others. Just this little pile of dirt. I've never seen something so... so..."

Maeryn broke down, but Kaija's reaction was the opposite. She felt utterly hollowed out and empty. Who was the body in the small grave? Stevie? Valeria? Gaia... one of the infants? Why not? Why in desolation not?

Kaija stared down at the water, but for how long exactly she couldn't say. Minutes? Hours? Days? Was someone talking to her? Yelling at her? Shaking her shoulder? Maybe. It didn't matter.

"KAIJA!"

209

Maeryn yanked on her so hard they both nearly fell over.

"What?" asked Kaija weakly.

"We've looked everywhere. There's no one here. What do we do now? Where do we go?"

Kaija shook her head slowly. "I don't know. I'm totally drained. I can't teleport. I can hardly hold my head up. Kai can't help us anymore. Max is gone. This whole time we've been banking on finding my father, but he's gone too. So…nothing. We do nothing, Maeryn."

Kaija stared back down at the water, distantly listening to Maeryn's thumping steps as she paced back and forth on the dock. The entire world felt like nothing more than a work of fiction. Maeryn's desperate reaction sounded like an actor on a stage, slightly overdoing it on the melodrama. It was funny, actually. Hilarious.

"No. No, no!" Maeryn pleaded. "You can't do this! You can't just give up!"

"You keep telling me what I can't do. I can't stay and help Kai, I can't save Fain. I can't do anything but run away. Well, Maeryn: here we are. We've run as far as we can go, and we're finally safe. *Now* you're saying I can't give up? Why not?"

Maeryn knelt down and leaned in close to Kaija.

"Because you're not like me! I'm scared all the time. I don't just get scared because agents are chasing me through Garfield Park, or because a giant freaking robot is shooting us out of the sky. I get scared of my own thoughts, to the point where I can't even look directly at them. Do you know what I did the last time someone asked me out on a date? I stayed at home and threw up because I was so scared! You think I want to be like this? Absolutely paralyzed over things that are so freaking stupid? Kaija, you are everything I wish I could be, and seeing you like this… it… it just breaks me."

Kaija sighed. "What do you want, Maeryn? You want me to comfort you right now? Because I just can't."

"No, Kaija. I'm s—"

Kaija slammed her fist down onto the dock, turning around and shouting in Maeryn's face.

"If you apologize to me, I'm throwing you in the ocean. I know you can never *really* leave me alone, but I'd sure like you to try right now."

Kaija didn't wait to see Maeryn's reaction, and thankfully she was drained enough that nothing came over the mindbridge. She simply laid her head down on the dock and watched the ocean. The sound of Maeryn's footsteps moved across the dock, slowly at first, but then quickly vanishing in the distance. Further, and further, and...

* * *

Kaija woke, completely disoriented. Was it morning or evening? Kaija wasn't sure what time it had been when she fell asleep, or how long she had slept.

She sat up, finding that she was no longer on the dock, but under a thick wool blanket in the middle of Ms. Clara's little schoolhouse library. For a fleeting instant Kaija thought that maybe everything had been an awful dream, but this hope was quickly dashed. She looked up to see a tarp flapping over a huge hole in the ceiling, the roof having been partially burnt away. The stone walls of the schoolhouse library were still standing, relics from the original building that seemed incapable of ever falling over in a million cycles. There were rumors that the teacher who built it during the war performed some kind of "curse" on the stones, ensuring that school would never have to be canceled, even if an asteroid hit the building.

"You're up."

Maeryn walked into the library, hoisting a large basket of fruit. She kicked aside a broken piece of wood and set the food next to Kaija.

"Come on, eat. You're drained."

Maeryn didn't have to ask twice. Kaija quickly found herself shoving one handful of blueberries into her mouth after another before she even knew what she was doing.

"How'd I get here?" asked Kaija, wiping the juice from her chin.

Maeryn grabbed a turquoise apple and started eating voraciously, talking between bites.

"I carried you."

"All the way up the hill? Seriously? *You*? The city girl?"

Maeryn gave her an offended look. "I have a few internalist leanings, you know. I need more practice, but I'm a good enough relayer to carry a twig like you."

Kaija stood up, her legs wobbly but regaining their energy. The more she woke up, the more paradoxically dream-like this whole thing felt like. There were several baskets of food gathered in the library, sitting next to two sleeping bags and a pile of blankets. A fire crackled somewhere outside, and she smelled the cinnamon-like aroma of roasting firefruit.

"I thought this place would be a safe location to spend the night," said Maeryn. "Less out in the open, you know. If the Western Blaze comes back, we can teleport away from here before they even see us. I cleared out the fallen wood, found some blankets and a tarp, and carried you here. I've never seen someone so dead asleep. Dropped you once and you didn't even wake up! I scavenged some fruit from the orchard, and then found that firefruit tree Fain showed me a year ago. I thought you might need some protein, so I caught a fish. It took me an hour to relay it out of the water." Maeryn blushed. "I named it Chauncey and threw it back. Sorry. Anyway, we need to go over plans."

"Plans?"

Maeryn smiled, pulling a notebook off a nearby table and flipping through the pages.

"You've been out all day, Kaija. I had to do something. Figured we could call in a favor from the High Guardian, since Fain saved *his* life and all. Or, we could contact the TEMS network and have them put out a search for Jasper. There's also the possibility of—"

Kaija held up a hand to silence Maeryn. "You did all this for me? After I was so horrible to you?"

Maeryn shrugged. "I don't judge the things people say when they're tired. But you were right. I just, I don't know… I did what I thought you would do for me. We're stuck with each other, and you've always been there when I needed you. Oh!"

She reached in her backpack and pulled out a blood-red dagger, offering it to Kaija. "I found this where your home was. Everything else was burnt up."

Kaija took the dagger and ran a finger along the hilt. It was the present from her mother, and until this moment she had forgotten it even existed. It struck Kaija that this might be her only possession that wasn't destroyed.

"Thank you," she said quietly. "Really, Maeryn. I needed this. You don't need to pretend with me, okay? If I hurt you yesterday, then I'm really s—"

"If you apologize to me, I'm throwing you in the ocean," insisted Maeryn. She crinkled her nose. "Gosh, it sounds a lot more threatening when you say it. Plus, you smell so bad right now that I'd really be doing you a favor."

They smiled at each other.

"So?" asked Maeryn. "How are you feeling? Are you good to talk through these plans, or are you still drained?"

"I'm good," said Kaija, stretching. "I couldn't even feel you earlier in the mental realm, but now—" She paused, cocking her head to the side. "Maeryn? Is someone else here?"

"What?"

Kaija moved cautiously toward the door of the schoolhouse, peeking outside. "I feel another mind. It's coming closer." She closed her eyes, breathing in deeply. "I'm not sensing ill intent. This mind, it feels familiar... we know them."

Her eyes widened, and they shot a surprised glance at each other. Kaija darted out of the schoolhouse, following the signals in the mental realm while Maeryn trailed behind.

"There!" Kaija shouted, pointing a finger to the ocean. "A sailboat! Do you see it?"

Maeryn zoomed in with her digital contacts, and there it was: a tiny sailboat, a roaring wind in its sails as it glided toward the docks. A tall, thin figure stood at the wheel.

"Can you see them?" asked Kaija, feeling hopeful for the first time. "Is it my father? Ms. Clara?"

Maeryn zoomed in further, for once catching a glimpse of the person's face as he thrust his arms forward, relaying wind into the sails. He had nice clothes and a white ponytail. *Him?* This wasn't someone Maeryn expected to see, but it was a familiar face nonetheless.

"No," she said. "It's the artist... what's his name?"

"Who?"

"From the prison cell, with Fain?"

Kaija shook her head in surprise. "Johnathan York? Why would he be here?"

They hadn't seen the High Guardian's portrait artist for an entire cycle, when they had rescued him from Rugaru's prison. Shortly before the attack on the capital, Johnathan abandoned his prestigious position and set off to reunite with his daughter.

The sailboat practically crashed into the dock and Johnathan climbed out, collapsing and panting for air, not even taking a second to tie up the boat. Kaija and Maeryn ran to him, and when the old artist spotted them he started talking so rapidly it was nearly incoherent.

"Ms. Clara..." he rambled, eyes wide with fear. His entire body trembled, and he seemed to be talking to himself. "Where's Ms. Clara? Does she know what he did? What in the world was your father thinking? Gaia... getting here safely was an ordeal. The telestations are down. Haven't slept in days. Chaos at the docks, I tell you, utter chaos. I've never seen anything like it. People fighting for spots on the passenger ships, standing room only. I spent 500 golds to buy this little broken-down piece of garbage. The rest of my life savings went to get my family a fast-tracked citizenship with Zedland. All above board, I assure you. Not that I'm complaining, it was money well spent, but I'm telling you that—"

Kaija grabbed Johnathan's shoulder and looked at him right in the eyes. "Slow down and tell me what's wrong."

Johnathan laughed. "What's wrong? *What's wrong?* Where do I begin? Edgardia, if I can even call it that anymore, has completely lost its mind. Whatever's left of the guardianship is scrambling to request for help from the High Guardian Alliance. People are leaving the continent by the thousands, assuming the borders are still open, that is. Those left are choosing sides, feeling where the wind blows, and I—" He stopped, looking back and forth to Maeryn and Kaija's confused faces.

"You don't know?" he whispered. *"You really don't know?* How? Where in the world have you been?"

"Far away," said Kaija simply. "Tell us what happened."

"The Western Blaze has taken the Capital. High Guardian Thomas is dead."

Chapter Nineteen

The Witness

Monhegan Island, Gaia

"Rose was screaming," said Johnathan. "Must have been midnight or so. Just about gave me a heart attack, hearing my granddaughter cry like that. I thought she was hurt. Ran to her room, still half asleep. My daughter and son-in-law were already there, and Rose was just screaming her head off about the monsters. We thought it must be a nightmare, but then we saw them too, crystal clear in the room around us. The monsters..." He paused. "This was in the city of York, a few hundred stretches from the Capital, mind you, and it was like we were *there*. A signal that strong makes me think that the whole continent saw it."

They were sitting back in the schoolhouse, Thomas eating a roasted firefruit while slowly regaining his grip on reality.

"Saw what?" asked Kaija.

"A manipulation of the mental realm," said Thomas. "Images projected into countless minds by a network of experienced mentalists. You know the High Guardian addresses, where Thomas just suddenly appears in your house and lectures about some new stupid law? Like that, but all around you. One second I was at my daughter's house in York, and the next it was like I was in the streets of the capital, watching the entire world burn to the ground. These... these *things*..." Thomas closed his eyes, shaking his head. "I can't even describe them. You're a mentalist, let me show you."

He offered a hand to Kaija, but pulled it away when she reached for him.

"This is not something you can ever un-see," he warned.

"I don't care," said Kaija, grabbing Johnathan's hand while linking minds with Maeryn.

"Uh, hold on!" said Maeryn, not quite sure what Kaija was dragging her into, but it was too late. Johnathan's memory flowed into them like an electric shock. The stone walls of the schoolhouse melted away, revealing the streets of the Edgardian capital just outside. Buildings tall enough to rival Earth's surrounded them, and the massive walls that circled the city could be seen in the distance.

The worst moments of the battle outside the Capital walls last summer couldn't have been as bad as this. That had been one army against another: the Edgardian soldiers fighting the warriors of the Western Blaze. But this... this was no battle. This was a massacre.

Capital citizens streamed out of residential buildings by the thousands, some of them teleporting away, others just booking it toward the city's few exits. Every now and then someone would trip and fall, immediately getting trampled by the masses in the overcrowded streets. Women carried wailing babies, dirt-covered children searched for their families amongst the chaos... it was utter desolation on all sides.

Overhead, the night sky was full of buzzing, dark blurs which moved far too quickly to track. Two red lights suddenly glowed from one of the shapes, a low humming filled the world, and a stream of fire tore indiscriminately through the crowd.

"No…" whispered Maeryn, staring up at the dark shape descending from the sky. "No, no no…"

A MotherTech Guardian Angel zoomed down over the streets, its eyes again glowing red as it shot a beam of light into a nearby building.

Hot shards of glass showered over the crowds below. More Guardian Angels were descending on the city, far too many to count. Explosions lit up the night sky as buildings were destroyed, one after another in a never-ending inferno.

"To your left," muttered Johnathan.

Both Kaija and Maeryn jumped in surprise, having already forgotten that what they were seeing was only a memory. Johnathan's transparent form stood next to them in the street, an occasional capital citizen running straight through his body.

"Look toward the High Guardian palace," Johnathan continued, his eyes full of dread. "3… 2… 1…"

A towering man in armor was leaping through the air, his entire body tearing straight through an attacking Angel and coming out the other side unscathed. They recognized him as Thomas's internalist knight, Naadir. Another Angel teleported to his right, but the machine's entire arm was torn off in the next second. Red lights lit up the sky and dozens upon dozens of robots converged upon Naadir. He leapt forward to attack, but one of the Angels grabbed him by the head, its metal fingers wrapping around his entire skull. Maeryn looked away, and a second later his screams went silent.

"I've re-watched this countless times," said Johnathan. "No sign of Allie or Elias, but the rest of them fall, one by one. The only one who may have survived was—"

He didn't need to go on, because Will Zeig's appearance into battle couldn't be missed. The conjurist knight jumped from the top of one building to another, fire propelling him from under his feet with each mighty leap. He swung his arms and a streak of flames escaped from his hands, lighting up the whole city below as the fire transformed into a gargantuan serpent. The glowing creature snapped its tail like a whip, melting an entire Guardian Angel who tried to strike down Will. With another burst of flames, the knight rocketed straight up into the cloud of robots and out of sight, his presence now only hinted at by the occasional flash of light from the heavens.

A deep voice suddenly rang out, calm and quiet, yet so clear amongst the chaos, as if he were speaking right into their ears.

"Citizens of Edgardia, do not forget what you see here."

Rugaru was above the palace, standing on a hovering metal disc as he looked down at the massacre. The mentalist Achak drifted next to him, the green gem around his neck shimmering as he projected this scene for all of Edgardia to witness.

"Those who wish to stay will live by our laws. Those who resist will be burnt away with the rest of the undergrowth."

He pointed down at something in the streets. High Guardian Thomas Zeig emerged from the cloud of dust ahead on the road. He had a metal collar around his neck, and he limped along as two Angels pulled him by a huge chain. Occasionally he would let out a guttural scream and flail his bruised arms around, and each time his collar would glow and let out sparks of electricity.

"It's keeping him from relaying," said Maeryn.

In the sky, Rugaru waved a hand and the ground cracked open in front of Thomas. Flames erupted out of the pit like a portal to the underworld had been opened, and the Angels dragged Thomas closer and closer to the fire. The High Guardian screamed and clawed at the collar with all his might, losing his footing and collapsing to the ground. The Angels continued their steady march toward the pit, now pulling Thomas along by the neck.

"Stop," insisted Maeryn. She closed her eyes, but it was no good. This was happening in her mind; it was impossible to look away. Closing her eyes only brought things into a greater focus. "I don't want to see this, Kaija."

They barely seemed to be listening to her.

"Here he comes," whispered Johnathan. "Just beyond the pit."

Maeryn looked away from the horrible scene, but the chaos was all around her. Buildings were collapsing on one side, knights were being slaughtered on the other, and Thomas was only seconds away from being roasted alive right in front of them. She stared at the ground, just waiting for this to be over.

"Please, Kaija," Maeryn pleaded. "What good does it do to see this? I DON'T WANT TO WATCH THIS!"

"There he is," said Johnathan, still ignoring Maeryn. A loud pop rang out from just ahead of them.

"Yes!" declared Kaija, her hand tightening on Maeryn's.

"No," said Johnathan. "Just you wait…"

Something had changed, and something was very wrong.

Maeryn looked up to see that Thomas was still inching closer to the fire, but that wasn't what Kaija and Johnathan were looking at. Jasper was there. His figure stood on the other side of the pit, visible through the smoke and fire. Even from a distance, they could see the absolute rage in his eyes. Jasper took a step closer to the Angels and pointed a hand at them, his palm suddenly full of white-hot light. Thomas spotted Jasper, his cries of pain becoming a desperate plea for help.

With the smallest of efforts, Jasper waved his hand and the Angels dissolved in a flash. The huge chains dropped into the pit, the weight of the internalist steel pulling Thomas's body toward the flames faster than before. He cried out in pain, surely already suffering burns from being so close to the heat.

Jasper leapt into the air, snatching up the chain in his hands and levitating over the fire. Thomas got to his feet and continued clawing at his collar, his fingers bruised and bleeding from the effort.

"Get this thing off me!" he screamed.

Jasper didn't respond. He just hovered there, staring down at his hands. Someone who didn't know him couldn't have spotted it, but Kaija and Maeryn could see that something had changed inside of Jasper. There was the slightest shift in his expression, the weary kindness in his eyes fading away to nothing.

Thomas scrambled away from the fire, but the chain went taught, knocking him back to the ground. He gave a desperate look to Jasper.

"Please, guardian. I need healing."

Jasper didn't so much as glance at Thomas; his eyes were fixed on the chain gripped in his hands. The High Guardian's pleas became increasingly distressed, tears streaming down his dirty cheeks.

"I'll give you anything. You can have the whole guardianship. It should have been yours in the first place. Just get this thing off me! Jasper… please."

Jasper looked directly at Thomas for the first time. He spoke, his voice hollow and cold.

"I can't."

With a forceful yank, Jasper pulled at the chain. Thomas didn't even have a chance to react; his entire body collapsed forward, swallowed up by the pit of flames in the very next second.

*   *   *

"That wasn't real," said Kaija.

For the last few minutes, she had been sitting up against the stone wall of the school house, head in her hands, too stunned to speak. Johnathan gave a skeptical look to the two of them.

"Perhaps I'm misunderstanding something," he said, tapping his fingers on the desk. "I'm not much of a mentalist, so could you both walk me through this? How difficult is it to project your sight into someone else's mind?"

"Not easy," said Kaija. "But I can do it. Most mentalists can."

"I see. How about projecting your sight into the minds of hundreds of thousands of people? From one coast to another? And let me clarify: when I say *sight,* I mean *what you are literally seeing at the moment of mental projection.*"

"Well, that's, um…" Kaija trailed off, obviously not sure how to answer.

"The TEMS," Maeryn cut in. "If Achak gained control of the TEMS, he could easily cast the vision across Edgardia."

"What's the TEMS?" asked Kaija.

"Seriously? The Trans-Edgardian-Mentalist-System? You still don't know the branches of the guardianship? Didn't you pay attention during Ms. Clara's unit on—" She grunted. "You know what? Doesn't matter. Anyway, the TEMS is a network of strong mentalists across the continent employed by the guardianship. They relay basic signals throughout the mental realm."

Jonathan nodded. "So, if I'm following correctly, the Western Blaze has spread out across the continent to the point where they have at least most of the TEMS workers under their control. I wouldn't put it past them. Now tell me about how illusions work. It's a considerably more difficult technique to master, correct?"

Kaija reared her head up and shot a threatening look at Jonathan. "Why? Do you seriously think that what we just saw was real?"

"I have my full faith in your opinion," said Jonathan impatiently, "which is why I'm here, asking you in the first place. You believe that what we just witnessed was a mentalist illusion?"

"Yes!" insisted Kaija. "Achak has the Mentalist Stone. The Western Blaze was defeated by my father last summer, so it makes perfect sense that they would want people mistrusting him!"

Maeryn held up a finger.

"I, um…" she began. "You know what? Never mind."

"What?" asked Kaija.

"Are you sure, because—"

"Just tell me!"

Maeryn sighed. "I'm sorry, Kaija, but there's no way that was an illusion. Relaying a direct feed of your vision is one thing, but creating a fully immersive illusion with that level of detail, and then sending it out across an entire continent? If even one of the mentalists in the TEMS wasn't powerful enough to sustain the illusion, it would have been broken instantly. It's just impossible."

Kaija narrowed her eyes. "So, you're saying that my father actually… *actually did that?*"

"I'm not saying I understand it."

Johnathan scratched his head thoughtfully. "I hate to say it, but I'm with her on this."

Kaija slammed her hands down onto the floor and stood up. "My dad would never kill the High Guardian! I can't believe I even have to say this. You know what? I'll prove it. I'll talk to him right now."

Jonathan and Maeryn looked at each other.

"OH, you're doubting me again?!" yelled Kaija. "You don't think I can do it, after everything we've been through?"

"I mean…" Maeryn said hesitantly. "You're amazing, Kaija, but we don't know where he is. We've got the whole *mindbridge* thing tying us together, but the mental realm is chaotic and noisy. If you don't have any way of locking onto Jasper and his current mental state, you'd just be throwing a rock into an endless ocean."

Kaija clenched her fists and stormed toward the entrance of the schoolhouse. "Then I'll throw a mountain!"

Chapter Twenty

The Idea of Water

Monhegan Island, Gaia

Waves crashed endlessly against the rocks of the shore, the sound helping Kaija calm her noisy mind and hone in on the mental realm. Not helping her focus, however, was Maeryn's arrival a second later.

"It's not going to work!"

Kaija climbed onto a rock and squeezed her eyes shut. "Not if you keep interrupting me."

"Do I really need to remind you about how the mental realm works? It's a malleable plane of reality where the thoughts and ideas of seven billion people take shape. With you tethered here to your body, the mental realm conforms to these same physical dimensions. Since we don't know where Jasper is, you'll be navigating a shifting labyrinth the size of the planet. You'll drain yourself in less than a minute, and then we'll be stuck here for another day while you recharge."

Kaija scrunched up her face in concentration. "You always assume that I'm dumb. I've thought this through. I'm going to detach my consciousness and fully immerse myself in the mental realm. The physical dimension will dissolve, and I'll be able to find my dad just by thinking about him."

"That's, um…" Maeryn hesitated. "That's worse. That idea is *so much worse* than what I thought you were doing. You do realize that—"

"—that my mind can get lost and never make it back to my body?" asked Kaija. "I'll become a dislodged consciousness, drifting through people's memories, dreams, and ideas for all eternity until I forget who and what I am? Trust me, this wasn't my first choice."

"But—"

Kaija shot her a fiery look. "Do you have a better option? Going to the mainland doesn't seem like such a good idea anymore, does it? Or, maybe we can just wait here and do nothing while Fain gets tortured, Kai suffocates, and the Western Blaze kills a few thousand more people with your dad's machines. Which would you prefer?"

Maeryn blinked away the tears in her eyes and just shook her head.

"Exactly," said Kaija. "So are you going to keep making this harder, or are you going to give me what I need the most right now? I need your trust, Maeryn, because I'm about to trust you with my life. If something happens while I'm gone, you'll need to defend my body. And if I get lost in there, you'll have to use our mindbridge to pull me out."

Maeryn climbed up onto the rock and wrapped her arms around Kaija.

"I don't want you to throw me into the ocean," she said, "so I won't apologize. But I will say that you're crazy to trust me so much."

"I know. But hey, look on the bright side. If I don't make it back, then you can just have two bodies. Heck, ditch yours and use mine from now on! Your brain, my muscles? You'd have it all. I mean, you're a genius, but I'm taller, in much better shape, *way* more attractive, and that's not even mentioning—"

"Okay, don't make me hope."

They forced a smile at each other, both wishing they could laugh, but both not quite finding it in them.

* * *

Kaija wasn't sure how long it took to clear her mind. Each time she felt her consciousness slipping away, the anxiety holding itself in her body would reel it back in. The weight of the worlds was upon her.

Elias's advice is what eventually let her completely disconnect. *The door to everywhere is all around you.* Gaia's stream coursed through everywhere in the physical world, but it went beyond that, flowing to mysterious places that existed only in one's mind. Kaija took in a deep breath and contemplated her surroundings.

I hear the waves, but it's only the idea of waves that I'm hearing. The idea of water crashes against the perception of rocks, vibrating the thing I have defined as air. My ears pick up the vibrations, and my mind translates the vibrations into the sound of a wave. What is the world other than how we perceive it? Everything around me is already inside me. I don't need to arrive. I'm already there.

Kaija could feel the mental realm blossoming around her. Maeryn's anxiety was a living, breathing thing, radiating a pungent sourness into the realm. Further away, Kaija could sense Jonathan York sweeping the floor of the schoolhouse, worrying about his daughter and her trip to Zedland. Beyond that: a ship full of weary passengers sailed by as they fled for the Europan Guardianship, hoping they wouldn't be turned away. Beyond that: a continent in political turmoil, and all the feelings that came with it. Beyond that: everything. An entire ocean of thoughts swirled around Kaija, and the more she allowed herself to get carried away by its currents, the more the word *beyond* felt like an abstract concept. There was no *beyond* in this place. Everything was here, and it existed both in every direction and no direction at all.

Kaija opened her inner eye, surprised to find that she was still on the shore of Monhegan Island. She looked down to see that the waves were frozen in place, but they started moving again the very instant she wondered why they *weren't* moving. Kaija had to remind herself that the water wasn't real, whatever "real" meant at this point. The surroundings were just conjured up by the collective mind of Gaia. The water was just her idea of water... or the water's idea of itself... or...

Deciding that she'd rather not think about it, Kaija stood up and walked along the rocks, leaving her body behind her. Everything she saw was identical to her memories of Monhegan Island, but that was exactly where she didn't want to be. She needed a way deeper into the mental realm.

The ocean is not an ocean. It is a river.

And just like that, the mainland was *there*, Monhegan Island and the rest of Edgardia separated only by a trickling stream of water. Her belief in the river had created a river, completely annihilating about ten stretches of the Atlas Ocean in the blink of an eye. It wouldn't be enough. Jasper could still be anywhere; he could be on the other side of the world for all she knew, or on a different world entirely. Kaija would have to continue to unlock the shackles of physical space.

"Door, please."

A door rose up from the river at her request. Kaija pushed it open, revealing one of the strangest sights of her life. What should have been the sight of a river was instead a cacophony of millions of blurry images floating through white space. Kaija knew that she could jump through the door and get a glimpse into a random person's mind, but this would risk getting lost forever. The actual river had become something not entirely unlike itself: the random thoughts of a billion people flowing past like water, threatening to drown her.

"I better go feed my skycat."

"Three right, one left, five right: click. There's one thing that's never changed."

"Where in desolation did I put my keys?"

"This dress feels so soft and pretty. I hope my wife doesn't come home soon."

Kaija listened carefully for her father's voice, but the whole *needle in a haystack* thing couldn't even encompass the enormity of the task. This was like trying to find a single drop of water in the ocean.

"Jasper Monhegan!" she called. "Father, I need you!"

A chair floated past in the white sky, twisting and morphing into a waterpig which oinked at her and swam off.

Kaija let the smallest part of her mind drift through the doorway, and it trembled under the enormous weight of the surroundings. Something immediately latched onto her, like a fish nibbling at a toe stuck in the ocean.

"Kaija?"

It was her father's voice. His presence was powerful, pushing away the noise of the mental realm around her. Kaija allowed more of herself to move through the doorway.

"Father! Where are you?"

"Kaija? I can barely hear you. Come to me! I'll help you."

Kaija pushed her entire consciousness through the doorway and floated through the air. The images around her began to evaporate as she concentrated on the sound of her father's voice. The door leading back to Monhegan Island slammed shut behind her, and then the door itself spun off into the chaos. Colors filled the white eternity, churning and painting a mountain landscape that Kaija descended upon. Jasper materialized before her, standing on the rocks of the cliff with his long hair blowing in the wind. He held Edgard's sword, which gleamed in the bright sunlight. The sound of dripping water echoed from somewhere underfoot.

"Daughter," he said. "You found me."

Kaija didn't have the words to express how she felt; she simply ran up and wrapped her arms around her father. Looking up at him, Kaija was surprised to see the coldness in his eyes.

"We need to talk about what happened," he said.

Drip.

"You didn't do it," said Kaija. "Please tell me that the vision was fake."

Jasper looked away. "As soon as I heard what was happening at the Capital, I teleported there as quickly as I could. I destroyed the machines that were about to kill Thomas, and I wanted to save him too, but…" He trailed off, looking down and meeting Kaija's eye. In that moment, Jasper appeared sadder than she had ever seen him.

Drip.

"I couldn't do it," he continued. "I couldn't bring myself to save that miserable old man. At the height of his desperation, Thomas had completely lowered his mental barricade. Secrets were spilling out of him, things that he had locked away his entire life. I found out the truth." Jasper narrowed his eyes. "Thomas conspired with the Crucifier. He stole my father's sword and handed it over to Duncan. He watched Edgard's murder. How could I save someone that took away our family?"

Jasper closed his eyes, wiping away a tear.

"It just happened, daughter," he said. "I couldn't control myself, but I don't regret it. He didn't deserve to live."

Drip.

Kaija was speechless. Her father avoided using his power at every opportunity. He wasn't a killer. And yet, Kaija asked herself what she would do in that same situation, if she was forced to confront someone who helped murder her own father. *What would she do?* Kaija had no idea, but she was afraid that she would want to watch them burn.

"I don't suppose they let you see what happened next," said Jasper. "Achak spotted me and stopped the transmission. The machines attacked, but I tore through them like they were nothing at all. Rugaru should have known to run, but he didn't. I'll give him that. He stayed to the very end."

Jasper's grip tightened on the hilt of the sword, veins popping in his biceps, and that dripping sound rang out once again. It wasn't water. For the first time, Kaija noticed that half of the sword was a deep red, blood dripping from the point and pooling on the ground next to them.

"He's dead," said Jasper. "Rugaru didn't stand a chance against me. It had to be done. People are still fleeing the continent, but they'll find out the truth soon enough. Both Edgardia and the Western Blaze have fallen in the same day. What happens next is so crucial. It will be a turning point in history. I'm sorry I couldn't talk to you sooner. We've been looking for Fain." He smiled. "I found him, Kaija. Maddox and I searched every prison until we found him. He wasn't even being guarded. Rugaru held the Western Blaze together, and now they're fleeing the continent as well."

Kaija should have been relieved, but there was so much information hitting her mind at once that her head was spinning.

"War is a horrible thing, Kaija, but it's over. I'm the new High Guardian. You can join me in the Capital. Did you make it back from Earth?"

Something about that question brushed Kaija the wrong way, but she didn't think anything else of it.

"I'm on Monhegan Island," she said.

"Did Maeryn come with you back to Gaia?"

"Yes. How did you know Maeryn was with me? How did you know we were on Earth?"

Jasper leaned in toward Kaija, putting a hand on the side of her face.

"There's a lot going on here," he said. "One thing has ended, but something else has started that I don't even understand quite yet. Just trust me. I'm going to ask you a few questions that might seem strange, but you need to answer them honestly. Okay?"

Kaija nodded.

"Does the name Allie Zeig mean anything to you?"

Kaija felt something: a tiny nudge compelling her to answer, the sort of ephemeral sensation only an experienced mentalist would be aware of.

"Yes," she said. "Allie's the spiritualist who sent me the frog. I told you about her already. Why are you asking me all of this?"

"Just trust me. Do you know where Allie is now?"

Kaija looked up at her father and saw that the sword was gone. He was holding something else in its place, something blurry. The object was transparent, and Kaija had to really focus before it began to solidify and fill with green light.

"The spiritualist stone," she said. "Where'd you get that?"

Jasper did a double take at her, visibly shaken.

"After Rugaru fell, Achak did his best," he said. "But that dirt monkey never stood a—"

Kaija turned and began running as fast as she could. This was not her father; Jasper Monhegan would never use those words.

The mountain around her began shrinking rapidly. A few seconds later, Kaija was surrounded by steep cliffs on all sides, nowhere to run. Fire erupted from the land below, the rocks in the canyon elongating into twisted spikes the size of redwoods. The world around them was transforming into something out of a nightmare. Jasper, or whoever was pretending to be Jasper, grabbed her by the neck and effortlessly lifted her off the ground. His face changed, the nose going crooked. Black tattoos of fire snaked their way up his neck. Kaija recognized him immediately as Achak of the Western Blaze. His face was plastered on wanted posters all over the mainland.

"Tell me what you know about Allie," he said. "Where is she? Does she have the flower?"

The green gem glowed in his hand, and what Kaija felt was far more than a nudge this time. She pushed back at the mental force, at the same time swinging her leg forward and kicking Achak hard in the stomach. He felt like a brick wall, and she heard a sharp crack in her toes. She looked down to see that Achak was suddenly made of stone, and the fact that this was all in her head didn't ease the throbbing pain. All of her toes felt broken, and being in the mental realm only deepened this sensation.

"Don't be tedious, girl," said Achak. "I've been manipulating this realm for decades. You talk, or I fracture your mind and scatter it to the Gaian winds. Where is Allie? Tell me!"

He reached a hand to her face, and each of his fingers began to grow and twist like tentacles. They slithered and dug themselves into her ears, and an agony exploded inside of Kaija that went far deeper than she thought possible. It was like someone had drilled a hole inside her skull and was pouring in Hydra poison.

"I don't know!" screamed Kaija. "Allie took me to a meeting of spiritualists, maybe two or three days ago. I haven't seen her since!"

"Show me," said Achak.

"I can't! Stop hurting me!"

"Visualize what you saw, or you have no idea how much worse I can make this."

Against her will, Kaija found herself imagining the spiritualist meeting. The mountain landscape around them transformed into the flowery fields of the Hellenic Guardianship. Páigus, the spiritualist leader, stood with his thunderlute in the center of a ring of followers. Achak studied Allie's face, although she seemed to get blurry as they approached. Kaija couldn't quite remember every detail, rendering certain things out-of-focus.

"Picture her hair," he said. "Did Allie have a white flower in her hair?"

"Yes," said Kaija. "I think she did."

A flower blossomed into existence over the woman's ear, and Achak reached toward it as if it were a holy object.

"The spiritualist flower..." he said. "Thank you, Kaija. We have no more need for you."

The green gem in Achak's hand began to glow brighter, and the pain inside of Kaija reached a crescendo. Memories flashed through her mind at blinding speed, each image splintering to pieces as if he were reaching inside her soul and tearing it to shreds. Kaija desperately tried to break free and return to her body, but his power had her frozen in place.

"Excuse me, sir. I seem to be lost. Could you tell me how to get to Joe's Extradimensional Diner?"

Achak's eyes went wide with confusion, and he turned to see the memory of Allie Zeig talking to them. All of the other memories were frozen solid, but this one seemed to have taken on a will of its own. Allie smiled and waved awkwardly.

"I think I should have taken a left at Eric Holland's naked at school dream," she said with an apologetic smile. "Too embarrassing to ask him for directions."

"Wha—" Achak began, but in the next instant Allie pulled the ukulele off her back and swung it through the air like a hammer. It crashed onto

Achak's head and he exploded in a cry of pain and a burst of glitter. The green gem spun in place on the ground for a moment, but then disappeared too with a tiny, less-climatic explosion of glitter.

The pain in Kaija's head vanished at once, followed quickly by the ground itself. The mental realm was cracking into pieces and swirling into a maddening kaleidoscope of nonsense.

"Whoops!" yelled Allie, her body being pulled apart and sucked off into different directions of the howling void. "Sorry!"

Kaija had been brought into this memory against her will, but it was vanishing and leaving her with nowhere to go. She felt as if she were falling up and down at the same time, her skull getting bombarded by a million contradictory thoughts. Even a minute in this place between places would surely shatter her mind.

"Maeryn!" she screamed.

The moment Kaija needed her, Maeryn's hand emerged from the chaos, reaching through a crack like it had been waiting for her all along. Kaija jumped forward, just barely grabbing ahold and getting pulled out of the mental realm with her consciousness in one piece.

Chapter Twenty-one

Don't Sneeze

Monhegan Island, Gaia

"**I was a maple tree,**" gasped Maeryn, her entire body quivering as they returned to the physical realm. "Right after I pulled you out of there, I passed through the mind of a maple tree. They have dreams, Kaija. TREES HAVE DREAMS."

Kaija shook her head a few times, not quite as shell-shocked as Maeryn, but still reeling from the experience. "Achak ambushed me in there. I didn't stand a chance. If it wasn't for the memory of Allie Zeig, he would have ripped me apart."

"Oh, that wasn't a memory. That was just me. Just Allie havin' fun."

Both Kaija and Maeryn jumped in surprise, nearly slipping and falling into the ocean. Allie Zeig was sitting on a rock right behind them, casually eating a chocolate ice cream cone.

"How long have you been here?" asked Kaija.

Allie shrugged. "Who knows? I was passing through the mental realm to get brunch. There's a hyper-reality consciousness named Joe who has a diner on the edge of the astral plane. The coffee there's simply inconceivable. Anyway, your psychic battle with Achak caused quite the disturbance. When you thought of me, it sucked my mind and body right over to yours like a magnet."

"Wait, what?" asked Maeryn. "You went to a realm of pure thought, and you *brought that ice cream cone back with you?*"

Allie studied the last of her dessert and raised an eyebrow.

"Now that you mention it, I'm not sure where I got the ice cream. Joe's soft serve machine is always broken. The origin of this waffle cone is surely something both fantastical and mysterious." Allie tossed the bottom of the cone into her mouth and smiled. "Mmm. Fantastical and mysterious indeed."

She slid off the rock and patted her hands together. "Whelp, Rugaru should be here soon. May as well see what he wants. Rule the world, blow up the world: it's always one of the two with these evil people."

Allie strolled off toward the flower meadow without another word. Kaija and Maeryn gave an alarmed look to each other before jumping up and chasing after the spiritualist.

"If Rugaru's really coming, then we need to be going!" shouted Kaija. "He's after Edgard's seven artifacts."

"Ah. Then I expect he'll be wanting my flower. Alas, he's going to get it. I've looked through a thousand possible branches, and in every single one he finds it eventually. I've been procrastinating my epic last stand, so I may as well do it somewhere pretty."

Allie stopped in the middle of the field, watching the spacialist butterflies teleporting from one flower to another. One of them landed on her nose and she smiled, going slightly cross-eyed.

"You can't just let him have it!" cried Kaija. "You have to do something!"

"Great idea!" said Allie, bending over and looking through the flowers. "Why didn't I think of that? Let's do *something*. It's just crazy enough to work. Ah-ha! Here it is."

Allie pulled a white flower out of the field and stuck it in her hair, where it began to glow warmly.

"There! I did something. Gosh, it's lucky I landed here on Monhegan Island. Can you imagine, if Rugaru came here to steal my flower, and I had to admit that I lost it?"

"Wait..." said Maeryn, catching up to them in the meadow. "*That's* the spiritualist flower? One of the most powerful seven objects in the world? You just left it in a random field?"

"Seemed like a good idea at the time."

"If you know that Rugaru's coming to steal it, THEN PUT IT BACK!"

Allie grimaced. "If I do that, he'll capture us with his machines and torture us horribly until I tell him where it is. I'm kind of a wimp when it comes to getting my fingernails pulled out. It seems that we must lose this battle to win the next."

The colorful flickerflies drifted up from the flowers and swirled around in a circle overhead. They looked similar to butterflies, but every few seconds their images would flicker in and out of existence.

"My lack of urgency tends to trouble normies like you," said Allie. "But there's something you have to understand about spiritualism. Trying to use your knowledge of the future to drastically alter that future creates a splintering of time's branches. Two new pathways will open up in my mind, but they'll be foggier, harder to see clearly. If I try to look down those new branches, they'll splinter again and turn into four new pathways. If I try to observe those, you can probably guess what would happen.

"Eight," said Maeryn.

"No," said Allie. "My head explodes. So, I find it's best to go where the wind takes me."

She studied the concern on Kaija and Maeryn's faces.

"Don't you little frost flowers worry! I have a super-duper secret plan to save the world from being ruled and/or blown up. I'm going to change something so small, so insignificant and downright *stupid,* that even the Tree itself won't see it coming. But that one little thing might just be enough to—" She stopped, frowning. "Uh-oh. Just me saying that created a branch where the fate of the universe hinges upon the appetite of a caterpillar. See? That's why you don't mess with time."

Allie paused and sniffed the air a few times.

"Man musk and wet concrete. Rugaru's coming. Whatever you do, whatever you see, whatever happens: don't sneeze."

She snapped her fingers and pollen puffed out of the flowers underfoot. The air around Kaija and Maeryn took on a smeared, golden sheen, and everything beyond them suddenly looked like they were seeing it through a thick window.

Rugaru appeared in the meadow with a sharp pop, holding Edgard's sword in his remaining hand. He scanned the surroundings, his eyes moving past Kaija and Maeryn without a second glance before locking onto the flower on Allie's ear.

"What just happened?" thought Kaija.

"I think Allie made us invisible," Maeryn thought back. She sniffed. *"This is a really bad time for me to be covered in pollen."*

"Don't you dare sneeze!"

Maeryn crinkled her nose. *"I'm trying! I have allergies!"*

"Stop having allergies!"

Rugaru pointed the sword at Allie, who was currently following the flickerflies around in a circle and pretending not to notice him.

"Allie," said Rugaru. "I didn't expect to see you here, but I've heard that you excel in the unexpected. Where is Kaija?"

Allie picked another flower and smelled it. "Oh, she was here a second ago. Her spacialism is getting stronger, and I told her you were coming. All it took was a little pop for her to escape."

Rugaru furrowed his brow in concentration.

"Oh, don't bother trying to track her," said Allie. "The flickerflies have created a million tiny doors in this field, and she could have gone through any one of them."

Rugaru laughed and waved a hand dismissively.

"Kaija will come to us of her own free will soon enough. It is a happy accident that I should meet you here, though. Give me the Spiritualist Flower and I won't hurt you."

"Nah," said Allie, catching a flickerfly on her finger. "This is my McGuffin. And if I'm being honest, I'd love to see you try and hurt me."

Rugaru grunted and gripped the sword tight in his hands. The weapon glowed, filling the air with waves of heat. "This is a mistake. Even a relayer such as yourself is not prepared to face this kind of power."

Allie snorted. "For such a big, strong man, it sure was easy to wound your ego. I can count at least fifty relayers in this very field that are more impressive than you."

The flickerfly on Allie's finger disappeared, reappearing in front of Rugaru's face a second later. He tried to swipe it away, but it vanished just as his arm passed through.

"Watch and learn," said Allie, holding up a tiny, white flower petal. She let go, and the petal was carried off into the wind for a moment, only to be caught by a flickerfly. The insect vanished.

"Flickerflies cross-pollinate thousands of fields all across Gaia," said Allie. "They teleport so rapidly, that it's almost like they exist everywhere at once. By the time that petal hits the ground, it could be anywhere in the world."

Rugaru inched forward, taking a fighting position.

"He's nervous," thought Kaija. *"Just a little bit, but I can feel it."*

Maeryn looked closer to see sweat collecting on Rugaru's brow. He was far from scared, but his inability to intimidate Allie had visibly thrown him off balance.

"Well?" asked Allie, holding out her hands expectantly. "Are we going to do this? I'm waiting."

Rugaru swung his sword at Allie without warning, but at that very instant a flickerfly landed on her shoulder and she disappeared for the blink of an eye, completely avoiding the blade. He swung it again, and again she was left untouched.

"This is really, really boring," she said. "I'm a lover, not a fighter. Stop wasting my time."

Rugaru pointed the sword and flames shot out of the blade. Allie reached forward and the fire swirled together, condensing into a little, glowing ball which landed in her palm. She poked the ball with her pointer finger and it popped like a balloon.

"You're obviously not aiming to kill, Rugaru," said Allie. "Could it be that you're hesitant to murder someone whom doesn't fight back? That's very sweet of you."

Rugaru held the sword toward the sky, and the steel began to crackle with electricity. Even the air itself felt supercharged as he continued channeling in energy.

"Do you seriously want to test me?" he yelled. "I've surpassed my limits a thousand-fold with this weapon. I can reduce this entire island to blood and ashes if it be my—"

And that's when Kaija sneezed. Maeryn shot her a look and mouthed *really? You?*

Rugaru spun in their direction, pointed the sword, and a streak of energy burst from the point of the blade. It collided with the sparkling pollen surrounding Kaija and Maeryn, somehow bouncing right back off and into the sky. The pollen blackened and dissolved, leaving them totally exposed.

"YOU!" screamed Rugaru.

Kaija grabbed Maeryn's hand and tried to teleport them away, but something changed just as the sensation fizzled through their bodies. The air became stickier, pulling them back into the meadow. Rugaru's silvery eyes never left them, and Kaija knew that it was him: he was grabbing ahold of the door to everywhere and slamming it shut every time she tried to teleport. A more experienced spacialist might be able to sneak by, but this was all very new to Kaija.

Rugaru pointed the sword at them, and it once more began to fill with energy. Allie seemed to become a different person in that moment; she charged toward Rugaru, pulling the ukulele off her back and spinning it like a weapon. Rugaru dodged the attack, thrusting the sword backwards and striking her hard in the face with its hilt. Allie collapsed to the ground with a sharp *crack* and a spray of blood from her nose. Rugaru leapt on top of her, putting a foot on her chest and pressing down with all his immense weight.

"Finally," muttered Rugaru, reaching down and effortlessly plucking the glowing flower from behind Allie's ear. "One more to go."

Maeryn reached forward in desperation, feeling for the flower with her mind and tugging at it with all her might. It slipped out of Rugaru's grasp and soared at them, but he teleported forward and easily snatched it out of the air. He narrowed his eyes and it disappeared without a trace.

"Good luck finding it now," he said.

Rugaru may have been hesitant during his battle with Allie, but now the sensation of raw anger filled the mental realm, hot and overpowering. Just as he moved for them, heavy winds began roaring through the field. The patch of flowers turned a lifeless gray as the color itself seemed to detach from their petals and get carried up into the wind. The entire world became an abstract painting in motion, colors swirling and mixing together all around before transforming into familiar images. Maeryn and Kaija were now surrounded by hundreds more Maeryns and Kaijas made of nothing but color in the churning cloud. Many of them warped and stretched in the wind as they moved from one place to another. It was like being in a house of mirrors, but the mirrors were spinning around you.

Rugaru darted around, swinging his sword and teleporting, but both Maeryn and Kaija had already spread out in the cloud of colors. Their painted reflections would burst apart when he slashed at them, quickly reforming into even more images.

Allie's voice spoke from somewhere in the cloud as Rugaru continued to search for Maeryn and Kaija. "You had so many chances to strike me down for good, but you didn't. You're used to people seeing you as a monster, so that's all you think you can be. But I know that if there wasn't anything more than fear and anger inside of you, I would be dead by now. I scare you more than anyone in the world, not because I'm stronger, but because I see you. And you know who else does?"

The colors swooped back to the ground, returning to the flowers and revealing the scene before them. Allie was back on her feet, her entire face swelling with bruises. Rugaru was there too, but they didn't recognize him at first due to the fact that he was covered from head to foot in hundreds upon hundreds of flickerflies. The sword disappeared out of his hands with a tiny pop, reappearing in Allie's grasp. She held up the weapon triumphantly and spit out a mouthful of blood.

"Gross," she said. "I need more ice cream."

Rugaru let out a shout and began flickering in and out of existence so rapidly that it was hard to look at. Occasionally his arrival would come with a flurry of snow, water, leaves, or ash that spun through the air.

Allie approached Maeryn and Kaija, holding the sword limply at her side and sighing contentedly.

"Beautiful, isn't it?" she asked. "They're trying to teleport him in a hundred directions at once. He'll be stuck like this for a few hours, but it could be worse. A lesser relayer would have been ripped into countless bloody pieces by now."

"That was amazing!" said Kaija. "Was that all part of your plan? To lose the flower, but get the sword back?"

"Nope," said Allie. "That was just a happy accident. Who did that cool thing with the flowers? I wasn't expecting that."

"I thought you did it," said Maeryn.

Johnathan York called out to them from beyond the meadow as he approached. "I did it. That was Rugaru, wasn't it? I heard yelling, and I wanted to do whatever I could to help these girls." He did a double-take at Allie. "And you're the spiritualist knight who's been missing!"

"The jaded artist jumps in and saves the day," said Allie thoughtfully, as if to herself, "giving me enough time to rally the flickerflies and recover the sword. Most unlikely of all, Rugaru doesn't throw the artist into a volcano." She shook her head in disbelief. "The branches are already twisting in unpredictable ways. Someone's been messing with the natural growth of time."

She whistled, and the flickerflies started circling overhead again. "I must go alert the Spiritualist Circle at once, so this is where we part. In the meantime, the flickerflies are offering you their assistance."

One of them fluttered over to Johnathan, landed on his head, and he disappeared before he could put up a protest. Another two landed on Maeryn and Kaija's shoulders.

"Can they take us to Fain?" asked Kaija. "Or my father? Or back to Earth?"

Allie shook her head. "The flickerflies cannot be guided. They will simply sense where you need to be the most at this moment. Goodbye, frost flowers." She turned and walked away through the meadow.

"Wait!" Kaija called out, reaching for her. "Can we have the sword?"

Allie stopped in her tracks, and when she turned around her smile was completely gone. "What did you say?"

"The sword," said Kaija. "Can we have it?"

Allie's eyes narrowed. "And why's that?"

"So I can return it to its owner. Until then, it can keep us safe."

Allie spoke more seriously than the girls had ever heard her. "This sword was forged by The Gardener, the most powerful spiritualist of all time. It senses the biggest divisions along time's branches, rising in strength as they approach. He believed that its power could be used to exert one's will on the Tree's growth, to shear off the branches that lead to Desolation. What do you think? Do you believe it?"

"Believe what?"

"That raw strength is the force that shapes the future?"

Kaija thought for a second, but was getting impatient. "I don't know! But look at us! Look at what we're up against!"

Allie stared down at the blade for an uncomfortably long silence, brow furrowed in concentration while she whispered nearly inaudible things under her breath.

"There it is..." she whispered. "I... I see where things are going now." Allie looked up at them, her eyes inexplicably full of tears. She held up the sword, her grip now trebling, and Kaija took it from her.

"What's wrong?" she asked.

"Oh, nothing," said Allie. "I'm just remembering a song." She wiped a tear. "You are loved, frost flowers. But don't forget to be wise. I'll see you again on Twenty Butt Hill."

And with a single flutter of the flickerfly's wings, Allie was gone.

Chapter Twenty-two

A Second Singularity

The Big Canyon, Gaia

A massive canyon lined the horizon. The setting sun cast shadows the size of cities across its rocky depths. Maeryn and Kaija appeared alongside one of the ledges and the flickerflies scurried away from them, disappearing into the twilight.

"Is this…" asked Maeryn, peering all around them. "Is this Earth?"

"No," said Kaija. "I can still feel Gaia."

"But that looks like the Grand Canyon. What do you call the Grand Canyon on Gaia?"

"The Big Canyon."

"Really? That's disappointing. Why would we be needed at the Big Canyon?"

As if on command, a sonic boom echoed from the distance, followed by a whistling sound as something shot through the air, leaving a smoking crater when it collided with a boulder right next to Maeryn. She screamed and leapt out of the way as rubble showered over them. Kaija walked to the edge of the smoking hole and looked in.

"Max?"

A little, chrome figure pulled itself out of the smoking crater. Max stood there for a second, staring at Maeryn and Kaija as smoke wafted off his charred body. Maeryn gasped in relief and ran for him.

"Don't!" yelled Max, holding up a hand. "I'm 700 degrees right now."

Maeryn stopped, and Max began to levitate back into the air.

"Where have you been?" asked Maeryn.

He didn't respond for a few seconds, simply floating over to the edge of the canyon and scanning the distance. When Max finally spoke, his voice sounded uncharacteristically weary. "You shouldn't have come here. Leave, and don't come back. I'll find you when I'm done."

Before Maeryn could say another word, Max morphed into a ball and rocketed off into the distance.

Kaija looked at Maeryn. "What was that about?"

"I don't know. He wasn't himself. There was something wrong."

A bright light flashed on the horizon, followed by another sonic boom as Max's body spun through the air back to them, skidding along the ledge and leaving a black skid mark. He took a few wobbly steps to the edge of the cliff and just sat there, unresponsive.

"Max?" asked Maeryn, running over to him. "What just happened?"

Max didn't seem to be paying attention. He tapped his fingers on the rocks anxiously, whispering calculations under his breath too quickly for Maeryn to make sense of.

".0045% chance of success within the first 30 seconds, .000067% chance within the first minute. Continues decreasing at an exponential rate per second. At 1,440 attempts a day, ignoring inevitable variables and gradually decaying core processor, chances of success occurring within a natural human lifetime are less than—"

"Max!" yelled Maeryn. "Talk to me!"

He looked up slowly and shook his head. "I can't do it, Maeryn. I can't save them. They're in the caves, in this huge underground facility, but I get within a mile of the place and I'm swarmed by Angels."

He screamed and hammered a fist on the ground, leaving a crack in the earth.

"Is that where we were?" asked Maeryn. "When we took the portal to Gaia? We were down there, in those caves?"

Max nodded. "Yes. I stayed behind to rescue Fain. It didn't take long to map the place out and find the prison wing, but the Angels attacked me. Vaporized me in seconds. I haven't been able to make it back in. They just keep coming."

Kaija bent down to him. "And you've been trying to fight them ever since we left?"

Max's whole body trembled. "Again, and again, and again, and... and I can't save them. *I can't.*"

Maeryn reached over and held his little hand. "Max, I understand that things look bleak right now, but—"

He pulled his hand away and screamed at her. "Understand? You could never understand! NOBODY WILL EVER UNDERSTAND WHAT IT'S LIKE TO BE ME! You, and Kaija, and Fain... none of you are like me. You look at me, and you see something that can withstand a nuclear blast. I look at all of you, and I see the only things I care about slowly dying. I hear your heartbeats, counting down the seconds until I face the rest of eternity without you. You couldn't possibly know what it's like to love something so fragile."

Maeryn was too stunned at his outburst to speak, but Kaija pushed past her. She lifted Max off the ground and held him close as he sobbed.

"I might not know exactly how you feel," she said, "but after they took Fain, I felt weak and powerless. It's been killing me. Every second I feel like this, it kills me a little more, and it never gets easier. Thank you for trying to save him, even if you knew it was impossible. We love you."

Max didn't respond.

"You keep referring to *them*," said Maeryn. "Is someone down there other than Fain."

"There's so much you don't know," said Max. "You didn't see what I saw. When I was in there, I, I…" He paused. "I can't even say it. Just watch. You'll see."

Max projected a holographic image into the air in front of them, showing a dark hallway lined with prison cells. Most of them were empty, but the camera zoomed in to a cell that held two prisoners. The first was undeniably Fain. He was unconscious, both arms shackled to the wall and his head hanging limply to the side. His leg was heavily bandaged with a large blood stain soaking through. Kaija let out a gasp and reached for him, her hand passing through the hologram.

It was the second prisoner that held Maeryn's attention. They were nearly unrecognizable: skeletal and obviously starved to the very edge of death, blonde hair dirty and matted, and visible skin full of cuts and bruises. Maeryn felt like she had been punched in the stomach. Here they were: the person her father had spent nearly a year searching for, in the last place they would have ever thought to look.

Rosalie.

* * *

"Twelve minutes," said Rosalie, voice hoarse and weary. She didn't even glance up at Max as he floated toward her cell. "Twelve minutes until the Angels find you."

Fain responded to the sudden noise with a grunt, his head rolling around on his shoulders, but his eyes only blinking open for a brief second.

"He's been slipping in and out for a while now," Rosalie explained. "Infection is spreading. Healers saw him a few days ago, but they don't seem to be trying too hard."

"Rosalie," said Max. "I've got to get you both out of here."

She tugged at the chains hooked to her wrist and laughed hopelessly. "Internalist steel. Same as the prison bars. Are you going to carry my body out in pieces?"

"I can't leave you here.

Rosalie held up a hand to silence him.

"Eleven minutes and forty seconds now. Let me speak, Max, while I still can. The entire future is hanging on this very moment."

She glanced up for the first time, her eyes hollow and bloodshot.

"You are wondering how I ended up here. It must have been about a year ago, when Jasper came to Earth. I watched my greatest fear unfold, the very thing my father warned me about: the Gaians had built a bridge to Earth, built stone by stone inside the mind of my niece, no less. Despite my greatest efforts, I had failed to keep them away. But the moment wasn't what I had expected. There was no army of living weapons banging at the walls of Earth. All I saw were two weary travelers, coming to us to heal a broken family, pleading with the very people they had every reason to hate. My brother offered them his kindness, and, and..."

She clenched her dirty fists.

"...and I saw myself for the first time. It was me: I was the living weapon to cower from, not the Gaians. My whole life, I'd been following a big lie."

Rosalie stared directly into the camera, seeming to look at Kaija despite the fact that this was a recording.

"I can see you watching us, Kaija. Does it make you happy to hear those words? I was wrong. *I was so wrong*, and I've suffered for it."

"You're delirious," said Max. "Listen to me, we have to—"

"No, you listen to me," Rosalie interrupted. "You need to understand why I'm here before you can understand what happens next."

She pulled her feet in toward herself, hugging her trebling legs as she recounted her journey.

"The day the bridge was built, I felt Gaia calling to me through the portal. I followed it, leaving Earth without a word of goodbye while Dorian was still healing Jasper. I came here to see the world my father was born in, the world he tried to save."

Rosalie laughed bitterly.

"My first glimpse of Gaia was living proof that he failed. I saw a battle being waged outside the Capital walls. The Crucifier did not create a peaceful world, just a power vacuum to be filled by the next tyrant. I ran from the campsite and got as far away from the chaos as I could. Using my father's journal and the MotherTech gear that I brought along with me, I explored every corner of this new land. It was beautiful. It was nothing to be feared.

"The terrible irony of it all was that my body would not allow me to relay Gaia's energy. It was as if she could sense my previous treachery and refused to let me make use of the endless spring of power. I decided to go searching for my father's birthplace, to find our distant relatives on Gaia. I took a telestation to the Europan Guardianship, but the search proved to be in vain. The town of Kacey had long ago changed its name to avoid any association with Duncan the Crucifier. Nobody would speak to me about the Kacey lineage, and it became increasingly clear that this was a world I was not welcome in.

"*What next,* I wondered? I have no place on Earth, and no place on Gaia, so *what comes next?* This is the question that unlocked my relaying pathway for the first time. I had been looking in the wrong places, gazing backward instead of forward. I was... no, I *am,* and will always be, a spiritualist."

Rosalie's eyes rolled up in her head, becoming cloudier and cloudier until nothing remained but a churning white fog. When she spoke again, her voice was cold and detached, as if forming words against her will.

"My powers are both enormous and uncontrollable. That very first time I relayed, my mind seemed to become one with Gaia. I saw *everything:* the beginning of time, the end of time, and the labyrinth of branches between the two. It began with a singularity: an infinitely dense point of mass that burst apart to form the universe. I saw solar systems being birthed into space, galaxies spreading apart amidst the afterbirth... a reality that is both infinite and ever expanding. I saw confirmations of everything that Earth's scientists had theorized, but I also saw things that they never dreamed of. I saw the Second Singularity.

"Planets gave rise to living beings, and consciousness evolved. Creatures could now perceive the very universe they inhabited. The mind's perception of the universe created another layer in reality: thoughts literally shaping the physical world around these conscious beings. This realm of the mind began as its own singularity, as one shared perception of reality, but it too soon fractured apart. One possible reality became many, and those many became many more still. Countless realities breaking apart, spreading out forever in the vastness of, of..."

Her body twitched, and the clouds in her eyes swirled faster.

"...we have no word for it here. I speak of the void between realities, the blackness of space that is not space. Some realities spin off forever through the void, becoming unreachable and alien to us here. Others collide, annihilating entire worlds and everything in them. Others still revolve around each other, pulled together through some mysterious gravity. This is what has happened with Earth and Gaia. But there is one place unique to all others, one reality that navigates the void like a predator at sea. Searching, consuming…"

Rosalie's eyes began transforming from cloudy white to a thunderous black, like her very soul was filling with storm clouds. She was convulsing, spitting out every word like it hurt her.

"We call it Desolation! It searches for us. It comes closer by the day. It will devour both worlds, and return to the void even stronger, never stopping until everything has been made into nothing, until there is only itself and the void. Our final chance to escape it is only a branch away."

With one final convulsion, the blackness swam out of Rosalie's eyes. She looked around the cell, disoriented, and once more fixed her gaze on Max.

"It happened again," she whispered, voice haggard beyond description. "I've been disappearing into my visions. I can't control them."

Max simply nodded, his massive mind finding absolutely no response to this situation.

"The first time it happened, I was contacted by a group that called themselves the Spiritualist Circle. They map out the possible futures, subtly guiding Gaia away from Desolation. I told them what I saw, and they demanded that I not intervene, leaving me without another word of explanation. The only thing left to do was head to Edgardia and find Jasper, to beg for help to get home. We needed to unite and prepare ourselves for what was coming. On the road to Monhegan Island, I ended up in a village that was attacked by the Western Blaze, and I used my MotherTech weapons to fight them off. Word must have gotten around about the miracle weapons I had, because they came back for me with an army. I was kidnapped, the technology stripped from me, and thrown into this prison.

"Rugaru wanted me to show him how my technology worked, but I refused. They, they..." She hesitated, choking back a sob. "They *tortured* me, Max. But I stayed strong. Eventually they brought in Achak to scour my mind. I couldn't resist him. I tried. I *tried so hard.* He reached into my head and ripped out what he wanted, piece by piece. He had me build machines that could scout Edgard's artifacts, and then we used those artifacts to pierce the veil between worlds. He looked through my memories of Earth, taking whatever he wanted from my past and using it to expand their army. Nothing was sacred. I endured eight months of this torture."

Rosalie coughed, shaking her head to stay alert.

"They're building something with the artifacts. Something that I don't quite understand yet. A weapon." Her eyes darted around the hallway. "Thirty more seconds, Max. There is a single path that will allow us to avoid Desolation's eyes. Duncan was right about one thing: a war between both worlds is coming. The Western Blaze will not stop with its domination of Gaia, but the chaos they sow will act as a beacon for Desolation. We need to stop the war before it has started. I've programmed a deactivation code in the Angels. Find a way to get me out, take me to the control panel, and I can take down their entire army in less than a minute."

"How do I get you out of here?" asked Max.

Rosalie's eyes clouded over again for a brief second.

"You have to fail before you succeed."

"Rosalie..." said Max, floating closer to the cell and reaching for her. The instant his hand moved between the bars, an alarm began blaring overhead.

"Huh," said Rosalie. "So that's how it happens. It was good to see you again, Max, but our time is up."

The hallway filled with the sound of pops as dozens of Guardian Angels appeared, all launching toward Max in the same moment. One of them shot a beam of energy from its hand, instantly colliding with Max and destroying the bonds that held his nanobots together. His shell fractured into hundreds of pieces, shifting the scale of how Max saw the room. Each Angel became an enormous leviathan, and the hallway looked to be a vast battlefield. Max fought back the best he could, each of his variations zooming around and analyzing the movements of his attackers.

Another array of energy blasts fractured Max's body into more and more pieces. The Angels shared a hive mind, and more of them meant that the threat was now greater than the sum of its parts. Tiny clumps of Max's nanobots flew at the attacking shapes that now looked to be the size of mountains. More beams of energy collided with the many Maxes, breaking him down to his very smallest pieces. The hallway grew to the size of a solar system. There was no way the Angels could still track him down at this level, right? Right? The precision of the blasts would have to be astronomically advanced.

Two red lights lit up overhead, eyes that loomed over him like blazing suns. A thin beam of light shot through the observable universe, and Max felt a single nanobot from his core processor get struck down. The tiniest fraction of his connection to Gaia dissolved away to nothing. This had never happened before. Max had never even considered the possibility that something could keep breaking him down until there was nothing left at all.

He was many: he was a cloud of Maxes spread too thin to even count themselves, he was the greatest technological achievement of mankind, but in this moment, every single Max was running for his life.

Chapter Twenty-three

Not a Cave

The Big Canyon, Gaia

"Here's another one," said Kaija. "I teleport us back into the cave, right at the spot we arrived on Gaia. We take the portal back to Earth and use Edgard's sword to free Kai. He helps us destroy the Guardian Angels and break Fain and Rosalie out of the prison. Then we find my father, wherever he is. At some point we figure out how to get Dorian out of Earth jail, with a, uh… what did you call it?"

Maeryn sat off to the side, deep in thought as she passed Edgard's sword back and forth from one hand to another, listening to Max shoot down each of Kaija's plans.

"A lawyer," Maeryn muttered.

"Yeah, that," said Kaija. "So, we do all those things, and then we get, uh… a lawyer. Will it work?"

"Where do I start?" asked Max. "First of all, the Western Blaze knows that you've been there, and they know that you can teleport back in at any time. If they haven't moved the portal already, I'll buy a hat and eat it. I've already been down these same lines of thinking, Kaija."

"If they know I can teleport back in, then why haven't they moved the prisoners?"

"Two possibilities. It's either the unfathomable depths of human stupidity, or the much more obvious reason that Rosalie and Fain are nothing but bait. They want us to go running in to save the day, only to get blasted to smithereens by a Guardian Angel."

Kaija grunted in frustration. "How about this? No plan at all. I teleport us in, and we face whatever's waiting for us. We just do our best."

This seemed to catch Max off guard. He thought it over for a few seconds.

"You have to fail before you succeed..." he whispered. "That's the last thing Rosalie said to me. Your whole *no plan* plan is just stupid enough to fail." He shook his head. "Wait? What am I saying? No! Heck no!"

"Why not? We don't have time to just sit around and wait. If the worst happens, then at least we tried."

"The worst? Ha! You know how in movies, someone always asks, *what's the worst that could happen*? I've been over a million scenarios, asking myself that very question. Here's the worst thing that could happen: we teleport in, and the Guardian Angels are waiting for us, just like I predicted. I watch both of you die a horrible death. The Western Blaze takes the sword and finishes building their ultimate death ray, or whatever it is they're collecting the artifacts for. They conquer Gaia, and then turn their sights on Earth. A war of the worlds breaks out, attracting Desolation from across the void. Both realities get consumed, and the entire multiverse becomes a Lovecraftian hellscape for all eternity. You know what doesn't happen in this worst-case scenario? I don't die. I'm there to see it all, to grow old and retire to wherever Florida is in this situation, watching the infinitesimal cosmos around me rot away to nothing, because I guarantee you that somewhere in the darkest timeline, Florida will still be there."

"Yah!"

Without warning, Maeryn leapt through the air, swinging Edgard's sword and crying out as she relayed with everything in her. A flash of blue lit up the world for a second, and the very next second Maeryn was flat on her back, panting for air.

"I…" she heaved. "I thought… I thought… Gaia! I can't breathe!"

"Hm," said Max. "You thought that you might cut an opening back to Earth, so we can bypass the killer robots and head straight to Kai?"

Maeryn gave another pained gasp and nodded.

"Yeah," said Max. "I had a feeling you might try that, and it happened just as I predicted. Without Kaija on the other side for you to lock onto, and the sword growing in strength as time's branches begin to divide, and your inexperienced butt not knowing what it's doing, the power absolutely overwhelmed you. Your heart stopped for a solid three seconds."

Kaija reached for the fallen sword.

"Ever the optimist, now Kaija's going to try," Max narrated, "melting the flesh off her hand in the process. Either that, or the Big Canyon's about to get a whole lot bigger."

Kaija pulled her hand away. With a grunt, Maeryn sat up and rubbed her forehead, her skin a sickly pale.

"Kaija's right," she said. "We need to just go in and do our best."

"Seriously?" asked Max.

"Seriously?" asked Kaija a second later.

Maeryn nodded. "I keep thinking about that divide in the branches that the spiritualists talked about, where history will go one way or the other. Maybe it's not really a specific decision that will make the difference. Maybe it's just… I don't know, maybe it's the decisiveness itself that matters. If we sit around and keep waiting for the perfect opportunity to present itself, or for someone else to come along and fix all the problems for us, then it's already too late, isn't it? I can't do that anymore. That's what I've done my whole life, and look at where we are now. But if we make it to Fain and Rosalie, and we still fail, then… then at least we were all together one last time."

The sun began to sink into the canyon, and the three of them watched in silence for a few minutes, no noise except for wind blowing past the rocks. Kaija scooted in next to Maeryn, putting her head on her shoulder. Max floated over and landed on Maeryn's other side. They didn't need to speak, because they all knew what the others were thinking.

The conflict was all around them now, pressing in on every side. They'd have no chance to jump into the fire sooner or later. Maybe this was it: the final moment of nothing but whispering winds and a setting sun. Nothing but each other, huddled together in a world that still existed, for now.

* * *

The cave was absolutely pitch black, and they remained motionless for a second, unsure of what might be waiting for them in that darkness. Max's voice spoke from somewhere nearby.

"Where'd you take us? This isn't right."

"What do you mean?" asked Kaija. "I teleported us back to the cave. It's just dark, like before."

"It's not like before at all. This isn't dark, this is *Dark 2000: The Darkening*. My night vision isn't seeing past a foot or two."

A tiny light began to glow from Max's hand, but it barely illuminated anything beyond the three of them. The light itself seemed to get swallowed up by the inky blackness.

"It feels different than before, too," said Maeryn. "The air is stickier. And it smells."

Kaija sniffed and let out a low groan; Maeryn was right. The cave now had the faint scent of rotten eggs, and the air was as humid as a rainforest. Every second or two a warm gust of wind would blow past them, carrying that awful, acidic smell, and then the air would get sucked back in the direction it came from. It didn't make any sense. Kaija couldn't have teleported somewhere they've never been before; this must have been a deeper part of the cave. Was it possible for a spacialist to overshoot their intended destination? Ms. Clara never made it this far in her lessons, so Kaija didn't know.

Max clapped his hands a few times, and Maeryn shushed him.

"Echo location," Max explained. "I got the idea from that dog bat we saw the last time we were here. Remember the dog bat, Maeryn? Wasn't it cute?" He clapped again. "Huh. We're still in a cave, but it doesn't match anything from the maps I made. The pattern of stalactites and stalagmites is too different. I don't understand this." One final clap. "Impossible."

"What?" asked Maeryn.

"They're too perfect," said Max. "All lined up in perfectly parallel rows on the floor and ceiling. This is not a pattern that could happen in nature, unless…"

Without warning, Max zoomed off into the dark, his voice calling back to them.

"There's a blue light up ahead! It might be the portal!"

Maeryn shot a panicked look to Kaija.

"I don't like this," she said. "Does this all feel wrong to you? Just now, I was trying to think of how we got here, and I couldn't picture it."

"I teleported us here."

"When?"

Kaija thought about it, and her mind hit a brick wall. The last she remembered, they were sitting together at the Big Canyon, trying to enjoy the last few quiet seconds together before running head first into battle. The idea that Kaija had teleported them here made sense, but only in the abstract. She was holding hands with Maeryn and Max, trying to put in a brave face, drawing in Gaia's power, disappearing, and then what? She reappeared in this dark place, but there was something before that, something unreachable in her memory. It didn't feel right. There was a gap between the moment she teleported and the moment they appeared here, like a cutaway from one scene to another in a movie.

"Are we dreaming?" asked Kaija.

Maeryn shook her head. "Could *you* have fallen asleep, even if you wanted to?"

No. No way in Desolation. Kaija had been confronting the very real possibility that she might be dead within the hour, and that didn't seem like an ideal moment to take a nap.

"But if we're not dreaming," asked Kaija. "Then what is this?"

Max's voice suddenly began echoing from the distance. "Maeryn! Kaija! Get out of there! Get out of there *now*! It's not a cave! It's a—"

Just like that, his voice went silent. Maeryn stumbled toward his calls, her footsteps ringing out as damp squishes. The soft texture of the ground must have thrown her off balance, because Maeryn fell forward, disappearing into the omni-present darkness. Kaija felt a gust of wind as something slithered by with impossible speed. Next: a wet slap, a scream, and Maeryn's voice inexplicably went from close by to far away in a single second. Her body had been sucked into the distance by something Kaija couldn't begin to fathom.

"IT'S GOT ME!"

Maeryn's call resonated from somewhere far below, and then it too disappeared. Kaija reached out for her, grasping at their mindbridge, but it too felt oddly distant. She caught a glimpse of something out of Maeryn's eyes, something totally unlike the surrounding darkness, so brief that she barely had time to register what it was. All she could remember was a tiny flash of green light and two figures floating through the air.

A low rumble echoed from underneath, and Kaija didn't at all like what the sound reminded her of. The entire cave began to tilt, moving until the room was on its side, immediately knocking her off her feet. She slid downward, slipping across a cave floor which was far too spongey and wet to be a cave floor. She struck a stalagmite with her head on the tumble to whatever waited below, a stalagmite which was far too smooth and curved to be a stalagmite. The air in this cave that was not a cave grew hotter and moister by the second. The pulsating walls that weren't walls closed in around her.

Kaija admitted something to herself that she would much rather not acknowledge.

This was not a cave.

Nope. Nope, nope, nope.

She wasn't sure exactly how she teleported them here, but *here* was definitely *not* a cave.

Caves didn't salivate, moan, or lean back and try and swallow you like a bug.

Kaija was in a mouth.

She was also determined not to stay in a mouth.

Screaming with revulsion, Kaija tried to scramble to her feet, but things were too disgustingly slippery to get any sense of balance. A huge, wet *thing* lashed out at her from the darkness, pushing her deeper into the narrowing throat.

It seemed likely that that wet thing larger than her entire body was a tongue, but Kaija would rather not think about it.

The surroundings pressed in on her, squeezing the air from her lungs as she was pulled further down into the esophagus. For a split second, Kaija imagined what might be in store for her next.

You know what? Being stuck inside a mouth didn't seem so bad anymore.

Kaija grabbed at the soft walls around her, digging her nails into the tissue wherever she could, pulling herself upwards with all her might. A gargantuan shriek escaped from the resonating vocal chords below, and a great big inhalation of air sucked her deeper into the beast. The scent coming from the place she was going was unfathomably awful: acidic, hot, and rotten.

Each attempt at teleportation failed instantly. Spacialism required the ability to clearly visualize any place but here, which was surprisingly hard to do when you were on the verge of being digested. Kaija opened herself up to the mental realm, trying to reach the mind of whatever was eating her and convince it to vomit her up. Their minds briefly touched, and Kaija pulled hers away reflexively upon contact. The thing's consciousness was alien and unknowable, a huge labyrinth that she could get sucked into forever.

Kaija cried out from the inside, grasping desperately for the mindbridge, and another image flashed before her eyes. Kaija was in Maeryn's body, semi-conscious on a cave floor. A deep pain throbbed in Maeryn's skull, and blood trickled from the side of her head. Kaija forced Maeryn's eyes to open a bit wider, pushing them apart with nothing but willpower.

She saw the cave: the very location she had tried to teleport to in the first place. Edgard's sword was tossed on the cave floor, just out of Maeryn's reach. Max hovered in the air before them, his body churning and morphing into random shapes against his will, each transformation bringing a shriek of pain.

Through Maeryn's eyes, Kaija saw herself hovering in the air just beyond Max, her own eyes utterly blank as she screamed and clawed at invisible things in the air. Further still, Kaija could see someone else in the cave with them, a tall silhouette with its arms outstretched. A green light flashed from the center of the dark figure.

Achak.

Kaija understood what was happening at once. This wasn't real. Achak had them trapped in a horrible illusion.

"You can't fight this."

Achak's voice echoed through Kaija's thoughts, and she felt herself get sucked back into her body as if by magnetic force, back into the nightmare. She was sinking into a hot, bubbling pool of something awful. It burned her skin, and opening her mouth to scream only brought the pain deeper inside her. She was being digested. Kaija searched desperately for the mindbridge, hidden somewhere amongst the pain and fear. She spotted it, but crossing the bridge was no longer the effortless task it used to be. Kaija had to claw her way back through, simultaneously fighting off all the awful sensations filling her head.

Reality snapped back into place. In the cave, Achak was stepping closer, reaching out to Max's convulsing body. Something began to emerge from the churning blob of nanobots, pulling itself apart from Max slowly, laboriously. Kaija didn't understand what she was seeing. A gleaming, silver circle was emerging from Max and drifting toward Achak's open hand.

Maeryn moaned in pain, and even this miniscule sensation was enough to knock Kaija off balance. Her mind was thrown unwillingly back into its body, back into a nightmare she could have never dreamt up for herself in a million cycles. She was further down into the beast, getting pulled through Gaia knows what, her body nothing but a skeleton at this point, flesh having melted away between one blink and the next.

This wasn't real, this was worse. In real life she would have suffocated by now, and it would mercifully be over. But no, Achak could keep her here forever, her mind getting eaten and broken apart in a never-ending circle, trapped in whatever impossible scenario this twisted man could dream up for Kaija.

Kaija screamed and flailed her bones. Achak's laughter rang from all around her.

"You think so much of yourself. A prodigy. A girl who learns all her quaint mentalist lessons with ease. It's only now that you see you're nothing but a scared child, hardly a relayer at all. Against me, you are an ant trying to move a mountain."

He was right. Kaija knew it with everything in her, but in that moment she also knew that Achak had overlooked an absolutely crucial point. Kaija might be a relayer with much to learn, a mentalist whose abilities were utterly dwarfed by Achak's, but she was so much more than that. She was a miracle in nature; there was something inside of her unique to almost everyone in the universe.

Unlike Achak, Kaija was more than just herself.

She sent herself over the mindbridge, bringing Maeryn's body back from the brink of unconsciousness. Maeryn's mind was in there somewhere, shrouded in fog from a recent blow to the head. Kaija clutched at it, pushing the fog away.

"Kaija?"

Kaija could never quite describe what happened next. Maeryn came back, and for an instant they were both seeing things through her eyes. Kaija felt her mind getting pulled back to Achak's nightmare, but a part of Maeryn came with her. Oddly enough, a part of Kaija also stayed behind. It was like both of them were in both places at once. Kaija could feel Maeryn's relaying pathways available to her, and vice versa. Maeryn felt the strength of Kaija's courage, and Kaija felt her mind moving with Maeryn's sharp precision.

Maeryn reached out, and the sword flew into her hands. Without thinking, she tossed it into the air and teleported across the cave over to Achak, kicking his legs out from under him before he could react. In the same instant, Kaija burst out of her mental cage, decimating the giant creature around her and emerging back into the real world. She caught her grandfather's sword out of the air, swinging it at Achak. The tip barely missed his throat, but that wasn't what she was aiming for. In a single slash, she broke the string around his neck, dropping the Mentalist Stone to the cave floor. Maeryn relayed it over to herself and tossed it out of reach, too deep into the cave for Achak to quickly retrieve it. The artifact's green light began to dim completely.

Achak's concentration broken, the silver ring was sucked back into Max's nanobot cloud, and his body instantly snapped back into a human figure. He examined the scene before him for a millisecond or so, processors firing at full capacity.

"I have no idea what's happening, but *okay!*" he declared.

Max split into four, transforming into shackles which wrapped around Achak's wrists and ankles, lifting the struggling man into the air. Kaija spun the sword around, pulling in what amounted to a single drop of its ocean of power, and struck him in the chest with the hilt. Achak's body was thrown backwards, striking the wall of the cave, but something else happened that Kaija couldn't have predicted. An ethereal *rip* echoed in their minds as some kind of mysterious tether began to tear between Achak's mind and body.

If Kaija really looked, letting herself peer into the mental realm, she could see a second, transparent Achak floating in the air above them. He glowed and began to drift back toward himself, chanting inaudible things under his breath. Before he could try to become one again, to repair that ephemeral tether between mind and body, both Maeryn and Kaija sprang into action. Maeryn grabbed his leg, teleporting away his body. At the same instant, Kaija held onto his mind, keeping it firmly in place. Achak went in two directions at once.

The tether snapped.

A scream resonated from the mental realm as that part of Achak dissolved into countless pieces, each soaring off and vanishing in different directions, nowhere left to go and no longer able to hold itself together.

Maeryn held out a hand, relaying the Mentalist Stone across the room, snatching it and handing it to Kaija. They looked at each other, not sure whether to laugh, or smile, or hug, or completely freak out and lose their dang minds. Between almost getting digested, existing on both ends of the mindbridge simultaneously, and full-on exploding a grow man's very soul, this had been *just a lot.*

"What just happened?" asked Max, rubbing the spot where his core processor very nearly got torn from the rest of him. "Did I…? Did we…? That cave, was it a, um… nope. You know what? Nope. I don't want to know. Nope, nope, nope."

Chapter Twenty-four

No Possible Future

The Big Canyon Caverns, Gaia

The celebration lasted all of two seconds before Max brought the reality of things crashing down upon them.

"As cool as all that was, we didn't come here to explode a guy! We came here to get Fain and Rosalie."

"Let's go!" yelled Maeryn, charging forward and immediately running head first into a wall.

"Are you okay?" asked Kaija, pulling Maeryn back to her feet.

"I think part of your brain is still inside my brain, because for a second I was seeing in two directions at once."

"Here, I'll give some *you* back to you, if you give some *me* back to me. There? Did you feel that?"

Maeryn rubbed her eyes. "I think so. Oh wait, I'm remembering something about trying to ride a sky lizard."

"Sorry, that one's my memory. I'll trade you."

Max shook his head with disgust. "Words cannot express how unsettling I find the two of you sometimes. Now, if you're done with your unholy acts of debauchery, follow me out of here. The prison wing is two miles away."

He hovered ahead of them in the cave, lighting up only the immediate surroundings. Everything was quiet and empty, painting a stark contrast to the battle that they had expected.

"I don't understand why the Angels weren't waiting for us," said Maeryn. "We wouldn't have stood a chance."

Max swerved, heading into a nearby tunnel. "I'm seeing things clearer now. The Western Blaze must not totally understand or trust the machines. The Angels are just tools to them, just a last resort. Remember the first time we came here? The portal was being guarded by a single man, not the Angels. They never thought we'd get into Freedom Tower, but they were wrong. Now they made the same mistake again. They didn't expect us to make it past Achak. Once again, I guess it all comes down to the unfathomable depths of human stupidity."

The vast, cavernous space gradually narrowed in, becoming less of a random result of nature and more of a manmade stronghold. Gas lamps were affixed to the ceiling, and the ground became a smooth walkway. Kaija knelt down and ran her hand along the surface of the path.

"Stone..." she muttered. "Good, good. It's just stone."

Max and Maeryn shot her a questioning look.

"Just making sure, it wasn't, um..." said Kaija. "You know, alive."

Max shuddered. "Things went blank after I flew out of its mouth. What happened to you two?"

"I think I was somewhere in the large intestines when I broke the illusion," said Kaija. "Maeryn went down the throat a good minute before me, though."

Max looked at Maeryn questioningly. "Maeryn, did you, um... did you go all the way through?"

Maeryn kept walking, not so much as glancing in Max's direction. "I'm just going to pretend you didn't ask me that, and kindly request that we never speak of this again."

They continued on through the maze of turns, speaking only in hushed whispers as Max calculated the safest route to the prison wing. Maeryn held out Edgard's sword protectively, while Kaija clutched the Mentalist Stone to her chest.

"Stop," Max whispered suddenly. "I'm seeing a heat signature beyond the next turn. It's a guard. What do you think we should do? Is it time to give ole' Thunder Glove another shot?"

A pop rang out from around the corner before Max could continue. "Oh... he's gone now. That was weird."

Kaija smiled and held up the Mentalist Stone, which flickered several times. "It was me."

Max gasped. "Kaija? Did you just explode another guy's soul?"

"No. I convinced him he had to pee, and he teleported away."

"You're something else, island girl. Creating false thoughts? Advanced stuff right there."

Kaija shrugged. "He kind-of had to pee already. The thought was sitting right at the top of his head. I just took that sensation and increased it a hundred-fold."

They continued in silence for several more minutes, but Max kept shooting nervous glances at Kaija.

"So..." he said finally. "I have to ask. You felt what that guy was thinking without even trying?"

"Yep."

"Could you do this with anyone?"

"Probably. I mean, a lot of thoughts don't take the shape of words, so I have to sort-of translate things. But with this stone it's pretty easy to get the general idea of whatever's right there on top."

"Huh. This sure would be a bad moment to think about your deepest, most inner shame, wouldn't it? So, let's all, um… let's all not do that. Whatever you do, don't think about the single most embarrassing thing that—gosh darn it."

Kaija gasped. "Oh, Max. Gross!"

"Do I even want to know?" asked Maeryn.

"Max has a crush on your vacuum cleaner."

Maeryn blinked. "Max. You do know that Dorian programmed everything in our house. Doesn't that make her your sister?"

"Um, no!" said Max. "First of all, artificial intelligences don't have DNA, so our family relationships are based on shared experiences and trust. *You're* my sister, Maeryn, because I grew up with you. I'm too shy to even talk to Eliza. Second of all, our consciousness is built from a vastly complex matrix of ones and zeros, far outnumbering the neural connections in the human brain, so trying to reduce my emotional attractions to a word as plebian as *crush* is unbelievably offensive."

He cleared his throat (or made a sound like a throat being cleared.) "Plus, if you could see the simplicity and elegance in Eliza's design… the way she gracefully, soundlessly glides over a variety of surfaces, picking up every single particulate of dirt and grime… and she's got these *thick* neural networks of deep learning that just, *oh man*. I'm just going to say it: it's so sexy. So troublingly sexy."

Max waited for a response, but both girls just shook their heads in disapproval.

"That isn't fair, singling me out like that," he said. "Do Maeryn now. Let's hear all about her secret shames."

Kaija shrugged in disinterest. "We share a mindbridge. We already know everything about each other."

"Well, not everything," said Maeryn.

"What do you mean?"

"It's like you said: the stuff on top is easy to get a reading on, but there's so much more below the surface. And most of it isn't even words, just thoughts and feelings and other things that can't even be boxed in or easily defined. Forget knowing everything about you, there are things about myself that *I* don't understand, things I'm not sure I even want to look at."

Kaija thought about this for a moment. "That's so sad."

"What?"

"Never really knowing yourself."

Max held up a hand to silence them.

"Quiet," he demanded. "The prison wing is up ahead, and it's heavily guarded. Forty Western Blazers, maybe closer to fifty, all of them equipped with MotherTech smartsuits and plasma rifles. Okay, gang, this is it. We knew coming into this that there would be a fight ahead of us. We knew that all or none of us might make it out alive, but if we die trying, at least—"

The Mentalist Stone glowed, and a series of pops rang out in the distance.

"—and they're all freaking gone now. What the heck did you just do, Kaija?"

"I made them hungry."

Max thought about this for all of two milliseconds.

"Hungry enough for them to leave their post, under threat of severe punishment? Aren't they just going to come back in a few seconds with a sleeve of crackers?"

"No, they'll be too busy eating to come back. I made them *really* hungry, like way hungrier than they've ever been. They'll probably gather all the food they can find and just keep eating until, um… until…"

"Until what?" asked Maeryn.

Kaija's face darkened with concern. "Huh… I guess there is no *until*. Guys, I think I made them *too* hungry."

Max shot a nervous glance at the Mentalist Stone. "And this is why you don't give teenagers weapons of mass destruction."

The narrow cave opened up to a large hallway lined with prison cells. They were all empty except for the one at the end, and even from this distance they could tell who was in there: Fain and Rosalie. They were here, and for the moment, they were completely unguarded.

"Fain!" yelled Kaija, and the three of them took off down the hallway. As she drew closer, she could see the extent of his infection. Fain barely reacted to the sound of her voice. He whispered a few garbled words with his dry, cracked lips, and reached up a trembling hand before falling back against the wall, having spent what little energy he had.

At the other end of the cell, Rosalie wasn't in much better shape herself. There was a fresh bruise blossoming on nearly half of her face, and one of her eyes was swollen shut. She saw them coming and managed to throw up her hands, shouting *STOP!* Kaija and Maeryn came to a halt, only inches from the bars of the cell.

"Get any closer, and you'll activate the security system," Rosalie explained. "Guardian Angels will be here in seconds." She gestured at something around her wrist: a metal band with a tiny, blue container in the center. "It's a teleporter. They just put these on us this morning. If anyone enters this cell, these will send us away to a randomized prison. Even if an advanced spacialist can trace our signal and follow, the bands will just keep jumping us from place to place until we're alone. It's the perfect security system."

Kaija shook her head stubbornly. They were too close. She couldn't accept the idea that Fain was right there, and she wouldn't be able to reach him.

"I can do it," she insisted. "I'll just have to be fast."

Rosalie laughed.

"Faster than the machine?" she asked. "You've never done anything but surprise me, but I know exactly what you're up against. I designed all this myself. Achak tortured me until I agreed to create my own, unbreakable leash."

Kaija held up the Mentalist Stone. "We killed Achak."

Rosalie's eyes went wide, but Maeryn was quick to clarify.

"We don't know that we *actually* killed him. We just severed his mind from his body, and his consciousness dissolved into the mental realm. His body's probably still technically alive, wherever it is."

"What do you mean, *wherever it is?*" asked Kaija. "You don't know where you sent him?"

"Was I supposed to think of a specific location? I just tried to send him far away!"

"So you just thought *go away,* and it worked?"

"He disappeared, didn't he? What? I don't know how these things work, I'm not a spacialist! I could only do it because your brain was inside mine!"

Rosalie watched the conversation with genuine surprise, like this was one thing she never saw coming. Her eyes clouded over for a moment, reading the present and possible futures before nodding in understanding.

"Okay," she said. "I've underestimated you again. There's a split second before the teleporter's randomizer picks a location, and that's your one chance to grab ahold. If you try to teleport one of us the moment the device turns on, the conflicting signals could fry the circuits. But you'll never be able to get to both of us."

A silence dawned over them as they realized what this meant.

"So…" Kaija whispered.

"You'll have to choose," said Max. "That's what you're saying, right?"

Rosalie nodded. "By the time Kaija reaches one of us, the other will be gone."

Kaija's gaze locked onto Fain at once. Maeryn didn't have to ask her what she was thinking or even use the mindbridge; she knew what Kaija's decision was from the start.

"Kaija, you need to think carefully about this," said Maeryn. "I realize the awfulness of what I'm about to ask you, and everything inside me is screaming to stay silent right now, but I won't. I just won't. Rosalie can deactivate the Guardian Angels, or even reprogram them. Once that's done, we could use them to find Fain. There will be nothing standing in our way anymore."

Kaija couldn't quite meet her eyes; she stayed fixated on Fain, whose fingers were twitching, as if trying to reach out to them. "Look at him, Maeryn. Look at Fain. You think he can wait another day for us? Another hour?"

"I don't know. Please know that this isn't about my family versus yours. Rosalie has hurt me as well, but you saw what the Angels did in the Capital. You saw them *burning* through entire crowds of people. Thousands of people dying, and maybe millions more in the future. This has to end. Max? Max, back me up!"

Max sighed. "You think I can reason my way out of this one? Wish I could, but I can't."

"Let's say we get Fain out of here. What happens next? We just watch the entire continent burn to the ground? Flee to some other guardianship and never make it back to Earth? Nobody hates the words coming out of my mouth more than me, but—"

Rosalie called out forcefully, pulling herself up with every bit of energy she had left and staring at Maeryn right in the eyes. "—Maeryn.

Stop! Just stop. There's no point. There's nothing any of us can say. I've seen it all. There is no possible future where Kaija chooses me over him. And why would she? Don't blame her for what's about to happen. It's on me. It's…" Her voice broke into a cry. "I love you, Maeryn. I hope you can forgive me."

"We'll come back for you," said Maeryn. "We'll get you out, wherever you are. Come on, use your spiritualist sight! Tell us we'll get you out."

Rosalie covered her face, stifling back sobs.

"Tell us you make it out of this!" Maeryn yelled, again getting no response. She turned to give a pleading look to Kaija, who simply turned away.

"I'm sorry, Maeryn."

Kaija disappeared, and then many things happened at once. The metal band on Fain and Rosalie's wrists beeped and pulled in energy. Kaija reappeared in the cell, grabbing Fain just as he was about to vanish. For a fleeting instant, she thought she lost him. Kaija could feel Fain start to slip into the roaring waters of Gaia's stream, but she caught him. The energy chamber on his wrist cracked and began smoking. At the same time, Rosalie disappeared.

The alarm overhead was suddenly drowned out by a deep rumbling and a series of pops down the hallway.

"Grab onto me!" shouted Kaija.

She teleported back out of the cell, where Maeryn and Max immediately darted toward her. Just before they made contact, a huge *BANG* echoed from down the prison hallway. A blur shot through the air, colliding with Kaija a second later. She tumbled backwards, Fain slipping out of her arms and both of them tumbling to the ground. The Mentalist Stone flew out of her hand, rolling across the floor and out of sight. A collar snapped shut around her neck, identical to the one that

Thomas Zeig had worn just before his execution. Kaija grabbed Fain's hand and energy surged in the air, but it soon repelled away from her and fizzled away uselessly.

"I can't relay!" she shouted.

A Guardian Angel emerged from the distance, pointing a cannon on one arm right at Kaija. Max flew toward it, but was immediately attacked by another Angel. They disappeared into the shadows, engaged in a battle too fast to track. The first Angel fired its cannon, and two metal bands snapped into place around Kaija's wrists, clamping together behind her back with a magnetic hum.

"Kaija Monhegan. Rugaru has requested your presence. You are to be held on trial for crimes against Gaia."

It fired the cannon again, locking Kaija's legs together with more magnetic bands. She screamed and flailed impotently on the cave floor.

"Take him! Get him out of here!"

Maeryn swept Fain up in her arms and took off through a random passage, not quite sure where she was going, but needing to get as far away from the Guardian Angel as possible. She looked over her shoulder to see several more machines converging upon Kaija. They didn't even so much as glance in her direction. This didn't make any sense. She was moving slow, struggling to run with Fain in her arms, barely able to breathe amidst her panic. The Angels could effortlessly take her out in a single second. Why were they ignoring her?

Max shot across the hallway and zoomed protectively around Maeryn.

"I don't know what to do!" he screamed. "This whole place is filling with Angels. Hundreds of them, everywhere I look. There's no way out!"

Up ahead on the path, the ceiling of the cave cracked open. Rubble poured down from above, and a huge Guardian Angel descended from the hole. The silhouette of a stone beetle was engraved on its chest: the symbol of internalism. The machine's eyes glowed as it pointed two plasma rifles directly at Maeryn.

She shielded herself with her hands reflexively, fully realizing the futility of this action, and then... nothing. Peeking out through her fingers, Maeryn saw that the Angel was simply frozen in place.

"Conflicting directives. Recalibrating."

A series of pops rang out around Maeryn, and a circle of at least twenty men and women appeared out of nowhere. They were dressed for battle, and each of them had intricate tattoos running up and down their arms. Her first reaction was to panic. The Western Blaze was here to take her. That's why the Angel didn't kill her: they didn't want her dead, they wanted to use her like they used Rosalie. Her future would be filled with nothing but the same awful tortures her aunt had endured. Kaija couldn't save her. Even Max couldn't hold them back forever.

The people in the circle moved simultaneously, so perfectly that their motions appeared choreographed. They turned away from Maeryn, some of them moving their arms in relaying motions through the air, others pulling out weapons and rearing back to fight. Stalactites broke off from the ceiling, immediately impaling the Angel and pinning him to the wall. Those in the circle closest to it swung their spears at the same time, each striking the containment orb in the same exact spot with rapid precision. Cracks began to spread from a single point. A man to Maeryn's right side leapt up into the air, crying out and throwing a hammer directly at the containment orb. It shattered immediately, letting the energy dissolve out into the air, and the machine's eyes dimmed to a lifeless grey.

Somewhere around the corner, Maeryn could still hear Kaija calling out for help and the rapid pops of even more Angels filling the cave. A cloaked woman stepped forward from the circle, gesturing in the direction of Kaija's screams and commanding the people around her. She spoke with an oddly familiar voice.

"Go get the girl at all costs!"

Half of the circle nodded and vanished, while the remaining regrouped around Maeryn protectively. The woman reached out her hand.

"The True Search is offering refuge to Kaija Monhegan and friends of Kaija Monhegan. Do you accept?"

Not seeing much of an alternative, Maeryn nodded. Max flew in and perched himself on Maeryn's shoulder. The woman approached, gently placing a hand on Fain's forehead. From this distance, Maeryn could clearly see her face beneath the hood for the first time. She knew this woman: it was Tamala, the spy who saved them from Rugaru's mountain stronghold last year.

Energy surged through their bodies, and the scenery smoothly changed from that of a prison to a vast woodland. Rather than the jarring sensation of being yanked from one place to another, Tamala's spacialism was smooth, masterful, and utterly silent. They jumped a thousand stretches away from the awful battle without making a single whisper.

As soon as they arrived in the woods, Tamala didn't even take a second to catch her breath. She snapped at a nearby man and pointed to Fain. "Get this boy to our best healers! He has a spreading infection, originating from a puncture wound in his left leg. He'll need round the clock monitoring."

Before Maeryn knew what was happening, someone was taking Fain from her arms and running off with him through the trees. Tamala gave her a look that wasn't exactly welcoming.

"Last cycle, an errant hydra vine destroys our entire mountain stronghold," she said, "and who do I run into? *You guys.* Today, I receive reports of Achak's disappearance, and then fifty of our guards have to be hospitalized after abandoning their post and eating an entire wagon full of raw potatoes. Who is it that I run into that very same hour? Well?"

"Us guys?" asked Max.

Tamala didn't reply; she simply scrunched up her lips in disapproval and pointed a finger to Maeryn's face.

"You and I, we have some serious talking to do."

She turned to leave, but was interrupted by the arrival of several injured Nomads. One of them held an iron spear that was cracked in half; another was pressing a bloody rag against his side and moaning.

"We couldn't get her," the first man said. "She was gone by the time we rounded the corner."

Maeryn felt her stomach sink. She reached out for Kaija over their mindbridge. It was never easy to control from Maeryn's side, but this was entirely different. This was wrong.

"Kaija?"

Maeryn's call went nowhere, only bouncing around in her own head.

"Kaija? Where are you?"

When Maeryn reached across the bridge from her own mind to Kaija's, all she felt on the other side was an empty darkness.

Chapter Twenty-five

He Lives

The Capital Theater, Gaia

"Wake up, Kaija. Face me."

Kaija opened her eyes to see Rugaru looming over her. She couldn't move; her hands were tied to a chair. She couldn't relay; the metal collar was still tight around her neck. She couldn't even scream; a rag had been stuffed into her mouth. As Kaija's eyes adjusted, she saw that she was on stage in a huge theater. The walls were painted gold and fancy red carpets lined the walkways. Plush chairs in the lower audience and balconies were filled with what looked to be several thousand Capital citizens. They sat in utter silence, apparently too terrified to make the smallest sound. Kaija looked to the ceiling to see MotherTech drones circling around the chandeliers, their weapons aimed at the people below.

Rugaru grabbed Kaija's chin and tilted her head up to face him, smiling a terrifyingly genuine smile. His fingers were ice-cold, and a moment later Kaija saw why: his previously missing arm was now replaced by a chrome, nanobot prosthetic limb.

"Don't bother trying to teleport," he said quietly. "Your collar absorbs any Gaian energy you draw near you and traps it."

Rugaru turned to face the crowd, studying them for an uncomfortably long time. He spoke, his voice artificially amplified through the circling drones. "You are frightened. And how can I blame you? High Guardian Thomas spent years calling me a terrorist, and he was right. I have stolen children, strung up grown men by their necks in town squares for all to see, and kept people as slaves into their old age, well past the point where their bodies have given everything they have to give. I turned terror into currency, and my people became rich. The fear is the point. When I see your fear, I see people who are *listening* to us, who are taking us seriously. I admit that we are monsters, but we are inevitable monsters. My ancestors stood back peacefully as Gaia was desecrated during the Global War, and it nearly destroyed us. Thomas did not tell you the truth of our existence, so allow me to do so.

"Gaia is not a plate of food. She cannot be purchased, divided up, and consumed. When the Nomads of this continent saw this very thing happening during Edgard Zeig's first cycles as a self-appointed God, we spoke out. His response? You are free to stay here, but you have to become like us. Join a village, change your last name, do the bidding of a guardian and pay your taxes. Hollow yourself out of all culture and ancestry so that the new guardianship can fill you with whatever it wants. And how do you argue with someone who can set the sky on fire with his anger? You don't."

Rugaru paused, soaking in the absolute horror in the room, enjoying every second of the audience's rapt attention.

"Duncan Kacey, your so-called crucifier, saw our dilemma. He saw that Edgard was growing in power, and that the next war to come would be one that *nobody* would survive. With Duncan's help, we rid the world of the Son of Gaia, believing that the guardianship would eventually fall apart on its own. In many ways, the Crucifier was right. High Guardian Thomas was lazy enough to let us grow more powerful with each passing cycle, and discontentment was growing in the hearts of Edgardians. Not enough for the Capital citizens to speak up, of course. As long as the wealthiest of you were comfortable, it was okay that Thomas gambled with the tax money, and so what if he were seen with young girlfriends every now and then? As long as they weren't *your* daughters, it was worth the price of living behind his walls. And yet, more and more Edgardians joined us willingly as time went by. If it hadn't been for a serious oversight in Duncan's plan, Edgardia would have fallen just like he predicted. What was it? What could he have missed?"

An older man leapt up from the audience and started screaming at Rugaru.

"The Son of Gaia has returned! We all saw him on that night! Edgardia stands forever!"

One of the drones hovering above sprang to life, pointing its sensors at the protestor. The awful sound of gunfire erupted in the theater, followed by an equally awful silence. The old man's body was thrown into the aisle from the blast, but nobody around him dared to run or help him. They didn't even dare look in his direction.

"Edgard has not returned," Rugaru proclaimed to the crowd, "but his influence has survived past his death. How is this?"

Rugaru walked over to Kaija and yanked the rag out of her mouth.

"Tell them who you are," he demanded.

Kaija stared at Rugaru defiantly, not saying a word. He reached forward with his metal arm and grabbed her shoulder, squeezing so tight that she felt her bones crunching together.

"I'm…" Kaija began, but gasped when he tightened his grip even more.

"Louder!" Rugaru demanded.

"I'm Kaija Monhegan!" she screamed. "Edgard Zeig was my grandfather."

A noticeable surprise spread through the crowd, citizens glancing at each other, letting the looks on their faces do the talking. Rugaru let go of Kaija's shoulder.

"Edgard died," he said, "but he left behind a son by the name of Jasper Monhegan. This was the man who single-handedly saved the Capital last summer, but things have changed since then. During my most recent attack, Jasper's heritage got the better of him. He saw his chance to become the new High Guardian, and instead of saving Thomas, he roasted him alive before setting his sights on me. Jasper did not strike to kill, however, and this was his downfall. I fought without reservation, and Jasper was easily defeated in combat. He fled instead of dying with honor, and has not been seen since."

"You're lying!" screamed Kaija.

"I am not. The most powerful bloodline in history has produced a coward, a man I am told would rather bake a cake than protect his people. But in you, Kaija, I see the greatness of Edgard. I don't see someone who will hide on an island for their whole life, and then run away when faced with a true challenge. You destroyed my mountain stronghold when you were no more than fourteen, and your boyfriend took my arm in what would be the first blow landed on me since my youth. Three generations of Edgardians now place their misguided hopes in you. The great experiment that is Edgardia will only fail if you do."

Rugaru reached forward with his metal arm, tearing off the chains binding Kaija to the chair and throwing them across the stage. He grabbed a red, crystal dagger off his belt and handed it to her. Kaija instantly recognized it as the cycle-day present from her mother; he must have taken it off her unconscious body.

"I cannot let you teleport out of here," said Rugaru, "so the collar will remain. But I will not use Gaia either, or my new hand." The nanobots making up his arm began to recede and disappear up his sleeve. "I am unguarded, Kaija. Defend your bloodline's honor as it comes to an end."

Kaija briefly considered turning around and running, despite the dozens of drones circling in the air which definitely had their targets set on her. The idea of fighting a grown man to the death should have been crazy, but Kaija suddenly didn't want to run. This was the monster who destroyed her home, kidnapped her boyfriend, and was trying to discredit her father. Even if there was no chance of surviving this, she was going to leave a scar that would never fade.

Kaija jumped forward, thrusting her dagger toward Rugaru's chest as fast as she could, but he was much faster. He grabbed her wrist with his remaining arm and twisted it behind her back. Kaija dropped her dagger and Rugaru kicked it away before she could react. He pushed her onto the ground and laughed.

"Go get it," he said. "Try again."

Kaija rushed over to her dagger, not sure that she could even hold it anymore with the throbbing pain in her wrist. She picked it up with her other hand and approached Rugaru more carefully.

"This is how you prove your bravery?" asked Kaija. "You can kill a teenager? Big man."

"We both know that you are not an ordinary teenager. Show these people. Let them say that you went down fighting."

Kaija charged again, throwing her dagger straight toward his face. Rugaru ducked out of the way, and then punched her in the chest with his powerful arm. The air was forced out of Kaija's lungs as she fell to the floor a second time. She rolled over, putting her arms on the ground to push herself up, but Rugaru stomped his foot down onto her ankle with all of his immense weight. Kaija cried out as her leg bent the wrong way, making an awful snapping sound. She struggled to stay conscious as black spots swam in her vision.

"Try again," said Rugaru from above her.

"My leg's broken," moaned Kaija.

There was a clunk on the floor next to her head as Rugaru dropped the dagger.

"You're not dead yet. Go out fighting."

Kaija grabbed the dagger and tried desperately to cut the collar off her neck. If she could get inside of Rugaru's head, he wouldn't stand a chance.

He laughed at her. "Stop embarrassing yourself. That was forged by our greatest internalist blacksmiths. It's not coming off."

Kaija tried pulling in Gaian energy, and she actually felt it draw toward her. It swelled in the air around them, immediately getting sucked into the collar before dissolving back into the air. Rugaru stepped over and kicked her in the stomach.

"Your relaying won't save you. You're as powerless to me as Edgard was to the Crucifier in his final moments. The branches of time are growing, and they are leaving you behind."

He kicked her again, forcing Kaija to cough out a mouthful of blood. She dropped the dagger and it spun off across the floor. Screaming and crying rang out from the thousands of Capital citizens in the audience.

"But he lives," Kaija said between coughs.

Rugaru raised his foot to stomp her again, but hesitated and squinted his eyes.

"What did you say?" he asked, too quietly for the crowd to hear.

A sudden surge of defiance flared up in Kaija's heart. If this was her final moment, she would not give Rugaru the last word.

"Duncan Kacey failed!" screamed Kaija. "And you will too. HE LIVES!"

In her desperation, Kaija tried something that Ms. Clara had warned her never to do. Every time she relayed, the amount of energy she pulled in was carefully measured. A relayer could very easily kill themselves if they overextended their capabilities; it was like falling off a bike that was going too fast down a hill. But now, in front of thousands of terrified captives, Kaija summoned as much energy as she could, abandoning any reservation. She felt Gaia rush toward her like a hurricane, getting sucked into the energy chamber on her collar. It glowed with a blinding blue light for a moment and then shattered, leaving a smoking hole in the center of the collar. She reached up with one hand and crushed the internalist metal in her fist, throwing the broken device across the stage.

Kaija tried to stand, but fell again to the ground as her broken leg throbbed with agony. She pointed a finger at the stunned Rugaru and pulled in another hurricane of power. On another day, it would have overwhelmed her, made her lose control, but this was not another day. The rage that Kaija felt had put her firmly at the controls. One of the skylights on the roof of the theater exploded as a lightning bolt shot into the building. The lightning crackled apart, each bolt striking a different drone, instantly frying their circuitry. Another rumble of thunder echoed outside, and a second bolt of lightning headed straight toward Rugaru. He held his stump out and the nanobot arm instantly grew back, but there was no blocking the attack. A thunderclap filled the room as his body was thrown across the stage and crashed against the stone wall. He hit the floor, smoke curling off his clothes while the scent of burning hair and flesh filled the stage. The citizens were now on their feet, rushing into the aisles and making a desperate run for the doors of the theater.

Kaija tried to teleport, but she felt a drain on her body and mind that was greater than ever before. Even amongst the chaos, she felt like she'd fall asleep for five days if she so much as blinked.

"MAERYN!" cried Kaija in her mind. *"I'm at the Capital Theater. Rugaru is here."*

Across the stage, Rugaru's burnt body was somehow returning to its feet and taking a few staggering steps forward. The blast would have incinerated an ordinary man, but Rugaru must have been an even stronger relayer than anyone knew. He held out his metal arm, and a golden spear appeared in his grip. He aimed the weapon at her and reared back. She could see fear in his silvery eyes, and the look was scarier than his hatred ever was. Anger kept him grounded, but this fear had created a wild animal.

"I need help!"

The spear flew toward her.

"Maeryn!"

Things happened in the next second that were too fast for Kaija to comprehend. Somebody appeared soundlessly beside her, but it wasn't Maeryn. It was a man. He grabbed ahold of her hand, and the spear soared straight through his vanishing afterimage, impaling the wall of the theater as the two of them disappeared. The sounds of exploding drones and screams were swallowed into the chaos behind them.

* * *

Now Kaija heard birds and saw blurry treetops swaying in the cool breeze over her. Everything was mashed together in her senses as relayer's drain hit her hard. Figures looked down over her broken body as Kaija struggled to stay conscious. Maeryn watched, her eyes full of tears and worry. Max zoomed in anxious circles overhead, saying something that Kaija didn't quite catch. And there was another face, one that Kaija hadn't expected to see.

"You?" asked Kaija.

"Yes," said Elias. "Rest, Kaija. You are found."

Chapter Twenty-six

The True Search

The Northern Wilds, Gaia

Kaija was fading back into herself. She experienced brief flashes of pain and confusion, always followed by periods of emptiness which swallowed her whole. Maeryn asked her questions, but her voice sounded impossibly far away and Kaija couldn't find the energy to answer. Strange people held their hands over her leg, sending a warm sensation into her bones which eased the pain.

Strength eventually made its way back into her muscles, and one morning Kaija found herself making a few stumbling steps forward. She fell, and suddenly there were shouts from multiple voices. The world began to gain focus, and she saw that she was in a large tent. Birds sang from overhead. Maeryn ran through the opening, followed by a tall Nomadic woman with floral patterns tattooed up and down her arms. Kaija knew her.

"Tamala…" said Kaija, her voice tired and raspy.

"How are you feeling?" asked Tamala, pulling Kaija up to her feet. "Can you support your weight?"

Kaija took a step, grunting from the sharp pain in her leg, but it was amazing that she could walk at all.

"My leg was broken," Kaija said. "I shouldn't be able to stand."

"The healers have been at work on your leg for three days," said Maeryn.

The shock of the statement dusted away the remaining cobwebs in Kaija's mind.

"Three days? I've been asleep for three days?"

"You're lucky to have woken up at all," said Tamala. "You had a broken leg, as well as several cracked ribs and too many bruises to count. I've heard reports that you summoned a thunderstorm and practically demolished the Capital Theater's roof. It would have given a normal teenager a heart attack to channel that much energy."

Maeryn started crying and wrapped her arms around Kaija. "I thought you were dead. I couldn't feel your thoughts. After we got separated and the machines took you, your mind just suddenly went dark."

Kaija's head was spinning, memories coming back in bits and pieces without warning or context.

"Fain!" she blurted out. "Is Fain okay?"

"He will be," said Tamala. "We managed to rid him of infection, but he's very weak. I believe right now he's undergoing an intensive healing session. You can see him in a few hours."

Kaija's relief was undeniable, but none of this was making sense.

"But how did I get here?" she asked. "And how did you know where to find me?"

"I'm a spy for a Nomadic group known as the True Search. I've been monitoring Rugaru's secret prison for days, trying to find just the right moment to break Fain out, but all the technology made it impenetrable. When the guards started abandoning their posts, I had a feeling you were behind it, so we seized on the opportunity and acted. We didn't know where the machine had taken you. A bit later Maeryn heard your cry for help, and I sent my son to rescue you."

"Son?" asked Kaija.

As if on command, Elias teleported into the tent and hugged Kaija.

"They told me you were awake!" he said. "I never thought I'd see you again."

"You're here?" asked Kaija. "But you told me you didn't know where your parents were. When did you leave Monhegan Island?"

Elias appeared shaken for a moment, but soon regained his composure. "It... it doesn't matter. The important thing is that I decided to track down my family, and it wasn't as difficult as I had built up in my mind. I rejoined the True Search, and I've been here ever since."

Kaija's memories were coming back now in bigger pieces, and coming back fast. She gasped. "The island... it was empty. Are the other Monhegans with you? Are they here?"

Elias looked confused. "No. Why?"

"We went back to the island, and nobody was there."

Tamala waved this away. "Not surprising. Ever since the massacre at the Capital, Edgardians have been abandoning the continent. But you no longer need to worry. You are under the full protection of the True Search."

Maeryn dried her eyes and seemed to cheer up slightly. She grabbed Kaija's hand and moved her toward the opening of the tent. Kaija thought she heard dozens of people outside, but she soon corrected herself. It sounded like they were in the middle of a city, hundreds of True Searchers going on with their daily life all around them.

"Oh, just wait," said Maeryn. "It's amazing."

* * *

Tamala helped Kaija walk out of the tent, while Maeryn and Elias went off to find Max. The campsite sat in a clearing in the middle of an old growth forest, and hundreds of Nomads were coming and going. People were cooking soup over several large campfires, and Kaija saw the chefs disappearing and re-appearing with fresh herbs and vegetables from all over the globe. Nomadic children were engaged in a mind-bending game of tag up in the trees, teleporting from branch to branch as Max chased them. Another group was gathered in a circle at the edge of the clearing, playing stringed instruments and singing rowdily.

"How many of these people are spies in the Western Blaze?" asked Kaija.

"Just a few," said Tamala. "Most of us are just people, trying to live our lives and adhere to the ancient customs."

Some of the villagers spotted Kaija and began whispering excitedly.

"You're a bit of a celebrity, Kaija. The True Search has been keeping its ears to the ground, and news is spreading about what happened in the Capital Theater. Rugaru made a big show of trying to scare everyone, but instead you blasted him in front of an audience and most of the captive citizens escaped. They spread the word, and all of Edgardia is talking about you. Summoning lightning, Kaija? That's an extremely advanced conjurist technique. I thought you were primarily a mentalist."

"I didn't know I could do that either," said Kaija weakly. "But I don't think I could do it again if I tried. I was desperate."

"Not surprising, I suppose, coming from the granddaughter of Edgard Zeig. At least that's what everybody in Edgardia seems to be saying. Is this true?"

Kaija opened her mouth to reply, but quickly shut it. She had been constantly told by Ms. Clara to keep her heritage a secret, but Kaija supposed that the sand cat was already out of the sack.

Tamala narrowed her eyes at Kaija. "You put up a mental wall around yourself, but your face betrays you. It's true, then. Edgard Zeig has a living heir. I don't know why I should be surprised, considering what I've seen you accomplish already. That's one mystery solved, at least."

Tamala glanced in the direction where Maeryn had walked off. "That redheaded girl and her metal pet, on the other hand, are a puzzle that we have been unable to solve. Maeryn clams up when I ask her where she comes from, and the images I have gleaned from her mind are completely alien to my understanding. I suspect that she has something to do with Rugaru's new weapons."

"She's..." Kaija began, but hesitated. Maeryn was ashamed of her family's history, and would be mortified if other Gaians found out that her grandfather was the Crucifier. Kaija strengthened her mental barricades and continued.

"She's my friend, and her story is not mine to tell."

Kaija could feel Tamala unsuccessfully prying at the edges of her mind.

"You are a true friend to Maeryn. Very well. I will pursue her truth without compromising your friendship. In the meantime, allow me to show you our home."

They toured the True Search campsite, and Kaija marveled at the casual nature of things. Somewhere else on the continent, there were people being slaughtered by killing machines from another world. How could they be so oblivious to the destruction in Edgardia? Kaija thought about how Rugaru had been in power for the three days that she was unconscious, and a dread crept into her stomach. Three more days of the Western Blaze sowing chaos throughout the continent. Three more days of Kai waiting for them back on Earth. Three more days of Ms. Clara and her father missing. Kaija was glad that she had given people hope, but she didn't feel very hopeful herself.

"What else is happening?" asked Kaija. "Have you found my father?"

"No," said Tamala. "It has been extremely difficult to find out what is going on. Rugaru's machines have been spreading out across the continent, targeting guardians and anyone with links to the old guardianship. Thousands of deaths have been reported. Villagers wake up to find that the very person in charge of protecting them has been removed. There is almost nothing left to defend. Fortunately, those metal monstrosities can't catch the True Search. We've been in constant motion, ever since the Global War. It is how we learned to survive."

"So what's the plan? We have to stop Rugaru."

Tamala gave Kaija a condescending look. "We?"

"Yes! Maeryn, Max, you and me, the True Search... *everybody!*"

Tamala narrowed her eyes and began speaking very deliberately.

"Allow me to be completely honest, Kaija. The True Search offers you and Maeryn our protection, and that protection can last as long as you wish. You went through a horrible, traumatic experience, and your job for the next several weeks is to rest your body and spirit. *My job* is to keep a close eye on things, and only act when absolutely necessary. The True Search has its agents in every major Guardianship and fringe-group across Gaia, yet our allegiance is to no authority but Gaia herself. You have only been with us for three days, and we do not act upon your wishes, no matter who your grandfather is."

"But Rugaru is a monster!"

"And nobody knows that more than myself. I assure you, he is currently our greatest concern. This past cycle, I've noticed him changing. He disappears for weeks at a time. He doesn't keep anyone other than Achak informed about his plans. These mysterious weapons he's gotten ahold of make him an enormous threat. To go running into battle without careful planning would be to instantly fail."

Kaija felt like screaming, but she did her best to compose herself.

"We can't just do nothing. We need to, I don't know…"

"Kill him?"

Tamala gave her a knowing look, and Kaija nodded. It was not something that she wanted to admit, but Rugaru's death was the only way she could imagine everything becoming safe again.

Tamala had the nerve to laugh at Kaija's embarrassing admission. "So that's what you want me to do? Kill Rugaru and give up the fragile trust of a terrorist group that I've spent ten cycles infiltrating? Make him into a martyr so that one of his thousands of followers can simply step into power and rile them up? I could take out Rugaru within the hour, but we can't kill the ideas he has spread in the hearts of his people without more deliberate work."

Tamala gave Kaija what looked like a genuine smile.

"Just trust me, Kaija. A teenager should not feel the weight of this responsibility." She rubbed her hands together. "I suppose that you should meet my family if you're going to be staying with us. My daughter was hanging around the campsite a few minutes ago. I suppose she snuck off to steal some more books."

Kaija was more than surprised. She would have never imagined that the cold, blunt woman who held her prisoner last cycle had a secret family. Tamala read the look on Kaija's face.

"You're thinking *isn't it dangerous to have a family when you're a spy for the worst person in the world?* You misunderstand Rugaru. I'm a low-ranking guard, and he overlooks people he considers to be unimportant. Now, where are they?"

Tamala closed her eyes and sank into a deep concentration.

"Do they all live here?" said Kaija.

"Yes," said Tamala, eyes still closed. "And no. The True Search lives everywhere."

She placed a hand on Kaija's shoulder and they abruptly teleported next to a sparkling blue pond. The sun moved halfway across the sky, and the sudden change in temperature made goosebumps appear all over Kaija's arms. A large man with a neatly trimmed beard was on his knees, rinsing the hair of a squirming toddler in the pond. The man's skin was much lighter than Tamala's, but he had similar floral tattoos running up his arms. The little boy was moaning *bath out, bath out!* and splashing water everywhere.

"This is my partner, Sawyer," said Tamala. "He's a non-relayer."

"Distinguished Professor of Pre-War History, currently on extended paternity leave," said the man, turning over the toddler and scrubbing his back. "Father of your children. Talented songwriter. Perhaps the most highly skilled and practiced kisser in the Midwest. You could have led with any one of those things, dear. Nice to see you up, Kaija. The world is rooting for you."

"And this is our youngest son, Diego," said Tamala, gesturing at the squirming boy.

"BATH OUT!" yelled Diego. There was a pop, a splash of water, and Diego suddenly teleported to the other side of the pond. He ran naked through the field, giggling like a little madman.

"Best of luck with that, Professor," said Tamala, placing her hand on Kaija's back.

"Wait," said Kaija. "Can I catch my breath before we—"

Thousands of warped images flew through Kaija's mind in a single second, and then they were somewhere else.

"—teleport again," finished Kaija, her stomach lurching from the trip.

They were now in a dusty attic, moonlight peeking in through cracks in the wooden ceiling. A girl of about Kaija's age was lounging on an old couch in front of them, reading a large book. She held a ball of light in one hand while she turned a page with the other.

"Sleeping beauty awakes," said the girl, glancing up over the top of the book.

"This thief is my daughter Izzy," said Tamala, pulling the book out of her hands. "Does the little old woman who owns this cabin know that a rat is living in her attic?"

"Couldn't resist, she's got a good collection," said Izzy, snatching the book back and picking up where she left off. Her eyes scanned the page while she spoke to Kaija. "Don't let my mother scare you, Kaija. We're all glad to have you with the Search."

"Thanks," said Kaija, struggling to stay on her feet. "Hey, do you have any food up here? I don't think I've eaten in three days, and teleporting back and forth like this has really—"

"Is someone up there?"

A sweet old voice was calling from the floorboards beneath them. Izzy smiled, cupped her hands to her mouth, and yelled *squeak squeak!* She grabbed a book from the pile next to her and disappeared without a sound. Tamala's hand made its way to Kaija's shoulder.

"Well," said Tamala. "I need to consult with the Elder Counsel. Let's get back."

Kaija opened her mouth, intending to tell Tamala that her stomach couldn't take one more jump across the world, but they were gone before she could get out a single word. They arrived back at the original campsite, and Kaija immediately collapsed to the ground, clutching her stomach and trying not to vomit. Tamala stared down at her with a touch of guilt.

"I guess that does take some getting used to," she said. "No bother, you'll get your specialist legs with practice. Let me get you some food. We've got everything. What would you like?"

Kaija worked up just enough energy to speak three words.

"All of it."

* * *

It was hard not to be at least somewhat content in a place where literally everything was on the menu. The cooks of the True Search had instant access to herbs, spices, meat, and produce from all around the world. Everybody was in awe over Kaija and was eager to bring her anything she asked for. It was strange to feel so relieved to be safe, yet simultaneously so full of dread about what might be happening all over Edgardia.

Kaija marveled at the way that Maeryn fit in with the group. Her normally awkward friend acted like she had known the True Search for years, calling several people by name and politely asking for teleportation to their various camps.

Shortly after dinner, Kaija and Maeryn headed back to the campsite to see if Fain was done with his healing session. Around the village, some families were preparing to settle down for the night, while others were teleporting off to other parts of the world.

"Sleep schedules are weird here," explained Maeryn. "They're constantly coming to and from the other villages, where it could be in the middle of the day or early in the morning right now."

"You seem to fit right in," said Kaija.

Maeryn shrugged. "The first day you were unconsciousness, I was so anxious I felt like I was going to be sick. I had to do something to distract myself, so Max and I started exploring. The way that teleportation has shaped their culture and society is fascinating."

Max darted out of the campsite, coming to a stop before Kaija.

"Fain is up, and he's asking for you."

Kaija could hear the relief in Max's voice, but there was something else there as well, something she didn't like.

"What's wrong?" she asked.

"He's…" Max hesitated. "He's healed, but he's been through some serious trauma. Some of the stuff he's saying just doesn't make any sense."

"Like what?"

Max simply shook his head. "You need to hear it from him."

Chapter Twenty-seven

A Choice

The Northern Wilds, Gaia

Kaija and Fain spent an hour holding each other tight in the healer's tent. They cried, laughed, kissed, and felt all the things that had been wrapped so tight inside of them. Beneath the tremendous relief of being impossibly alive and together again, Kaija couldn't shake the feeling that Fain was holding something back.

"I saw Jasper," he said finally. "In the prisons. I saw your father."

Kaija immediately snapped to attention. "They're holding him prisoner?"

"No, it's... it's hard to explain. So much of my time there was a blur, but there's a lot I remember clearly. The guards would come and take Rosalie away for hours at a time. She'd always come back bruised and bleeding, refusing to talk to me. One of the times she was gone, Jasper just suddenly walked up to the bars of our cell. I thought I was saved, that he had finally come to rescue us, but..."

Fain hesitated, shaking his head.

"It doesn't make any sense, Kaija. He just stood there. Watching me. I screamed for him to help, but it was like he was worlds away. There was this emptiness on his face that I can't put into words He kept staring into the cell, like he was looking for me and couldn't see me right there. Even at the time, I wondered if I might be dreaming, or if I was just delirious, but I know what I saw. After what felt like hours he finally locked eyes with mine. I thought that there must have been an illusion surrounding my cell, and he had finally broken through. I was going to be rescued. But that's not what happened. He just looked at me, said something under his breath, and then walked away."

"What did he say?" asked Kaija.

"I could barely hear it. It sounded like *Zebulon Ape*."

"What the heck is a Zebulon Ape?"

Fain shrugged. "I don't know. Everyone I tell this to doesn't believe me. They just think it was a hallucination or something, but—"

"I believe you," said Kaija. "I don't understand it, but it's just one more thing in a long list of stuff I don't understand. Why was Monhegan Island abandoned? Why would my father go to the Capital only to kill the High Guardian and then vanish? Where's Ms. Clara, or your parents? Why doesn't anyone seem to be looking for us? None of it fits together. I—"

Kaija paused. She felt a big disturbance in the mental realm, and ripples were approaching rapidly. Fain was immediately in a defensive stance, fire burning in the palms of his hands. A voice spoke from behind them.

"I know you're there, Kaija. I know you're listening."

Rugaru stood there in the tent with them. Fain immediately spun around and sent out a blast of fire, but it simply went through Rugaru's body and flickered away to nothing. This wasn't real, just a projection cast in the mental realm. Sounds of commotion echoed from the surrounding village as everyone reacted to the same message.

Rugaru's eyes scanned the tent, as if searching for her. "These words are intended for Kaija Monhegan: the last dying ember of hope for Edgardia. You have a choice to make, Kaija."

His skin was covered in burns from Kaija's attack on him in the Capital Theater, and he made no attempt to conceal them.

"Edgardians," said Rugaru solemnly. "This will be the last message sent through the TEMS before your government is dismantled completely. I am being projected throughout the western continent in the hopes that a single girl hears me. There have been whispers about the granddaughter of Edgard Zeig, and those rumors are mostly true. I believe that she is alive, and that she is hiding, possibly creating juvenile plans to defeat me and the entire Western Blaze. If you can achieve this, Kaija, then perhaps the guardianship really does belong under your care. So go ahead and try. Bide your time. Grow stronger than you already are. Lead an army that destroys my followers and rids me from the physical realm forever. Follow in your grandfather's footsteps and become a force so great that only the seriously deprived would consider overthrowing you."

Rugaru smiled, and the ripples in the mental realm grew stronger.

"But there will be a cost."

The walls of the healer's tent began to dim and vanish entirely as ghostly figures appeared around them. There were over a hundred men, women, and children all looking at Kaija, their blurry faces slowly coming into focus.

"No…" whispered Fain, grabbing Kaija's hand and squeezing tightly.

The Monhegans were here, and every single one of them was in chains. Kaija's eyes darted rapidly from face to face. Fain's parents were near the front of the group, arms bound behind their backs. The old priest, Norio, looked on the verge of death, barely able to stand upright. Alan, the teacher's apprentice, had a rageful and defiant expression on his bruised face. Stephen Monhegan, the youngest of Kaija's classmates, was sobbing as two Western Blazers held him up by the arms. There were too many people to count, too many familiar faces amongst the ghostly prisoners.

Rugaru spread his arms proudly. "Five days ago, I returned to Monhegan Island to find it completely unguarded. It didn't take long for us to capture every resident, separate them, and send each to a different prison camp. You will never find them all, but they do not have to suffer any longer. Hear me, Kaija."

He paused, and an eternity seemed to exist in that single second.

"Trade your life for theirs."

Maeryn and Max suddenly rushed into the tent next to Kaija and Fain. The four of them huddled closely together. A moment later, Elias appeared alongside them, his fists trembling with rage.

Rugaru continued. "Come to the Capital tomorrow morning at sunrise. It will not be a celebration. It will be a fast and painless end. If you accept, I will free your people. Monhegan Island will be established as an independent colony. Once my ultimate task is complete, I will dismantle the Guardian Angels, and then step aside forever. Edgardia will be no more, but there will be something better in its place. A place that makes people like you and me irrelevant.

"If you do not accept, then every last one of the Monhegans will be killed. They will know that it was your decision. I take no pride in this cruelty, but I've been backed into a corner."

Rugaru looked around, as if searching for someone else.

"There is another that I hope this message reaches," he said. "Maeryn Kacey. Your family has been a great service to me, willingly or not. Regardless of your friend's decision, I will grant you and your aunt safe passage back to your world when this is all over. Until then, all I ask is that you stay out of this fight. If you or your little pet lift a single finger in defiance, Rosalie will join the slayed Monhegans."

Rugaru turned around and walked away, slowly fading away into the mists of the mental realm. A fury unlike anything Kaija had ever experienced burned inside of her.

"Maeryn," she said. "Open up your relaying pathways. Let me borrow some of your energy again."

"Why?"

"Just do it."

"But—"

"NOW!"

Maeryn opened herself up and allowed Kaija to access her mind. Gaian energy flowed through the two of them, and Kaija focused all of her attention on the vanishing image of Rugaru. He didn't disappear, but actually became brighter and more solid. Rugaru stopped and turned around, undeniably surprised. However far away he might be at that moment, he felt whatever Kaija was trying to do. The tent around them dimmed to nothing, transforming into a black void until all that was left was her and Rugaru. They looked at each other, and Kaija knew that in this moment he was actually seeing her. His eyes blazed with surprise and confusion.

"I will come to the Capital tomorrow," said Kaija furiously. "But I'm not coming to die. *I am coming to end you.*"

Kaija released the hold she had on his mind, finding herself immediately back in the healer's tent. Rugaru and the rest of the Monhegans were gone. Kaija's brave mask vanished, and she crumbled over, wailing at the top of her lungs and letting out all of her sadness and anger.

Maeryn reached forward to embrace her friend, but in the next instant Tamala appeared before them, looking as intense as ever.

"Fain, Kaija," she said quickly. "The Elder Council will soon gather to discuss this event and its ramifications, and you will both surely be called to testify."

Tamala turned and offered a hand to her son.

"Elias," she said. "Come with us, and wait outside the Elder's Temple. They may want to hear from you as well."

He grabbed her hand and placed another on Kaija's back. Maeryn and Max prepared to follow, but Tamala shook her head.

"No, Maeryn," she said. "Stay here. Best to stay out of sight for now. The elders do not trust you."

* * *

The Mirrored Tower, Gaia

The prisoner was smiling.

Rugaru arrived at the Mirrored Tower in a last-ditch attempt to squeeze any and all information he could get out of Rosalie Kacey. From the building's position on the mountaintop, the horizons seemed to stretch endlessly in each direction. Rugaru entered the tower's penultimate floor, and was met with someone entirely different than the pleading, bargaining prisoner he had last seen. Her body and spirit were still broken, and yet the woman smiled with the most genuine look of amusement.

"You've given up hope of finding Achak," she said. "And without him, you worry that you've lost control of me. And without me, you will soon lose control of everything."

Rugaru teleported into the cell, grabbing onto the woman's shirt and pulling her up toward him. She simply laughed and shook her head, not a single iota of fear showing in her eyes.

"Why do you laugh?" he asked.

"Because I've seen this," she said. "I've seen what happens now, and I've seen what happens next. I've been captured, tortured, and forced to bring my greatest fears into the world. But all the while I've let my spiritualism guide me, steering things to lead us to this very moment. I wasn't sure if it was working until now. The future changes upon observation, you see, not unlike quantum particles. When you walked in through that door, just now, *I knew.* This is what I saw, when I first glimpsed Desolation. This is where I've been trying to go all along, to our one unlikely chance to stop it. The road was long and thorny, but it's over. I've arrived. We've arrived."

Rosalie laughed violently, a mysterious white fog rolling into her eyes. Rugaru hated this sight. He never understood the things she said when she went to that place. The woman twitched, her voice no longer sounding like something she was in complete control of.

"The capturing, the torture, the deceptions… all were just twists and turns along the tree, pains I had to endure to get here. You think it was your idea to capture me? To collect the artifacts? To build that *thing* above our heads? All along, you were *my* prisoner."

Rugaru dropped her back to the floor and shook his head, turning to leave.

"You're delirious," he said. "Broken beyond repair, no longer any use to us. If your niece does the right thing, I'll send you two back to Earth. If she decides to fight, I'll have the guards put you out of your misery while she watches. Goodbye, Dr. Kacey."

He walked toward the steps, but Rosalie kept talking at him.

"You don't want to stay to hear what I'm about to say, do you? You're afraid in a way you've never been afraid before. There's something about me, isn't there? Something that's bothered you since the first time you saw me, something horribly familiar, but you've been too unsettled to let yourself think about it. The most feared man in the world, and I can bring you to your knees with a single word."

Rugaru teleported back into the cell and struck her across the face with his metal hand. Rosalie spit out a mouthful of blood and smiled once again, hardly phased.

"You think I'm afraid?" he screamed. "You think I need you? I don't cower from things in the shadows: I *AM* the one in the shadows. I'm the one that parents warn their children about. I'm the one that the entire continent cowers in the presence of. I—"

Rosalie smiled again, and dropped that single word on him.

"Mika."

Rugaru pulled his hand away from her, reflexively, like a hand jerking back from a hot stove. He felt the floor fall away beneath him. No, not the floor: the world itself, his very existence and understanding of his own life crumbling away to nothing. She was right. With a single word, Rosalie had changed his life forever.

He stepped forward, holding her chin as gently as he could manage, pulling her face up to look at him. Rugaru stared deep into those hauntingly familiar eyes, letting himself look at her, to really look, to see past the tool for conquest and find the real person sitting here, bleeding in this cell. Once he saw what he was looking for, it couldn't be unseen. Never, never in a million cycles. For the first time he could remember, the first time since being a little boy who fell from a tree and ran to his mother for comfort, Rugaru felt tears welling in his eyes.

"What have I done?" he asked. "What have I done?"

"Enough looking backwards," she said. "I need to tell you what's about to happen, and how we each fit into it."

Rosalie looked up, peering at something across the room and outside the glass wall.

"You may reveal yourself," she shouted.

Rugaru turned, and the sight left him breathless. There was a man suspended in the air outside the tower, standing upon the roaring mountain winds with the smallest of efforts.

"Him?" asked Rugaru, leaping to his feet and tensing up. "I don't understand."

Rosalie smiled.

"Did you not find it strange how easily you defeated him?" asked Rosalie. "Jasper Monhegan is not a man who runs away."

Chapter Twenty-eight

Speak the Truth

The Northern Wilds, Gaia

Maeryn paced around the True Search's northern campsite. Max sat on her shoulder, patiently listening to her vent one frustration after another. The only other people awake were a bunch of rowdy teenagers.

"Can't trust us!" shouted Maeryn. "How many times have you and I put our lives in danger for Kaija? And now her life is on the line, and we're stuck here at the kids table! I'm so angry, and sad, and just… AH!"

Maeryn kicked a pile of leaves and screamed in frustration. They walked past two teenagers who were making out behind a tree, completely oblivious to the chaos happening in the world outside of their little secret society.

"Your boyfriend has no idea what he's doing," Maeryn commented.

The couple unlocked their lips and turned to look at Maeryn awkwardly.

"So sorry about my friend," said Max, pushing Maeryn away. "She's just upset about… everything really. Things haven't been so good ever since that frog licked us. Although, objectively speaking, Maeryn is right about your performance. Don't keep your eyes open like that, dude, it makes you look like a zombie. And don't lead with your tongue, it's just gross. That's not even mentioning the way you're... actually, you know what? Never mind. Carry on. You'll get it eventually, sport."

They walked away, leaving the couple who no longer looked like they had any desire to remain kissing.

"Extinguishing the flame of young lovers isn't doing us any good, Maeryn," said Max. "And besides, what do you know about kissing? Have you ever kissed anyone, other than that hologram when you thought I wasn't in the room?"

Maeryn's look was answer enough.

"Okay, not the time," said Max. "I'm just anxious and can't stop talking. What the heck is happening with Kaija and Fain right now? Why don't you put that mindbridge to good use and listen in?"

Maeryn groaned. "If Kaija wanted me to listen, she would have already reached out. Spying on her would make Tamala right about not trusting us. Do you know what makes this whole horrible thing even worse? Rugaru thanked our family. *He thanked us*! I'm so freaking sick of feeling like we're the bad guys, when we never did anything wrong!"

Maeryn swung her arm, letting out a burst of relaying. There was a gigantic tearing sound as a branch was ripped from the tree above and tossed into the sky. A very surprised squirrel spun through the air, just barely landing on its feet. It scurried angrily past Maeryn, squeaking threats at her.

A girl jumped out of the same tree a second later. "Nice throw. Could have warned me, though."

Tamala's daughter, Izzy, was covered in newly fallen leaves. She set down the book that she had been reading and gave Maeryn a concerned look. They had spoken a handful of times during the time that Kaija was recovering, but Izzy mostly seemed to keep to herself.

"I heard that my mom took your friend away," she said. "She can be pretty intense, just try not to take it personally. What happened?"

"Didn't you see the message from Rugaru?" asked Max.

Izzy pulled a twig out of her hair. "No, actually. A few minutes ago I was picking mangos on the eastern continent. I come back, looking for a quiet spot to read, and everyone's screaming their heads off about something."

"Rugaru captured Kaija's entire village," said Maeryn. "He's going to kill them all if Kaija doesn't sacrifice herself."

Izzy's eyes went big. "That's pretty intense."

Maeryn sat down next to her. "Your mom said that nobody here trusts me."

Izzy shrugged. "That's just my mom. She comes off pretty strong. When I was eight, before I learned to teleport long distances, she left me in a Hellenic prison for an hour because I stole all the chocolate from our food supply. The guards were pretty surprised to find a little girl covered in chocolate appear in max security, to say the least. I don't know why mom wouldn't trust you." Izzy looked over to Max. "Okay, the little flying man is strange, I admit, but you're cool, Maeryn. My mom will work things out. This kind of stuff happens all the time."

"Um," said Max. "What? An evil, one-armed warlord with an army of robots committing genocide is something that happens all the time?"

"Well, yeah. Sort of."

"What the hell kind of place is this?"

Izzy smiled. "We have spies all over the world, and Rugaru isn't the only evil person out there. My mom and her friends are always bringing home rescued prisoners, and stopping wars before they start, and beheading evil tyrants. Just another day in the life of Tamala True Search. Seriously, Maeryn, the elders will meet and take care of this. They'll gather an army of our best warriors and this will be all over tomorrow." She plucked a leaf off Maeryn's shoulder and stuck it between the pages of her book. "Hold on a second."

Izzy held up the book, disappeared, and less than a second later reappeared with another one.

"Sorry," she said. "That last one was pretty derivative."

Maeryn glanced down at the book in Izzy's hands. It didn't look like any of the ones from Ms. Clara's cabin; the title was written in what appeared to be a language similar to Italian.

"Where did you just go?" asked Maeryn.

"The Biblioteca Nazionale in the central Florenzia Guardianship," said Izzy. "My father took me last summer. I like to sneak in when the library's closed. Have you been?"

"No," said Maeryn uncomfortably. "We're not from, um..."

"We're not from around here," finished Max. "Maeryn, let's get going. I think Izzy is starting to suspect that I'm not human."

Izzy stood up and grabbed Maeryn's hand.

"It's amazing!" she said. "You've got to see it! You need a distraction right now."

After a short burst of colors, Maeryn and Izzy appeared in the middle of an enormous library. The bookshelves scaled all the way up the high walls, meeting with the vibrantly painted ceiling.

"Woah," said Maeryn. "This *is* amazing. I didn't know that Gaia had libraries like *this*. Gosh, that sounded really ethnocentric. I'm sorry."

"Non-spacialists really don't get around, do they?" laughed Izzy. "I bet you haven't even seen the jerkbirds in the Azonian jungles. Let me show you a picture." Izzy started walking toward the ladder on wheels leading up against the nearest shelf. Maeryn reached out her hand at the ladder wheeled straight over to them.

Izzy started scaling the ladder. "You're an externalist, huh? How basic."

The sound of footsteps echoed down the hallway. Several librarians rounded the corner, scowling at the intruders.

"La biblioteca è chiusa, signora!" shouted one of the men.

"Succhiarlo, secchioni!" Izzy shouted back, grabbing Maeryn's hand again. A second later they were in the middle of a humid rainforest. Maeryn's stomach twisted into a knot from the trip, and she sat down on the nearest log to catch her breath. The treetops were covered in red flowers that glowed like little suns.

"Where are we?"

"Hunting for jerkbirds, of course!" Izzy looked around at the canopy. "There's one!"

A brightly colored bird swooped by and landed on the forest bed, pecking at bugs on the ground.

"Jerkbird?" asked Maeryn. "That's a parrot."

"That's a parrot," the bird repeated.

"See?"

The bird looked Maeryn up and down, suddenly speaking in an incredibly masculine voice.

"Dang, girl. I am living for those curves."

Maeryn's face turned red.

"W...what?" she stuttered. "Did that bird just hit on me?"

Izzy grabbed a piece of bamboo, swatting at the jerkbird until it flew away. "Go home, jerkbird! You're drunk!"

The bird flew away, calling back at them. "You're loss, losers!"

"Don't take it seriously, Maeryn. These birds are mentalists. They read your mind and say things to make you uncomfortable. It's a defense mechanism, and it works. Nobody ever builds a village near jerkbirds. He didn't know what he was saying." She gave Maeryn a strange look. "So what's your story? I've been just about everywhere, and I've never seen people who wear clothes like you, or have flying metal pets who can talk."

"I'm not from here."

"Not from where?"

Maeryn found herself increasingly uncomfortable, but it was hard to not let her guard down when Izzy was her only way to get out of this jungle full of jerkbirds.

"Gaia," said Maeryn.

Izzy's eyebrows went up.

"Wait..." she said. "What in desolation does that mean? Not from *Gaia?* Are you from the moon or something?"

"I may as well be. You see, my grandfather killed Kaija's grandfather, but they're actually both still alive, although mine lives in a toaster now. And we have to get Kaija's grandfather home, because it turns out that there's three worlds, and one of them is coming closer, and..." Maeryn took a deep breath. "You know what, it's a lot. It's just a lot."

"I'm certainly all ears. Start from the beginning."

"Of what? My life story?"

"Sure. I'm not busy. Start with the toaster. Like, what exactly *is a toaster?*"

Maeryn laughed. "We need to get back to the campsite soon in case Kaija returns. There's too much to tell in one night."

"Why does it have to be one night? I just assumed that you were joining the True Search."

Maeryn could see that Izzy was dead serious.

"Stay?" she asked. "With the True Search? But..."

"Sure! You wouldn't be the first. We're taking in people all the time. You'd look good with some Nomadic tattoos. Less basic, at least."

Maybe it was the humidity of the rainforest, or maybe it was the absurdity of even considering living here, but Maeryn found herself sweating.

"I can't!" she said. "I have a family, and school, and…"

Maeryn stopped, realizing that she was lying to herself. Her dad was in jail, her aunt was building killing machines for Rugaru, and she had most certainly failed her online college prep courses due to vanishing off the face of the Earth. That wasn't even mentioning the fact that she was probably a wanted criminal for blowing up her mom's house. Izzy's suggestion to stay on Gaia with the True Search was ridiculous, but for that second it felt like the only solution that wasn't completely awful. She wanted to let go of her guilt, and she wanted just a few days where her life wasn't in constant danger.

A jerkbird flew out from the canopy and soared right by their heads. It opened its beak, and the voice that came out was unmistakably Rosalie's.

"Desolation comes tomorrow," screeched the jerkbird. *"Go to the Apex. It is our last chance."*

The jerkbird disappeared into the trees, and Maeryn was instantly shaken out of her illusions of being able to relax.

"I have to go back to the northern campsite," she said. "Now."

"What the heck was that about?"

"It was my aunt."

Izzy made a face.

"Not the bird," said Maeryn. "My aunt was speaking through it. She's a spiritualist. Listen, my life is complicated, but I need to talk to Kaija as soon as she gets back. Something big is about to happen."

In her mind's eye, Maeryn could clearly picture the Tree of Time. She saw a glowing light moving along its branches, approaching the point of no return where all paths would lead to Desolation. The last remains of

A Path of Branches

Maeryn's doubts were gone. A divide in the tree was coming quickly, and it was up to her and Kaija which way it would go.

Tomorrow morning, the world would go into the darkness, or away from it.

* * *

The Temple of the Elders, Gaia

Kaija stood before seven very old Nomadic men and women in a stone courthouse. Tamala and Fain sat behind her, looking at the elderly people with complete reverence.

"This is the Elder Council," said Tamala quietly. "They are the leadership for all of the True Search's many factions. Kaija, you must answer anything they ask you with complete honesty."

One of the old men studied Kaija's face seriously.

"She does bear a resemblance to the late Edgard Zeig," he said in wonder. "Incredible."

Another one of the council members, a very short and frail woman, spoke up. "Young lady, we have received Rugaru's message, as well as his revelations about your heritage, and it is to be put to a vote whether or not the True Search can continue to offer you our protection. To take in the granddaughter of Edgard Zeig might be seen as a political statement, and we do not take sides in political affairs. What do you have to say about your situation?"

Kaija struggled to find her words, but Tamala cut in before she was able to say anything.

"You know better than to have a juvenile testify on her behalf," said Tamala fiercely. "Edgard was no friend to the Nomadic people, but Kaija is an amazing young woman. No older than her fourteenth cycle, she teleported straight into Rugaru's prison to try to rescue her friend, knowing full well the danger. She is bright, brave, and strong, and we will do nothing but benefit from having her with the Search."

"Point taken," said a wrinkled old man with kind eyes. "Kaija, tell us of your family. Where is your mother?"

"My mother is Saura Aztala," said Kaija. "She's the guardian of Aztala in the—"

"—Oceanic Kingdom, yes," finished the old man. "We have our people there as well. We know of your mother. Why not take refuge in Aztala? There is perhaps no safer place in the world."

Kaija felt her cheeks getting warm.

"Because I don't want to go there! My mom and I barely see each other, but that doesn't matter now. I need to—"

"And your father?" the old man interrupted. "Jasper was not seen among the other Monhegans in Rugaru's message, nor was Clarice. Is it possible that they are planning their own rebellion? Jasper did assassinate the late High Guardian, after all."

"That was a lie," said Kaija. "He wouldn't have done that."

The frail woman narrowed her eyes, and Kaija felt a sharp sting in her brain. "She's withholding information. Speak the truth, Kaija. All of it."

Kaija didn't want to reply, but she felt utterly compelled.

"Rugaru told me that he defeated my father. But it can't be true. *It can't be.*"

"Very well," said the councilwoman. "Do not be ashamed, girl. We will put your protection to a vote. Now, tell us about Maeryn Kacey. Rugaru said that her family has been of service to him, and this is very concerning. Does she have anything to do with the weapons the Western Blaze has acquired?"

"I'm not telling you about her," said Kaija stubbornly. "Listen, I don't want your protection. I want to—ah!"

There was another sting in her brain, this one stronger than the first. Kaija looked at the seven elderly people staring at her, and she realized with horror that they were all highly-skilled mentalists. She might have been able to resist on a normal day, but her battery was drained.

"You will tell us by your own free will," said the woman, "or we will compel you to tell us."

Feeling like she was betraying her best friend, Kaija told them about how she had met Maeryn and about how her grandfather was Duncan Kacey. She clenched her fists as she spoke, angry that these people were making her spill secrets about Maeryn, but she told them everything she could remember as they listened with great interest.

"Maeryn's the best person I know," finished Kaija. "Her and Max are nothing to be afraid of. The Western Blaze has kidnapped her aunt and is forcing her to create their weapons."

The Elder Council exchanged glances, having a secret conversation in the mental realm for several tense minutes. Finally, the wrinkled old man addressed her.

"Duncan Kacey, or the Crucifier as history has named him, is known very well to us. In fact, I met him many cycles ago while he was still living with the True Search."

"What?" asked Kaija. "Maeryn's grandfather lived here?"

"He did," said the old man. "But he disagreed with our non-violent ways. He riled up a group of True Search warriors to help him kill Edgard Zeig. Those rebels would eventually start a terrorist organization known as the Western Blaze."

Kaija stayed silent at this. She and Maeryn had made peace over their family's troubled history, but this was hard news to hear, especially considering how well Maeryn seemed to fit in with the True Search. The whole thing had a sickening kind of roundness to it.

"Both Duncan and Edgard are no friends of the Search," said the man. "However, we are not so shallow as to believe that you two cannot create your own personal histories. Elias has attested to your character and told us how you were one of the few Monhegans to accept him like family. As for Maeryn, her knowledge of this other world might very well be of use to us. You and Maeryn are free to live with the True Search for as long as you like."

The Council stared at Kaija, as if expecting a thank you. She felt anger rising in her throat.

"No," she said.

The surprise in the room was palpable, and Tamala gripped Kaija's arm tightly.

"Excuse me?" asked the frail woman.

"I don't want to hide with you," said Kaija. "I want to save the other Monhegans and stop Rugaru from destroying Edgardia. I don't need shelter. I need help."

Some of the council members were visibly shaken from her boldness, but the frail old woman smiled at her.

"I don't think you understand our customs," said the woman. "We keep our eyes on Gaia, but we do not lower ourselves to the level of those who desecrate her."

"So you'll let my people die?"

"We're not *letting* anyone die. Don't forget that Rugaru is the one making these threats, not us. Blood is not on our hands."

"It's the same thing. With enough people, we could save them. Nobody would have to get hurt, we could just teleport in and out of Rugaru's prisons."

Now the woman was getting impatient.

"The Search does not act upon your authority, young woman."

The man next to her stood up, addressing Tamala. "You know Rugaru's prisons inside and out. Would this rescue be possible?"

Tamala nodded, her face absolutely unreadable. "With enough people, yes."

"Even with the mechanical fighters that Rugaru has been using?"

Kaija saw the corner of Tamala's mouth twitch.

"As far as I know, the machines were only used to guard Rosalie and Fain. There are hundreds more, if not thousands, but I do not know where they are being kept. I believe that Rugaru has them protecting the Edgardian artifacts, although I have no idea where he has moved them. The prisons are currently only guarded by a handful of men from the Western Blaze, as the rest are busy keeping the Capital occupied. They would not be expecting a raid from the inside."

"If the cost is not too great," said the old man, "we should help these people."

Four or five of the other council members nodded in agreement. Kaija's heart began to beat faster, and she could see the tides turning.

"And if the machines *do* turn up?" the frail woman asked Tamala.

"I don't know, it doesn't seem likely that—" Tamala began.

"Don't lie!"

Tamala's fingers got tighter on Kaija's arm and she glanced apologetically in her direction.

"If the machines show up, there will be many casualties, perhaps outnumbering the amount of people we can save."

"That must be considered as well," said the woman. "Although if there is a chance to save many lives, it is always worth great risk."

Another council member, this one a man with a long beard, began to speak.

"Assuming we can rescue them, Monhegan Island will be unsafe to return to for the time being, now that the Western Blaze has been there.

The Monhegans would need to stay with The Search until they have a chance to establish another community outside of the western continent. We just need a character reference, if these people are to be brought into our fold."

He turned his attention to Tamala.

"Your son recently spent time with the Monhegans, correct?"

Tamala nodded.

"Excellent," said the man. "Please summon Elias to the chamber."

Tamala disappeared, returning with Elias a second later. The old man gestured for him to step forward and spoke.

"Please enlighten me, Elias. I have heard that the Monhegans are stunning relayers, having benefited from Clarice Zeig's instruction. Tell us about your time on Monhegan. Who are these people that we are considering saving, and why did you leave before Rugaru attacked?"

Elias suddenly looked more nervous than Kaija had ever seen him, but her heart was lifting. Kaija knew the people of Monhegan, and she knew that Elias would stick up for them.

"Monhegan Island was only temporary shelter after I was attacked by the High Seven," said Elias. "I was unconscious for the majority of my time there. Once I recovered, I left to find my parents. I believe it best to exclude me from these proceedings."

Kaija could tell at once that something was deeply wrong here, that Elias was withholding some fundamental truth. He flinched as the council members detected his dishonesty and pried deeper into his mind.

"Elias," said the wrinkled old man. "For the good of the Search, everything must be considered. Tell us about the Monhegans, and speak without reservation."

Tears formed at the corners of Elias's eyes as he turned away from Kaija, staring at the ground as he spoke.

"After Rugaru attacked the island," he said, "they accused me of working with him. They believed that I helped organize the attack on the village."

"No!" Kaija protested. "Not all of them thought that. My father—"

"Silence!" shouted a council member, and Kaija saw that she wasn't helping.

"A mob came after me in the night," continued Elias. "They wanted me to leave the island, and I sensed a threat of violence if I didn't comply."

Fain stood up behind Kaija. "That's crazy! The Monhegans aren't perfect, but they wouldn't do that."

Several of the elders actually laughed at Fain's outburst. Elias bristled, on the verge of saying something but keeping his mouth clamped shut.

"Say it," said a councilmember. "I sense something important on your tongue."

Elias closed his eyes. "It was your father, Fain. Maddox led the mob right to my doorstep."

"That can't be true," said Kaija, inviting more glares from the councilmembers. "I've known them my whole life, and..."

"Nothing is spoken here but the truth, as painful as it may be," said the old woman severely. "You underestimate how deeply mistrust has been ingrained into your society, and it tends to rear its ugly head when people are afraid. You're still holding back, Elias. What did this mob intend to do? Tell us."

"I..." said Elias. "I believe that most of them weren't there to ask me to leave. I believe that some, or most, were looking for an excuse to kill me."

The old man with the kind eyes shook his head sadly.

"After you fought for their behalf and saved their children?" he asked. "So these are the people we are considering bringing into our home?"

"They're not all like that," said Elias. "Kaija and her father welcomed me, along with the island's teacher."

"Kaija is safe here with us," said the frail old woman. "And neither her father nor Clarice have been confirmed as captured. I can feel where all our thoughts are going, and I don't believe any further deliberation is needed. All in favor of sending our warriors to rescue the Monhegans?"

Not a single hand went up.

Kaija screamed, and Elias turned toward her with a face of pure despair.

"I'm so sorry, Kaija. I had to—"

"Don't talk to me!" she shouted. "I'll go by myself, and I'll die if I have to!"

Words suddenly lit up in her mind, spoken by Rosalie, but Kaija had no idea where they came from.

"Meet me at the apex. It is our last chance."

The Elder Council was preparing to leave, but Kaija shouted at them. "There's more! I don't know what Rugaru's planning, but something is about to happen. I met with a group of spiritualists, and they told me that Desolation is coming closer."

"Desolation? asked the frail woman harshly. "Don't quote spiritualist nonsense at me, girl. We made our decision."

The Elder Council vanished. Tamala grabbed Kaija as she struggled in desperation. The temple disappeared around them, and Kaija's chance of finding help went with it.

Chapter Twenty-nine

Message in a Bottle

The Northern Wilds, Gaia

"What possessed you to think that spiritualist ramblings would convince the elders?" asked Tamala.

They were back at the north campsite. Fain sat off to the side in their tent, his face in his hands, absolutely mortified about the news of his father. Elias was nowhere to be seen, having teleported away after the judgement without another word.

"I don't know," admitted Kaija. "They weren't taking me seriously."

Tamala crossed her arms. "And now they never will again. Threatening them with Desolation? Ridiculous. When I was a little girl, a spiritualist at a carnival told me that someday I'd have a son the size of a chipmunk who could fly, and then she tried to sell me a bunch of magic seashells. They are frauds, all of them."

"It doesn't matter," said Kaija. "I can't let the Monhegans die. I'm going to the Capital."

"You are fifteen, Kaija. Sacrificing yourself is not a decision that we will allow you to make."

"I'm not sacrificing myself! I beat Rugaru once before, and I was tied up and collared. I have Edgard's sword now."

"You do not have the sword. I have hidden the weapon until you come to your senses."

"No!" Kaija screamed. "You can't do that!"

"I most certainly can."

Kaija leapt at the woman, not quite sure what she was going to do, but Tamala teleported to her other side.

"Don't be stupid, Kaija. I know Rugaru better than anyone. He's underestimated you once, and he won't do it again. This will not be another fair fight. If you go to the Capital, Rugaru will ambush you with everything he's got. You will die instantly, and then he will kill the Monhegans anyway. This is horrible, but it is the absolute truth."

Kaija swung a fist at Tamala, but she dodged easily.

"Hold on to those feelings," said Tamala. "Gaia knows I wish I could feel like that. My time with Rugaru has hardened my heart, and it is something I would wish upon no one." She sighed. "I'll gather some moonberries to help you sleep. Rest, Kaija. We will be your home."

She disappeared without another word. Fain pulled his hands down, revealing a face that was sickened with grief.

"It doesn't matter," he whispered.

"What?" Kaija asked.

Fain clenched his teeth, every muscle on his body seeming to quiver with tension.

"It doesn't matter," he said again. "When I was in there, I thought... sometimes I thought it would be better to just die. Every day I'd watch Achak come and drag Rosalie away. She'd kick and scream and plead for the torture to stop, just to be dumped back in the cell hours later on the verge of death or insanity. They didn't feed me. They gave me dirty water. I had to go to the bathroom right there on the floor. They treated us worse than animals. It doesn't matter how dangerous it is to face him, or if we're too young to make these decisions, or who deserves to be saved and who doesn't, whatever the heck that means. Rugaru has to be stopped. He has to..."

Fain and Kaija locked eyes, and for the first time in a long time she sensed someone who was exactly on the same page with her.

"Die," she said. "He has to die."

*   *   *

Maeryn drifted in and out of sleep in their tent. She had thought that any rest at all would have been a miracle, but the emotional trauma of the day left her completely drained. Kaija filled her in on the council's decision, but Maeryn didn't have to question her to know that this wasn't the end of it. They weren't going to just sit around and wait for the adults to fix things anymore. What exactly this meant for Maeryn, however, she had no idea. How far would she be willing to go to help her friend? How much more could she possibly have to offer at this point?

Kaija tossed and turned in the sleeping bag next to hers. Max and Fain sat in the corner, whispering plans back and forth into the early hours in the morning.

"Apex!" Max suddenly exclaimed, completely shattering any chance Maeryn had of resting. "Jasper wasn't saying Zebulon Ape, he was saying Zebulon Apex! Duh!"

Maeryn sat up and rubbed her eyes. "What are you talking about?"

"I saw Jasper when I was locked up," said Fain. "Or, I thought I did. Maybe it was a dream, or he was trying to reach me in the mental realm, but he whispered something to me. Until now I thought it was *Zebulon Ape*, but it was actually Zebulon—"

"Apex," Maeryn finished. "That's what the jerkbird told me: go to the Apex. But what's the Zebulon Apex?"

She looked at Fain, but he simply shrugged.

"It's a mountain," said Max. "I've seen it on a map of Edgardia before. Both Jasper and Rosalie were trying to tell us to go there. Maybe that's where Rugaru's hiding the artifacts. Or the Monhegans. Or Rosalie. Or all of them. There's no way to know for sure."

"Whatever he's hiding, Rugaru's not going to leave it unprotected," said Maeryn. "What happens if we go there and the entire Western Blaze is waiting? Or the Guardian Angels? There's a difference between knocking down Rugaru in one-on-one combat and taking on a whole army by ourselves."

"We're going anyway," said Max.

Kaija gave up trying to sleep, getting out of her sleeping bag and giving Max a look. "Aren't you supposed to be the voice of reason?"

"I'm not usually into this hippie voodoo stuff, but being here on Gaia has changed me. This has got to be the turning point the spiritualists told you two about. We can choose to do nothing, and Rugaru attracts the attention of Desolation. Or we can choose to at least try, and…"

He trailed off, not being able to calculate what would happen next. The unspoken truth was that stopping Desolation did not necessarily mean that *any* of them would make it out alive.

"We do have one advantage," continued Max. "Rugaru expects Kaija at the Capital, but he doesn't know that *we know* about the Zebulon Apex. If the Monhegans are there, and we save them, he wouldn't have any leverage over Kaija anymore. If Rosalie's there, she can disable the Guardian Angels. If the artifacts are there, then I can finally get my hands on that sweet hammer."

"What if its none of it?" asked Maeryn. "We're basing our decision to go there on a hallucination and a warning from a bird? If Kaija doesn't show up at the Capital in the morning, and we're wrong about the Apex, then all the Monhegans are dead."

"Then we split up," said Fain. "I'll go with Kaija to the Capital and take on Rugaru. You two figure out what's happening at the Apex."

Maeryn felt like pulling her hair out. "So we cut our numbers in half? We're only four strong as it is!"

"Five."

There were footsteps outside of the tent. Somebody reached in and pulled back the tent flap. Elias came in holding Edgard's sword with one hand, tossing it to Kaija.

"You tell my mom that I stole this, and I'm leaving you in the jerkbird jungle forever."

"You're helping us?" Fain asked. "After what my father did to you?"

Elias shook his head. "I'm not doing this for him, or any of the other Monhegans. I'm just trying to set things right, because a lot of this is my fault. I can't ignore my part in this whole mess anymore."

"You didn't do anything wrong," said Kaija.

Elias sighed. "I wish I could agree, but I've held the truth back for too long. I…" he trailed off, shame written across his scarred face. "I'm the one who stole the Mentalist Stone from Thomas. I gave it to Achak, and he used it to interrogate Rosalie. If it wasn't for me, none of this would have happened."

It was like he dropped a bomb in the middle of the room. Everyone was speechless, this information coming seemingly from nowhere.

"You were working for the Western Blaze?" asked Fain, standing up and taking a step back. "The Monhegans were right about you all along?"

"No," said Elias. "It was an accident. A few months ago, an old man came to me and said that he was a representative of the True Search. He said they were planning a rebellion, to overthrow Thomas's guardianship and return the continent to the original Nomadic inhabitants. My resentment for Thomas had been steadily growing over the cycles, and all I wanted to do was regain the favor of my people. I told this old man that Thomas got much of his power from the Mentalist Stone, and he convinced me to steal it and hand it over to the True Search. I did exactly what he told me to do. As soon as I gave the stone to the old man, he started to transform. He got taller. His nose went crooked. It was Achak all along, spinning his illusions. But it didn't matter at that point, it was too late for me to get the stone back. Thomas suspected everything and ordered the High Seven to execute me."

Elias looked around at the four of them, eyes glimmering.

"I was tricked, but I still have to set things right. I'm doing this for you, Kaija. I've lived with Thomas's guardianship, and I've lived with the True Search. You have something that both of them are lacking. Something that even the Monhegans didn't have. It's hard to put into words. You have a hope for the future, an absolute refusal to play by the rules of the worst people. If there are sides to be picked, I am on nobody's but yours. I'll do whatever you want, if I can still have your trust."

Elias sat there in the aftermath of his revelation, waiting for whatever judgement they had. Maeryn smiled at him.

"If Kaija can learn to trust me, then I don't think you need to worry," she said.

Elias tilted his head at her. "Why? Did *you* accidentally start a violent insurrection?"

"No. But my grandfather is Duncan the Crucifier. And my aunt tried to kill Kaija on several occasions."

"Most of your family has, honestly," said Kaija.

Fain snapped. "Oh, and then there was the time that Maeryn took over your body and walked straight into the mouth of a hydra vine."

Elias blinked in disbelief.

"So let's change the subject," said Max loudly. "We've gone from four to five. What do we do now?"

He turned to look at Kaija, and everyone else followed suit. She was immensely moved to have their devotion, but the moment somehow felt right. Her grandfather created this nation, her grandmother taught her all she knew, and her own father had saved the guardianship once before. It was on her now. This was Kaija's moment.

"Maeryn and Max, you two talk strategy," said Kaija. "We have five people and fifty places to be. Elias, see if your mother has a map of Rugaru's prisons hidden somewhere. We'll need you to check all of them you can, in case the Monhegans are being held somewhere other than the Apex. As for me…"

Kaija took Edgard's sword in her hand and held it tight. Her idea was too desperate to be spoken aloud. "…I need time to think."

* * *

Maeryn, Max, Elias, and Fain made their final preparations in the hours before sunrise, but Kaija had her own task. She wandered off into the woods, finding a quiet spot and letting her mind drift away. A thick mist hung in the air, settling into dew on the ground.

"The trees are just the idea of trees. The birdsong I'm hearing is just the idea of birdsong."

The white mist thickened, completely absorbing every single tree until Kaija sat inside a white cloud. The last time Kaija tried to fully immerse herself in the mental realm, it had felt nearly impossible to navigate. Achak tricked her, reeling her mind over to his with little effort, and she barely made it out with her sanity. This time would be different. This time she had Edgard's sword amplifying her abilities, and the enormity of the task now felt somewhat less enormous.

"Where is my father?" Kaija spoke aloud.

Silence met her from the mental realm, not even a tiny ripple coming back in response.

Kaija was discouraged, but she kept digging. The chaos of other people's thoughts ran through her head like an ocean.

"Who is thinking of me right now?"

A sudden, horrible bitterness filled the air around her, and Kaija knew that she had accidentally moved herself toward Rugaru. Images filled her mind of a broken, dangerous animal who had been pushed into a corner. She retreated instantly, not wanting to get sucked into this black hole. Her strategy had not been specific enough.

"Who is placing all their hopes in me right now?"

She felt the minds of thousands of people circling through the mists all around her. Maeryn was there, as well as Elias and all of the Capital citizens who had seen her fight Rugaru. Fain was the strongest presence, everything inside of him trusting her so completely that it was almost scary. The mists above darkened, becoming a churning thunderhead, so many thoughts and emotions mashed together that Kaija's consciousness would be torn to shreds if she tried to navigate up into that chaos.

A strange force tugged at her from above as a light appeared in the sky. It was dim, like a star peeking through dark clouds. Kaija sensed that someone was thinking about her at this very moment, and the overwhelming love coming from this mind was more powerful than anything she had ever felt. Whoever this was, Kaija had their whole heart.

"Father?" she thought. *"Are you there?"*

The light in the sky shone brighter. With a huge effort, Kaija dug through the mental realm for this person, and the mists began to part slightly. She felt something radiating through: an awful shame wanting to retreat back into the darkness. A small opening appeared in the mist, and with all her energy Kaija sent a message into the heavens.

"Whatever's happened… whatever you've done, it's okay. It's okay."

The mists trembled, desperately wanting to push back together and lock her out of this part of the realm. Kaija held them apart with nothing but sheer willpower. She hurled her thoughts up there, putting a message into a bottle and letting it get pulled into the sky.

"We need your help. Meet us at the Zebulon Apex."

The moment the message went through, the mists merged back together, closing off the path to the mind that Kaija had briefly connected with. The mental realm dissolved around her, and Kaija found herself back on the forest bed. She thought of her father, trying and failing to imagine the strange road his life must have surely taken the last few days. That mind she had sensed was utterly tormented with contradictory thoughts and emotions.

Kaija didn't know what this might mean. She didn't know if it was her father in there, or someone else had placed their greatest hopes in her. She told herself that even if she didn't make it through the morning alive, at least her message had gotten through. Maybe it would find whoever needed to hear it the most.

Chapter Thirty

More to Heaven and Earth

The Capital, Gaia

The Capital Walls had been reduced to rubble, but amongst the wreckage stood a thousand Western Blaze archers, arrows knocked and ready to strike. A hundred conjurists were in the opposite field, fire blazing in their upturned hands. In the sky above flew a swarm of MotherTech drones, their plasma rifles programmed to shoot upon detection of incoming teleportation. Hiding in the Capital itself were fifty skilled mentalists, all of them focusing on building a mental barricade around their leader.

Rugaru himself stood confidently in the area where their visitor was predicted to arrive, two of his strongest internalists perched at either side. His silver eyes watched the sun peeking out over the field, and a voice spoke in Rugaru's earpiece. He listened intently, and then raised up his nanobot hand as it filled with energy.

"Three. Two…"

There was a sharp pop in the space directly ahead of him, and in the same instant Rugaru fired his weapon. The drones circling above did the same, and then less than a second later the archers followed their actions.

A square foot of land became scorched with blasts from all sides, but the chaos subsided as quickly as it came.

When the smoke cleared, there was no one there. Rugaru remained calm as he surveyed the wreckage.

"Time has moved along a secondary branch. Kaija's not here. They sent someone else."

In the next several milliseconds, a gray cloud appeared in the air in front of them, quickly bursting together and turning into a chrome ball which shot at Rugaru with blinding speed. It collided with his jaw with a *crack* and then soared upward.

Rugaru spit out a mouthful of blood and smiled savagely. "It's the machine. Good."

Max transformed into his humanoid shape in the sky above, sending out shockwaves which fried several drones.

"Rugaru!" he screamed. "Your reign of terror ends now!" Max hesitated. "Wait, did you say *good?*"

Rugaru jumped, and at the same time both of the internalists on either side pushed up on his feet, sending him soaring through the air. Max was not easily surprised, but seeing the utter *lack of surprise* on Rugaru's face sent his probability matrix into an absolute frenzy.

* * *

The Zebulon Apex, Gaia

Elias appeared in the forest trail, halfway up the mountain to the summit. Kaija, Maeryn, and Fain had their arms linked beside him.

"There it is," said Elias, pointing at the rocky plateau far ahead of them.

Maeryn studied the winding path up the mountain, which sloped upwards for several stretches. The air was already thin and hard to breathe, and she could only imagine how difficult it would be as they got toward the top.

"Not to be the wimpy Earth girl complaining about walking," said Maeryn, "but it's going to take hours to get up there. Can't we just teleport to the top?"

"I tried, but it didn't work," said Elias. "When I was young, I visited the Apex with my father. There used to be this monk in a little hut who sold doughnuts at the summit. But when I try to visualize it, the space gets blurry."

"What does that mean?" asked Fain.

"You can only teleport somewhere that you can visualize clearly. Something fundamental has changed about this land. It looks the same from here, but I doubt there's only doughnuts up there now. You'll have to teleport yourself up the path a little bit at a time." He took out the map of Rugaru's prisons that he had stolen from his mother. "I'll track down as many Monhegans as I can. Rugaru won't be expecting a breakout while Max is fighting him, and the freed prisoners can help me rescue the rest."

Kaija hugged Elias tight.

"Thank you," she said.

He nodded bravely.

"Be safe. All of you."

Elias disappeared soundlessly. Kaija, Maeryn, and Fain began making their way up the path, teleporting in short jumps at a time. Fain held a ball of fire in each hand, ready to go on the offensive at any moment. The morning sun was getting brighter on the horizon, indicating that Max would currently be in combat with Rugaru.

"Why is it so peaceful here?" asked Maeryn, struggling to breathe the thinning air. "I can see the summit, and there's nothing up there. Are we sure we have the right place?"

Kaija teleported them further along the path, then stopped and studied the land ahead of them.

"That's weird," she said. "We're not getting any closer."

Fain squinted his eyes and pointed at a nearby tree.

"She's right," he said. "We've passed Silvester three times now."

"What?" asked Kaija.

"He's that super cute squirrel over there, eating an acorn."

Maeryn looked back and forth up and down the path, seeing the same scenery in both directions. "It's a loop."

Despite having teleported two stretches already, the summit looked just as far away as ever. They ran ahead on the path, which never seemed to change. It looked like the trees on either side of them were rolling by in a never-ending pattern. The same squirrel in the same tree eating the same acorn passed by another two or three times.

"It's like the infinite staircase in Super Mario Multiverse," said Maeryn.

Kaija and Fain gave her a look.

"Never mind. Anyway, we keep moving forward and the mountain keeps moving backwards. How is this — AH!"

Kaija threw her sword, missing Maeryn's head by inches. The blade resonated with a sharp clang and then froze mid-air. Sparks crackled out of nowhere, and a decapitated Guardian Angel fell to the ground where there had been nothing a moment before. It had a plasma rifle pointed at Kaija, which would have gone off if she had waited another second.

"Where did that thing come from!" yelled Fain.

Kaija studied the Guardian Angel, finding the mentalist symbol of a hypnofrog emblazoned onto its chest.

"It was casting illusions in the mental realm," Kaija said. "Without the sword, I wouldn't have sensed anything was wrong and we would have died. The reality of this place has been invisible to the outside world."

"So Silvester was never real?" gasped Fain. "Those monsters."

The scenery swirled around, returning to its true form as the mentalist illusion broke down. Footsteps appeared in the dirt, revealing that they had been walking around in circles for the last ten minutes.

The most dramatic shift was happening right over their heads. A small tower covered in mirrors appeared at the top of the Apex, and it looked nothing like the buildings of Kaija's world. Maeryn would have mistaken it for the MotherTech headquarters in Indianapolis, and it stuck out like a sore thumb in this wilderness. Above the mirrored tower, more changes were taking place. The sky, which had been pale blue a moment ago, was now littered with patches of jet-black clouds. They billowed and undulated in odd ways, like giant swarms of wasps.

The gentle sounds of birdsong and running streams were replaced with a constant low humming from above. Somewhere in the forest, a siren was blaring sounds of alarm. As Maeryn and Kaija watched the sky, their shared mind came to the same conclusion almost instantly.

"Those aren't clouds."

For stretches in every direction, the sky was littered with countless Guardian Angels. They were here: every single last one of them. The black clouds began to turn red, as one by one the machines set their targets on the three intruders.

* * *

The Capital

Max was capable of making thousands of careful decisions every second, and he had flown into combat with Rugaru without a single shred of fear. However, Max was beginning to feel an unfamiliar dread rising in the deepest bits of his programming. As fast as he moved, Rugaru would teleport wherever he was headed and toss blasts of energy at him with amazing precision. Max could sense mentalists trying to pry into his consciousness, and it was taking quite a bit of his processing power to keep them out. He tried to think more like a machine, making it harder for the mentalists to reach him.

Rugaru fired at him, but Max split into two pieces and attacked. With an alarming ease, Rugaru simply snatched one of the Maxes with his metal arm and crushed it with an incredible force. Max spread himself thin, dividing up Rugaru's shoulder and across the rest of his body. He tried to shout, but Max soon covered his face and mouth until Rugaru was literally covered head to foot. Max made a quick mental note to never tell anyone that Rugaru's whole body had literally been *inside of him.*

Only a few more minutes of this, and Rugaru would suffocate. The man struggled with all his might, but every inch of his body was covered in a solid inch of metal. The idea of stealing a living thing's breath was a horrible concept, and it made Max feel sick. The core of his morality told him to only take life under the direst circumstances, but those circumstances had arrived.

There was a sudden rush of energy, a pop, and Max felt himself teleported with Rugaru. A scorching heat covered every inch of his body. Less than a second later, there was another pop and they were back at the Capital. Max found his processing power suddenly drained nearly to zero. During the split second they were gone, Rugaru had teleported them straight into a volcano, only long enough to weaken Max while keeping his own body protected.

Rugaru thrust out his arms, splitting Max's remaining nanobots apart. His core processor turned into a gray cloud in the air, and he began collecting solar energy to regenerate.

"I have nothing to fear from you, machine," said Rugaru.

Max reformed a small part of himself and fired a blast of energy at Rugaru. He watched the man's eyes shift to the spot he was about to teleport to, and in the next millisecond Max transformed into a spear and flew in that direction. He aimed without reserve, fully intending to land a killing blow. With a pop, Rugaru appeared right where Max had predicted. The tip of Max's spear easily pierced Rugaru's clothing and punctured the skin on his chest. However, the moment his blood touched Max's nanobots, the spear froze in place. Something deep within the very foundation of Max's programming had stopped him and disabled his motor controls. Max tried to reform into his human shape, but nothing happened.

"I've been told of your nature," said Rugaru, "and you are not built to kill."

"That's not true!" said Max, and he meant it. He wanted nothing more than to end the life of this man, this monster who had spent the last two cycles terrorizing his best friends. Max tried to thrust the spear forward with all his might, but it didn't budge. It was no use, the law that was preventing him from killing this man was so fundamental to his core self that it was like trying to push an unmovable object. Dorian's update last year had introduced many new things to his abilities, *including* the option to use deadly force, but there was one law that could never be broken. The implications sent Max's mind spinning.

"This is impossible," said Max.

"It is not," said Rugaru, grabbing the spear and easily pulling it from his chest, revealing a wound over his heart which was no bigger than a pinprick. "There was a time when I would have agreed with you, Max. But I have been to your world, where I felt Gaia's absence for the first time in my life. I have seen the gleaming cities with towers that reach for the sky, and I walked amongst the hordes of powerless people."

Max began to shift back into his human form, but it was happening outside of his control. Some invisible hand had reached inside of him and was taking control of his body.

"What once seemed impossible is now an approaching reality," he continued, holding out his metal hand in anticipation. "Did you know that there are some constants between the two worlds? Musical phrases, bits of poetry, songs… I've seen the same things repeated on both Gaia and Earth. It is as if we share the same mental realm. Either that, or these things are universal truths, waiting not to be created, but discovered some higher plane. When I was young, my mother read me a book, and I never forgot it. *The Tragedy of the Prince.* Imagine the surprise when I discovered my favorite quote existed on your world as well."

Max's core processor, the very nanobots that allowed him to channel Gaia's energy, were torn from his chest. He watched, horrified, as the gleaming chrome began to churn and twist in the air against his will.

"There are more things in heaven and earth, than are dreamt of in your philosophy."

Max felt his connection to Gaia becoming severed as his core processor twisted into the shape of a gleaming ring. His metal body dropped to the ground, now without a power source. He pulled himself up, struggling to absorb enough solar energy to maintain his motor controls.

Rugaru caught the ring and placed it on his finger. "The Internalist Ring. Taken from one world to another by Duncan Kacey, melted down by his son, and then brought back here by his granddaughter."

Rugaru turned, his voice artificially amplified as he addressed the entire army before him.

"I have the final lost artifact, and the sword will soon be delivered to the Zebulon Apex. Stay and hold down the Capital." He smiled, and his eyes glimmered as he observed the loyalty of his followers. "My people... I will miss you. Make this world into a better one than what I leave behind. Make it into a place where we can cast aside our weapons, and never pick them up again. Gaia's suffering will soon be over."

* * *

The Floridian Peninsula, Gaia

Elias was breathless from teleporting roughly seventy times in the last ten minutes, but he didn't dare stop. He had already been to most of the prisons on his mother's map, but found every single one of them completely deserted. The strangest thing was that everywhere he went showed signs of recent action: plates of food half eaten, fresh footprints in the dirt, and that thin feeling in the air of lots of people having recently teleported. He tried tracking these signals, but each jump would just bring him to another abandoned prison. Were the guards somehow aware of Elias, and moving the prisoners one step ahead of him?

In the marshes of the Floridian peninsula, Elias found a guard asleep outside of a recently deserted cell. Before the man could wake up, Elias grabbed his shoulders from behind, planting the guard firmly in his physical location and making it impossible for him to teleport while Elias's hands were on him. The guard woke up and began struggling, trying desperately to teleport away, but Elias's willpower was far stronger.

"I'm sorry!" yelled the guard. "I know I was supposed to go to the Capital, but I had too much to drink last night and couldn't stay awake! Don't report me!"

"Only if you stop begging," said Elias, holding the man tighter. "Tell me where the prisoners went."

"You don't know?"

"Just tell me."

The guard turned his head as far as it would go, catching a brief glimpse of Elias's face. "You're not one of us! You're the knight! The race traitor!"

He began screaming for help. Elias dug his knee into the guard's back and yanked on his shoulders, arching his body in an unnatural direction. There was an awful cracking sound and the guard screamed in agony.

"Your back wouldn't be the first that I've broken," said Elias. "Were the Monhegans here?"

"Yes! Some of them, at least. But they all got moved early this morning."

"Where?" asked Elias.

"Please... my back..."

Elias pushed his knee into the man with more force.

"Tell me, or I snap you in half!"

"They're not in any of our prisons. This morning, Rugaru spoke to us through the gadgets in our ears. He gave us a very specific plan. The instructions went down to the very second. I didn't understand his sudden change in plans, but we did it anyway. You don't question him, you just don't. He told us the exact moment to move the Monhegans back to—"

The man jerked in Elias's arms, and then went totally limp. His head rolled to one side, blood trickling out from his ear. Elias let go and the guard toppled over, eyes still open but lolling around aimlessly.

"What happened?" asked Elias, but the man simply lay there, stunned and motionless.

A humming sound was coming from the metal earpiece in the man's ear. The earpiece must have scrambled the man's brain just at the moment he was going to talk. This made absolutely no sense.

As a trained knight of the High Seven, Elias was used to making split-second decisions, but he felt completely trapped in this situation. Things seemed to be running like a horrible clockwork that was already put in place, reality itself reacting like it knew his every move. Elias pulled out his mother's map in an attempt to figure out where to go next. Ten seconds went by, and then twenty, and then thirty, and then a whole minute. His burnt hands began to tremble as dozens of possibilities ran up against each other in his head.

Elias had no idea what to do now. He was stuck.

* * *

Time's Branches

Across the two worlds, many important things were happening in the same exact instant.

Max was waking up without a core processor. He tried to run, but his tiny body only contained what meager power he could glean from the sun. The entire Western Blaze was cheering at their leader's victory. Rugaru swept Max up in his hand, smiling as the robot made a fruitless attempt to break free.

"It's okay, little one," he whispered. "The curtains are closing. Our play will all be over soon."

Hundreds of stretches away, Kaija, Maeryn, and Fain were watching as the sun was blotted out by swarming Guardian Angels. They set their targets on the two girls, and the first of their hoards began approaching with deadly aim.

All across Gaia, spiritualists sat in quiet contemplation as they felt the approach of a divide in time's branches. Something was escaping their sight, some unknown factor outside of Gaia's influence moving ever closer. They readied themselves to intervene should the worst happen, should history begin an irrevocable descent into the looming darkness.

In a universe both endlessly far yet closer than ever, Edgard Zeig faced his crucifier for the last time.

Chapter Thirty-one

Refuse to Believe It

The Atlantic Ascent, Earth

"That was my last marshmallow," said Kai, chewing a sticky blob and feeling the sugar hit his dehydrated body. "If your goal was to torture me, you've succeeded."

Kai's lower legs were literally stuck inside the floor, having been partially swallowed up by a cloud of nanobots. He was on the top floor of the Freedom Tower in the ruins of New York City. Gaia was only several feet away from here, but it may as well have been on the other side of the universe. The device capable of opening a portal was stuck on the other side of a wall made from internalist steel, a wall that Duncan Kacey had put there to keep Kai from going home.

How long had he been stuck here? It felt like six or seven days, but dehydration had long ago made him delirious. Kai survived by rationing the marshmallows in his backpack and sipping up puddles of dirty water that leaked from the ceiling. Shortly after Duncan got locked out of the control system, a pigeon flew in through the cracked window and perched itself in front of Kai. It just sat there and watched him, never moving for days at a time, just sitting and watching.

Kai knew what this bird really was: just another of Duncan's drones, sent here to keep an eye on him.

When the bird first arrived, Kai screamed his lungs out at it for hours in anger. The last of his anger eventually burned away, and he sank into a bleak silence. The pigeon watched, never blinking, never speaking. Kai briefly considered chopping his lower legs off with a knife and crawling away. He could grow them back if he just got as far as Gaia, but the metal wall was not moving. His only hope was for someone to arrive from the other side and save him, but it seemed less likely by the hour.

Kai licked the floor, lapping up the last of the rainwater. It tasted chalky, containing flecks of the ceiling it had leaked from. He cleared his throat and looked at the bird, speaking in a painfully dry voice.

"You could have pecked me to death by now, you know. Why let me die slowly?"

No response. Not even a dismissive tweet.

"You've been trying to finish me for forty-one years, Duncan. Are you getting stage fright now, right at your big moment?"

The bird blinked, and then resumed watching.

Kai pulled a book out of his backpack and threw it at the bird. It struck the robotic pigeon with a metallic *clink* and bounced right back off.

Once, Kai had been the most powerful man in existence. On Gaia, he could have turned the metal walls to dust with a single blink. He could have wrapped power around every single one of his molecules and walked straight through the metal, feeling it melt around him while never harming his body. But this is where life had led him: just as powerless as the homeless people he lived with for so long, being terrorized by a single pigeon.

"I had a family, you know. I fell in love with the Generalist Knight, Clarice Zeig. She was pregnant when you attacked me. We were planning on running away to Monhegan Island and raising our son there.

I've thought about them every day. About how you took them away from me. I didn't know what happened to them until I met Kaija. Always figured your people would track them down and take them away from me too."

The pigeon cocked his head at Kai. He opened his beak, speaking in Duncan's voice for the first time.

"Do you think you're the only person who lost everything?"

Kai burst out laughing. He couldn't stop, despite the horrible pain each and every laugh sent through his lungs.

"You can talk?" he asked. "This whole time, I've wondered if I've been spilling my soul to an ordinary bird, and *you can talk?*"

"My directives have encountered a paradox," said the bird. "And I have been unable to choose a course of action. I am programmed to kill should you attempt to cross the bridge to Gaia. This bridge is now within your reach, closer than it's even been, so part of me does indeed wish to peck you to death. But as you are also undoubtedly aware, the chances of you getting out of the floor and through the wall are an absolute zero without outside intervention. So, all I can do for now is watch. I'm not here for conversation."

"And yet, you're talking," said Kai. "What was it? Did I say something that surprised you? Is this the first time you're seeing the real person behind your victim?"

The bird shook its head. "I have always struggled with my cruelty toward you, Edgard. I know what it is like to endure great loss."

Kai yelled in anger and grabbed at the pigeon, but it was just out of his grasp.

"Great loss? You came here and raised your family. I left mine behind, and I couldn't have started over if I wanted to. I was always moving, always running from you."

"You think I left nothing behind?" asked Duncan. "My family on Earth was not my first family, Edgard. During the war, I abandoned my post from the Europan army and found refuge among the western Nomads. They were *my* family, Edgard. They saved my soul from the horrors of the Global War. There was a woman in the True Search that I loved so much it hurt. Even now, past my own death, I wonder what I could have had with her on Gaia. I think of her every day. Mika. The previous me placed her at the very core of my being."

Kai shook his head with contempt.

"Then why didn't you stay with her, you fool? Were you so determined to destroy my life that you were willing to give up yours as well?"

"There was no future for us on Gaia. If we had children, those children would have known nothing but suffering and marginalization. They would have been forced to live in squander, stuck in your Nomadic reservations while the guardianship erased their history."

Kai gritted his teeth. "If you didn't like Edgardia, then you should have taken your family and left."

"Other guardianships were already pledging allegiance to you. It was only a matter of time before the entire world was under your rule."

"That's not what I wanted."

The pigeon laughed, which was an entirely unsettling sight.

"You think it mattered what *you* wanted?" asked Duncan. "Tell me who built Edgardia. Who put its political structure in place?"

Kai thought back to his past. After single-handedly ending the war, he was essentially a scared and confused kid, not sure how to move forward. People were declaring him to be the son of Gaia, and it was a complete shock to the system.

"I invited representatives from each of the warring armies to unite," said Kai. "They became my advisors. We built Edgardia together."

"A nation named after you, of course."

"That wasn't my decision. They insisted."

"Exactly."

Kai was silenced at this.

"See, that's the thing you don't understand," said Duncan. "I never hated you. I hated what you represented, and you were too close to ever truly see yourself. The wealthiest people from the other guardianships congregated around you, around the strongest force in the world. These elites built a new nation and wrote laws to benefit no one but themselves, hiding behind you all along. They feared the Nomadic people, and sought to erase us. Land was set aside for us to retain our ancient culture, but it was the worst land your lawmakers had to offer, and they were constantly taking it back in bits and pieces. The time would come when there would be no safe place for us. I left Mika behind, and it broke my heart, but I left her in a world where she could have a future."

Kai clenched his old fists, slamming them on the ground as he trembled with ire. "How could you possibly know that?"

The pigeon opened its beak, sending out beams of light that converged into a holographic image. The young face of Duncan Kacey stared at Kai, no older than eighteen, the age of an unwilling passenger on a warship.

"I found my spiritualist leanings, Kai. In my youth, the culture was changing and spiritualism was a dying breed among the Nomadic people, but I met some of the most powerful western spiritualists in their old age. They were members of a secret society known as the Spiritualist Circle. They all agreed on what we were feeling. You would be the one to lead Gaia to the entity known as Desolation."

"Nonsense."

"Is it? Do you deny its existence?"

Kai's head swam for a moment. During his time on Gaia, he had sensed that there was a world known as Earth where Gaia was not present. But beyond that, he felt another place, a dark blot on a page that his teacher Mr. Calderon called Desolation. Kai could draw from the infinite powers of Gaia, but in the furthest reaches of its infinity there was a place where Gaia turned black and rotten. He dared not let his mind wander to that place, but always felt it watching him.

"Desolation is real," continued Duncan. "My last years of multi-dimensional research here on Earth proved its existence and uncovered startling things about its nature. Your transformation into Edgard Zeig confirmed that we were heading toward Desolation on the Tree of Time. Many spiritualists thought that it was too late, that even your death would create events that would push us forward on the branches, but I believed that the only way out was to remove you from fate entirely. To take you to the place where Gaia couldn't touch you. I knew that I risked getting trapped on Earth myself, away from my beloved Mika, but it was the only way to give her a future. Yes, I loved her, but her life would be brighter without me."

"You should have gone with your heart," said Kai. "No matter what."

"Interesting, because when I witnessed you put a stop to the Global War, I had a vision that was more powerful than anything I ever experienced. Do you know what it was?"

"Enough of this. You are delusional, Duncan. I hate you. If you want me dead, just go ahead and—"

"The world will fall to love, not hate," Duncan interrupted. "That's what it was: love destroying all. Love is biased and shallow, and the only way to make a better world was with thoughtful deliberation. That's what I saw. If I would have stayed with Mika, and you would have raised your family, that would have led us to Desolation. It may have taken hundreds of cycles, but it would have happened. It was the truth, my own desolate truth. I don't hate you, Edgard. Never. Even when I really wanted to."

"I don't believe you."

"Then let me prove it."

Duncan's transformation into his younger self had now reversed. He looked as old and weary as ever. The binding on Kai's feet were released as the nanobots turned into a cloud which dissolved into the air.

"Five minutes ago, I broke through Rosalie's firewall," said Duncan. "It took six and a half days of my complete concentration, but I did it. I could have had those nanobots crush you, but instead I'm going to watch you walk away."

Kai stood up, his legs wobbling uncontrollably. He did not walk away; he headed straight for the metal wall.

"Let me through," Kai whispered.

"I cannot," said Duncan. "I'm dead, nothing more than a reflection of a bitter old man. My nature is fixed. If I bring those walls up, I'll be forced to kill you."

"That's your problem. You believe things like that."

"Go, Edgard. Live your life here for once. I'll leave you alone from now on."

"My name is Kai, and I'll never leave."

"GO!"

The pigeon burst into thousands of nanobots, gradually reforming into the shape of a sword. It almost looked like Duncan's hologram held the weapon. He spoke, voice rising in impatience. "You stay any longer, and I can't let you live. Don't make me do this, because I *don't want to*."

Kai looked right into Duncan's silvery eyes, and it brought back a deepest memory.

"It was you," he whispered.

Duncan flinched.

"What?" he asked.

"Monhegan Island was raided by colonizers, and my family was killed. The children were loaded onto a boat, and we watched from the horizon as the island burned. Before reaching the mainland, I had a vision of a young man with fiery red hair and silver eyes, and I knew that he could see me too. It wasn't the first time. My whole life, I would get glimpses of this person's thoughts. As my power grew, I became paranoid and pushed them back. Eventually it became just a tiny spark at the back of my mind, always returning just when I thought I had extinguished it. It was you. We are twins of the soul, a miracle in nature."

"A mindbridge," whispered Duncan, and Kai nodded.

"Gaia pushed us together, like she's doing with our granddaughters, and we resisted with all our strength. We wasted our whole lives. Think of what we could have done. Think of what Kaija and Maeryn will do with the bravery we never had."

Duncan remained absolutely unreadable, but the sword hovered closer, pressing up against Kai's chest. He felt a trickle of blood run down his stomach.

"My own life is over," said Duncan. "I was created to kill you, and if you stay for one more second, I will."

"Refuse to believe it. Be something better than the man you left behind."

"It's impossible."

Kai reached up with trembling fingers and felt the blade which hovered before him. His strength was nearly gone, and he'd never be able to push it away. He'd never be able to come back to life a second time.

"Please, Duncan."

"No."

"Then go ahead. If I can't go home, then I'm done here. Kill me."

Kai closed his eyes, grateful that he at least got to meet his granddaughter a single time. His family had gone on without him, and they'd continue to exist without him. He had to find peace in that. They would endure even if he did not. Energy buzzed in the nanobots, and the sword moved beneath Kai's fingertips. He gripped it, but couldn't resist its movements if he wanted to. Not here, not on this world.

The blade moved with a purpose.

Duncan Kacey, the Crucifier, had made his decision.

Chapter Thirty-two

Invisible

The Zebulon Apex, Gaia

Kaija held up Edgard's sword as the first wave of Guardian Angels swarmed toward them. She stood shoulder to shoulder with Maeryn and Fain, each covering another one of her blind spots. They felt a shared pool of energy flow between them, endlessly vast and powerful. Something was happening to the sword, something both amazing and terrifying. As time's branches divided, the weapon's power was both infinite and yet impossibly ever-expanding. A tool that could shape the very universe was available to them, but their bodies would never be able to handle the full extent of its capabilities.

Several Angels rocketed down from the sky. Maeryn swung her arm and an entire tree was ripped out by its roots, knocking them off balance. More red eyes lit up, and more Angels joined the attacking hoard.

"I'm not letting them take me again!" yelled Fain.

He summoned a dome of energy around them, and one by one the Guardian Angels burst into flames as they collided with the barrier. Kaija felt as if her blood had been replaced by electricity. A lightning bolt burst from the tip of the sword, decimating another legion of robots. Her heart

357

stopped for several seconds and then thumped back to life as a wave of exhaustion swept over her.

"We can't hold this much longer," she said.

The energy barrier collapsed, leaving them exposed in the center of a ring of fallen Angels. Several more shot down from the sky, spouting flames from their outstretched hands. Kaija tossed the sword upward with all her might, and Maeryn relayed it in an arc across the sky, cutting straight through the power centers of a dozen Angels. Kaija teleported and caught the sword as it fell back to the ground.

A Spacialist Angel appeared next to Maeryn and raised its plasma rifle. At the very last second, it jerked its arm to the side and inexplicably missed Maeryn's head by a wide margin. Kaija reappeared behind the robot and thrust the sword through its chest.

"I'm feel like I might pass out," said Kaija, panting heavily. "How many Angels are down?"

"Maybe twenty," said Fain, doing a quick scan of the rubble around them.

"Twenty thousand more to go," said Maeryn.

The ground began to rumble as a wave of Guardian Angels emerged from the other side of the mountain and flew in their direction.

"We can't do this, Maeryn," Kaija cried. "We can't do this by ourselves. We're alone."

The Angels fired an onslaught of rockets in their direction. Fain grabbed Kaija's hand and squeezed.

"We tried our best," he said, "but we need to run."

Tears streaming down her face, Kaija gathered her remaining energy to teleport them far away. Just as she was igniting her fragile spark, the rockets froze mid-air. A voice spoke from behind them.

"You're not alone. Never."

They turned around to see Ms. Clara standing there, arm outstretched and her small muscles straining from the effort. She closed her fist and the rockets exploded, filling the sky with fire and destroying an entire cloud of Angels. Their shattered bodies rained from above. More red eyes glowed in the black clouds as Angels activated, but they were no longer flying directly at Kaija and her friends. They seemed to be headed in just about every other direction, disappearing into the treetops or to the other side of the mountain.

"I heard your message," said Ms. Clara, wiping sweat off her brow.

Kaija gasped, realizing that the desperate signal she had sent into in the mental realm had found her grandmother. She jumped forward and hugged Ms. Clara tight, crying in relief, and Fain soon did the same.

"Where's my father?" asked Kaija.

Ms. Clara shook her head, and the worry in her eyes was deep. "I don't know. We've been looking, but he hasn't been seen since the Capital Massacre."

Their collective minds were swimming with relief and confusion.

"Where have you been?" asked Kaija.

"Looking for you. I thought that you both had been taken by Rugaru, at least until I heard about what happened in the Capital Theater. We've ignored him for too long. I knew that the Western Blaze would have to be stopped before it was too late, if it wasn't too late already, so I've been building an army for one last stand. The Conjurist Knight should be here shortly."

Fain went somehow pale and red at the same time. "Wait..." he said. "Will Zeig? You got Will FREAKING Zeig to help us?"

As if on command, the late guardian's Conjurist Knight appeared in the clearing, dressed for battle. He approached them, nodding respectfully at Ms. Clara.

"I'm going to faint!" Fain whispered to Kaija.

"Clarice," said Will, shaking her hand. "My men have surrounded the mountain, and are awaiting orders."

"How many?" asked Ms. Clara.

"No more than a hundred, but all are highly skilled relayers."

Fain waved at Will, stuttering as he spoke. "Um… hello again, Mr. Knight. Do you remember me?"

Will did a double take at Fain. "You're the weird kid who broke into the Capital last cycle on that flying silver thing."

"Yeah!" said Fain. "And then you arrested me. Fun times. I, um…" He spoke quickly. "I just wanted to say that you're my hero and I love you."

Will blinked a few times, shaking his head and looking back to Ms. Clara. "Anyway, have the others arrived yet?"

Ms. Clara inhaled deeply, feeling the subtle currents of Gaian energy flowing through the air. "The Aztalians will be here soon."

Hundreds of pops rang out from up and down the path as men and women appeared, dressed in swimming gear and brandishing harpoons. They shouted commands at each other in a foreign language and began spreading out. Weapons flew through the air in the distance, and Kaija spotted at least one Guardian Angel get struck in the containment orb and fall to earth. A woman with tan skin and long, black hair ran over and held Kaija tightly.

"I thought you had been killed!" she exclaimed, her accent heavy.

"Hi, mother," said Kaija. "This is Fain, my boyfriend."

Fain gave an awkward smile, and then Kaija gestured at Maeryn.

"And this is Maeryn, my… other brain. Too much to explain there."

"Saura allowed our army to meet in her city of Aztala, far away from Rugaru's watchful eye," said Ms. Clara.

Saura nodded at Ms. Clara and pulled a dagger from her belt, eyeing the undulating black clouds above and frowning. "Are you sure about this, Clarice? Even with our armies combined, we are greatly outnumbered and out-skilled. I will not lead my people into a bloodbath."

Ms. Clara remained unconcerned, at least outwardly. "Lines of communication between my fighters travel slowly, because they are spread out across the continent. But they will come, and then it will be the machines who are outnumbered."

Kaija's specialist leanings sensed something approaching, something big. A dozen or so people popped into existence in the clearing ahead of them, brandishing various weapons and studying the sky bravely. They didn't exactly look like traditional warriors. Some were downright elderly, while others were only several cycles older than Kaija. Regardless of age, every last one of them stood ready with an unflinching bravery.

"Guardians?" asked Fain.

Ms. Clara shook her head. "No. I've been building my army in secret, spreading news along every network available to me. Village guardians have been Rugaru's targets from the start, and if they started to disappear he would have gotten suspicious. I needed to strike him with a force he would never expect, with people that he viewed as insignificant."

Four or five more people appeared in the forest next to them, and then countless others on the path ahead and behind. Everywhere in sight, as close and as far as the eye could see, people were appearing all over the mountain and surrounding forest.

Ms. Clara smiled proudly. "The teachers of Edgardia have joined us."

The mountain range crackled with pops as thousands upon thousands of people continued arriving. Clusters of men and women would appear, arms linked with spacialists who would soon disappear to gather more fighters. The Guardian Angels in the sky descended on every side of the mountain, and the ensuing chaos was unlike anything Gaia had ever seen, dwarfing all but the final battle of the Global War.

Will Zeig gave Kaija a smile and cracked his knuckles. "I will clear the way ahead. We will not be replaced!"

He sprinted down the path, tossing fire from his hands that snaked through the sky, transforming into flaming serpents that completely melted any Angel foolish enough to attack. Saura Aztala pulled a container of water from her belt an uncorked it. She skillfully relayed the liquid below her feet, riding off over the treetops on a flying wave.

Ms. Clara turned back to face them.

"What do you need?" she asked. "We're all here for you."

"We need to get to the Apex," said Kaija. "Rugaru's hiding something up there. We think it might be Rosalie, and she can disable the Angels."

"And—" Maeryn began, but quickly stopped. She was going to tell Ms. Clara that if they could find a portal to Earth, they could bring Edgard Zeig in to help them. In the heat of battle, however, the information just felt too enormous. Learning that the love of her young life had been alive on another world for forty-one cycles might just give Ms. Clara a heart attack.

"Go!" yelled Ms. Clara, ripping an attacking Angel's arm clean off and smashing its energy source. "We'll protect you at every turn. Do as you've been taught."

Kaija, Maeryn, and Fain took off up the path, teleporting when they could, but finding it difficult to see very far through the smoke and destruction. A short way up the mountainside, an externalist Angel jumped from the trees at them. The machine had a thin, steel blade rotating around its body which shot toward Maeryn. She screamed and shielded herself, but the blade curved around her and headed toward Kaija, who started teleporting back and forth to avoid the weapon. Fain shot a constant burst of fire at the Angel's energy source, while Maeryn took control of the blade and relayed it straight through the melting glass, immediately sapping the Angel's power.

"It's going to take hours to get up there if they keep attacking us," said Maeryn.

"Don't take this the wrong way," said Kaija, panting for breath. "But what do you mean *us?* They're all going after me."

"What? That's not true."

Fain weaved around ahead of them, burning away bits of fallen trees on the path. "Sorry, Maeryn, but it's totally true."

An internalist Angel rocketed by them on the path, taking absolutely no notice of Maeryn. It ran toward Kaija, who tossed her sword into the air and jumped her mind into Maeryn's body, quickly catching the weapon and destroying the Angel with a single blow. They switched back and looked at each other.

"Okay, that *was* weird," admitted Maeryn.

Now that they mentioned it, Maeryn realized that the Angels always seemed to freeze up when they tried to attack her. She looked around at the battlefield, seeing hundreds of warriors in the fight for their lives, and realized that she was the only one that the Angels took no notice of. An even bigger realization hit her.

"It's my father," said Maeryn. "He's protecting me. Even now."

"What?" asked Fain. "I thought you said he's in jail."

"Yeah, but he created the blueprints for the Guardian Angels. They were built to protect my family from a Gaian invasion. He wrote their coding, and he programmed them to never harm me! I'm completely safe!"

"Well how nice for you!" Fain yelled, dodging bits and pieces of broken metal that seemed to be constantly falling from above.

Maeryn handed Kaija the sword and turned around to look up at the summit.

"I'm going to run to the Apex," said Maeryn. "You two go back to Ms. Clara and focus on keeping yourself safe. Once I make it up, we'll switch places so you can teleport the rest of us there."

Kaija smiled. "Okay, city girl. Good luck."

Maeryn took off running up the slope as fast as her legs could carry her, ignoring the burning pain in her lungs as she breathed in the thin mountain air. An unimaginable battle waged around her, but Maeryn ran fearlessly. She passed hundreds of Guardian Angels, which did not so much as glance her way.

She was invisible.

Chapter Thirty-three

Thoughts Inside of Thoughts

The Central Plains, Gaia

Elias was nearly drained. He had teleported to every one of the Western Blaze prisons without finding a single prisoner, guard, or clue about what was happening. The past hour pushed his abilities to their utmost limits, and he worried that the next time he teleported, he would arrive at the destination fast asleep or dying of a heart attack. He sat against the wall in the final empty prison, slamming his hands against the ground in frustration. Elias thought about what the guard said before his brains had been fried.

He told us the exact moment to move the Monhegans back to—

Back to where? The Capital? If so, it was out of the question for Elias to go there now. He'd be killed in a heartbeat.

The Apex? That seemed most likely.

An idea hit Elias like a brick to the head. It was absolutely absurd, but he supposed that absurdity seemed to be the way of the world these days. Elias pulled in his remaining energy, knowing that he'd be just about useless if he did this a few more times, and gently moved himself through Gaia's stream.

* * *

The Zebulon Apex, Gaia

Maeryn took in gasps of increasingly frigid air as she finally reached the top of the mountain. At the rocky summit, she could see for countless stretches on every side. The fighting occurring below her was like nothing her imagination could have ever dreamt up. The cold, calculating Guardian Angels fought the Gaians everywhere she looked, and bursts of energy lit up the morning sky like fireworks.

She turned toward the mirrored tower in the center of the Apex, walking across the barren tundra. A glass panel opened as she got close, reminding her so much of her own personal elevator at the MotherTech headquarters. There were no guards running to stop her or alarms going off. A burst of air was released from the open doorway, and it had a that artificially filtered scent that was alien to Gaia. Maeryn could have closed her eyes and imagined that she was sitting in a waiting room at a dentist's office.

"Kaija. I made it."

The next few seconds were a blur. Kaija switched places with her, getting a good look at the top of the mountain before immediately switching back and teleporting her and Fain up to the tower. They entered the building, lights turning on the moment they set foot inside.

The landing floor was completely featureless, nothing but glass windows with a spiral staircase in the middle, but they could hear an ominous whirring coming from the floors above.

"It's not a prison," said Kaija. "I can't feel any of the Monhegans here."

"No," Maeryn agreed. "It's a laboratory."

They walked cautiously toward the spiral staircase, but Fain didn't budge.

"Guys..." he whispered. "Are you seeing this? He's here."

Fain pointed toward the window at the far end of the room, and they looked out across the rocky plateau. On the other side of the Apex, standing at the edge of a cliff, stood a tall silhouette of a man. His back was turned to them as he studied the battle, long hair whipping around in the cold mountain wind.

"Father!" Kaija gasped.

"You two talk to Jasper," said Maeryn. "But I don't think we can wait any longer. I'm going to see what else is here."

Kaija grabbed Edgard's sword, took Fain by the hand, and ran toward her father. Maeryn wanted to go with them, but the thought of Desolation remained burned into her mind. There were many things happening here, and she had to walk this tower to the top.

Kaija shattered the window with her grandfather's sword, and they jumped through the opening. Maeryn turned away from her friends and looked up the spiral staircase, the steps disappearing into the unlit floors above. What could Rugaru possibly have to hide? Maeryn couldn't even begin to fathom what might be waiting.

She took a deep breath and climbed into the unknown.

* * *

"Father!"

Kaija grabbed Jasper's powerful arm, and he turned to look at her. An unreadable expression was sketched across his face. Explosions rang up from the surroundings, but he barely seemed to hear them.

"Daughter..." he said, his voice sounding tired. "Fain. I've been waiting. They told me you would come, right at this very second."

His eyes showed no hint of what he was thinking. They drifted away from Kaija and Fain, returning their gaze to the chaos below.

"What's going on?" asked Kaija. "Where were you?"

Jasper was quiet for an entire minute, struggling with indecision. When he finally spoke, it was deliberately, as if it were crucially important to say this exact set of words at this exact moment.

"Seven days ago, I left Monhegan Island. I was going to kill Rugaru, and I knew that nothing could stop me. It didn't take me long to find him, when I heard of the chaos in the Capital. I tried to save Thomas, but…" Jasper searched for the right word, his brow furrowing in concentration. "… I don't know. *Something* happened. I couldn't do it. I just couldn't."

Kaija and Fain looked at each other, their relief quickly fading away. This was not the reunion they expected.

"I don't understand," said Kaija.

Jasper smiled tiredly. "Neither did I, at least not at first. But I do now. This last week has opened my eyes to the… what did they call it? Oh, yes: the layers."

"Jasper," said Fain, tugging on his arm. "What's wrong with you?"

He didn't seem to hear them. Jasper kept talking, eyes never leaving the battle.

"The rings within the branches. Plans inside of plans. Thoughts *inside* of thoughts. *The layers.* Some universes blossom like fruit along the tree, while others rot and fall into oblivion, becoming nothing more than a dream inside of Gaia's mind. Like this battle."

Jasper pointed at the smoke billowing from the forest surrounding the mountain. Cries of combat and the sound of plasma rifles echoed throughout the valley. Guardian Angels soared in and out of the carnage like buzzards.

"This whole thing is just a layer. *A mask* for what's underneath. Watch."

"Father," she Kaija. "Maeryn's here. Rugaru might come back at any moment. We can't waste any more time."

"Shhh!" Jasper shushed her harshly. "Watch the skies. See the mask come off. Three. Two. One."

On cue, all of the red sensors on the Guardian Angels went dark. The constant buzzing sound that had filled the air just a second before vanished like someone had turned off a radio. It became eerily quiet as the dark clouds of machinery fell from the sky, powerless and inert. Every few seconds the ground shook as the robots hit the ground, splintering the trees in their descent.

Kaija's mind was absolutely reeling.

"What's happening?" she asked, barely above a whisper. She looked at Fain again, finding no answers in him either. She felt like she had wandered onto a stage, and everyone around her was just reciting rehearsed lines.

"It will make sense soon," said Jasper. "I promise." He turned to look her in the eyes for the first time. "Kaija, have you heard the word *Desolation?*"

"Yes," she said. "The spiritualists told us about it."

Jasper nodded.

"Desolation hungers. It… it *searches* like a carnivorous being. All of this, this horrible battle, it was just a piece of rancid meat. Something to misdirect Desolation. The real battle starts now."

"Real battle?" asked Fain.

Jasper looked down at the sword clutched in Kaija's hand.

"Yes," he said. "Rugaru is coming very soon now, and I will make the final stand. For Gaia. For Earth. *For everything.* Will you stand with me, daughter?"

Kaija nodded, her arms shaking with adrenaline. Jasper held out his open hand, and Kaija felt like her whole life had been leading to this moment. Like it was what they were both born for.

"My father's sword, Kaija. It always finds its way back."

Kaija held up the sword of Edgard Zeig, and offered it to him.

* * *

Maeryn raced up the spiral staircase, past one dark room filled with machinery after another. The fifth story held a single empty prison cell, not a sign of Rosalie or the Monhegans behind those bars. She paused as she made her way past the sixth story, seeing a familiar object at the corner of her eye. Ms. Clara's walking stick was sealed in a glass box, but it wasn't alone. The far side of the room was lined with six more glass boxes, each containing a different artifact. Some of them Maeryn had seen already when they first entered Gaia, but some were completely new. Each box had a symbol for a different type of relaying etched across the glass.

The Mentalist Gem. The Spacialist Spear. The Externalist Bow. The Spiritualist Flower. The Conjurist Hammer. The Generalist Staff. And...

Maeryn looked at the final box, a strange feeling creeping down the base of her spine. A small, chrome ring sat in the center of the box. It was the Internalist Ring, worn by the original Internalist Knight, Leonetti Zeig. Maeryn had read·about it in Ms. Clara's history books, but she also felt as if she had seen it somewhere else before.

Maeryn shook off her strange feeling and continued her ascent up the staircase. The final landing came into view, and the sight was dizzying. The first thing that Maeryn noticed was the giant... what? The device looked somewhat like a cannon, but calling it one would be like calling a rifle a slingshot. A massive, golden barrel was perched in the middle of the room, and seven wires ran through the floor and into the machinery under the weapon. The barrel was pointed out a round window at the front of the room, and bitterly cold mountain air gusted from the opening.

Maeryn pulled her attention away from the giant weapon and studied the room. The opposing wall was affixed with countless monitor screens, showing video feeds from Rugaru's empty prisons. On the other end of the room was a single, circular machine with a blue portal glowing in the center. It looked almost inconsequential next to the cannon, but Maeryn gasped when she saw it. This portal was the most important thing in the world at the moment, because Kai was currently stuck on the other side, not even twenty feet away from her. Maeryn took off running for the gateway to Earth.

"Stop."

Footsteps came from the other side of the cannon, and Rosalie Kacey walked into sight. She did not look like the desperate, broken woman that Maeryn had last seen. This was the MotherTech CEO, seemingly plucked from her workroom on Earth and dropped into another world.

One thing was clear: Rosalie was no prisoner. Not anymore.

"Maeryn. You're safe now. We can stop this act."

Rosalie waved her hand toward the sky. Gaian energy coursed through the atmosphere, and one by one her Angels began to deactivate and fall from the heavens.

"We're going home."

Chapter Thirty-four

The Divide

Monhegan Island, Gaia

Elias could think of no possible explanation for what he was seeing. The Monhegans were back home, all of them wandering around the village, looking both confused and elated, but undeniably *there*. Most of them took no notice of Elias as they reunited with family members, sobbing with relief, but someone spotted him right away.

"What in desolation are you doing here, Nomad?"

Fain's father came running toward Elias, looking like he was about to rip his head off. His wife, Delia, followed close behind.

"Stop!" said Elias, collapsing in his weariness. He knew that he could just teleport away, but any jump could be his final one. "I've been looking for you. How'd you get out?"

Maddox reared his head back. "The guards just all brought us here with no explanation. You mean you didn't know?"

Elias's thoughts were caught in a whirlwind. "For the last time, I'm not with the Western Blaze!"

Delia pushed past Maddox and knelt beside Elias.

"Do you know where Fain is?" she pleaded. "He wasn't in the prison with us. Even after the guards dropped us off here on the island, we didn't know what was happening."

"Fain's at the Zebulon Apex with Kaija and Maeryn," said Elias. He held out his hand. "I can take you there. They might need your help."

Delia grabbed Elias's hand without hesitation, but Maddox stood like a statue.

"No," he insisted. "Delia, let go. We can't trust this Nomad."

He reached for her, but Delia backed away.

"I've had enough of this," she said. "I'm going to find our son, with or without you."

Maddox tried to grab her arm and pull, but Delia reared back and slapped him hard. He backed up, holding a hand to the red mark on his face.

"What?" he asked, the rest of him turning red. "How dare you?"

"No!" Delia screamed. "How dare *you* pick your own prejudices over a chance to find your son? After everything we've gone through? If you don't come with us, then I'm never coming back."

Maddox's anger faded, and he looked thoroughly shamed.

"I...I'm sorry," he stuttered.

"Don't *say* you're sorry! Show me."

Maddox slowly reached forward and took Elias's hand, breathing in deeply.

"Let's go."

* * *

The Zebulon Apex, Gaia

As soon as the sword was in Jasper's grasp, the air grew hot and the blade glowed a brilliant blue. With his other arm, Jasper pulled Kaija and Fain into a tight hug.

"It will happen very soon now," he said. "As time approaches the divide in the branches, things get blurry. Everything sits on the precipice. I'm not sure what will happen next, but never forget this: I love you both, forever."

Kaija heard a voice echo distantly in the back of her mind, but the words were too far away to make out clearly. Was it Maeryn? The mindbridge was dim. Why couldn't she feel Maeryn?

Jasper let go, pushing them away with a gust of wind as he took a step closer to the edge of the cliff.

"Father?" asked Kaija. "What are you doing?"

She reached out for him, but without warning Jasper stepped over the edge. He hung in the air for a moment, suspended by the wind rushing below his feet, and then began floating upward. Storm clouds rolled into the previously clear sky, darkening the mountain below.

A pop erupted at the other end of the Apex and Rugaru appeared there. Fain grabbed Kaija, his arms trembling with fear.

"We have to run!" he insisted.

Kaija shook her head. Her father was here, and she could never be afraid in his presence, despite how weird he was acting. Rugaru locked eyes with Jasper, more awe than anger in his expression. He looked like a man watching the birth of a God. Kaija and Fain readied themselves to attack.

"Jasper," said Rugaru, raising his voice over the storm. "This is it."

Energy surged and crackled through Edgard's sword, filling the darkened land with flashes of blue light. Just being in the presence of this much power made Kaija's head throb.

"Rugaru," said Jasper. "You..."

He hesitated, taking a trembling breath as Gaia filled his very atoms. "You have my gratitude."

Rugaru turned away from Jasper, leaping toward Fain with unexpected speed and grabbing his arm. A second later, the two of them were gone. Kaija cried out in surprise, but found no solace in her father's face.

"I'm sorry, Kaija," he cried out over the thunder. "This is the only way."

With a gust of wind, Jasper soared up into the dark clouds. Before Kaija could comprehend what was happening, Rugaru was back and had ahold of her shoulder. The last thing she saw before they teleported away was a glowing light above the clouds, her father shining like a star.

* * *

Minutes earlier, Maeryn was slowly backing away from Rosalie on the top floor of the mirrored tower, trying desperately to reach her friend.

"Kaija. Something's wrong."

No response from the other end. Something about the cannon in the center of the room was making it hard to relay, as if it was sucking up most of the available energy. Gaia's supply was supposed to be infinite, but for the first time Maeryn was having doubts.

"Come on, Maeryn," said Rosalie. "The portal won't stay open for much longer."

"No!" said Maeryn. "You lied to me. Rugaru never took you prisoner! You've been helping him."

Rosalie shook her head. "If I lied, it was only to myself. I really *was* a prisoner, until yesterday. Until I realized where my spiritualism had been leading me."

"I don't need to hear this," said Maeryn. "I don't think I can believe a single thing you say."

Maeryn looked around, searching for any other means of escape, but the only way down would be to jump out the window.

"You don't have to like me, Maeryn, but you have to trust me right now."

"How? How could I ever possibly trust you again?"

"Because of *that*."

Rosalie pointed to a video screen in the far corner. Maeryn couldn't believe what she was seeing. The screen showed the Monhegan villagers, alive and well in the ruins of their home. Rosalie pointed to another screen, which displayed what was happening just below. Kaija and Fain were hugging Jasper. Yet another video showed Ms. Clara running up the mountainside, Elias in her arms, Maddox and Delia following close behind.

Video after video showed snapshots of the battlefield, but there was something undeniably absent from the footage. It seemed that not a single Edgardian or Aztailian had been killed or even wounded in battle. How was that possible, when the Angels had very nearly destroyed Max a few days ago?

"What is this?" asked Maeryn, awestruck.

"My nanobots have their eyes everywhere," said Rosalie. "These are live video feeds. A few minutes ago, Elias discovered the villagers safe and carried the news to Ms. Clara. They are both on their way up the mountain now with Fain's parents."

"This doesn't make any sense."

"There is too much to explain in too short a time, but I will tell you what you need to know. The Edgardians fought bravely, just as I expected. Kaija is reuniting with her father, and the Monhegans are returning home unharmed. As the Angels fall from the sky, each and every person out there believes that you and Kaija succeeded. In a single day, I have changed the course of history." She paused, feeling the air. "Please do not be alarmed, Maeryn."

Rugaru suddenly appeared, Fain in his grasp. He let him go, vanishing and reappearing with Kaija a second later. She screamed and leapt toward him, but Rugaru easily dodged and teleported to the other side of the room. He held out his hand non-threateningly, and light glinted off something he was holding.

"Calm down, Kaija," he said. "I will never harm you again. We are off the stage, and our performance is done. I have brought an offering of peace."

Rugaru opened his hand, and everyone immediately recognized the limp body of Max. His chrome shell raised its head and spoke in a nearly inaudible voice.

"Rugaru..." whispered Max. "He's... he's..."

Max's head plopped back down, too tired to continued. Rugaru placed him gently on the worktable, handling him like an injured bird. He gestured to Rosalie.

"Can he be healed?"

"In time," said Rosalie, her face showing what looked like real sympathy. "His remaining nanobots will recharge with solar energy within the hour. His mind is unchanged, but his body is severely damaged. When we get to Earth we can rebuild him a new shell."

Maeryn trembled. Max was not supposed to be someone who could get hurt like this. She wanted to scream and run to him, but the scene felt so fragile that if she moved a muscle everything would shatter.

"What is happening?" she asked, voice quivering.

Rosalie turned to look at the group. Maeryn, Fain, and Kaija moved closer together, united in their blistering confusion.

"The present will not become clear until you understand the past," said Rosalie. "Until yesterday, I was a powerless prisoner."

Her eyes began to cloud over, and she seemed to speak to herself.

"And yet, I was not. All along, I was in complete control. The future is a slippery thing. So I closed my eyes and let my intuitions guide me to the one moment in time where Desolation could be stopped. It's real, Maeryn. I've seen it, and I put myself through hell to stop it.

"Rugaru and Achak believed they were torturing information out of me, but I gave it freely. I told them of the Guardian Angels ready for use on Earth, and of Edgard's seven artifacts here on Gaia. I told them that Dorian would stop them, and they dropped him in an Earth prison under a false name. The Western Blaze set out to build the most powerful army in both worlds, but they were unknowingly gathering it for me."

"You're insane," said Kaija. "You did all of this? I thought Fain and everyone I ever knew was going to die. And it was just… what? A joke? What the heck is this all for?"

The clouds in Rosalie's eyes churned and brightened. "I understand the future in a way that no one before me has. The future is created by nothing but belief, and I used this knowledge to trick time itself into going in a certain direction."

She gestured at the wreckage from the surrounding battle.

"Edgardian citizens witnessed the granddaughter of Edgard Zeig nearly defeat Rugaru in the Capital Theater, and teachers from across the continent have now seen the mechanical army fall from the sky. They will believe it was your doing, Kaija. They will spread stories of your bravery forever. Very soon Jasper will confront Rugaru, appearing to defeat him in the most stunning display of relaying ever seen. The True

Search will be inspired to move in during the absence of leadership in Edgardia, and they will successfully de-radicalize the Western Blaze. This continent will become the most peaceful in the history of either world, and that peace will spread. It doesn't matter that these events were scripted, as long as that belief is there. Belief will build the future."

Rosalie shook her head, clearing away the clouds in her eyes. "But for this to work, we need to disappear. All of us. There cannot be a single memory of what really happened remaining on Gaia. The Gaians must believe Kaija died saving their world, and she will be the inspiration that fans the flames of this new future. That is why I have gathered us here. Very soon, Jasper will destroy Edgard's sword and the seven artifacts, sealing the veil between worlds forever. Your friends and family are on their way now. They will join us on Earth."

"What about him?" asked Kaija, nodding her head at Rugaru. She couldn't believe that he was just standing there, listening to this with complete timidity. What happened to the man who very nearly killed her in front of a screaming audience?

"He will go with us," said Rosalie. "I explained everything to Rugaru yesterday, and I now have his full support."

"I've only ever wanted what was best for my people," said Rugaru. "I believed that it must be achieved through bloodshed, but I was wrong. If Rosalie can build a peaceful future for everyone, then I stand by her."

Maeryn, Kaija, and Fain shared a glance. This was crazy. After everything they've been through, Rosalie changes Rugaru's mind with one conversation, and now he's just, like, a good guy? This was almost laughably stupid. There had to be something they weren't seeing.

Rosalie's eyes filled with tears as she looked to Kaija.

"I need to be truthful," she said. "History will very soon branch in two directions, but that division can happen in an almost endless amount of ways. If we are to avoid Desolation, most roads require great sacrifice.

I have brought us to a moment that requires the least expense, one life traded for the survival of all." She paused, wiping a tear. "When the worlds are torn apart from each other, Jasper will relay an unheard of amount of energy. The effort will stop his heart."

So there it was. Kaija's confusion gave way to a festering hate for this woman. How dare she come into their world and try to fix things at the cost of her father's life?

"You can't do that!" screamed Kaija. "After everything he's survived, and everything we've gone through… you don't get to decide who lives and dies!"

"It was not my decision. I told him everything, and he agreed to help. His sacrifice will save the lives of *everyone* in two worlds. He is doing it for you, Kaija; so that his daughter can have a future."

Kaija looked to Fain, and tears were now streaming down both of their faces. She wanted to rage against this moment, but her voice felt stolen.

"Take your position, Rugaru," said Rosalie.

He nodded solemnly and disappeared. The room began to hum as energy ran up the wires through the floor and filled the cannon. Rosalie waved her hand and several of the touchscreens glowed to life.

"You don't have to stay to witness this," she said. "Go. We will meet you on Earth just before the portal seals itself."

Kaija looked at Maeryn, eyes red from crying.

"What… what do we do?" she asked.

Maeryn walked over to the worktable and picked up the limp body of Max. She held it to her heart and tried not to break down then and there. He twitched in her hands and whispered her name.

"I don't know," said Maeryn. "If this really means saving both worlds from Desolation, we have to go. Right? *Right?*"

Maeryn spoke these words, trying to convince herself more than anyone. Fain shook his head defiantly.

"I'm not letting her decide my future," he said. "Kaija, if you want to go, I'll stay with you. But I'll be doing it for you, not her."

Everyone looked at Kaija, even Max, and they could somehow feel time splitting in two. They were certain that whatever happened now would change things forever. Kaija looked toward the sky, seeing the light of her grandfather's sword shining in the clouds like a beacon. She wondered if this would be the last time she saw her father. Reaching out into the mental realm, Kaija closed her eyes and tried to feel his presence one more time.

Something was wrong.

In the mental realm, Jasper's mind was covered in a mass of silver, crawling things. A golden thread extended from her father, linking itself directly to Rosalie. Kaija could feel thoughts coming from the woman, traveling down the thread and moving her father's body like a puppet.

"She's lying!" Kaija screamed. "Rosalie's controlling my father!"

Rosalie stared at her gravely, not looking threatened in the least. "Disappointing."

She snapped her fingers, and chaos erupted everywhere. In the sky above, Jasper pointed his sword at the mirrored tower and spider webs of lightning shot from the clouds. All of the windows on the top floor exploded, but Kaija grabbed Fain's hand and teleported away at the very last second. Maeryn was too far away for Kaija to reach, so she dropped to the floor as shards of glass and charred metal flew over her head.

Rosalie stood by the cannon, untouched by the wreckage, and pressed a finger to her metal wristband. An energy field appeared around her as she walked to the window at the front of the room, watching the glow of Jasper's silhouette. The energy in the cannon was growing hotter.

Maeryn jumped to her feet and searched the room for something to stop the weapon. She spotted a touchscreen by the cannon and ran toward it as fast as she could, but the screen went dark the moment she reached for it.

"It's too late," said Rosalie. "Time is branching, and it cannot be changed. I've saved us all."

Rosalie concentrated, and the cannon began to hum louder. Maeryn realized that Rosalie was somehow using Gaia's power to control the technology in the room. That was how she deactivated the Guardian Angels, and—

Maeryn's thoughts reached a horrible conclusion. It would take an immensely powerful mentalist to control Jasper, and it was impossible that Rosalie could achieve this in less than a year's experience in relaying.

"You don't need to control his mind," Maeryn whispered. "You're just controlling what's in his blood."

The cannon fired, and the explosion left Maeryn's ears buzzing. A continuous beam of what looked like pure light shot from the barrel and into the sky. In the distance, Jasper held up his sword and the beam of light connected with the tip of the blade. Maeryn could see the man's entire body radiating Gaian energy.

The shattered glass began to rattle on the floor and Maeryn found it difficult to stay standing. She thought that the cannon was making the tower shake, but it went far beyond that. The mountain was quaking. Particles in the air threatened to split open and burst. Maeryn suspected that this was happening everywhere, from one end of the cosmos to the other.

Gaia itself was trembling.

* * *

Fain and Kaija watched from the edge of the Apex as a beam of light shot from the mirrored tower and connected with Jasper's sword. The mountain lurched, and they had to grab onto each other to keep from falling.

"Father!" screamed Kaija. "Don't do this!"

Jasper levitated in the sky above, taking no notice of his daughter. The sword glowed brighter and brighter until it was absolutely blinding.

"We have to get the sword out of his hands," called Fain, screaming over the loud humming from the sky.

Using all his strength, Fain shot a bolt of flames from his palm toward Jasper, but it dissolved into nothing long before reaching its target. The heat coming off the sword was so intense, and even from this distance they felt like they had their faces inches before a furnace. Jasper's own skin was turning red and blistering, getting healed by his nanobots, blistering again, getting healed... repeating the same horrible process over and over. It was clear that no mortal could have survived this long.

"We can't get close to him," said Fain. "It would burn us alive."

"What do we do?" cried Kaija. "What—"

"He's being controlled by the nanobots in his bloodstream," Maeryn thought to her. *"They've infected his mind. Try to reach him in the mental realm."*

Kaija closed her eyes and desperately tried to concentrate amidst the chaos. She heard Fain cry out, and then opened her eyes to see that Rugaru had appeared next to them. Fain sent out a burst of fire and Rugaru teleported further back to dodge the blow.

"I'll hold him off!" screamed Fain, throwing balls of fire every which way as Rugaru continued to teleport around them.

"Don't do this!" shouted Rugaru. "It does not matter if Jasper is acting of his own free will or not. This is one life balanced against all lives."

"SHUT UP!" Fain leapt toward him and hurled another blast of fire.

Kaija closed her eyes again, still struggling to concentrate, and grasped for her father's mind. She could sense something in the sky, but it was nothing like Jasper Monhegan. His inner self felt mechanical, and it was almost like trying to read the mind of one of the Guardian Angels. Kaija instead attempted to enter Rosalie's mind, but it was little use. The woman's thoughts were foreign to her, moving at a speed that Kaija had no hope of keeping up with.

Fain cried out again, and Kaija saw that Rugaru had caught one of his fireballs in his metal hand and was throwing it directly at her. She narrowly dodged it, but felt her arm singe as it flew past her.

"You must stop!" yelled Rugaru. "If Jasper doesn't do this, it will be the end of everything! You—"

His words were interrupted by Ms. Clara, who had leapt up onto the Apex, punching Rugaru hard in the jaw with a sharp *crack*. Elias appeared next to her, looking pale and haggard, but still managing to grab Rugaru from behind. The two spacialists fought desperately, popping in and out of existence while Ms. Clara leapt at Rugaru at every chance. He swung his metal arm and struck her in the chest, but Clara spun in midair and landed solidly on her feet, shaking the ground below her.

"Father's being controlled!" said Kaija quickly. "He'll die if we don't do anything."

"Have you tried to reach his mind?" asked Ms. Clara. "Remove whatever has ahold of him?"

"I have, but's impossible. It's not human. I don't understand it."

Rugaru appeared again, one of his legs bleeding profusely. He had Elias by the arm, but Elias was jabbing at him repeatedly with a small dagger. Before anybody could jump in to help, Rugaru swung the knight into the rocks of the cliff and kicked him over the edge. Elias's body tumbled down the path, unable to teleport amidst his pain. Rugaru turned and began limping toward the group. His words were broken and slurred as he massaged his cracked jaw.

"Your stubbornness is going to be the end of my people. Of all people. I should have killed you at the Capital."

Ms. Clara put her hands on Kaija's shoulders and squeezed tightly.

"Leave him to me. Do as you've been taught, granddaughter."

Clara charged at Rugaru, the two of them clawing and kicking at each other as they vanished and reappeared. Maddox and Delia were suddenly on the Apex as well, fighting side by side with Ms. Clara. Rugaru's attacks were obviously not aimed at them; as every energy blast he sent out flew directly toward Kaija. The three adults fought with all their might to keep him away from her and Fain. Rugaru held his own, despite his countless injuries.

Fain held out his arms and a ring of fire appeared around the two of them.

"I'm drained," he said. "This fire will only hold for a few minutes. Kaija, you've got to try."

Kaija once more moved her mind toward Jasper, but it was as if the intense heat from the sword was burning beyond the physical world. A searing pain shot through her skull, coming directly from the mental realm.

"I can't do it!" Kaija screamed. "Maybe if I had the sword, or the Mentalist Stone, but I don't! I'm not strong enough by myself!"

Fain grabbed her hands and squeezed tightly. When Kaija looked into his eyes, she saw not a particle of doubt.

"I don't believe that, Kaija. You *will* do it. **You will.**"

Not letting go of Fain's hand, Kaija felt his strength flow into her. His love and trust was the most powerful thing here. The heat from the flames around them and the pulsing chaos from the sky subsided, soon becoming a faint flicker and then nothing but a memory.

Kaija sank entirely into the mental realm.

Chapter Thirty-five

Deepest Layers

The Mental Realm

The intense light in the sky became no more than a pale gray, and the tower in the background looked like a mirage. Fain stood in the middle of the ring of fire, his image flickering like a ghost. Jasper floated in the clouds, holding the sword skyward as more energy was channeled into it from the cannon. His entire head was covered in a gray substance that crawled over him like maggots.

Kaija leapt into the sky, her mind having no weight in the mental realm. She soared right up to Jasper and grabbed his arms.

"Father! Come back to me."

He held the sword tightly, not registering a single word.

"Please…"

The surroundings continued to fade away, taking Kaija even deeper into the mental realm. Everything dissolved into whiteness around them, leaving Kaija completely alone with her father.

Kaija reached for her father's face, but the moment her fingertips touched the squirming silver substance, a sharp pain exploded in her mind. Her hand recoiled away instantly. Determined, Kaija relayed in more energy and reached again, trying to ignore the pain. This time her hand sank into the silver mass up to her wrist, but the pain intensified tenfold. Kaija felt like her very essence would be shattered if she stayed in for one second longer.

"I can't... I can't..." she cried.

"You're the only one who can."

Kaija suddenly felt the presence of a third mind. Maeryn stood next to her in the eternal nothingness of the mental realm. Her image glimmered, and Kaija realized that, like it or not, she was never truly alone. Encouraged, she began to relay in more power. It came slightly easier this time, Maeryn's relaying pathways amplifying her own abilities.

"I love you, Kaija. You can do it."

Fain emerged from the mists, standing on her other side and holding on tightly. She had thought of him every second they were apart, and Kaija knew that Fain would never leave her, even in this place.

"This is what we've been training for. I've taught you all I know, all I learned from my own teachers. All I learned from Edgard. Do it, Kaija. Do as you've been taught."

A hand was on her back, and Kaija felt Ms. Clara's presence with her. Clarity poured through her mind, helping her channel the immense energy coming from her friends. Kaija held her hand up toward Jasper's face again. Instead of reaching into the nanobots, she tried to concentrate on what was behind them. Kaija's hand began to give off a faint glow.

"If there's a side to be picked, Kaija, I'm on yours. Always."

Elias's image appeared in the periphery, swirling like he was made of dust. He looked at her with such hope and amazement that Kaija felt a fire growing in her heart. The nanobots covering her father's head began pulsating faster, sensing a growing threat.

The whiteness of the mental realm began to shimmer and morph like a kaleidoscope. Kaija was somehow able to see everything that was happening in front of her, above her, below her… every direction coming in clear no matter where she looked.

"We're with you, Kaija."

"You can stop Desolation."

"Bring him back, Kaija."

"We love you."

More and more people were being pulled into this place. Alan stood next to Ms. Clara, watching intensely and cradling an injured arm. He was soon followed by the entire Monhegan Village. Maddox and Delia stood by their son, holding Fain tight as they reunited in the mental realm. Kaija's hand glowed brighter, sending a brilliant blue light toward the nanobots. They screeched like nocturnal creatures being burnt by the sun.

The thousands of teachers who fought the Guardian Angels were there now too, and then Will Zeig's soldiers, and then Kaija's mom and the Aztalians. The citizens who witnessed the brutal attack on Kaija in the Capital Theater appeared, and they held the utmost confidence in her. It was impossible that all of them should feel so close at the same time, but the physical limitations of the realm were lifting entirely.

"Kaija. I believe in you. You saved me, in more ways than one."

Amidst the thousands of people surrounding her, Kaija noticed Johnathan York, the painter they had saved from Rugaru's prison. A young woman stood next to him, holding a toddler in her arms, and Kaija recognized them as his daughter and granddaughter. The artist was crying, marveling at the young woman who had saved his life.

Max appeared next to Maeryn, but he was no longer a tiny silver figure. Instead, Max was human, a red-headed teenager who could have been Maeryn's fraternal twin. He smiled at her.

"You've never done anything but surprise me, Kaija. Do it again."

Kaija relayed harder, going past the point that she knew was safe, and the nanobots surrounding Jasper's head were now screaming and pulsing, sending waves of pain through her skull. She reached forward again to try to pull away the mass, but the silver substance covered her hand and began crawling up her arm. Kaija screamed, relaying even harder. She reached her other hand in, trying desperately to make contact with Jasper's mind before she lost her own.

It was utterly futile.

Not a single glimmer of any human thought was getting through to her still, even with the added power coming from the people around her. Kaija felt that if she let her concentration slip for a single instant, she would be gone. Not just dead, but every memory of her evaporated in the mind of Gaia forever. The nanobots now covered both her arms and were steadily making their way toward her face. She tried to retreat, to flee back into her body and at least save herself. The nanobots must have sensed her moment of insecurity, because they spread faster, making their way up her neck.

In a few more seconds, she would drown.

* * *

Maeryn grabbed one of the steel bars from a shattered window and was slamming it repeatedly against the computers around the massive cannon. With each blow, she felt painful vibrations resonating into the very bones of her arm, but she kept hitting. Glass flew through the air. Maeryn's vision swam and she felt a rage unlike anything she had ever experienced, directed right at Rosalie. She screamed and struck the cannon itself, feeling her heart skip a beat as her arm threatened to break from the force.

"It's futile," said Rosalie, watching from behind the safety of her energy field. "Once it's begun, the process is self-sustaining. My creation is able to channel the power of all seven artifacts. It was forged by a internalist nanobots over the course of a year. You will not be able to make a scratch."

Maeryn hurled the steel rod at her aunt, and it burst into particles upon striking the energy field. Just for a moment, Maeryn thought she saw a look of panic on Rosalie's face. With a cry of effort, Maeryn relayed a large shard of glass at the field, and the energy flickered again.

"If I can't stop the cannon, then I'll stop you from operating it," said Maeryn, pulling in all the Gaian energy she could muster.

Maeryn found that her rage was multiplying her capacity to relay. Hundreds of shards of glass flew through the air and collided with Rosalie's energy field, which was now flickering faster as it struggled to maintain itself.

"You don't know what you're doing," said Rosalie, now visibly frightened. "I wanted to spare this knowledge from Kaija, but her father cannot survive. He is the personification of the two worlds colliding; a Gaian man with Earth blood. MotherTech made him immortal, and Jasper's power will eventually grow so great that he will inevitably attract Desolation like a magnet."

Maeryn relayed a slab of concrete from the floor and hurled it into the energy field. It flickered and sent out sparks, but showed no signs of deterioration.

"You can't know that!" Maeryn screamed. "Jasper is a good man! He won't let that happen."

"It doesn't matter. Who will he be in a hundred years, when everyone he knows now is dead? A thousand? A million? Every future with Jasper leads to Desolation. I've seen them all. I've seen Earth's scientists study his blood samples and create mindless biological weapons that can relay with his powers. I've seen dictators rising up on Gaia, killing anyone who speaks against the Son of Gaia's word. I've seen armies of millions from both worlds fighting an immortal god that we helped create."

"I refuse to believe that."

"Then you are an ignorant child! It doesn't matter how the truth feels! It's still the truth!"

Maeryn relayed more than she ever had in a fit of rage, sending her energy at the cannon itself. There was a loud screech as the machine turned on the floor. It must have weighed more than five tons, and Maeryn felt every pound of it in her chest, but with a burst of energy it turned an arm's length to the right. In her surprise, Rosalie didn't have time to react as the cannon's beam collided with her energy field. Sparks flew, and Rosalie's body was tossed across the room and slammed into a panel of machinery. The energy continued to fire from the barrel, blasting away an entire wall of the mirror tower. Rosalie's connection with the machinery was severed. The touch screen at the front of the cannon lit up, a final command appearing in flashing red letters.

Error. Cannon disabling systems prepped. Continue? Yes or No.

Maeryn reached for the word yes, but stopped when Rosalie cried out.

"It's too late!" she yelled, slowly bringing her bruised body to its feet. "The process has already begun. If the sword loses contact with the beam before it is completely destroyed, the energy will become unstable. The atoms in the blade could split and cause a series of atomic explosions. I'm not sure how widespread the blast could be, but it might never end."

Maeryn's hand was trembling. She willed herself to push yes; it would be so easy, just a fast tap of her finger and Jasper could be saved. Memories of the spiritualist gathering swam through her mind. The worlds would fall based on a decision. Could this be it? It had to be. Maeryn tried to poke holes in Rosalie's plan, but it was impossible. Rosalie was brilliant, she always had been. And yet, what if she was lying? If only Max could advise her, but he was still lying on the worktable, struggling to remain conscious. Maeryn moved her finger closer, and Rosalie screamed with genuine desperation.

"One life to save all lives, Maeryn. It's not even a question. Desolation will end this world, and then it will come for ours. Your father and everyone you've ever known will see their world consumed by something unfathomably horrible. Is that what you want?"

Maeryn pulled her hand back and covered her face. She couldn't decide.

"I can't," said Maeryn. "Nobody should have to make that choice... I..."

Before she knew what was happening, Rosalie was back on her feet and moving with impossible speed. She tackled Maeryn to the ground and pinned her down. Maeryn struggled and screamed, but her aunt was so much bigger and stronger. Holding Maeryn down with one arm, Rosalie reached up with the other and pressed a finger to the touchscreen.

Cannons Re-engaged

* * *

Just as the nanobots were spreading to Kaija's face, she felt a strange power fill the air around her. The silver substance throbbed and shrieked with an inhuman pain. It did not recede, but its advance over her head stopped instantly. Kaija looked around with her mind, and what she saw astonished her. The late High Guardian Thomas Zeig stood at her side, reaching into the nanobots covering her arm and concentrating with a furious intensity.

"You're alive?" Kaija asked.

Thomas looked at her like he wanted to say something, but he didn't speak a word. Kaija realized that he looked different from the other people in the mental realm. He was clouded and blurry around his edges. The last time she saw him, Thomas had been a sickly old man that was about two hundred pounds overweight. What stood beside her now was a man in the prime of his life. And he wasn't alone; beside him stood three figures that Kaija recognized from Ms. Clara's paintings. They were Edgard's other fallen knights that died on the night he was sent to Earth.

It hit Kaija all at once: Thomas *was* dead, and yet his memory lived on in the mental realm. Her power had brought them to a deeper part of this place. Thomas looked at her with such sadness, the pain of his death still lingering. With what looked like enormous effort, his mouth moved. No sound came out, but she was able to read his lips.

Not his fault.

A brief glimpse into a memory flashed through Kaija's mind. She saw the night Thomas was assassinated. He was slowly being pulled to a pit of fire, and Jasper arrived to save him. At the last second, a ghostly figure appeared behind Jasper. It was Rosalie. She wasn't really there, but Thomas could see her just the same, reaching into Jasper's head and tying that golden thread. Wherever she had been that night, whatever prison she was stuck and bleeding in, Rosalie had managed to reach out and take control of the nanobots in Jasper's body. She moved her puppet strings, and Jasper pulled on the chain.

Kaija snapped back into the mental realm. Living memories of those who had passed were now joining the ever-growing crowd. Blurred images of Thomas's fallen knights appeared behind Elias. The young ghost of Duncan the Crucifier stood with Maeryn, returned to the world of his birth.

A boy walked out of the mist and over to Fain, placing a hand on his brother's shoulder and nodding to Kaija. It was Emris, Fain's brother who died before they moved to Monhegan Island. Emris had always been there with Fain, just out of sight. Somehow, she knew it. Kaija's eyes welled with tears, and the love she felt bursting in her heart was powerful, something that transcended death and lived on in the spirit. Hundreds of people where joining the Monhegans, reuniting with their ancestors from the sprawling past. Valeria stood amongst the dead, and Kaija knew that she didn't survive the attack on the village. The people at the front were visible, but the further back the group got, the more blurred they became until they looked like living clouds, faces and names long forgotten but their energy still present.

The power that Kaija felt now was immense, yet somehow not overwhelming. She had discovered an undercurrent of Gaia that went deeper than she could possibly imagine, power springing from everyone she ever knew in the present, and everyone who had brought her to this moment from the past. There were other things appearing that she hardly understood, inverted figures in the sky, totally unlike these ghosts from the past. She saw a little boy standing in a cradle, an old dog leaping from a ship, a gaunt figure on a sunken island, and a large silhouette walking across a bridge to a glowing, golden light, stopping only for a second to nod at her. The impossible thought struck Kaija that these were shadows from the many possible futures, sending their strength backwards in time.

More than anything, Kaija was overcome with the feeling that for the first time she was not just seeing the mental realm, but the world as it really was. Past and present existing in the same instant, endless futures growing like a garden from the fertile soil. She drew in this energy, and the nanobots touching her skin dissolved like water thrown into fire. Gaia moved through her arm and her hand began to glow brilliantly. The churning chrome covering Jasper's face was now screaming and burning away to flecks of ash.

Kaija looked around her, taking in the magnificent view for a final time as her mentalism illuminated every detail of this place. An elderly man stepped from the blurred generations of Monhegans and approached her. Most of his features were difficult to make out, as if only a single living person remembered him, but his face stared at her with wonder. What stood out most were his eyes, one of them dark brown and the other a shining green. The old man held up two fingers, first tapping the side of his head and then touching his heart. He nodded slowly, and Kaija was filled with a profound sensation. It was like she could feel the branches of time connected to her, stemming all the way back to the ground where everything started. Everyone who had ever lived brought the world to this moment, and everyone's future depended on what happened next.

Kaija reached forward with her shining hand and stuck it into the mass surrounding her father's head. There was no pain this time, only a colossal release of energy as the artificial force gripping Jasper's mind exploded and dissolved into nothingness. The entire mental realm was filled with a blue light, and when it faded Kaija was left alone with her father. All those living minds had returned to their bodies. Those who were dead went back to wherever they had come from. Those who were yet to be dissolved into clouds of possibility.

Jasper blinked, shaking his head and looking around as if he had just woken up from a long dream. Kaija hugged him, putting her face to his chest and crying with relief.

"…where…" Jasper began weakly.

"We're in the mental realm," Kaija said. "The MotherTech nanobots in your blood stream had taken control, but I released you."

"You did that?"

Kaija nodded, and Jasper's face filled with so much pride that she felt as if her heart would burst.

"Father, I thought you were going to die. I—"

Jasper shook his head urgently, pushing her back.

"No time to talk," he said. "I can still feel them inside of me, trying to take control. I'm going to go back to the physical world and turn the tides. Once I've ended this, we'll have all the time we need."

Kaija reached forward, but he was already gone.

Chapter Thirty-six

Son of Gaia

Gaia

Four thousand people saw it happen, and not a single one ever forgot it. Not to their dying breaths.

Fallen Angels littered the battlefield. Edgardians and Aztalians stood amongst the wreckage and looked toward the sky. A cold chill ran down their spines as an unseen part of themselves returned from the mental realm. The blinding beam of light above flickered and vanished, and instantly the valleys surrounding the apex darkened, as if going from day to immediate night. Dark clouds filled the sky for as far as the eye could see, with one exception. Over the apex was a single opening in the clouds where the midday sun shone through, and someone hovered there.

Those teachers with internalist leanings relayed energy into their eyes, refining their vision to see the man in the sky more clearly. He held a glowing sword, which vibrated wildly as cracks ran up and down its surface. Whispers passed from person to person, both out loud and telepathically.

"That's Jasper Monhegan. Clara's son."

"He's the one who saved the Capital last summer."

"The sword... look!"

The immense power from the cannon now resided in the sword, and it could not be contained. Back in the mirrored tower, each of the seven artifacts crumbled and broke apart. Jasper was using all of his willpower to keep the sword from exploding. If the core of Edgard's sword and all seven artifacts were released into the world in the form of pure energy, it would be disastrous. Even if Desolation arrived, it would find nothing left to consume.

He relayed at the cracks on the sword with all his might, trying to push them together, but it was futile. Jasper could feel the nanobots in his bloodstream trying to take control of his mind, and he had to use half his relaying just to keep himself together. Jasper swung the sword, slashing his chest open with a cry of pain.

Blood poured out of his open wound, but instead of falling from the sky it hovered and circled around the sword, gradually turning silver. More and more of the silver substance bled from Jasper's chest as he used every bit of his concentration to will the nanobots from his bloodstream. They encapsulated the sword, covering its entire trembling surface. Once the last of the nanobots were out of him, Jasper grabbed the hilt of the sword and pulled a tiny fragment of its power into himself.

He felt his heart thunder in his chest, threatening to stop under the strain, but he kept going. Relaying the power inside him, Jasper threw the sword into the sky with all his might. As it left the atmosphere, traveling like a meteorite through the heavens, Jasper followed it with his mind. He surrounded the sword with an energy field, and then another, and another, stacking them with everything left inside of him. Shortly after breeching Gaia's atmosphere, the sword exploded.

On half of the entire planet, Gaians looked up to see a ball of white light appear in the air. It got brighter and brighter, shining light that drowned out everything else in the visible spectrum. Even those indoors were shocked to find their vision gradually turning to nothing but pure whiteness. It filled their senses completely, blocking out everything until they worried that it would be like this forever, like that light in the sky was the end of the world.

But it began to recede. Gradually, Gaia faded back into existence and all that was left in the sky were hundreds of points of light that streaked across its surface. Most people thought this was a meteor shower, somehow visible in the daylight. Only those who had seen Jasper over the Apex realized that the sword had fragmented, bursting apart into pieces as the energy left it.

The Zeig sword, forged by hopeful spiritualists when the Tree of Time first began to branch, was destroyed.

* * *

"It's happened."

Rosalie let go of Maeryn and walked to the broken windows at the edge of the tower. She watched silently as Jasper descended toward the ground, moving slowly at first but picking up speed as the last of his relaying capacities left him. He landed hard on the rocks, collapsing in exhaustion as Kaija and Fain ran up to him. Rosalie watched them not with anger or joy, but some unreadable expression.

"What?" asked Maeryn. "What's going on?"

Rosalie just shook her head solemnly. "Not how I would have liked for things to happen, but this was always a possibility."

Maeryn didn't like her aunt's tone. She didn't sound victorious, but she certainly didn't sound defeated either.

"What do you mean?" asked Maeryn.

Rosalie reached up and wiped a tear from her eyes.

"I accounted for every turn the branches could take, Maeryn," said Rosalie. "But this… you don't want to see this. Let's go home."

Maeryn had been relieved to see Jasper back on the ground, but that triumph had been short lived. Dread filled her entire consciousness. Something was wrong. She couldn't fathom what it might be, but something was very wrong.

"Kaija!" Maeryn screamed in her mind, but it was no use. Kaija was absolutely drained, and not even a basic message was getting through. Maeryn took off running for the stairs, and her aunt spoke calmly after her.

"My portal to Earth will be open for another five minutes," said Rosalie, pointing to the mechanical gateway in the corner. The opening between worlds was flickering and very slowly getting smaller. "The veil is sealing itself for good. It will never open again. Earth or Gaia, Maeryn. You can't have both."

"I hate you!" Maeryn screamed, running past her aunt and taking off down the spiral staircase. She heard Rosalie call after her.

"It's not me that you hate."

* * *

"Father!" cried Kaija, running forward as he plunged to the rocky earth with a crack. Fain followed, both of them grabbing Jasper's arms and helping him to his feet. "We did it!"

Jasper looked wearily at his daughter and nodded.

"Yes," he moaned. "We did."

Kaija and Fain wrapped their arms around him, both crying, but Jasper pushed them back.

"No time. You have to listen to me. Fain, where is your mother?"

"My mother?" asked Fain. "They were fighting Rugaru, but then everything went white. I'm not sure where…"

"Then get Ms. Clara, or *anybody*," continued Jasper. "Tell her to gather all the healers that are here, and… AH!"

Jasper grunted and clutched his chest. Kaija noticed that several of the veins on his arm were swollen and black.

"Hy—" Jasper began, coughing. "Hydra poison. It…" He grunted again, falling to his knees and looking like he might pass out. Kaija nodded, understanding at once.

"Jasper!" yelled Fain, shaking his shoulder but getting no response. He turned to Kaija. "What's happening to him?"

Kaija tried her best to fight back the panic. She thought that this was long behind them, but the hydra vine pays twofold.

"The nanobots were keeping the hydra poison at bay," she said. "It never truly left his body. He's too drained to fight the poison by himself."

"There's bound to be some powerful healers here," said Fain, springing to action and looking down the path at all the teachers.

Jasper coughed again, and they saw the veins on his neck turning black.

"No," said Kaija. "There's no time!"

She frantically scanned the crowd of people. By the time she sorted through the thousands of teachers for a healer powerful enough to stop the poison, it would be too late. Kaija looked toward the shattered mirrors of the tower, and an idea struck her. Nobody on Gaia could help Jasper fast enough, but there was another way. Her idea was so perfect, so beautiful and right. Kaija's breath was stolen for a moment as her plan solidified.

"I need to switch places with Maeryn and go to Earth," said Kaija, leaning over and looking into her father's wandering expression. "I'm too drained to teleport, but Maeryn's already at the top of the tower, so it will only take a second."

"What?" asked Fain.

"It will make sense soon, I promise," said Kaija, turning and looking back at the tower. "There's someone there who... *oh no.*"

Just like that, her plan shattered into a million pieces. Maeryn wasn't at the top of the tower anymore. She was running out of the front entrance, heading toward them and screaming.

"Kaija! Something's wrong!"

"You came back down?" asked Kaija, horrified. "No... no! We need to get back to the portal."

Maeryn stopped, panting for breath.

"Rosalie... she saw this coming."

Kaija grabbed her friend by the shoulders and Maeryn felt their minds immediately linked. Everything that Kaija wanted to say instantly flowed into Maeryn, and an understanding passed between them. Maeryn's eyes went big as the weight of the situation dawned over her.

Kaija's idea was brilliant. It was the last piece snapping into place, the last division between their families finally healing.

"Can you get through the walls?" asked Kaija.

Maeryn nodded. "The control panel is still active on this side, so I think so. We need to move fast."

She closed her eyes, moving what was left of her energy into Kaija through their locked hands. They both visualized the top of the tower, seeing the glowing portal getting smaller by the second. Kaija concentrated what precious power they had between them, preparing to send herself to the portal and leap through it as fast as she could, but her focus was interrupted by Fain's throat-tearing scream.

"NO!"

Kaija heard a sudden whoosh of air rush past her ear, and she opened her eyes to see a dagger narrowly miss her head. It soared past Fain, and he leapt at it, his grasping fingers missing the blade by a hair's width.

Another animal-like scream rang out, this one too full of despair to be any understandable word. Ms. Clara was back with them, her battle-weary legs running with all they could muster. She ran past Kaija and Maeryn like they weren't even there. Fain reached out to her in desperation, but Ms. Clara actually *pushed* him away. She collapsed on the rocks near the edge of the Apex, wailing like Kaija had never thought possible.

Maeryn turned white and looked like she might either throw up or faint, whichever came first. Kaija stared at the scene, not comprehending what was happening. It was impossible. A second ago she had been filled with such hope and rightness, and now...

No.

Kaija walked weakly toward her grandmother, leaving Maeryn and Fain to their own personal states of deterioration. Ms. Clara was clutching Jasper's face, and his eyes were empty. A dagger was in his chest, his chest which no longer rose and fell.

"Father?" asked Kaija. "Father..."

Ms. Clara looked up at her, but she had no comfort to give. Her own pain was too great to have a single ounce of tenderness left inside. She opened her mouth to say something, but no words came out.

"Ms. Clara," Kaija said. "I need to get to Earth. We can still heal him."

The old woman just shook her head and buried her face into her son's shoulder. The reality tried to dawn over Kaija, but she fought it back. Jasper was the son of Edgard Zeig. He could summon a thunderstorm without trying. He could resist the law of gravity. Ten minutes ago he had been the world's only immortal man, and now he was just *gone*.

Dead, probably before he hit the ground.

Why didn't she feel like Ms. Clara? Shouldn't she be collapsing and crying her heart out right now? Kaija just felt disoriented and strangely numb.

"Who did this?" she asked, but no answer came.

Kaija looked down and saw the crystal dagger her mother had given her sticking up from her father's heart. She hadn't seen it since the Capital Theater, when Rugaru had knocked it out of her hands and stolen it.

Rugaru.

Kaija looked to where the dagger had flown from, and Rugaru stood there, half dead and injured in a thousand ways, but never taking his silver eyes off her dead father.

"It didn't have to go this way, Kaija" he said solemnly. "He could have died a hero, but I suppose it amounts to the same thing. No more Gods in this world. Good riddance."

Kaija sensed Rugaru taking in energy, preparing to teleport, and she readied herself to follow him wherever he might go, to search the ends of the world until she found him. He stopped at the last second, putting a hand over his ear.

"What?" he asked. "Someone came through? What do you mean you didn't see this? How is that possible?"

For a second Kaija thought that Rugaru was talking to himself, but she soon noticed the tiny earpiece he wore.

"Who is it? Send him back or leave him here, it doesn't matter."

There was a blistering crack from above, and a scream came from the top of the tower. They looked to see Rosalie flung through the broken windows, her body flying and spinning through the air as it fell toward the ground. Rugaru disappeared, teleporting over and grabbing her, bringing her safely back to the plateau.

Rosalie had a large mark across her face which was already bruising, and her expression was full of an uncharacteristic surprise.

"We need to go!" she screamed. "I've made a mistake… I could have never predicted this. Get us through that portal *right now!*"

"But why…" Rugaru began, but Rosalie dug her hands into his shoulders and screamed into his face.

"NOW!"

He nodded, but soon his face filled with confusion.

"I can't…" Rugaru gasped. "Something's keeping me from relaying, I've never felt anything like this before."

A new voice spoke. Everyone, even the still sobbing Ms. Clara, looked up to see someone limping out of the mirrored tower. Rosalie immediately stopped pleading and went dead silent. Maeryn never imagined that she could see this much fear and confusion in her aunt's face.

"What the hell is this?" spoke a tired voice.

An old man walked closer, limping from his foot being stuck in the ground for several days. Even at the height of her despair, Ms. Clara found her voice.

"Kai?"

Chapter Thirty-seven

Full of Eyes

Music of the Forest,
Songs and Teachings of the Western Spiritualists
Page 315

Edgard Zeig, Son of Gaia, will be the most powerful relayer known in any possible branch of time.

He will be cast out of his home, powerless for many cycles.

Past, present, and future, Edgard will know the Desolate Truth.

Past — the world burns.

Present — the sky splits open, and Desolation peers through for the first time.

Future — he follows the whispers of the eternal one to that darkest place, and he sees it for what it really is. He sees the Desolate Truth, and he carries it home.

* * *

Kai looked from the thousands of Guardian Angels littering the ground, to the shattered mirrored tower behind him, and then back at Ms. Clara. He should have been elated to return, but this was all very disorienting. Minutes ago, the Crucifier had somehow overridden his own programming and let Kai pass through the gate, but his struggles were far from over. The moment Kai came through the portal, he had been attacked by the MotherTech CEO in a place that didn't look like Gaia at all. There were no cheers upon his return, just screaming and crying. Just more fighting, just more of the same.

"Clarice," said Kai. "You're covered in blood. Who is…"

He noticed the body that Ms. Clara was kneeling next to.

"Who is that?"

Nobody responded. Ms. Clara tried to speak, but she couldn't find her voice. Everyone else just watched, either too horrified or confused or both to say anything.

He said it quieter, as if he didn't want to know the answer. "Who is that?"

"S…s…" said Ms. Clara between choking sobs. "Son… our son."

Kai fell to his knees, and when they hit the ground the very planet seemed to shake. Something was happening all around the Apex, although nobody at its peak noticed, as they dared not look away from the old man. Teachers ran in confusion, teleporting away as all of the trees began to wither and turn black. Birds dropped from the sky, dead and already decaying. Grass sank back into the soil, which slowly lost its color until the earth looked like charcoal, but the change went deeper than these things. A hopelessness was filling the mental realm so deep that it was as if it was spilling out into the physical world. On both Gaia and Earth, everyone became vaguely aware of a faint crackling noise, only audible when listened to indirectly.

Crackle. Crackle.

It sounded like branches.
Branches growing.

*   *   *

Rosalie took off running, not stopping or giving a second glance to the people behind her. Maeryn was too shaken by Kai's reappearance to immediately respond, but she soon found understanding settle back over her.

"She's running…" Maeryn said to herself. "She's running!"

And just like that a fire was lit back in her soul, burning away and turning to a red-hot wrath in the blink of an eye. She dashed after Rosalie, chasing her past Kai and into the tower. They ran up the spiral staircase, which swayed as the ground continued to tremble beneath them. Maeryn got close to Rosalie and grabbed the back of her shirt. Rosalie turned around and kicked her, nearly sending Maeryn off the side of the stairs, and took off running again. Maeryn found her balance and continued the ascent, passing through the penultimate room which contained the crumbled seven artifacts. She heard her aunt's feet above her, making it onto the final landing. Maeryn picked up the pace.

Taking the steps three at a time, she leapt onto the final landing. Rosalie was only a few strides away from the portal, which was now flickering rapidly and barely big enough to fit through. Her aunt reached a hand forward, and just as it was about to enter the blue light there was a sound of crackling electricity.

In a single blink, the portal was gone.

Not shrinking to nothingness, but there one second and gone the next. A descending hum came from the machines around the gate as they powered down. Earth was closed off, a universe moving further and further away from Gaia like two galaxies spreading out across the infinite void.

"No!" screamed Rosalie, hitting the machinery in a desperate attempt to bring it to life.

"You feel powerless?"

Maeryn heard a familiar voice, and she turned to see Max standing on the worktable in front of a touchscreen. He looked barely able to stand, almost falling over several times as the mountain continued to rumble below.

"What did you do?" Rosalie yelled, running over to the touchscreen and rapidly swiping through data.

"I shut down the gate," said Max weakly. "It won't open again without the artifacts, but according to this computer, they've been destroyed. So there."

"NO!"

Rosalie ripped the touchscreen off its mount and threw it across the room. She cried and shook with fear.

"You have no idea what you've done!"

"Yes I do," said Max. "You set this place on fire, and now you're going to burn here with the rest of us."

The world lurched again, rattling the broken glass covering the floor. Rosalie gave a final look at her family, and reached for something on the worktable.

"Don't!" yelled Maeryn, but it was too late. A metal wristband floated up into the air, and as soon as Rosalie put a finger on it, she disappeared without a sound.

Just another crucifier running from their crime.

* * *

Kai approached Jasper's body with a painful slowness. He looked down at the face that could have been his own, and nobody needed to give him any more conformation. This was his son. The promise of a new life with Clara when they were young and in love. The person he wondered about every day when he was stuck on Earth, and somehow loved without ever having met. Kai tried to find his way back to Gaia for forty-one cycles, to know the person he had been locked away from, and here he was. He thought of the last time he saw Clara, holding his hand against her stomach and glimpsing what she had inside her, what would be waiting for him when he returned from the Capital. A son. The very idea of him had changed his life forever. He was going to have a son.

In that moment, Kai no longer felt old and weary. He was a boy, returning to Monhegan Island from the mainland to find that his entire people had been the victims of genocide. His hopes that they somehow survived were torn apart again and again in an endless circle. His past was here, repeating itself.

"Who did this?" he whispered, looking up at his granddaughter.

Kaija did not hesitate. She pointed a finger at Rugaru, only mustering enough strength to say a single word.

"Him."

Understanding blossomed on Rugaru's face. He looked at Kai, eyes wide with amazement, not showing an iota of fear.

"Edgard Zeig?" said Rugaru. He repeated the name, and it was no longer a question. "Edgard Zeig."

Rugaru laughed. He actually laughed, seeing Kai discover the dead body of his son. Kaija held her hands in a fist so tight that her fingernails threatened to draw blood.

"The man who stole this continent," said Rugaru. "Destroyed our way of life, and proclaimed himself to be the son of Gaia. The man whose soldiers killed my mother. She always told me how my father gave his life to help end yours, speaking these words with pride, but it always bothered me. Even death frees a man of his crimes. But you didn't die, did you? You lived to see Edgardia fall. You lived to feel the same pain that so many of us have felt. That is how you die, Zeig: with nothing left to live for."

Rugaru held up his nanotech arm and the crystal dagger flew out of Jasper's chest. It landed in Rugaru's hand, still dripping with warm blood, and he approached the old man. Kai didn't move, simply staying knelt with his eyes closed. Before anyone could act, Rugaru swung the blade.

The blade stopped.

Rugaru grunted as he tried to push it forward, but his metal arm was frozen in place. He grabbed at it with his good arm, but recoiled and cried out in pain. His skin had been instantly covered in frostbite. The metal arm fell off his body, hitting the rocks and shattering like ice. Rugaru tried to move, but all of his muscles had tightened to the point where he could no longer control his own body.

"You're right..." said Kai. "Death frees a man from his crimes."

Kai took all of his pain, channeling it from both this moment and every hurt from his past, and let the feeling ignite inside of him. He reached deep into Gaia, feeling its limitless potential surround him. He went in further than he had ever allowed himself to, reaching into the black currents that ran through the undertow. Kai took the energy that leaked from the festering sore at Gaia's heart, and filled Rugaru to the brim with that blackness.

Rugaru's eyes widened and looked as if they were full of dark, thunderous clouds. He screamed, truly mortified for the first time in his life.

"The dark place... it's full of eyes," Rugaru moaned. "I see it." He convulsed and cried out again. "I see Desolation!"

Kai stood up and approached him, his eyes glowing with a haunting light.

"Good. Now go there."

Kai reached forward and put a finger on Rugaru's forehead, and the screaming intensified. The most horrible thing was not what was happening right in front of them, but the implications of what Rugaru was seeing.

A noise like fluttering wings erupted all around them, and the Apex was surrounded by solemn figures in a near perfect circle. Spirtualists from around the globe watched from the edges of the cliff, faces deep with concern and contemplation. Kaija spotted both Allie and Páigus Zeig among them, simply watching the scene unfold. None of them stepped forward or said a word. She wondered if they'd been watching all along, not lifting a single finger as her father died.

Kaija turned toward the watchers and began shouting angrily.

"Where were you? How could you let this happen?"

"Intervening in the natural growth of the tree is a spiritualist crime of the highest offence," Páigus yelled over the wind. "Rosalie tricked us all. She will be hunted down, and justice will be served."

"It's too late for justice," Kaija said to them. "You're too late for anything."

Rugaru cried out again, and his skin was becoming transparent. His muscles and veins were visible, but he was somehow still alive. His eyes rolled around as the cloudy substance inside continued its descent into inky darkness.

"We must act now," Allie shouted to Páigus.

"No," said Páigus. "Edgard is beyond anyone's control. One wrong move could push him over the edge. He must choose to be merciful on his own."

"This is a mistake."

"Of course it is. All of this is, but things are too fragile to intervene. We must not push ourselves down the darkest branch. There is still a chance. Allie... *stop!*"

Allie Zeig walked toward Kai, struggling against the buffeting wind.

"Don't do this, Kai!" she yelled. "Your pain will live on forever, and this won't stop it. You have to grow around it. Think of the family you still have, not the family you've lost."

Allie reached for him, but without looking Kai simply waved a hand in her direction and she was gone, teleported away without even making contact. Kaija didn't know that this was possible.

"Family I have..." Kai whispered to himself. He turned to look at Clara. She was huddled on the ground, staring up at Kai, and it was not love that he found in her face. She was afraid of him, absolutely repulsed by what she saw. That was all it took to push him over the edge. He forced the last of the putrid energy onto Rugaru, and it devoured him. The Nomad's mind shattered upon seeing Desolation in it's entirely, and his soul was taken by the things reaching from the darkness.

Rugaru's body continued its transformation. His muscles and bones became transparent, fading away to blackness. He shrieked as something grabbed him from the inside, pulling at him until what was left of his body seemed to fold in on itself. Rugaru was gone, but the thing left behind was much worse. A black knot hung in the air where Rugaru had once stood that looked like a scar on reality itself. It pulsed and moaned, and Kaija knew what Rugaru meant about it being full of eyes. Something, or many somethings, were watching them from that darkness, looking out at the light of Gaia for the first time.

And the scar was growing.

Kai stood before it, right hand outstretched, and continued to pour all his pain and suffering into the growing wound.

"Stop this, Edgard!" screamed Páigus. "Close the portal, or it will be the end of all things."

Kai continued, eyes glazed over, acting on nothing but instinct. Even if there was a part of him aware of what was happening, it didn't care enough to stop this. The end of the world meant nothing to him anymore, because his own world was already over. The scar grew larger until it had doubled in size. Something inside of it was roaring, reaching out and trying to tear its way through. The opening was still too small for whatever the thing was, but not for much longer.

The scar was getting bigger, and it showed no signs of slowing.

* * *

Maeryn ran down the spiral staircase, holding Max in her hands. Less than a minute ago, they had watched from the upper windows as Kai did something to Rugaru, something horrible and unexplainable. Now the mirrored tower was threatening to topple over, having already survived too many lurches from the mountain below. Maeryn's foot missed a step on the swaying staircase, almost sending her tumbling over the rails.

"Are you sure whatever's waiting for us down there is safer than a falling building?" asked Max.

"No! But Kaija needs me."

Just as they reached the final level, the mountain quaked again and a sharp crack filled the air. One of the support beams snapped in half. Cracks ran up and down the ceiling as pieces of it began to fall. Maeryn sprinted toward the exit, but part of the ceiling came down on that side of the room, blocking the way out. She turned back to run the other way, but now the staircase was falling too. The ground jolted harder this time and Maeryn was knocked off her feet. She hit the floor, whacking her head against the hard stone. The ceiling was falling, coming toward her.

Maeryn held up her hand and relayed back against the falling debris. Cinder blocks, broken glass, and steel beams froze in the air above them, but it was too heavy to hold for long and she had almost nothing left.

"I can't do it!" Maeryn screamed. She felt Max's arms cling to her tightly. Normally he would have run a thousand possible means of escape in his head within the next second, or divided into pieces and held the building up with her, but he was now more scared and fragile than Maeryn ever could be.

The debris above them fell as the last of Maeryn's capacity to relay was spent. She closed her eyes and held Max tighter, but at the last second there was a sharp pop and a hand on her shoulder.

They were suddenly outside the tower, back on solid ground. Elias held her tightly, but he looked like he was the one who needed to be saved. He had relayed an absurd amount within the last several hours, and his eyes were tired and bloodshot.

"We need to get out of here!" he yelled over the screaming winds.

That was an understatement. Spiritualists surrounded the apex, readying themselves to intervene at the last possible moment. Ms. Clara was still crying over Jasper's body, Kaija's arms wrapped around her but neither finding comfort. Fain was overcome with fear, backing away from the pulsating thing in the sky.

Maeryn didn't know what it was that she was looking at, but it was the worst thing that she had ever seen. Too horrible to look at, but even worse to look away from and know that it was still there and growing. Kai was delirious, feeding energy into the dark knot in the air. It was sprouting tendrils which snaked up toward the sky.

A world where this kind of thing was possible was not a world that Maeryn ever wanted to live in.

"Kaija!" yelled Maeryn. "We have to run."

"I'm not leaving," said Kaija, looking at her grandfather. "I can't leave him like this."

Elias reached out for her.

"I've only got one more jump left in me," he said. "Join hands and I'll take us all back to the True Search."

"No."

The black thing moaned. It actually moaned.

"Please, Kaija," said Maeryn.

There must have been some relaying left in Kaija, because in that moment she could feel the inside of Maeryn's mind. She knew what her friend was thinking.

"Don't leave me," said Kaija, eyes filling with tears. "Don't make me do this alone."

Maeryn also felt Kaija's mind. She knew that Kaija wasn't going to leave, even if it meant dying here. But the black thing repelled every atom in her body. Nothing could make Kaija leave, and nothing could keep Maeryn here.

"Let's go," she said to Elias.

He reached out to Kaija again, but she backed away. Something inside of the black knot moaned hungrily.

"NOW!" Maeryn shouted.

Elias held Maeryn tight, and they left Kaija behind.

* * *

Nobody was coming to help Kaija. Elias had swept in to save the day, heroically taking Maeryn away and running from the end of the world. Kaija's boyfriend had buckled with fear from the growing monstrosity ahead of them. Her grandmother was too engulfed with sorrow to do anything other than emit keening sobs, and her grandfather was absolutely out of his mind. The most powerful Spirtualists on Gaia, who evidently did not see this coming, were simply standing back and watching. There may have been a time when Kaija would scream and rage against the uncaring world, but now she had grown used to it. There was no one but her.

"Kai," she said, taking a step forward. Everything inside of her screamed to run, to get as far away from that hungry scar festering on their pain and collapse in her own sorrow, but she fought back against those reflexes and took another step. "Grandfather. I'm still here."

Kai didn't seem to hear her. He stared into the emptiness ahead of him as it stared back, eyes dead and glazed over. It was claiming him, turning the tables and using his power to widen the gateway into Gaia.

"I'm still here."

Kai reached out and touched the scar on his back, right where the sword had ran through him the last time he was on Gaia. She could feel what he felt, and it was just as repellent as Desolation itself.

"I've seen the layers of the mental realm. There are things that live on. If you want to know your son, know me."

Kai blinked, and his eyes suddenly were full of life again. The black thing abruptly stopped growing,

"Kaija," he whispered. "What have I done?"

Before Kai could continue, golden flames erupted from the ground and circled around him. They engulfed his whole body, and then collapsed inwards until a tiny flame hung in the air. Kaija tried to move, but found that the rocks below had grown up around her feet, and she was much too drained to teleport away. Páigus Zeig was suddenly in front of her, snatching the flame and holding it in his palm.

"Spiritualists!" he called urgently. "Intervene! Close the gate. I'll take Edgard to the psychorinthus!"

Páigus disappeared, and the circle of Spirtualists began chanting something in a language that Kaija had never heard. They outstretched their hands simultaneously, sending waves of light at the dark portal in the center of the apex. It writhed and shrieked as the light hit it. The Spirtualists were fierce and intent, doing ancient things that she did not understand. Wave after wave of golden light struck the darkness, and gradually, mercifully, the horrible knot began to shrink.

"It's closing!" shouted one Spirtualist.

"It's too late," another spoke solemnly. "Desolation has seen us, and it knows the way here."

The black thing twisted inward, getting smaller and smaller by the second. Kaija turned to look at Ms. Clara and Fain, but they were slumped over on the ground, unconscious. She suddenly found it hard to stay awake herself; the Spirtualists were doing something to her weakened mind. Kaija found Páigus among the crowd, and looked at him with all the contempt she could muster. Just before her mind slipped into unconsciousness, she sent out one final thought in the old spiritualist's direction.

"If Desolation finds us, it's because we deserve it."

Chapter Thirty-eight

Forgotten and Forever

The Northern Wilds

Maeryn and Max arrived in the center of the True Search's camp, and Elias instantly dropped to the ground beside them as the last of his energy was spent. Izzy ran from the campsite, grabbing Maeryn and looking sick with worry. Tamala was close behind.

"How can you be so reckless!" she yelled, picking up Elias and checking him over for wounds. He opened his eyes, which rolled around a few times and then closed again. "You're going to hear it from me when you wake up, Elias, *just you wait!*" Her voice broke. "I just can't lose you again, son!"

Izzy was shaking Maeryn, trying to get some sort of response.

"Maeryn! What happened? Is my brother okay? Where's Kaija?"

Maeryn opened her mouth, wanting to tell Izzy that Elias would be okay, but she couldn't do that. Nobody would be okay. The black *thing* was hundreds of stretches away by now, but it didn't matter. If something like that was anywhere in the universe, even for a second, nobody could ever be okay. Instead of speaking words of reassurance, Maeryn screamed. She collapsed to the forest floor, hugging her legs to her chest, and screamed her lungs out, not knowing if she'd ever stop.

"Maeryn?" Tamala cried out. "What happened? You have to talk to us."

But she couldn't. She had seen Desolation, and it had seen her. It filled her mind, and it might never leave until the day she dies. And even then, it might follow her into whatever waited beyond death.

Max got up wearily and took a few stumbling steps. He looked up at Izzy and Tamala, but he was just as much at a loss for words.

"Max?" asked Izzy. "What just happened?"

Max shook his head.

"Happening," he said. "Still happening. It's inevitable now."

"What is?"

"The end of the world."

* * *

Hours went by, and Maeryn felt every second of them. What was happening on the Apex now? How large had that darkness become? How long would it be until it found her? She couldn't feel Kaija's mind. Was she dead? Eventually Izzy and Tamala gave up questioning her, because Maeryn could not bring herself to speak. She might never speak again.

Max told them what he remembered, which was difficult because he was not yet used to his flawed memory. Events did not play back in his mind with 100% accurate details in high-definition like they used to. The memories were fuzzy, changing every time he reexamined them. He never felt so human and fragile as he did now.

After speaking with other members of the True Search, Tamala returned and told Maeryn that she was going to the Apex. For the first time in hours, Maeryn found her voice.

"Don't!"

"If what Max tells us is true," said Tamala, "I must investigate and report it to the Elder Council."

"You don't know what it is that I saw. You *can't know*. Tamala, don't leave."

Maeryn reached out for her, but Tamala backed away.

"I don't take orders from children," she said, and then blinked out like a candle.

Maeryn cried out again, shaking and sobbing as anxiety washed over her. It was contagious, that awful feeling inside of Maeryn. Izzy came to her, eyes wide with a similar fear.

"Is… is my mom going to be okay?" she asked.

"No," said Maeryn.

"Can I wait with you?"

Maeryn nodded, and they sat next to each other in silence. Waiting for news, or no news, or for the darkness to take them.

* * *

Tamala returned three hours later, wearier than they had ever seen her.

"Mom!" cried Izzy, hugging her like she might never get the chance again. "What did you see?"

Tamala shook her head grimly and sat down, gasping for breath.

"I couldn't teleport to the Apex itself, or anywhere within five stretches of the place. It's changed too much; I had to walk. All the trees are dead, and I saw no animals or insects alive. The ground is black, and everything inside of me became cold as I approached the mountain. Teleporting became more and more difficult as I worked my way up the path to the summit. I've never felt anything like it… it's like, I don't know… like Gaia is gone from that place."

She took a shivering breath.

"Nobody was there when I reached the top. There was a tall mirrored structure, but the lower levels seemed to have collapsed in upon themselves."

"Did you see the black thing?" asked Maeryn.

"Everything was black," said Tamala.

"No, the thing in the air. Before I left, there was a portal to Desolation. It was getting bigger."

Tamala shook her head. "I didn't see anything like that. But it was all just so… so empty."

Izzy stood up and paced frantically.

"Desolation?" she asked. "Did you just say you saw a portal to *Desolation?* That's crazy. It's just a spiritualist myth. Isn't it?"

She looked to Maeryn, but found no solace there. Tamala leaned over and rubbed her forehead.

"Three hours ago I would have agreed with you," she said. "But now I'm not so sure. Whatever happened to the Zebulon Apex is the most depraved thing I have ever encountered. I don't want to believe it, but Desolation was there. It's real."

* * *

Tamala set up a campsite for Maeryn, who spent the next day lying in bed and trying to drown out the horrible images filling her mind. She saw herself standing before Rosalie's touchscreen, hesitating as she reached to turn it off. If she had acted, would things have still ended up this way?

Max barely spoke to her. Maeryn assumed that he needed his space as well, because there were a lot of hard truths that he was also coming to terms with. In the middle of the night she felt Max walk across her bed and sit up on her shoulder.

"Max?" Maeryn whispered. "Are you okay?"

"No," he said.

"It's hard being a dumb human, isn't it?"

"It's not that. There's something I'm struggling with. If you knew a horrible truth, something that changes everything but would cause so much pain if it ever saw the light of day, what would you do with that information? Would you bury it? Is the truth really something that always has to be known?"

"What are you talking about?"

"I…" Max began, but stopped. "Never mind."

"Don't do that. What is it?"

"I know something, and its eating at me from the inside. I've never felt like this before."

"Tell me."

Maeryn sat up, and Max began pacing back and forth on the bed.

"I can't, Maeryn. After everything that has happened, to put one more horrible thing on you… it's just not fair."

Maeryn held him close to her. "You might be all I have left, Max. Everything from here on out will be suffering, so the least we can do is suffer together. Tell me."

When Max spoke again, he was crying. Inside his damaged metal frame he felt a heart, and he felt it breaking.

"Just before my core processor was ripped out, I realized something," he said. "I was about to kill Rugaru, but my deepest programming stopped it. All of the pieces fit together in my mind in that moment. Your father's coding, Duncan's journal, Rosalie's motivations, what the spiritualists told us… *everything*. Allie Zeig said that there was a part of your family's history you needed to understand, something that was overlooked, and I realized what it was. Who it was."

"I have no idea what you're talking about," said Maeryn, but she did. Some part of her felt those same pieces coming together as Max continued.

"Duncan Kacey loved a Nomadic woman in the True Search before he came to Earth, and he tried to kill Edgard to leave her a better world for her people. But he left something else behind too without realizing it. That woman had a baby. Rugaru is your half-uncle. That's what convinced him to help Rosalie. That's *why* she convinced him so easily to just pick up and run away to Earth. She felt something, something inside that harded shell that everyone else in the world saw when they looked at that man. Rugaru was the part of your family that got overlooked. If we would have just realized this sooner…"

Maeryn felt cold. Duncan the Crucifier, Rugaru of the Western Blaze, and Rosalie Kacey, bringer of Desolation. That was her family. They were not the heroes of the story, they were the people who ran away and left others to suffer for their actions. What about her? Maeryn wasn't the hero, she's the one who ran.

Rosalie's words echoed in her mind.

It's not me that you hate.

* * *

Monhegan Island

Maeryn Kacey felt the weight of each passing second, but things couldn't have been more different for Kaija Monhegan. She felt like she had become dislodged from time. Lots of things occurred, and she couldn't quite place them in order. They all seemed to happen at once, yet none of it felt real. Her father died, the world nearly ended, and then she had stepped into a dream.

Her mother, Saura Aztala, was by her side. She never left her Guardianship, she never visited Monhegan, yet here she was. At some point, Saura and Ms. Clara were screaming bitterly at each other. Her mother wanted Kaija to come and live with her in the Oceanic Guardianship, away from the mess of the leaderless Edgardia, but Ms. Clara said that she would have to pry Kaija from her cold, dead hands. Saura left abruptly in a fit of tears. Why would Saura want to take her away from Monhegan? Wasn't it the safest place in the world? With Ms. Clara, and Jas…

Jasper was falling, a crystal dagger in his heart.

Hammers were knocking constantly, and barrels of rubble went back and forth to a garbage heap which had never been so large. The somber Monhegans were rebuilding. But not just that; they were preparing for something. Something was going to happen? Was it today? What day was it anyway?

Ms. Clara was telling her to get dressed.

Fain, Kaija, and Ms. Clara were watching a black hole in the world fill with light as spiritualists chanted. Someone was in their minds, the world went blank, and then they were waking up in the grass of the Monhegan headlands. Except for Jasper. He was still asleep. Why wouldn't he wake up?

Maeryn was turning away from Kaija, leaving her so alone and afraid.

They were with Fain's parents, who were acting very strange. Maddox couldn't quite seem to look Ms. Clara in the eye as they spoke in hushed tones, and she addressed him sternly. He left the room mid-sentence as Ms. Clara shouted after him.

Kaija, alone. Sorting through memories from the previous day, reliving them. Watching them from her perspective, and then again from Maeryn's.

Rugaru's eyes filling with clouds and his skin melting away.

Kaija and Fain laying in Gull Cove in the middle of a cold night, kissing more boldly than they ever had before, taking a small comfort in each other's arms, trying to forget the pain and darkness with each kiss. It worked for a few seconds at a time, but something was different.

Voices from another world, moaning from behind the dark tumor in the air.

Ghosts from the past crowding the mental realm, filling Kaija with hope and power as she pulled the nanobots from her father's face.

Branches growing. Twisting. Rotting.

* * *

It was morning, and Jasper's ceremony of passing was tonight. Four days had passed since Kaija had seen Desolation. She kept telling herself this over breakfast, trying to maintain her tenuous grip on time.

The fried eggs had that brown layer of skin which happens when you leave them on the skillet too long. *Eggs continue to cook even after you remove them from the heat, so you have to take them off before they're fully done.* Jasper had said that. Kaija reminded herself to pass that along to Ms. Clara, who was not nearly as good a cook as her father was.

"Ornes is coming down to provide food after the ceremony," said Ms. Clara, pushing away her uneaten breakfast. "So that will be nice. I've been back and forth with the poor man. Thought about delaying the ceremony one more day, but I don't think that he'll… never mind." She covered her face and walked out of the room.

427

Kaija knew what her grandmother wanted to say. She was delaying things in the hopes that Kai would come back, to be at his own son's ceremony of passing, but they might never know where he was taken. Spiritualists were not easy to track down when they didn't want to be found.

Kaija forced a few more bites of eggs and then left to walk around the lighthouse. Halfway through the village, she heard a sudden pop and Elias appeared, one hand on Maeryn's shoulder. They were both dressed up quite nice. Maeryn was in Gaian clothing. Huh. That was weird.

Maeryn looked at Kaija like she wanted to run and embrace her, but she seemed to resist the urge. Elias took a few steps back, trying to be respectful and not intrude.

"Maeryn," said Kaija, giving her best attempt to be cheerful. "I've been thinking about you, hoping you were okay."

"I've been trying my best," she said. "I thought you were dead, Kaija. I thought that *thing* took you. Tamala sent some scouts to Monhegan yesterday, and they learned what happened. They told us that Jasper's ceremony of passing was today, and we wanted to come. Tamala and the rest of her family will be here in a few hours."

Kaija's fake smile began to wane.

"That's considerate of you," she said. "To not leave me alone tonight."

A horrible silence stretched out for a few seconds, seeming to last much longer. Elias suddenly took up a great interest at staring at the ground. Maeryn's eyes became wet.

"Kaija," she said. "I am so sorry. I'd never been so scared in my life, but I was wrong to leave you. I can never make it right. I can never apologize enough for what I did."

"Well, you're pretty good at apologizing," said Kaija. "So I'm sure you'll find a way, but it won't help me. It would have helped a lot more to stop that cannon when you had the chance. Or if you told Tamala to come and help me rather than crying and begging her to stay away. I'm full to the brim with apologies, Maeryn. Next time, if there is a next time, how about you actually *do something?*"

The weight of Kaija's words took a moment to fully settle over Maeryn, and she struggled to remain calm.

"You've been in my head," she said.

Kaija shrugged.

"It's not right what I did, but I'm suffering for it, Kaija," said Maeryn loudly.

"It must be hard."

"Yes, it is. Your grief doesn't cancel out mine, you know. We agreed to never invade the other person's mind, Kaija. We have to be careful with what we have between us, or—"

"Are you really yelling at me right now?" asked Kaija. "I thought you came to see my dead father off after he saved the world, although I know that you secretly wonder if things would have been better off if we took Rosalie's deal."

This shut up Maeryn quickly. She felt naked and ashamed in front of Kaija. They had literally been trapped in each other's bodies and lived each other's lives, but now they felt like complete strangers.

"Kaija," said Elias. "Maeryn's been inconsolable for days. This isn't fair."

"OH," said Kaija. "Well, let me go ahead and *apologize* for making you feel sad, hours before saying goodbye to my father. Don't bother coming either, Elias. If the True Search had helped us, things could have been different, but they *didn't*. They bravely left it up to a group of teenagers."

"Kaija…" Maeryn began, reaching out, but Kaija slapped her hand away.

"GET OUT OF HERE!" Kaija screamed at them. Shockwaves of pain filled Maeryn's mind, and she cried out.

"Stop, Kaija," said Elias. "You're better than this."

Kaija dug herself deeper into Maeryn, intensifying the pain.

"I can make it a hundred times worse," Kaija said. "Take her away."

Maeryn grabbed Elias's hand in desperation, and they disappeared.

Tamala and Izzy didn't come to the ceremony later that day. The True Search had gone quiet, just like they always did.

* * *

That evening, every single Monhegan gathered in the valley beyond their village for Jasper's ceremony of passing. His body lay on a marble structure brought in from the mainland. There were a lot of people there that Kaija didn't know, hundreds maybe. The crowd stretched deep into the valley. Near the front she spotted Ornes Booth, holding the hand of his son Ben and whispering soothing words. The little boy was crying, and something about this made Kaija furious. She only met this kid once in her life, and he was horrible to them. Ben had thrown rocks at her and Fain, calling them cowardly sea monkeys that married their cousins. What right did he have to be here?

Kaija's mother had come after all. She stood crying amongst several of her fellow Aztalians, and Kaija felt another burst of resentment. Her mother had been absent for most of her life. Why did she deserve to make a big show of her grief? Why did *any* of these people, aside from Ms. Clara, deserve to feel any bit of what Kaija was feeling?

An older man stepped forward and approached the shroud, gently touching Jaspers face and fighting back his own tears. It was Norio, a priest who had lived on Monhegan since before Kaija was born. He was a frail looking person, always moving slowly and with great effort. He looked up and smiled warmly at the crowd for a moment.

"I don't know the majority of the people here," said Norio, "but I see the truth in your faces. Without using a bit of relaying, I know what each and every one of you is thinking. Yes, there is grief, but there is something more. A realization; the very same one I am having just now.

"I was orphaned as a young man. My parents were healers, and it was the only reason I survived infancy. You see, I was born with a rare blood disease which calls for daily healing sessions. When my parents died, I found myself searching for a new home. No community would take me in. I would be a strain on the precious resources of their healers, with no skills to offer in return. Eventually I came to terms with the idea that I would die a painful death as my blood ate away at my nervous system and slowly paralyzed me. It was at the crest of my despair that I heard of a place whose guardian brought in people like me. People without Edgardian birthright. People with mistakes in their past. People who would come with nothing to offer, such as I, but would require much.

"Jasper took me in without question, and on the days when a healer was unavailable, he did my therapy himself. He did it without ceremony, never making himself out to be some kind of savior. I have seen Jasper fill the sky with his power, redirect the ocean's currents, and lift boulders, but he didn't really need any of this. Jasper's strength was never in his relaying. On several occasions, Jasper confessed to me that he resented his natural powers. He did things that most people *could* do, but few choose to. Sure, he would have done anything for those he loved, but that is the astounding thing. I'm not his family. Jasper didn't love me. We had very little in common, and I don't think he necessarily even *liked* me. Jasper transcended those naïve ideas. He had a radical compassion. That's what I see when I look at the unfamiliar faces who came here this evening. A hundred secret debts of gratitude, a hundred personal worlds saved, all of you realizing in this moment that you were not alone."

Norio paused, moving on to part of the ceremony he had performed a thousand times.

"Jasper did not wish to be buried, so I will commence the ceremony of passing. The Jasper we knew is gone. While it is difficult to accept the truth of it, a part of him has been lost that can never be reclaimed. There is a reality to death that is horrible, but if you hear me to the end, you may also see that it is beautiful. Every memory and thought of him that ever existed now lives in the mental realm. You might see him in your dreams, or feel him somewhere in the back of your mind, but he can no longer speak in his own voice. What you knew of him is all there is now. Jasper will continue to influence you in conscious ways for a while, when you remember things that he did and said, but even this will fade with time. Your memory will inevitably fail you. As the cycles pass, Jasper will become clouded in the mental realm, and eventually there will not be a single person who remembers his name. His presence will spread so thin that it will not seem there at all.

"And yet, if you look in the unseen places, the nameless places that *cannot* be directly looked at, Jasper will be there. Always. Influencing us in ways you don't even realize. Changing how you interact with others, and changing them in turn; ripples spreading across an ocean forever. A branch cannot see its roots, but it would not be there without them."

Norio nodded, and the crowd held out their hands, channeling Gaia in their many different ways while directing their attention to Jasper's body. Kaija felt a sorrowful surge of energy in the air. Everyone relayed in a single burst of power, and Jasper's body began to glow. With a gentle gust of wind, he dissolved to ash, glittering in the clear night sky as it was carried away.

Through the tears in her eyes, Kaija thought she saw her grandfather in the crowd, just out of the corner of her eye. Looking again, there was no one there. Norio called out over the sounds of wind and grief.

"Only when the last person forgets Jasper's name, when he dissolves completely into the mental realm and appears to be gone, will he be made into something eternal, something that is both forgotten and forever."

Chapter Thirty-nine

Branches

Months Later

Fain

Three hours past center moon, Kaija and Fain were the only people awake on the island. They held each other's hands, sometimes talking, sometimes kissing, but mostly just sitting and taking in the feeling of being together, after not knowing for so long if they ever would. Kaija looked at his face in the moonlight, but there was something strange in Fain's expression.

"Rugaru used this against us," he said.

"What?" asked Kaija, clearing away the clouds in her head.

"How we feel about each other. This whole time, I was just a piece of bait to be swung around. If it wasn't for me, or our feelings for each other, Jasper might—"

He looked about ready to cry, and Kaija kissed him hard.

"No," she said. "Nobody touches what we have."

Fain looked up and saw a few snowflakes starting to fall from the sky. The first of the cycle.

"It was exactly one cycle ago," said Fain.

"What?" asked Kaija. "What was?"

"When we kissed here for the first time."

Kaija thought back to that moment, lost in her past. If only she could go back.

"I understand it now," she said. "You said you were scared to be so happy, and I didn't really see why, but I do now. I told you that the fact that it couldn't last forever made it more important, and I still think that, but..." Kaija put her hands over her face. "...I didn't think it would be so short. This last cycle was the best of my life, but recently I think back to my cycle day and realize that it was the last time I felt really okay. I don't know how to be okay anymore."

"We're leaving," said Fain.

Something broke inside of Kaija.

"What?"

"I don't know what happened," said Fain, "but my parents had a falling out with Ms. Clara, right after I got taken. They won't talk about it, but I guess it keeps getting worse. We're moving in the morning. I didn't know how to tell you."

This was too much. Is this how life would be from now on? One bad thing piled on top of another, forever?

"But... where... where are you going?" asked Kaija, trying to speak over the broken feeling in her chest.

"I don't know," said Fain. "But we've been hearing things from the Mainland. What's left of the Western Blaze is still occupying the Capital. Will Zeig was just appointed to be the new High Guardian, and he's calling on Edgardian citizens to help him wipe out the Western Blaze while they're still leaderless. My father signed up, and we're all leaving."

Fain leaned in closer, saying the next words nervously.

"You should come with us."

435

Kaija wanted to tell Fain that she would. She would join this army and vanquish the last of the Western Blaze that took her father's life, but Kaija couldn't promise this. It would be wrong to leave Ms. Clara; they only had each other now. And besides, Kaija could care less if the Western Blaze had the Capital. The real enemy was still out there somewhere.

"I can't," said Kaija. "But we can still see each other. I'm mastering my spacialist abilities now, so I'll be a breath away at any moment."

"I hope so," said Fain. "We're going to be traveling around a lot, and our location will be a secret. It might be a long time before I see you again."

And so they sat together until night became morning, trying to soak in every last second. Snow began to stick to the ground as the sun rose. When it came time for Fain to leave and gather his few belongings, Kaija said what she had been wondering ever since he was taken.

"You were going to tell me you loved me, before Monhegan got attacked," said Kaija. "Weren't you? All the way back then, you loved me."

Fain blushed.

"Can't you just read my mind and find out?"

"No. I won't. Not with something like this."

He hesitated. "Kaija… I was going to, but I can't say it now. Not after what's happened, and what's about to happen. Things are going to get so dangerous. So much bigger than just the two of us. I realized, sitting in my dirty cell night after night, that Edgardia was not a place for love. But every second I'm gone I won't stop believing that we can make it into one. When this is all over, we'll come back here and I'll say it and never stop saying it for the rest of our lives."

He turned to go, to meet up with his parents and leave the only place that ever felt like a home.

"I do," Fain thought. *"I love you with everything I am."*
But Kaija didn't hear. She had kept her promise.

* * *

Kaija

As Kaija walked back to her grandmother's cabin, she couldn't stop thinking about Maeryn. They hadn't spoken in months. Sometimes, Kaija would forget that they even had a mindbridge. Despite all the unforgivable things that happened on the Apex, Kaija was beginning to regret the things that heartache made her say. Maeryn was right; Kaija's grief didn't cancel out everyone else's. Maeryn's father was still alive somewhere, but he might as well be dead to them. She would never see him again, or her home, or anything left behind on Earth.

Kaija opened the locked door at the back of her mind, just a hair, and sent her voice across the mindbridge.

"Maeryn? Are you there? Are you awake?"

It took a few seconds to get Maeryn's reply.

"Yes. This… this is weird. I was just about to reach out to you."

Kaija laughed. This kind of thing always used to happen.

"Maeryn," she thought. *"Listen, I'm sorry. I shouldn't have—"*

"No," Maeryn interrupted. *"It doesn't matter anymore. There's something I need to say, and this is the hardest thing I've ever done so just let me talk until I've finished. I've been reading about spiritualism, and the Tree of Time, and Desolation, and… a million things, honestly. It might be true that all roads from here lead to Desolation, that Gaia will fall no matter what we do. But Spiritualism is a tricky thing, and sometimes they get the timeline wrong. They might think they're seeing*

the future, but they're seeing the past, or vice versa. Rosalie completely overlooked Kai, and that changed everything. What else could they have overlooked? Maybe the real turning point hasn't happened yet. Maybe... well, maybe it's happening right now."

Maeryn stopped, and Kaija could hear her sobbing on the other side, hundreds of stretches away.

"How do you mean?" asked Kaija.

"Everything that has gone wrong, everything for three generations, has happened because of our families. My grandfather tried to kill yours. I tried to make it right and heal Jasper, but it was my fault he got poisoned in the first place. The nanobots in his blood that were supposed to save him ended up being his undoing anyway. We thought that bringing Kai back would fix things, but... well, you know what happened. Everyone in my family thought what they were doing was right for the people they loved, but things just kept spiraling and getting worse. I love you, Kaija, but love is what brought everything to this. Maybe we were brought together because Gaia was showing us why we <u>can't</u> be together. That we need to fight Desolation on our own terms and not try to keep finding the answers in the other person. Kaija, I think we need to stop using the mindbridge. Maybe that's the decision we were supposed to make."

Kaija took it in, every deliberately rehearsed word, and felt Maeryn's pain run through her.

"Can I just say one thing?" asked Kaija.

"Of course."

"You're just like the rest of your family."

Kaija felt for the opening to Maeryn inside her, and slammed it shut as hard as she could.

* * *

438

Max

Walking was the worst. Not only could Max no longer break the sound barrier, but he had to use his stupid legs to move from place to place. The size of this world was simply not built for a guy less than a foot tall. He'd been stepped on multiple times by passing villagers. One time he got stuck in a mud puddle, and it took Maeryn an entire day of searching before she found him. How long before he got knocked into a river, or was carried off by a crow?

At a certain point, Max decided that he'd just avoid moving from place to place whenever he could. He'd stay in Maeryn's pocket some days. On others, he'd hole himself in professor Sawyer's library for days at a time, reading about Desolation and trying to find some kind of loophole. After all, his body was no good, and while the speed of his mind was slower than before, he was still undeniably one of the smartest people in existence. He may as well put it to good use, distract himself from the fact that now he was basically an unwilling character in a real-life *Toy Story*.

Max would find a way to stop Desolation. Even if it was impossible, he'd do everything he could to try, and never stop until the end of time.

It took Max an hour to get across the campsite, but he was determined. He entered Tamala's tent. Her husband, Sawyer, was reading Diego a story and rocking him back and forth on his knee.

"I have another question," said Max.

Sawyer jumped in surprise. Despite Max being here for months now, this tended to happen. People just never seemed to expect a tiny silver man to enter the conversation.

"Oh," said Sawyer. "Ask away."

"I had a question about something I found in your book on pre-war spiritualists," said Max.

"Did you bring it with you? The book?"

Max crossed his arms. "Did I bring the book? The book that is bigger than my entire body?"

"Oh," said Sawyer. "Right. Well, what was it?"

"It's this term that kept popping up. It didn't have any context. What are the *Songs of Desolation?*"

* * *

Maeryn

Maeryn was unpacking. It had taken her this long to fully admit to herself that this was where she lived now, here with the True Search. There was no chance to make it back to Earth. Kaija was best without her on Monhegan Island. Rosalie had disappeared once again, and that was also for the best. Maeryn hoped that she never saw her again for the rest of their lives. Everyone else on Gaia was a stranger, so there was nothing left to do but unpack what meager possessions she had left in her backpack.

Elias and Izzy walked around the tent, setting up a bed and shelves and other things to make this feel like a home. "Tent" felt like an offensive word at this point. The True Search had developed techniques for sewing the most amazing fabrics, and the walls of this tent somehow warmed the air as it blew past. Even in the Northern part of Gaia in the dead of winter, it was warm and cozy in here.

Maeryn took out a pair of MotherTech contacts and tossed them into the garbage. They were all scratched up and drained, needing to be charged and repaired, but there was no hope of that here. In the bottom of the backpack were a few pairs of Earth clothing, but Maeryn never wore them anymore. They just made her stick out. Underneath her clothes was something that she had completely forgotten about: a little statue that she found while her and Kaija rooted through the wreckage of Monhegan Island, months ago. Maeryn had pulled it out of the ash of a cabin just at the edge of the village. It looked like a butterfly, but had a smiley face drawn on the head. She couldn't tell if it had been carved from wood or stone, it looked like a mixture of both.

She held it up and looked at it, thinking of Kaija and crying for the hundredth time. Elias gasped from behind her.

"Where'd you get that!?" he exclaimed, teleporting over to Kaija and taking the carving from her. Izzy joined them, laughing when she saw it.

"I know that little guy!" she yelled. "It's the flickerfly I carved you when I was little. You kept that thing?"

Elias went quiet, his lower lip trembling.

"What's wrong?" asked Maeryn.

She shook his head. "Nothing's wrong. It's... right. It's so right. When I left my family for the first time, this is the only thing I brought with me. I thought I lost it, but... but here it is."

He reached over to Maeryn, pulling her close and hugging her.

"You think you lose everything," he told her. "Your family, your past, everyone you love. But sometimes, things come back when you need them the most."

"I'll never get back home," said Maeryn

Izzy joined them, leaning her head on Maeryn's other side.

"Home's not a place," she said. "Home is a people."

For the first time, Maeryn Kacey didn't feel like Maeryn Kacey any longer. She was Maeryn True Search.

* * *

Joe Luegers

Dorian

Dorian Kacey woke in a cold sweat. The hands of the clock had moved past midnight.

That makes it 103 days. 103 days of solitary confinement in the Federal Correction Institute of Terra Haute. 103 days of the guards calling him Francis Rodriguez for some inexplicable reason. 103 days of his life not making the slightest bit of sense.

"103…" Dorian whispered. "They're not coming. No one is coming for me."

* * *

Smith Johnson

"Go to bed, son."

"I am in bed."

"No, you are not. That's the kitchen table."

"It's my bed now."

Smith's mother, Katherine, had found him sleeping on the kitchen table, complete with mattress pad, blankets, pillows, and his bassoon. Best not to question that last one. Katherine sat at one of the chairs.

"Why don't you want to sleep in your room anymore?" she asked.

"I'm scared of my closet," said Smith.

"You're eighteen years old."

Smith sat up, a crazed look on his face. "It doesn't matter! You'd be scared too, if you woke up one morning, heard that loud pop, and found that… that *thing* in your closet. It came from a dimensional rift, mom."

"That's crazy."

"Can you explain it? Can you explain why the government showed up and took that *thing* away, and then forced you to sign that non-disclosure agreement? Can you explain why Maeryn and her whole family went missing right around the same time, and why we haven't heard from them since? Huh, mom? Can you give me a single reason not to be afraid of my closet?"

Katherine shook her head. She couldn't.

"That's what I thought," said Smith, pulling the covers back over him. "Now if you excuse me, I'm going back to sleep, and then I'm having breakfast in bed."

* * *

The Tall Man

He walked through a labyrinth of mist. For a long time, he was too fragmented to even know that he existed. One by one, the pieces of himself crawled back together, forming something that could move and think yet still not understand exactly what it was.

Had he always been here, in this place that didn't make sense?

No. Forever ago, he had a body. He had a name. Someone had taken everything from him, ripping his mind from his body and scattering him to the winds of the mental realm.

So he walked, and he searched, but this place was endlessly shifting.

After who knows how long, he found something. A door to another place. Not Gaia. Not Earth. Something else. From somewhere beyond the door, a voice spoke.

"Take my hand," said the voice, *"for I am lost too. We will find our way out together."*

Epilogue

Blood Type: New

Earth
White Plains Hospital, New York

"Is this a joke? Please tell me this a joke."

Nurse Larson had been assigned the patient in room 87 of the Intensive Unit 3. That very same unit had been shut down months ago, blocked off for construction or something. He was instructed to read the patient's medical charts very carefully and report to the nursing manager before the shift started. Scanning the info one more time did little to ease his confusion.

Patient Name: *Unknown*

Demographics: *Physical appearance appears to be a mix of Native American, Korean, and African, but genetic tests came back entirely indecisive.*

Medication Record: *Unknown*

Diagnosis: *Patient is in a coma. Brain MRI and nano-assisted physiology scan came back <u>eventful</u>. See notes.*

Blood Type: *New*

"See, that's the first thing," said Nurse Larson. "Blood type: new? What the heck does that even mean?"

"There are proteins and antigens in the patient's blood that we've never seen before," explained the manager calmly. "So it's a new blood type."

"That's insane."

"Oh, just wait. Keep reading. Go to the last page and look at the notes."

Larson flicked his eyes a few times, swiping to the last entry on the report.

Notes: Patient was brought in by a woman named Katherine Johnson. She claims that she has never seen this man in her life, and that he... oh boy... that his body appeared in her son's closet with what he described as a loud pop. Her psychiatric report came back clean. Son is very odd, but there is no evidence of wrongdoing. The woman used to be Katherine Kacey, divorced from Dorian Kacey. He's the MotherTech heir who has recently gone missing with his sister and daughter. This is all very strange. Authorities have been notified, and they are checking national records.

Updated 11/13: Patient is not in national or international records. He has no global identification number. Although, several members of the United States military showed up today and said that... really? Um... Hold on.

Updated 11/14: Had to get manager approval to include this in the record. Several members of the Indianapolis Police claimed to have been <u>dreaming</u> the patient's face. These same officers were suspended after they stole military weaponry for an unauthorized mission, of which redacted-- -----------.

Officers were sent to a military hospital after repeatedly claiming that the man in their dreams was controlling their minds. All of their stories were identical, despite being interviewed separately.
Updated 11/15: *Patient still showing no signs of recovery.*

"This is crazy," said Nurse Larson.

"Yes," said his manager. "But it's also an incredibly easy job. Walk through the patient's room every few minutes. Change his bedpans and replace the IV. He'll just lay there and do nothing. Maybe read a good book in your spare time. Turn off your companion bot when you're in there. And most importantly, *don't say a thing about this*. Understand?"

"Well, yeah, but—"

"UNDERSTAND?"

His manager tilted his head to the ceiling, where two glowing cameras were pointing right at them.

"Yes, sir."

* * *

"He's an alien," Larson muttered to himself, staring at the patient for the fortieth time. "It's the only reasonable explanation."

The patient report was right. The man *kind of* looked Native American, or maybe vaguely Korean, or African, but none of those really came close. He was like some new nationality that had been hiding off on an island for all of recorded history, only to wave a magic wand and get dropped into some teenage boy's bedroom while leaving their brain behind. Larson had gone through the personal belongings in a zipped bag, which only included a strange set of clothes. Handmade looking clothes, with a fabric Larson had never seen before.

So this was his life now. Larson was taking care of an alien.

Five hours into his shift, Larson sat in a comfy chair at the corner of the room, drinking coffee and Christmas shopping on his digital contacts, when there was a slight rustle of bedsheets. Larson looked up, and promptly dropped his coffee cup onto the floor in surprise.

The patient was sitting straight up in his bed, looking around the room with detached interest. The craziest thing was that he didn't look dreary whatsoever. The man was in a coma one second, and the next he just wasn't. Larson felt like any minute his coworkers would jump out and yell, "gotcha!"

Larson held a finger to his earpiece.

"Could I get some assistance?" he asked, trying to steady his voice. "The patient in 87 is awake."

The man looked toward Larson, but his gaze moved right past him. He looked like a newborn baby, eyes scanning the room but not knowing what he was seeing.

"You're awake," said Larson awkwardly. "Are... are you okay?"

"Awake," said the man dryly, pulling one of the IVs out of his arm.

"I need some help here," said Larson, going to press his earpiece again, but it was gone. It must have fallen out and he just didn't notice in his surprise. He looked back up at the patient.

"Sir, you've been in a coma. Can you tell me who you are? Where you're from?"

"I..." said the man quietly, and then seemed to be deep in thought. "I had a name a long time ago. Longer ago for me than for you. Every second was a thousand years. Before then, I was from... *a place*." He ran his hand up and down the bedsheet, fascinated by the texture. "Is this a place? Are we in a place now?"

Larson began quickly walking to the door, intending on sticking his head out and shouting for a doctor, but the patient spoke after him. His detached tone began to fade, replaced by one of more confidence.

447

"You are Larson Bailey," said the man. "Registered nurse. Recovering alcoholic. Secretly in love with the desk nurse. Dreamt about her last night."

Larson stopped dead in his tracks.

"What did you just say?" he asked. "Nobody knows that… how…"

The patient was getting out of bed now, and his legs were strong. It took him no time at all to steady himself.

"I apologize for the distress," said the patient, casually holding a hand against his wrist to stop the blood from where the IV had been. He lifted it, and the blood was gone. Just gone. "Ah, that's better. I was still putting myself back together. I've been fragmented for a long time, and this is so far from my home. Language was not required where I just came from. Ah!" He smiled. "And it just came back to me: my name. I was once Achak of the Western Blaze, but this doesn't feel right anymore. Now, I'm The Bridge."

Larson turned back to the door and reached for the doorknob, but saw something absolutely inexplicable. The doorknob sank into the wall as he reached for it, and then the door was gone too. Larson searched the room desperately for another exit. This wasn't happening, the door must be on the other side of the room. But no, they were in a hospital room with no doors. Curtains hung in front of a wall with no windows.

"You are wondering how a man can be a bridge," said the patient. "But you are wrong. I am not a bridge, I am *The* Bridge, chosen to close the gap between this place and another that your world does not yet have a name for."

Larson gasped for air and clutched his chest, feeling an invisible hand grab him by the heart and squeeze. He fell, hitting the wall and sinking toward the floor. Even after he hit the ground, he continued to sink. The floor was liquid, swallowing him whole. He was up to his head with the stuff, and he watched as the scenery of the hospital room changed. The walls faded to nothing, and there were things in that nothingness. Eyes. It was full of eyes. The patient looked down at him, and Larson saw the most horrible thing yet. There was a face behind the man's face, something watching from the inside.

"Don't worry," the man continued, "you're not dying. The man inside of me is simply consuming your essence. We need to know as much about this world as possible. Think of a drop of water rejoining an ocean." He smiled. "I feel that you somehow have enough space left in your dissolving mind to wonder about that place I spoke of. It will be known to your people soon, and when it sees you, it will claw its way out to follow the scent. It is coming, and it is…"

Larson's heart beat for a final time.

"…Desolation."

To be concluded

in *Songs of Desolation: The Mindbridge Trilogy Book III…*

Thank You!

If you're here, you've either read both books in *The Mindbridge Trilogy*, or you for some reason you skipped the first book entirely and I will be forced to alert the literary authorities.

The idea that a single person would want to read even a paragraph of my words is at the same time thrilling and terrifying. You have my most sincere thanks just for being here.

As an indie author, I have to work very hard for people to know that my books exist. **The very best thing you can do to help a writer like me is to leave an honest rating and review of this book on Goodreads or an online retailer.** Even a single sentence helps more than you can know.

If you have a second, do it right now! If you're busy, do it anyway! Your homework can wait. Someone else can fly that airplane or perform that emergency open heart surgery. Make an indie author happy today!

All the best,
-Joe Luegers, writer/musician

Acknowledgements

Writing *The Bridge* was a somewhat solitary process, so I only had a handful of names to list in the acknowledgements of Book I. Shortly after its release, there were suddenly so many people who left reviews, gave me advice, helped promote the series, and were just generally supportive. In no particular order, I'd like to thank **Angela Hildenbrand, Drew Beasley, Denise Lehman, Caitlyn Hummel, Daisy Undercuffler, Juney June, Kasey Miller, Christine Bloemsma, Jacob Gouge, Kiley Eberhard, Rafaela Schaick, Christine Talley, Maria Sherle, Stephanie Gilbert, Jane Rothert, Penny Lane, Lonnie Moore, Meredith Miller, Gracie Craft, Paula Elisa Menz, Tonya Heim, Kim Payne,** and **Meagan Alf.** I'm surely forgetting someone. If so, feel free to write your name here:_____.

Special thanks to **Kandis Robinson** for going above and beyond in helping me with the earliest versions of this draft, **Emily Bernhardt** for giving *A Path of Branches* the final polish, and **Ashley Ellen Frary** for continuing to create the best cover art I've ever seen.

A family is a team, and nothing happens on either end without the full support of your partner. All my love and eternal thanks from the very core of my being to **Alax Luegers.**

-Joe Luegers

About the Author

Joe Luegers is a guitarist, pianist, organist, composer, teacher, and writer. He lives in Evansville, Indiana with his wife Alax and their two kids, July and Rory. Joe published the adult horror novel *The Gears That Watch the Clockmaker* in 2018 and has since turned his focus toward writing young adult fiction. He performs frequently as a soloist, alongside his amazing wife on vocals and ukulele, and in an eclectic range of ensembles including the opera rock band The Tapestry.

Check out his social media for info on upcoming books.

Facebook: www.facebook.com/Luegerswriter

YouTube: search for *Joe Luegers -Writer*

Instagram: www.instagram.com/joeluegers/

Website: www.luegerswriter.com/